FRINGE THEORY

FRINGE THEORY
Amazon Kindle Edition

Copyright © 2018 by Chuck Driskell
Published by Autobahn Books
Cover art by Nat Shane

First Edition: December 2018

autobahn
BOOKS

FRINGE THEORY

CHUCK DRISKELL

Our country is now geared to an arms economy bred in an artificially induced psychosis of war hysteria and an incessant propaganda of fear.
—Douglas MacArthur

Part One

Le Criminel Solitaire

Chapter One

After seven long nights of surveillance, Max Warfield decided it was time to breach the strong room. Over the past week, six different Algerians had come and gone with regularity, almost always carrying a bag or container that was presumably full of cash—small, dirty bills, if Max had to guess. There were never less than two guards in the strong room at one time and, in the early evening hours, sometimes there were three or even four. Max had made notes about the times of the shift changes along with each of the men who guarded the strong room. He'd given them nicknames associated with their appearance. Most important, on six nights of seven, the midnight shift change had been sloppy—probably due to alcohol or narcotics. Each and every evening, Max had seen jugs of cheap wine carried in, the jugs discarded out the small window over the balance of the second shift.

Between the bad habits of the guards and all that he'd learned, Max was confident of his plan. It was similar to the plans that had worked for him so many times before: pick the most advantageous time to go in heavy, and hard.

So, unless tonight's midnight shift change was unusual, he'd breach the strong room alone with his shotgun and hopefully be gone within thirty seconds.

It was currently just after 8 P.M.

Max sat alone outside a small waterside food stand in the Les Crottes area of Marseilles. In front of him was a jar of cloudy water and a plate with olives, roasted Brussels sprouts, fresh bread and three cold hard-boiled eggs. Max studied his notes one last time, using the table's hurricane lamp for light. When the stiff ocean breeze made the protected flame flicker, he peppered his eggs and ate slowly. There was no need to hurry. As he ate, his thoughts were rich with the visions of Ludivine St Vincent, his Parisian girlfriend of the last year. In two days' time, he would be back in her cozy Neuilly-sur-Seine flat, enjoying her; smelling her; tasting her; loving her…

The strong room, Maxime. Your mind should be on the strong room.

Tonight would be Max's fourth, and hopefully last, breach this year. Based on the narcotic activity he'd followed in the weeks leading up to his discovery of the strong room, he believed there must be the equivalent of at least 10,000 new French francs in the room on a given night. The last drop of the night, and probably the largest, typically arrived in the early morning hours. But if Max waited until then, he'd have to deal with what appeared to be a more vigilant and sober guard force. So, despite the fact that the strong room didn't contain its peak cash at midnight, he felt his chances of success

1

were much better at that time. Max hoped his calculations about the amount were correct. Regardless of what he believed, anything less than 4,000 new francs would be disastrous. He'd have to go right back to work and find another strong room to breach by the end of November.

More breaches meant more risk, and more risk increased Max's chances of dying or, worse, getting captured.

He'd hit 14 underworld strong rooms since arriving in France. They probably all belonged to the crime syndicate known as the *Unione Corse*. The Corse, a.k.a. the Corsican mafia, was France's version of La Cosa Nostra. Certainly the Unione Corse were aware of Max's misdeeds, but in their stratospheric net worth he'd not stolen enough from them to appear too brightly on their radar. Even the regional crime lords, known as the *patron de la zone*, probably hadn't heard much about the thefts. If they had, the person committing the robberies was nothing more than a *petit chien*. But with each breach, Max knew his next job would grow more difficult. That's why he preferred to space his hits out by several months.

After tonight, security in underworld strong rooms would tighten over the coming weeks. But, when no more hits occurred, the men would grow complacent. They'd start drinking again—they'd become lackadaisical. The bosses would move on to the next problem, and the next. By the time everything fell back to normal, in the New Year, Max would be ready to strike again. He was toying with the idea of heading to Belgium for his next score—he'd think more on it while he spent the last six weeks of the year with Ludivine—sensual, voluptuous Ludivine.

The thoughts of his Parisian *bombe* warmed Max in the chill of the seaside evening.

About a year ago, he'd been stricken with the peculiar fear that he was being followed. It turned out to be unfounded, but during one of his evasive maneuvers, he'd literally run into a striking lady on a narrow aisle of a market in Paris' 16th Arrondissement. During his apologies, he learned her name was Ludivine. She laughed off the collision and Max had found himself unable to keep walking. An hour later, they enjoyed a bottle of rough wine together at a café near her flat. This led to another date, then another. That was nearly a year ago. They'd seen each other regularly since then.

Max longed for her company.

He finished the tasty and simple dinner, mopping the wax paper with his last bite of bread. Afterward, he swiveled around on the bench, resting his elbows on the picnic table and signaling the lady in the food stand to prepare him a coffee. Max enjoyed one of his Gitane filterless cigarettes as he waited. Behind him, in the waters of the port, gulls could be heard chirping frantically as they tussled over a fresh catch. Between drags on his cigarette, Max breathed deeply of the early November salt air. The weather here had been fine during his stay, with comfortable days and chilly, wood smoke filled nights. He wondered when he'd visit the sea again. Perhaps Ludivine would be with him.

"*Merci*," Max said to the worker as she handed him the cup and saucer. The vibrating tinkle of the cheap ceramic was due to his shaking.

He viewed the time on his Rolex Submariner, a watch he'd have never sprung for. Only a few hours to go before the breach.

Plenty of time…

Max rubbed the crystal of the Rolex, recalling the day when Captain Ortega had given it to him. Each member of the squad received one, inscribed with the twins' names on the back. He unclipped the band, turning it in the light to see the names:

Linda & Jeanie

He wondered where those girls were today. They had to be teenagers by now. When Max had briefly known them, they were toe-headed, frightened, screaming for their mother. He remembered the men who had kidnapped the twins. Max remembered what he had done to the men.

It was one of the few times Max had truly believed another man deserved to die.

There's time, Max, but let's keep our mind in the present.

He put the watch back on and focused his thoughts on tonight, and the danger that lay ahead. He needed a good breach, one where no one died, one that paid him well. Unlike what happened to the kidnappers, Max had no desire to kill tonight's men—he only wanted their drug money.

It's a good plan. It's always a good plan.

Max's hour was near.

***

Despite his vigilance, Max had no way of keeping tabs on the entirety of his surroundings. His concern was the strong room, its occupants, and anyone nearby. Two hundred meters away, two men—they looked like locals—sat in a beat-up, rusty Peugeot 403. Neither man smoked and they spoke only in whispers.

Their language wasn't French, but if confronted, they could *parlent Francais* like a couple of Marseilles natives. They wouldn't have been sent here if they couldn't.

The men had parked so there was no light behind their car that might betray their silhouettes. They were experienced operators, well practiced in the craft of long term surveillance.

Max would be disturbed to know that they'd watched him off and on for more than a year. They'd created reams of notes about his habits and activities—notes that were encoded and passed on to the higher-ups. They'd taken photos of him, and even film, all of which was on record at headquarters. They knew his routines; they knew his gait; they knew he smoked an average of 17.3 cigarettes per day. They knew he preferred an afternoon cup of coffee. They knew he preferred brunettes to blondes. They even predicted tonight was the night he would perform his breach.

They knew Max.

Though neither man would admit it to anyone else, they admired their mark, for his skill and for carving out such a niche that provided him a good living. On more than one occasion, the two men had discussed leaving their organization and picking up where Max left off.

Because tonight would be the last time Max Warfield ever breached another narcotics strong room.

As he smoked one of his 17.3 cigarettes, the men continued to keep watch over him.

Patience versus patience. Strength versus strength.

***

Khalil, *abn aleahira*, was late. Again.

Hakim swilled the harsh wine from the jug and rolled another cigarette. He blew on the paper to dry his saliva before he lit it. Then he dragged deeply on the tobacco, subconsciously satisfied with the popping sound as the rush of oxygen fueled the fire. As he exhaled smoke like a dragon through his khaki teeth, he muttered foul curses over enduring a minute of extra time in this stinking hellhole of a room. The hole in the floor hadn't been flushed with seawater in a week—the urine and excrement building to an unbearable stench.

More bored than disgusted, he fingered the bags of money, again pondering what might happen if he took it upon himself to steal the entire drop and leave.

"You'd better stop thinking about it," Mustafa warned. He sat across from Hakim, his chair leaned back against the wall. Because Mustafa's eyes were closed, Hakim had thought he was asleep.

"How'd you know what I was thinking?" Hakim asked.

"It's what you're *always* thinking."

"Because it's a lot of money."

"And you'd be dead before you made it to Aubagne," Mustafa countered. "Nothing in life is free. Ever. My father told me this every day until I left home."

"Your father spends his days knee-deep in goat shit."

"Doesn't matter. He spoke the truth."

"Who says I'd head to Aubagne? Maybe I have a boat waiting. Ever thought of that?"

"You don't have a damn thing."

"Don't you want to be rich, Mustafa?"

"I am rich." Mustafa laughed deeply. "Now roll me a cigarette, will you?"

Hakim tapped a fingernail on his cheap wristwatch. "When's that *chatte* going to get here anyway?"

Mustafa cocked his eyebrow. "What's your hurry?"

"I've got things to do. If I was paid overtime, it'd be different."

"Overtime? That'll be the day."

"It's happening all over France," Hakim declared. "We should all band together and demand it."

"Yeah, that'll go over real well. They'll find our remains floating in the Med, ripped apart by sharks." Mustafa snorted before narrowing his eyes. "Where are you going tonight when you leave? New boyfriend?"

"I'll have you know, there are women panting for me, all around the city."

"Goats or sheep?"

Hakim finished the cigarette and tossed it to his smart-mouthed friend. Hakim then took a slug of the wine, winced, and passed it to Mustafa. Just as Mustafa drank from the jug, the single light bulb overhead flickered out. Both men noisily grabbed their weapons, old STEN guns that may or may not work as designed.

"It's about damn time," Hakim hissed, watching the light.

The light came back on. Then off. Then a series of flickering on and off occurred, confirming the correct pattern.

"He owes us ten minutes tomorrow night," Hakim muttered, dropping his weapon on a burlap bag after the light burned brightly once again.

He waited until Khalil smacked the thick wooden door with his palm. Hakim unbarred the heavy door and pulled it open. "Where the hell have you been?" he asked.

Because of the light in the room and the bulb he'd just stared at, he wasn't able to see Khalil clearly in the black rectangle of the doorway. But Hakim did see the tongue of yellow-orange light. This was just before he was thrust backward as the shot from the shotgun blast struck him squarely in the chest.

***

During the seven days and nights of Max's surveillance, it had become obvious that the flickering light sequence was used as the code for entry, regardless of which shift was changing. Even in the daytime, the bright bulb could easily be seen turning on and off. Though Max had attempted to understand the pattern, he'd come to the realization that the code was changed on a daily basis. Thankfully, the old-fashioned throw switch was located in the adjacent alley, down by the water, just behind the strong room. The switch was situated behind a wooden panel that had to be removed before the person sending the code could access it. He'd shaken his head upon watching this process, because each courier or incoming guard had to stick their hand into the wall in order to the throw the switch.

The perfect vulnerable position. Only an idiot would have approved such slipshod security measures.

A half-hour before he blasted his way into the strong room, Max had padded quietly to the alleyway, hiding in the shadows just around the corner. No one had approached while he waited. Most locals knew what went on here, and dared not linger near this underworld hotbed for fear that they'd end up with their throat slit. At 12:06 A.M., the man Max had coined as "Hairy" had slipped into the alleyway and accessed the switch. Max palmed the leather-wrapped blackjack, waiting and watching the light in the small window. When Hairy finished with his code, just as he was pulling his arm from the black rectangle, Max lurched forward, hammering the sap onto the Algerian's thick skull.

The man dropped like a lead weight. Max caught him and quickly covered his head with a thick jute sack to muffle any sounds he might make. Judging by the smell of wine, Max would bet Hairy wouldn't stir until morning.

Max had then turned, listening. Nothing. No response from the strong room. He used a thick Ty-Rap to secure the Algerian's wrists—then Max lifted the bag containing the drop the Algerian had carried. Max set it off to the side. Going strictly by feel, he checked his shotgun, an Ithaca 37 Stakeout. Max lifted the gun and, mimicking Hairy's style, he smacked his palm on the door one time.

Then he took one step back.

Muffled voices could be heard, followed by the unbarring of the door. When it was pulled open, Max unleashed his first round of buckshot, watching with a millisecond of satisfaction as the one he called "Grumpy" was thrust backward as if he'd been struck in the chest with a wrecking ball.

Red wine went tumbling as the wide-eyed second guard, "Fatso," stood in alarm, a cigarette sparking as it tumbled from his mouth. Fatso took a shotgun blast to his ribs for his trouble. He smashed into the wall and crumpled unnaturally to the floor.

Damn, that'll hurt tomorrow.

As the smell of cordite and spilled red wine mingled with the disgusting smell of a pit latrine, Max dumped all the resident cash into his black bag, including the take from Hairy. Leaving both men writhing and groaning, and probably *wishing* they were dead, Max held the shotgun at the ready as he stalked through the mews and up the quay to his Triumph motorcycle. Once there, he placed his shotgun in the bag and secured it behind him. He tugged his 1911 up, out of his waistband, jamming it under the rubber strap on the side of the tank. He'd keep it there for the first few kilometers, ready to use it if needed.

Max slung one leg over the bike and turned the choke. It was cool tonight—he'd have to employ the choke for a few hundred feet. He gave the bike a smooth kick and it sputtered as the smell of fuel touched his nose.

"Not tonight, baby…please."

Kicked again. No ignition.

He looked back. Nobody. Above him and a short distance away, a heavyset young woman leaned out her window and watched. There was a faint amount of light coming from her flat. She moved away from the window. Max took another look behind him.

Still no one.

He let go of the throttle, kicking the bike five times, hoping whatever fuel was in the cylinder would burn out.

Finally, on his next kick, the Meriden engine grudgingly took hold, rumbling to life as the smell of gasoline filled the air. Max held the clutch and popped it into first, cruising slowly through the mews before whipping left onto the darkened Rue de Lyon in Marseilles' 2nd Arrondissement. He leaned down and slowly moved the choke open. The engine was now warm and pulled with great torque. It wasn't until he was kilometers away, in Pertuis, that he relaxed and slid his 1911 into his saddlebag. No one had followed him. No one had died. And judging by the weight of the bag that had cut into his shoulder on the walk to the motorcycle—certainly not a scientific indicator—tonight's haul was potentially significant. Max hoped that perhaps it would carry him all the way through to next summer, when he could reconnoiter his next breach in the luxury of warm temperatures.

His thoughts had drifted to summer weather because a significant chill had soaked into Max's bones over the steady climb from Marseilles. It was past 1 A.M. now—more than an hour since he'd taken his newest haul. Regardless of his take, he was rather satisfied with the buildup and result of this particular mission. Tonight was another shining example of why patience and planning are necessary for such precision. This might have been his finest work since the takedown in Nice last year. He wouldn't know until he counted the cash.

Max killed the engine and coasted the last 200 meters, parking his pearl gray/tangerine Triumph in the forecourt of the surrounding quad of tenement flats.

Stretching the knots from his back and legs, he lit a Gitane and surveyed the area. No movement or lights anywhere. His flat was paid for through the week and it was painfully obvious that the slumlord here wasn't doing a boom business. In fact, Max had only noticed two other tenants in the quad of 16 flats surrounding Max's temporary hovel. One flat was used by twin brothers—they were roofers and usually staggered in drunk and arguing by 11 P.M. The other flat was utilized by an obvious prostitute who seemed to have only two regular customers, one who typically visited in the morning, the other in mid-afternoon. Her johns always wore suits and probably worked nearby, able to slip here under the noses of their wives and employers.

Dragging deeply on his warm Gitane, Max alternated sliding his freezing cold hands up under his shirt, letting his body temperature warm them. He stood there, puffing his cigarette until it was gone and he could feel his fingers again. After slinging the bag over his back, he quietly took the wooden stairs up to his flat. Once he'd had a bite to eat, he'd count the money before rolling it tightly for the first leg of tomorrow's long ride to Paris. There was a chance he'd make the ride in one day, but the weather and traffic would have to be perfect. It's doubtful they would be, in which case he'd break the ride into two segments, especially with the looming prospect of significant time off with Ludivine.

He envisioned the upcoming winter with his lovely companion: cozy dinners, shows, perhaps even a trip to Normandy—there was much to look forward to.

Don't get ahead yourself, Max. What if she finds out about you?

He answered himself.

You've hid your secret successfully for a year. She won't find out.

Then, perhaps it's time to tell her?

Let's think about this tomorrow.

At the top of the stairs, under the solitary light on the stoop, Max scratched a match alight and eyed the bolt lock. The millimeter of brown thread protruded from the keyhole, just as it was supposed to. He removed it and knelt. On the threshold, the fine dusting of talc was undisturbed. No one had bothered his flat.

After keying the door, Max stepped inside and gently placed the bag on the floor. He locked the door behind him and crossed the room. Then, just as he was reaching for the light on the small bar, he was struck in the lower back by what felt like a baseball bat. From his left, he was tackled and dropped to the floor by a man who was much larger and stronger.

As he struggled, something hard pounded Max on the top of his head and knocked him out. Just before he took the blow to the head, Max concluded that these weren't mere robbers after his bag of money. They'd slipped into his flat via the window, bypassing his rudimentary precautions.

If this was the Unione Corse, or some other crime syndicate, seeking retribution for the money he'd stolen from them, Max was in for a torturous end to his tumultuous life.

But it wasn't the Unione Corse, and it certainly wasn't some smaller syndicate.

Max *was* correct about the torture. Quite correct. It would be indirect and bewildering.

The three men departed a half-hour later.

Their destination was hell.

Chapter Two

Consciousness returned to Max. Despite the blow to his head, he remembered what had happened in his flat. Based on the road noise, he knew he was in the back of a vehicle, lying supine on the cold metal floor. Several quick tugs revealed that his arms, his legs, and his midsection were bound to the floor by what felt like aircraft cables. His wrists were raw, the cable cutting into his flesh even without conscious tugging. He was dangerously cold, his teeth chattering fitfully.

Max's mouth was taped shut and a blindfold covered most of his eyes. It had slipped upward, giving him a sliver of vision. He lifted his head, realizing he was in a panel van of some sort. In front of him, a large man drove as a cigarette burned in the ashtray to his right.

Head pounding, Max made a plea through the tape that came out as nothing more than a hum. The driver turned, his crooked nose visible in the road light. He spoke English with what sounded like an American accent, telling Max to shut up. "And if you don't, I'll stop the van and beat you with a stick." In demonstration, the man lifted a stick from the floor—a shortened rake handle.

Simple yet effective.

Craning his neck, Max tried to glean other details but all he could tell was that he was tightly bound and could only see forward, barely, through the bottom edge of the thick blindfold.

Max's head pounded a steady tattoo. The exact spot where he'd taken the blow was resting on the hard floor. It ached, the pain shooting forward to his eyeballs. In fact, as Max's consciousness grew keener, the pain intensified. Freezing cold, bound securely, and with the dread of knowing he'd been captured, Max felt as miserable as he had in years, and he had no idea where he was headed. Or, who had captured him.

The driver's English sounded American. What the hell?

Max didn't sleep again during the ride. Sheer misery. The van stopped three times, twice for gasoline—made evident by the rushing sound as the gas entered the neck pipe of the tank. Each time the driver exited, Max made as much noise as he could. He garnered no response from anyone. After the third stop, the driver feasted on something that smelled so incredibly good. It had meat, and mustard, and onions. Worst of all was the smell of hot bread. Max was hungry. He was thirsty. He was in pain.

The long drive, combined with Max's discomfort, were complete agony.

It would soon get much, much worse.

***

His jail cell, if one were to call it that, was without light of any measure. There were no benches or beds—only a few cracks and crevices that Max discovered within minutes of being unceremoniously thrown inside. He'd taken significant time to touch and feel every inch of the space he could reach, all of it built from cold and gritty concrete. By this point, Max had no idea how long he'd been there—days for sure. Perhaps even a week. But there was no way for him to tell. No light. No routine. Nothing. There was a single bucket that was now overflowing with Max's syrupy piss and watery shit. Over the balance of his stay, he'd been given a grand total of six cups of water and three thick slices of hard bread that smelled of mold. After the first serving of nourishment—which arrived through a sliding steel slot in the door that betrayed no light—a large rat had materialized, though Max didn't know from where.

The rat was wily and, because there was no light, Max had yet to kill him. It wasn't for a lack of trying. Once, as Max slept, the rat tore into the flesh of his hand. Max had managed to grab the massive rodent but it squirmed away before he could do any damage.

So, Max began to accept that he and the rat were in this together. Despite their tenuous partnership, Max had attempted to catch the rat numerous times. The rat always knew when Max was sleeping, because that's when he'd risk a bite of Max's skin. Max now had six rat wounds in all, the most painful on his ear.

The darkness, cold, hunger and general discomfort had all begun to take their toll. Max was a hard man, but no man is hard enough to survive such conditions over the long haul. Delusions began after his second feeding. Shivers came and went. Paranoia. Max began to hear voices. His father was a regular visitor, only the visits weren't pleasant. He'd ask Max why he hadn't finished his chores, then he would backhand Max the way he always did.

After the third feeding, Max's vomiting commenced. It was explosive at first, soon followed by dry heaves and retching.

Then came the fever. Searing, burning hot fever that alternated between periods of heat exhaustion and freezing cold. His teeth chattered so hard they might have cracked.

Through his delirium, Max wondered if he'd developed sickness from the rat. For whatever reason, the rat hadn't taken a bite of him in quite some time. At this point, it didn't matter. Max's retching and coughing had gotten so bad that he wondered if sickness might soon claim him.

He couldn't live much longer in this condition.

His clothes were soiled and he couldn't get warm. The temperature in his cell fluctuated over what he guessed to be daytime and nighttime, but it was always cooler than what a person might find comfortable—probably from 50 degrees Fahrenheit on the low end to 60 on the high end. Too much exposure to temperatures like this, especially while sick, would lead to hypothermia and death.

Max knew all these things from experience, but he couldn't put his experience to good use. As time trudged on, his thoughts began to swing between utter despondency and sheer elation as his mind melded reality with fantasy.

At one point—and the vision seemed so *very* real—Max believed he was rescued by his old platoon-mate Jimmy Cooley, a hardscrabble southerner and perhaps the best soldier Max had ever served with. At first blush, most soldiers had taken Jimmy for a bumpkin. But once they'd served with him a bit, Max and his platoon mates had discovered that Jimmy was a fine sniper and a de facto engineer, able to build all sorts of useful contraptions from common items. And here, wherever this jail cell was, Jimmy breached the concrete wall with improvised explosives and spirited Max away into the bright sunshine. Max saw three guards, all with the same face of the van driver, dead outside the cell.

"Ignore them bastards," Jimmy said to Max, grinning ear to ear. "Follow me to heaven on earth."

The two men ran like hell. They crossed a great field, enduring machine gun fire, the tracers streaking overhead. After splashing through a creek, they entered a jungle similar to what Max recalled from the islands of the South Pacific. In minutes, they emerged from a tangle of trees and briars and found themselves on a warm beach with sugary white sand. Though Max had never been to Hawaii, this beach resembled the pictures he'd seen of the 50th state. Jimmy visibly relaxed and led Max to a sunny clearing in the middle of the windswept dunes. They sat facing one another, when Max noticed Jimmy was wearing his old uniform. His face was smeared with black shoe polish, just like they'd always done before battle.

"Ain't no one goin'ta shoot us here, bubba," Jimmy said. "Warm yourself. That cell looked cold as a witch's tit."

"You have no idea," Max said. "Got any food?"

From behind his back, Jimmy produced a giant pineapple.

"My eyes have never seen a prettier sight," Max muttered.

"You wanna do the honors, or you want me to do it?" Jimmy asked, lifting the plump pineapple between them.

"Go ahead," Max said, tilting his face back to the sky, letting the sun's radiance warm him. He wanted to lay back and bask, but his hunger outweighed his desire for warmth.

Jimmy began expertly slicing the pineapple with his trench knife. Max stared at the fruit, never wanting a sugary treat more than that very moment. When Jimmy paused, Max reached for a piece.

"Slow down, Frenchy," Jimmy said, using the moniker Max had gone by over the balance of the war. "This fruit ain't goin' nowhere. Be patient."

Jimmy twisted the fruit one last time, making a few final cuts to reveal only the tender pulp of the pineapple. "There," he said. "You hungry?"

"As hungry as I've ever been."

"Bone appetite," Jimmy said incorrectly, mocking a French accent.

Max accepted a jumbo slice and ate with gusto. The tangy sweet fruit exploded in his mouth, a taste bud bonanza he hoped might never end. He ate another slice, and another.

"Eat up, brother," Jimmy encouraged. "We can find us another one. No offense, but you look like you could use the nourishment."

"Thanks," Max mumbled, his mouth full of the tangy sweet fruit.

As the sugary juices ran down his chin and onto his neck, Max remembered witnessing Jimmy get killed early in the war. He'd taken a rifle round to the face. Despite the provisions of the Hague Convention, Max would have sworn Jimmy's face was ripped off by a hollow point bullet.

Holy shit, that's right…Jimmy's been dead for years. We couldn't even take his body with us. I had his dog tags in my pack until the end of the war.

Max touched his own skin.

And I'm not warmed by the sun. I'm still freezing cold.

He blinked his eyes, looking all around.

It's still pitch black.

I'm still in the cell.

As his hallucination came to a crashing halt, Max realized he wasn't eating a juicy pineapple after all. And those juices running down his chin weren't sweet and they definitely weren't tangy.

They were blood. And guts.

Max was feasting on the rat.

***

"Hear that?" the technician asked his partner.

"He finally got him," the partner answered.

The squealing of the rat was soon replaced by the sounds of frenzied mastication. Bursting into laughter, the first technician slapped the table.

"Damn, they said this guy was hard but I didn't think he was an actual wild animal."

"An animal or has he just gone crazy? Probably won't make it much longer. Winthrop needs to end this."

The technician pressed on his earpiece. "Listen to that…you can hear him crunching the bones. We better call."

His partner gagged and laughed at the same time. Then he phoned Mr. Winthrop.

***

Light.

It faded in gradually via an overhead bulb that was at least twelve feet up, well out of Max's reach.

As Max's eyes adjusted, he experienced a burst of energy as one of his senses awakened from dormancy to resume its usefulness. It was as if an entire new world opened up before him. From darkness to light, creation occurred, and Max indeed felt reborn. Most human beings take for granted how critical light is. Its mere presence made Max feel whole again.

He surveyed the room. The door was painted dark gray, just a bit darker than the concrete. Max saw the disgusting bucket and the soiled area of the floor where he preferred to sleep. His eyes moved upward. He now knew where the rat came from—there was a sizeable crack in the top corner of the room, out of reach. The concrete was rough enough that the rat had been able to walk vertically with his sharp claws.

Speaking of the rat, Max saw what was left of it on the floor—claws, a tail and most of its head. Despite his revulsion, eating the rat had quelled his retching, amazingly enough. Max turned away and viewed his own arms and legs.

He was, of course, filthy. The floor of the concrete cell was rather dirty, much of the dirt and soil now clinging to Max's skin and the jumpsuit he wore. His hands were a mess, especially the one that had been ripped open by the rat. It oozed green around the edges of the wound. Max's ankles were raw from the aircraft cable, made worse by the rat bites and scratches.

For what seemed an hour, he examined himself and the cell. Despite his condition and the drab concrete box, he was mesmerized and vowed to never again take his vision for granted.

Finally, there was a loud click before the door opened. A squat man in plain olive fatigues held the door, a shiny black baseball bat in his other hand. His face contorted when the stench touched his nose. Behind him was a slightly taller man in a gray suit. The man in the suit stepped forward. He was of average height and had grayish-dark hair and horn-rimmed glasses. His gray-blue eyes were a bit close together, giving him a hawkish appearance. He sent the soldier away before he placed his hands behind his back and greeted Max perfunctorily, in American English.

"I *do* apologize for the poor treatment. You will be cared for and fed, then I will be back to speak with you." He took on a reproachful expression. "Max, without your ongoing cooperation, you will be placed in this cell again and forgotten about. Do you understand?"

Max was dumbstruck.

"I'll take your silence as assent."

"Wait…"

"Yes?" the man asked.

"I haven't seen another person in…how long have I been in here?"

"Eight days. And during that time, you've had six pints of water, three slices of stale bread, and approximately three-quarters of a large black rat. Again, I must emphasize that if you don't cooperate going forward, you will be put back in this cell, and there will be nothing more to eat or drink. Ever." The man frowned. "I'm told you'll make it three or four more days before you die. So?"

"I'm, uh…"

"Not thinking clearly? It's understandable. We're not savages. We'll give you a chance to regain your bearings under more suitable conditions. You and I will speak again soon, Max. Things are looking up for you."

"I do understand," Max said, not wanting this moment to end.

The man appeared pleased. "Good. So, you'll cooperate with exactly what I request of you? I can assure you that what I have planned for you is well within your current skill set and modus operandi."

In a dark and repressed corner of Max's mind, he couldn't believe the words he heard escaping his own mouth in what sounded like an obsequious tone. "Yes, I'll cooperate."

"Very good."

Max's eyes drifted down to the rat's tail and the remains of his gnawed claws. The rat's glazed eye stared up at him. Max shivered. "And I don't ever want to come back here."

The man's eyes followed Max's. "I don't blame you."

"Please, sir. I'll do whatever you want."

"Good. If so, you shall not have to languish in this cell anymore."

"Thank you, sir. Thank you."

Despite all the years of training; despite his toughness; despite his reputation; Max Warfield had been broken by the man in the suit.

Or so the man in the suit thought.

Chapter Three

A clear voice awoke Max. It was the man. Max had not seen him in four days. During that time, Max had lived in a small apartment that was mere feet from his concrete jail cell. Despite their proximity, the two spaces couldn't have been any more different. In the jail cell, hardly any of his needs were met. Here, in the apartment, Max had just about everything he needed to survive in comfort.

When he was first removed from the jail cell, he was strapped to a gurney and given several IVs before being examined by two doctors who spoke English. This was done just outside the cell in a stark white hallway. There were no markings on the walls and no windows to see out of. Neither doctor responded to Max's queries unless they had to do with his physical condition. The doctors had taken Max's blood and given him several shots. One of them returned two days later and spoke through the sliding slot in the apartment door. He told Max his blood work was clean and he should require no further treatment. He asked about the bite wounds and also inquired as to Max's general state of health. Other than his complete bewilderment, Max felt almost back to normal after two days of liquids, food and rest. Now, four days after leaving the cell, Max felt fine although he knew he was weaker than before. His strength would return with time and exercise.

Max's apartment, as he'd come to know it, had no windows other than the sliding communicating slot on the door. The apartment was a simple square room with a comfortable single bed and a multitude of sheets and blankets. The walls were tan and the floor deep green linoleum. Most of the floor was covered by a gray area rug. There was an easy chair and a stack of old books about a variety of subjects. There were also magazines that were between one and three years old. There was a separate toilet adjoining his room and a small cabinet next to his wall locker. There was an adjustable radiator against the wall that kept the room quite warm. A multitude of snacks were stored in the cabinet, along with Max's brand of cigarettes. In the wall locker were two clean jumpsuits, underwear, socks and shoes. Max's captors checked on him every few hours and seemed to be responsive to his needs, although he correctly guessed their positive nature would change if he got out of order. On one occasion Max asked if he could go outside. The answer was a quick and plain "no."

Each day, Max's head was covered by a shroud as he was led to a nearby gymnasium. It had high windows well above Max's field of vision. The windows displayed cloudy skies and, on one day, rain. But the light of the sky aligned with the time of the clock on the wall in Max's apartment. The ability to comprehend the current time, despite seeming trivial, is extremely helpful in the managing of one's psyche. Max was now able to reconcile himself to a schedule and, after the second day, he'd attempted to be as vigorous as possible with his gym exercise.

Over the balance of his four days, he'd been provided with decent food and was given several choices for each meal. One night he'd even been fed a decent sirloin steak and a baked potato. Along with the available snacks and cigarettes, Max was offered beer or wine if he wanted it. He declined the alcohol. Other than his medical care, all of Max's needs were provided by men in plain olive fatigues. None of the men wore identifying name tags, rank or unit insignia of any type. But on more than one occasion, Max had heard military marching cadence being called in the distance. The cadences were all in English. This, combined with the bland construction of his environs, led Max to believe he was on an American military installation somewhere in Europe.

His assumptions were confirmed on the afternoon of the fourth day, when the man in the suit returned.

The man wore the same, or similar, plain gray suit. It appeared to have been expertly tailored. He wore a crisp white shirt and a thin burgundy tie with a plain gold clasp. His black wingtips were highly polished and his horn-rimmed glasses gleamed. The man's salt and pepper hair once again appeared to have been freshly barbered, and the man's face didn't show a trace of a whisker. His eyes were dull, blue-gray as Max had first thought, and he had small teeth that hardly showed when he talked. If Max met him on the street, he'd guess him to be an accountant or a banker.

"How do you feel, Max?"

Max shrugged. "Fine, I guess."

"May I sit?"

"Yes."

The man gestured to the two-seat table in the middle of the room. Before he sat, he removed his jacket and hung it on a hanger in the wall locker, leaving the locker open. He took his seat and eyed Max.

"You probably have some questions, Max."

"I do."

"We'll get to those. Before we do, will you please lift your sleeves to your elbows?"

Max knew what this was about, even though they'd already had a chance to view his tattoos during his medical exam. Regardless, right now was not the time to resist. Max pushed up each sleeve of the comfortable white jumpsuit, displaying both tattoos for his captor.

On Max's left forearm was a rather complicated tattoo of a black demon holding a red arrowhead that was inscribed with "USA" horizontally and

"Canada" vertically. Behind the demon were crossed arrows. Max and his platoon mates had gotten different versions of this tattoo aboard a ship in the Mediterranean.

On his right forearm was a skull. The skull wore a black beret and smoked a long cigar. As far as the quality of the tattoos was concerned, this one was better, performed by a drunken German woman in Garmisch-Partenkirchen, nine years before. Max had been alone when he'd gotten the skull tattoo, not too long before things went bad for him.

Max's guest tilted his head slightly backward, finding the right angle of his bifocals. Then, he touched each tattoo, tugging on Max's skin. When it seemed he approved, he sat back and crossed his arms.

"May I tell you a few things?" the man asked.

"Sure."

"I dislike that word," the man said. "It hints at uncertainty."

"Tell me anything you like," Max clarified.

Satisfied, the man nodded before he spoke. "You are Maxime Victor Warfield, but you've gone by the nickname of 'Max' since you were a child. You were born in Chicago, Illinois, to a first-generation French mother and a father of dubious English origin who was once a boxer. You're the youngest of six, two of whom have died." The man dipped his head. "If you didn't know your oldest sister died last year, I do apologize for having to be the one to tell you."

Max already knew.

The man pulled in a deep breath through his sharp nose. "You dropped out of school when you were fourteen and worked as a mason. Over time, you specialized in dangerous work at great height—probably a preview of the fearlessness you would often display later in life."

The man gestured to Max's hands. "Along with your tattoos, your other trademark is the size of your hands. If I didn't see the rest of you, Max, I'd guess those rough hands of yours belonged to someone four inches taller and forty pounds heavier. The doctors feel that you were probably malnourished as a child, the product of a whoring mother and a no good, apathetic father."

Max knew better than to respond to the insults. He blinked once.

"The discovery I find most striking, Max, is how utterly unaffected you are by your life and all you've been through. Though you can be violent, you're not a menace to society. You knock over criminals and steal their money, yet you preserve life. You're not shell-shocked from your time in the military, either. Your pathetic excuse for parents didn't seem to put much of a dent in your psyche. All in all, you're a normally adjusted human being—a bit of a loner...nothing wrong with that—who is simply making ends meet illegally because he's wanted for a crime."

Max stared.

"Part of the reason you were chosen is the fact you're not some broken individual with a myriad of problems."

"How did you learn so much about me?" Max asked.

The man removed a peppermint, carefully unwrapping it and sucking annoyingly for a moment. "That's the tip of the iceberg, Max. I know quite a bit more." He then flattened the peppermint wrapper, carefully smoothing it and folding it into a tidy square.

"What's next?" Max asked.

When the man was finished with the wrapper, he turned his head and spoke sharply, saying, "Bring it in."

One of Max's guards entered with something wrapped inside of a white sheet. The object was approximately the size of a shoebox, and rather heavy, judging by the way the guard handled it. The guard placed it on the table with a heavy clunk and departed. Without fanfare, the man slid the sheet off the box.

Max struggled not to react.

"You, of course, recognize this." When Max didn't respond, the man continued. "You buried this on the south end of Cemetery Saint Vincent, right on the border between Paris's Seventeenth and Eighteenth Arrondissements. It contains 1,500 U.S. dollars—probably your emergency fund."

Max struggled not to react because he'd buried it during the summer, at three in the morning. That had been five months ago. He'd left no map of its location—memorizing it in his mind. To Max, this proved that he'd been watched for a significant amount of time.

Just before he crunched the peppermint, the man winked confidently and said, "Just the tip of the iceberg."

"Impressive," Max said, struggling to remain passive.

"I don't leave items to chance, Max."

His ego is showing through. Perhaps an opportunity later?

Changing the subject, Max attempted to learn a bit about his current situation. "What's your name?"

"I'm Mister Winthrop."

"So, Mister *Winthrop*, am I on a military installation?"

"Irrelevant."

"Fine. Then tell me what it is you want from me."

Mr. Winthrop smiled warmly and flattened both palms on the table. "Right down to business. This is the type of interaction that I prefer." He pointed at Max. "You went AWOL soon after being transferred back to the States, when you were stationed at Fort Ord, in California."

Max said nothing.

"You're wanted for murder although, in my opinion, the worst you'd have gotten from a jury of your peers was manslaughter. Had you gotten yourself a good attorney, you might have made a decent run at self-defense. That gentleman you killed had a lengthy record." Mr. Winthrop wagged his finger. "But that ship has now sailed, wouldn't you say? You resurface, and they're going to put you away for murder."

Max didn't react.

"So, you lammed it. And although those mid-decade years are a mite muddy, it appears you began supporting yourself by knocking off criminal organizations and undesirables for their cash. A modern day Robin Hood, except you didn't donate your earnings to charity." Mr. Winthrop eyed the ceiling, recalling the information. "Best I can tell, you've had successful runs in Los Angeles, Houston, and a *long* run in New Orleans—no surprise there. You then jumped up to Boston before you finished out your American tour in Washington D.C. We may have missed you somewhere, because there were some gaps in what we were able to find. At the end of the decade, you popped up in Paris. The scent of your trail here in Europe is rather strong, Max. Smart to work in France, since you're fluent. Not smart to stick to one country, though, because sooner or later, you were going to get burned by the Unione Corse."

"They wouldn't have caught me."

"Think what you want. You've been under rotating surveillance for nearly a year, when you were chosen."

"Chosen for what?"

"We'll come back to that tomorrow." Mr. Winthrop tapped his watch. "I'll be here at ten in the morning. At that time, I'll provide a brief précis of what I want from you. You can decline, Max. But if you do, you go right back into that concrete cell," he said, pointing, "...where you'll remain until your death."

"You told me that already."

"I'm telling you again. We won't watch. We won't listen. We won't care."

Max believed him without reservation. "And if I cooperate?"

"You'll have one job to do. One," Mr. Winthrop said, displaying his vertical index finger. "It's difficult, but it has a reward component."

"After the job?"

Mr. Winthrop's eyes twinkled. "You'll be back on the run. There'll be no expunging of past crimes, or anything like that. I can't help you there. But you'll be well compensated for this mission. You're an old alley cat, Max. I suspect with the money you'll have, you'll be just fine."

Max was quiet.

"Oh, there's one more thing," Mr. Winthrop added. "In Marseilles, the last score you took..."

"Yeah?"

"The two men you shot and the one you knocked out in the alleyway, the three Algerians?"

"Yeah?"

"They're all dead."

Silence.

Winthrop continued. "As of today, the gruesome triple homicide is unsolved, but the pendulum could very well swing to you, Max."

"I didn't kill them."

A smirk. "Believe me, they're dead, Max. Shotgun blasts. And the shell casings that match your gun could turn up at any moment, quite near the strong room. There's a woman nearby who saw a man who looked just like you speeding away on his Triumph motorcycle. He almost didn't get it started. With her testimony, the shell casings, and your background, I'd say you're in deep shit." Mr. Winthrop rapped on the table twice. "See you in the morning."

"Wait. If I don't cooperate, I go back to the cell. So, why frame me for the murders, too?"

"If you accept this mission, you'll have certain freedoms. But if you try to escape, the murders come into play. The same applies after the mission. Once you're on the run, you can avoid any unpleasantness by simply keeping your mouth shut."

Max didn't reply.

"Do you understand?"

"Yes, I do."

"Good." Mr. Winthrop glanced at the door. "Would you care for some company?"

"Company?"

"A woman. You have needs."

Max's mouth opened but he didn't know how to respond.

"You can have intercourse with her, if you'd like. Tell you what, I'll arrange it. Anything short of violence is fine." Mr. Winthrop smiled and nodded—such benevolence.

After he called out, a guard opened the door and Mr. Winthrop departed.

Max put his potential woman visitor out of his mind and focused on what he'd just learned.

Whatever brokenness he had experienced in that concrete cell had faded away. And though his mind was relatively clear and his confidence mostly restored, there was still a certain measure of defeat that came with captivity. Even the most hardened criminal can puff his or her chest out, claiming to be fearless. But when one has no freedom, it robs that individual of a large measure of effectiveness. Because of that, Max couldn't help but be stricken by an undercurrent of dread.

Whoever this prick Mr. Winthrop really was, he wanted something significant from Max. All the planning that had gone into this stunt: surveillance for nearly a year; a deep background investigation; this private prison, replete with a staff of American guards and doctors in a foreign land. And the cherry on top: three dead men in Marseilles. It would be an open-and-shut case, especially with Max's history.

Who would go to such trouble to set up an operation like this? Whoever it was, the tab for the operation must have been enormous.

And it wasn't going to be a government or some shadowy organization left with the bill. No. Max knew exactly who was going to be stuck with the tab.

It was him.

***

Mr. Winthrop stood in his hotel room, his drapes open as a blanket of darkness fell over Stuttgart, Germany. He'd driven directly here after departing Panzer Kaserne. Winthrop was listed on Panzer Kaserne's VIP register as Timothy Pooler, Assistant Secretary of the Army (Manpower). Of course, he was not Timothy Pooler, nor did he work for the U.S. Department of the Army. That cover had been provided for him and had come off without a hitch. When he first arrived, several weeks before, along with a staff of twelve men, he'd had coffee with the toadying post commander, telling him he needed complete seclusion for his human factors project on the southwestern corner of the installation. The commander, an ill-informed colonel with great hunger for his first star, promised Mr. Pooler anything he needed.

Everything had since gone to plan.

Many months before, Mr. Winthrop had been certain there was a mirror operation taking place elsewhere. There was no way all the eggs were being put in the one Max Warfield basket. But after Max had been captured, Winthrop was assured his man was the only candidate for the mission. A year ago, when Mr. Winthrop had first discovered Max, he was certain this American with a French pedigree was the right man for the job. Max was skilled. Max was vicious. And Max was highly motivated—the concrete cell had taken care of that.

In other words, Max was perfect.

Mr. Winthrop poured himself a healthy shot of chilled vodka, shooting the drink as he awaited the call. Minutes later, at 1700 hours local, the call came in. He spoke briefly to his superior, Mr. Vickers, predicting that Max would cooperate without reservation.

After several questions, Mr. Winthrop answered neutrally. "I'm as certain as I can be, but one never knows how a man like this truly works." He listened for a moment. "Yes. I'd go forward with him today. As I've said many times, he's as good a candidate as exists, and he's a loner to boot."

Winthrop listened for a moment. "I'm pleased to know we're moving forward. Have a good evening."

Afterward, he made another phone call, removing his tie as he spoke to the concierge, who he'd tipped a small wad of money on his way in. The concierge had done as he'd been asked. Mr. Winthrop hung up and checked his watch. He shot two more cold vodkas as he awaited his guests, allowing the alcohol to disrobe him of his daytime inhibitions. His guests arrived shortly after 1800 hours. Displaying a rare smile of warmth, Mr. Winthrop, their well-paying customer, ushered them in.

The two young women accepted drinks from him. They listened to his flawless, university-level German as he described what he wanted. One of the women, the older one, asked for an additional 30 marks each, due to his special requests. Once everything was agreed upon, the women disrobed and stood before him. He had them turn around, slowly, one at a time. At his command, the two women moved to the bed. They waited.

"Einander lieben," Mr. Winthrop commanded, his tone low and throaty.

The women kissed. In moments, they writhed on the bed—all flesh and hair and scent—while Mr. Winthrop sat in the corner, watching quietly, ingesting shot after shot.

A fascinating show.

***

Max's guest arrived at 8 P.M. She was petite and pretty, but wore too much makeup. He guessed she was about 30 years old. Her hair was bottle blonde, her eyes hazel. She smelled good. Her outfit seemed ridiculous for the setting: a sequined cocktail dress with high black heels. She carried a matching clutch and introduced herself as Kathleen. She sounded American, but her accent beyond that was indistinct.

"What's your name?" she asked.

"Max. Where do you live?"

"I can't tell you that."

"How's the weather?" he asked, measuring his boundaries.

"Cool and rainy."

"Where are we?"

"I can't tell you that, either."

"Okay. Do you know where we are?"

The woman stared.

"Are you a government employee?"

Nothing.

"Would you like a drink?"

"A whisky on ice, please."

Max prepared the drink for his guest. She sipped it and nodded.

23

"What do you know about me?" he asked.

The question seemed to throw her just a bit. She tilted her head. "Almost nothing. I was told you're lonely and might like me."

"I am lonely. Tell me about yourself."

Zilch.

"So, what do you want to do?" Max asked.

"I'm here for you."

"What do you mean?"

She cut her eyes to the bed as one corner of her mouth ticked upward.

He sat there.

"What do you want to do?" she asked.

"I'd like to talk."

"Then talk."

Max gnawed on his bottom lip for a moment. After deliberating for a moment, he leaned back in his chair and began to tell her about his last job in Marseilles. He spoke in great detail, eventually getting to the part about being captured by the men who brought him here. No sooner had he begun to talk about being tied down in the panel van than the door to the apartment was roughly opened.

Two guards in olive drab fatigues entered, gesturing for the woman to exit. She complied. After she was gone, leaving the smell of her perfume in her wake, the older of the guards shook his head as he eyed Max.

"You are one stupid bastard. All you had to do was tell her to get naked and then you could tap her all night long. She was ready, for cryin' out loud."

Max tilted his chair backward and put his hands behind his head. "I didn't want to tap her. Now, would you two please leave?"

Grumbling, the two guards exited and bolted the door shut.

Though he attempted to appear calm, he wasn't. What he'd just done demonstrated he had the tiniest bit of control. Max's mind was awhirl with the possibilities. He slept very little that night.

***

Max had no choice. None whatsoever. Whatever options he had resided in the future, and they would be far away from this compound—this prison. In other words, he had to comply with whatever was in store for him. He'd deal with the consequences later, if it ever got to that. Max had thought the situation through in every conceivable direction and, in the end, he firmly believed Mr. Winthrop's promise that he would imprison Max again in the concrete cell and leave him to die. Second to that were the murders in Marseilles. Even if Max cooperated, they loomed henceforth over his head. But murders he could fight—a prison, he couldn't.

There was something cold and dead behind Mr. Winthrop's eyes—Max had known men like him in the military. Winthrop cared about Winthrop, and no one else. Right now, Max was a mean to Winthrop's end. Later, he'd dispose of Max the same as he'd squash an insect, never thinking about him again. On to the next personal victory, and the next victim.

There was but one path. Cooperate now, and search for a way out later.

Thus, at 10:02 A.M. on Sunday, on his fifth day in the apartment, Max acquiesced to the request Mr. Winthrop made of him. Winthrop, of course, didn't clue Max in beforehand as to what he'd be doing. He simply asked for complete and total cooperation, to which Max agreed. Mr. Winthrop seemed pleased, and now they were down to business. Though Winthrop sucked on another peppermint, Max was able to detect the cloying scent of last night's alcohol. Despite Winthrop's flawless appearance, right down to his hair and grooming, Max marked Winthrop's drinking as a chink in his armor—perhaps one that he could exploit later.

For now, Max focused on what Mr. Winthrop told him as they again sat at the table in the apartment.

"Max, there are certain elements to this mission that I cannot reveal to you until the actual mission commences. Do you understand?"

"If you say so."

"Yes or no."

"Yes."

"Very good. That said, there are a few limited details I *can* now share with you." Mr. Winthrop leaned back and crossed his leg over the other. He removed a piece of lint from his trousers, then spoke academically with the peppermint tucked into his cheek. "You will travel to Paris and perform a robbery that's quite similar to the thefts you've been performing on the narcotics strong rooms. But in *this* instance, there may be more resistance to deal with and far greater outside security."

"How many more people?"

"Three to five."

Max frowned. "And what sort of outside security?"

"Locals."

"Cops?"

"No. Private security."

"Will I be alone?"

"All alone on the breach."

Max leaned back in his chair and crossed his arms. He pondered this for a moment. "Would you mind laying the details of the job out for me? Just tell me what you can, from the time I'm on site until the time I leave."

"Certainly. You'll be driven via an automobile to the facility in question. At that moment, the two guards outside the facility will be immobilized."

"Where?"

"Paris"

"I know that. Where in Paris?"

"You'll learn that later."

"I know Paris quite well. It would be helpful if I knew where."

"Later," Mr. Winthrop answered in a firm tone.

"How will the guards be immobilized?"

"Irrelevant. But they won't be killed, if that's your question. This entire operation will work as your others have, without anyone dying."

Max lifted his cigarettes and Winthrop nodded. Max lit one. "Go on."

"You'll be masked when you exit the car. You'll rush into the facility with your shotgun. Inside, you'll likely have to disable three people on your way to a secure room." Mr. Winthrop removed a strange looking key from his pocket. It was large and circular at its tip. "You will access the room with this key. Inside the room, you will remove a dark gray steel briefcase that will be very heavy because it's lined with lead. It should be on the bottom shelf on the back wall."

"Tell me about the secure room."

"Let me finish. In addition to the briefcase, you'll fill your bag with cash, also in the secure room. I'd recommend you take the currency from the shelf on the right, as the money is worn from previous use. The currency on the left is new and too conspicuous."

"How much is in there?"

"Millions. I also wouldn't take too many bands of large bills. Get my briefcase first, then fill your bag, quickly. From there, you simply hurry back out and get whisked away."

"How heavy is the briefcase?"

Winthrop shrugged. "Forty-pounds, give or take."

Dragging on the cigarette, Max tried to focus on the task, and not the whys and wherefores. Regardless, he couldn't help but ask the next question. "What's in the briefcase?"

Mr. Winthrop hitched as if he was chuckling, but it was without humor. "The money is *yours*—the briefcase is *mine*. What are your questions?"

"Is the money marked?"

"No."

"Are the people I'm taking down French?"

Mr. Winthrop stared for a moment, nostrils flaring. After a moment, as if he'd come to some sort of conclusion, he shook his head. "Irrelevant."

If they were French, he'd have told me so. So, they're not French?

"I can tell you're overthinking, Max. That sort of thing will get you thrown back in your concrete dungeon," Mr. Winthrop warned. "I have options *other* than you."

The sharp tone he spoke the words with made Max believe him.

"It's not just that," Max countered. "I typically scope out a job for weeks before going in. And with something this involved, I'd probably case it for a month."

"I realize that it might seem a bit dismaying, envisioning a job blindly. Rest assured, you'll be able to practice on a full-scale mock-up. We will cover all contingencies. You will be impeccably prepared before you go in."

There were a million more questions to ask about the job itself, but Max decided to set those aside until later. Instead, he asked one that was currently rather unimportant, but didn't infringe upon the type of questions Mr. Winthrop had warned him about.

"Why me?"

Mr. Winthrop didn't react for a moment. Finally he said, "That's a good question."

"Well?"

"Plausible deniability."

"What do you mean by that?"

"You're a thief, Max—a known thief, who's also wanted for murder. You're going into this particular strong room to steal a pile of cash, and there's a mountain of it there, believe me."

"And the briefcase?"

Mr. Winthrop stood. "No one will ever admit it even existed, much less admit that it's gone."

"Are you going to rat me out afterward?"

"Rat you out?" Winthrop asked with a frown. "Now you sound like a common thief. I thought you were above such cellblock vernacular."

"Please answer the question."

"Why would I give you up?"

"So you don't get blamed?"

"I don't know if any organization knows your actual identity, Max. But your modus operandi is well known, so I will assume that the authorities will come to the conclusion that the man who's been knocking off the Unione Corse strong rooms is the same man who hit the secure room in Paris. This is to my advantage." Mr. Winthrop laced his fingers over his starched white shirt. "I'd recommend you go to ground and make your way elsewhere after this score. Perhaps Costa Rica, Australia, or someplace like that."

Then, it hit Max…

As soon as he came out of the target building with the precious briefcase, he was a dead man. Winthrop would have to kill him. If he didn't, Max might get caught. And when he did, he'd tell everything he knew about this operation.

I'm going to be killed.

"You're overthinking," Mr. Winthrop warned.

"I was thinking of where I might go. I wouldn't mind living out my life in the Bahamas."

"So, we have a deal?" Mr. Winthrop asked.

"Yes."

"A deal without reservation?"

"I'll do anything you tell me to do." Max extended his hand.

Mr. Winthrop's hand was cool and thin. "All I ask of you is to get me my briefcase. After that, you're free and on your own."

"Could you help me arrange transportation out of France?"

After a shrug, Mr. Winthrop nodded. "We'll have to build in some time to let things cool down. But, yes, we can do that. Bahamas?"

"I'll let you know."

"Very well." Now that the official portion was over, Winthrop gestured to the bed and cocked an eyebrow. "Am I to understand you didn't copulate with the woman I sent you?"

Max shook his head.

Winthrop's face darkened. "Do you feel well? Are all your systems functioning?"

"I wasn't attracted to her." Max twirled his finger around the apartment. "And even if I were, I had no desire to put on a show for your guards."

"From what I heard, she was disappointed."

Max said nothing.

Mr. Winthrop stood and walked to the door. "Be ready to leave in five minutes. We've a long drive ahead of us."

Max was again loaded into a panel van, this time with a shroud over his head. He was manacled and shackled, but was allowed to sit in a seat. The manacles were covered by fabric and had enough slack that Max could move around just a bit. The viewless drive took approximately six hours. Other than a few short conversations revolving around refueling, the ride was silent. Despite his relative comfort, the blind ride reopened some of the fresh mental wounds from his imprisonment. Max used all of his willpower to remain calm.

When the shroud was removed and Max's eyes had adjusted, he could see he was at a farmhouse. Mr. Winthrop told Max they were in France. He said the closest neighbors were several miles away. He warned of numerous guards around the perimeter of the property, each armed with high-powered rifles. Max eyed two of them—watched their movements—noticed how they held their rifles.

They appeared capable.

"Some you can see, some you can't," Winthrop added.

Max nodded his understanding.

"Do I need to tell you what will happen if you try to escape?"

"No, and I won't try to escape."

"Good. Are you hungry?"

"Yes."

"There's food in the kitchen, and coffee. Get settled in. We start work in ninety minutes."

After a quick trip to the toilet, Max gorged himself.

That evening, his training began.

Chapter Four

Over the following four nights, Max performed countless dry runs. He practiced at night because he would breach at night—in the early evening, actually. The evening shift at the secure room in Paris was lesser in personnel than the day shift. In addition to the shift differences, Mr. Winthrop indicated that Max would find the workers distracted. He wouldn't divulge *why* they'd be distracted. Of course, Max knew better than to persist. In addition to the workers inside, there were at least two guards posted outside. Just as he had in the apartment, Mr. Winthrop had promised that the outside guards would be incapacitated. They would pose no threat. Once again, he wouldn't indicate the method that would be used to take down the outside guards.

"Don't worry about it, Max. It's not in your scope of responsibility. But the inside workers, who are in your scope, will be armed and are highly trained," Winthrop had maintained. "Concern yourself with them, and don't let their appearance fool you."

"What's their appearance?"

"They'll look like businesspeople."

"What kind of place am I hitting? Is this a bank?"

"No."

"If you just tell me, it'll help me prepare."

"Not up for discussion. You'll find out minutes before you go in."

"Well, at least tell me if they're expecting to get hit," Max had pleaded.

"They're *not* expecting to get hit. In fact, the location you're hitting is unknown to most people, and has never been the target of any sort of violence that I'm aware of."

This gave Max a measure of comfort. But just a measure.

"Are the occupants armed?"

"Yes."

"And they're well-trained?"

"Again, yes. *Very* well-trained."

The comfort quickly evaporated.

All of his practice had been done at a mock-up. The mock-up was built to scale, according to Mr. Winthrop. It was located behind the farmhouse and was surrounded by a fence. Inside the fence was a plaza approximately 30 meters wide. At the opposite side of the plaza was a single-story building with a solitary entry.

The mock-up of the structure was rather impressive. Made of plywood and concrete block, it had been painted to resemble a stone building. It had actual windows, but there was no glass in the windowpanes. Mr. Winthrop told Max that the real windows weren't just bullet proof; they were bomb proof, too.

"During the breach, don't even think about trying to slip out through a window and escape. It won't work, and we'll know if you try."

"Why would I do that?"

Mr. Winthrop didn't answer with anything other than a knowing expression.

Outside of the mock-up was a wooden stick-built fence painted to look like black iron. In the front was a vehicle gate. Adjacent was a guardhouse with a pass through gate where Max would enter on foot.

"And the big gate will be closed but the pass through gate will be open?" Max had asked more than once.

"When my men disable the guards, they'll make sure the pass-through is open. Don't worry about it," Winthrop snapped. He was irritable after Max had asked different versions of the same question three times. "We *won't* breach if it's not open."

Behind the guardhouse and to the left was a small nook against the fence. It was approximately 2 feet by 3 feet and flanked by one of the fence columns. Max never mentioned it, but he took note of it during each breach. He noted many other curious fixtures and features about the mock-up, but the nook's seemingly hidden location intrigued him. Why was it there?

"Is this a retail establishment?" Max asked after his fourth practice breach in a row.

"No, dammit. I told you, it's an unmarked location that hardly anyone knows exists."

Max was unapologetic about the questions. "Who will the guards think I am?"

"What does that mean?"

"Am I a burglar? Am I coming in on a paramilitary insertion? Am I a crazy man off the street?"

Winthrop massaged the bridge of his nose. "Irrelevant. You're in and you're out. They won't have time to think."

"Is the area where it's located busy?"

Mr. Winthrop shrugged then nodded. "Pretty busy. It's Paris." Before Max could object, Winthrop cut him off. "Everything's been thought through. No one will know what you're doing because you won't show your shotgun till you're inside. Enough questions."

The plan wasn't too unlike Max's cash room takedowns. Per their rehearsals at the mock-up, Max would exit the car and walk naturally through the pass through gate. He would enter the building via the front door. Inside was a rather small anteroom with a buzzer entry on a reinforced metal door. Despite the pass through gate and guards, all personnel had to be buzzed in past the anteroom. Fortunately, this area was private from the outside. Rather than trying to get someone to admit him, Max would use his shotgun and expend a single frangible round into the metal door, at an angle just to the left of where the electronically activated bolt was located. Though he'd practiced with a dozen frangible rounds in the past week, this part of the operation created his greatest concern—and that was saying something.

Everything about the job gave him heartburn. But if the frangible round didn't work, the entire mission was blown. It meant he wouldn't gain access and he might have to deal with armed workers as he retreated.

"It *will* work," Mr. Winthrop remarked. "Nothing has been left to chance."

If that were the case, why do you need me? Max wanted to ask.

Regardless of reassurances, the frangible round remained at the forefront of Max's mind. He was concerned that the round might not work as advertised. In essence, a frangible round was engineered to disintegrate upon impact, after it had destroyed its target—typically a lock. The benefit of such a round is the fact that it wouldn't ricochet backward and harm the shooter. Allegedly, the round would weaken the union of the lock and door enough so Max could yank the door open with one swift pull.

Assuming he was able to breach the door, the remainder of the job was rather straightforward. Behind the door was a hallway. On the left side of the hallway were two offices and two restrooms. On the right was a meeting room. At the end of the hallway was a vault-like door that led to the secure room. According to Mr. Winthrop, Max would need to incapacitate two or perhaps three workers. These were the men who Mr. Winthrop predicted would be distracted.

"It'll probably be two," Winthrop replied for at least the third time.

"Just a few more questions. Will we know beforehand exactly how many workers are inside?" Max asked.

"No."

"Males?"

"Probably."

"So, there could be women?"

"Yes," Winthrop hissed.

They'd run the scenario with as many variations as they could come up with. Each time, at the start of the scenario, the two guards by the pass-through gate were on the ground, unconscious.

"What if they're not unconscious?" Max asked.

"They will be," Winthrop replied through clenched teeth.

"But what if?"

Winthrop glared.

Max couldn't count how many times he and Mr. Winthrop had had similar exchanges. Whenever Max took the questioning too far, Winthrop threatened him. Despite their bickering, Max had successfully negotiated the breach under every imaginable condition. Last night at 10:20 P.M. Central European Time, Mr. Winthrop had declared Max ready. The two men ate a celebratory dinner of steak, haricot verts and fried potatoes. Mr. Winthrop even removed his jacket as they ate. Max had yet to see the man without a starched white shirt and tie.

"You told me you had other options," Max said, just as they finished dinner.

"I did," Winthrop answered, dabbing his mouth with his napkin. "But you were chosen."

"Why me?"

"You've done well, Max. And we're almost finished. After the breach, you can go your way, and I can go mine." Winthrop tossed his napkin on his plate and prepared to stand.

"And my passage to the Bahamas?"

"It's all set up."

"May I know the details?"

"No."

Max threw up his hands.

"You'll know when you know."

"Where are you from?" Max asked.

Mr. Winthrop arched his eyebrows as if amused. "Do you honestly think I'll tell you that?"

"Why not?"

"I'm American, and that's all you'll ever know." He tapped his watch. "I've got some things to do. You need to rest."

Soon afterward, Max was barred in his farmhouse room just as he had been every night this week. The two windows had been sealed over with brick and mortar. There were two guards outside his room. He had to be let out just to take a piss. Unable to sleep, around 3 A.M., Max sat on the side of his bed and thought he heard the muffled sound of a woman screaming.

But the scream didn't sound like one of agony. It was a scream of ecstasy.

The sounds made Max think of Ludivine. He wondered if he'd ever see her again.

Max dragged deeply on a cigarette, thankful that this charade was almost over. Though he hardly slept, he was heartened because the breach would be finished in less than 18 hours.

One way or another, live or die, Max would soon escape the misery that is captivity.

***

On Friday evening, Max was back in Paris for the first time in nearly a month. He was in the backseat of a Mercedes-Benz 300SE. Mr. Winthrop was beside him. In the front seat was a lone driver, sitting quietly, wringing the steering wheel with his driving gloves. Next to the driver, on the seat, was a submachine gun. In Max's hand was his own Ithaca 37 Stakeout shotgun. It wasn't loaded.

They'd driven into the city an hour before and now waited. Every few minutes, Mr. Winthrop's radio crackled and he held the earpiece to his ear. He'd only uttered a single response word—"Roger"—each time the radio had transmitted. Although Max tried, he couldn't make out anything from the radio transmissions.

Instead, he eyed the quiet driver, a man who'd earned Max's trust over the past week. Strangely enough, he had never heard the driver utter even a single word. Max had only been around him during the test runs, when they would drive to the mock-up together and then race away afterward. The driver was always alone in the front seat, with Mr. Winthrop and Max in the back, just like tonight.

The driver was rather small and had a dark beard with a helmet of black hair. He had swarthy features, and could easily pass for Greek or Turkish. Regardless of how he looked, Max felt the driver was either American or understood English quite well, because he always followed Mr. Winthrop's orders to the letter and without a second's hesitation.

But it was his ability behind the wheel that set the driver apart. Over the past four nights, Max had clung to the door handle in the back of the Mercedes during all manner of evasive driving techniques, transitioning from sheer terror the first time to complete and total confidence in the driver. Max had watched in awe as the driver successfully performed a number of high-speed maneuvers, to include a bootlegger's turn, in the dark, in the rain, while aiming out his window with a MAT-49 submachine gun. The driver performed switchbacks, high speed cornering, rapid backing followed by whip turns—he'd done it all, managing each maneuver with aplomb. Max had yet to witness the man make a mistake.

Last night, just before Max's celebratory steak dinner, the driver had finished the final dry run by whisking Max and Mr. Winthrop away from the property after their simulated escape. This was the first time Max had left the farm property without a shroud over his head and it clued Max in to the farm's location. The driver sped down the curvy pitch black *Condécourt*, falling in elevation to the banks of the Seine. Max recognized the area, knowing they were northwest of Paris. After several kilometers, it was evident the man was showing off, hurtling the car through turn after turn. The only thing that could have killed them was equipment failure, but it seemed the powerful

Mercedes sedan wouldn't dare disappoint the driver who so effortlessly controlled it.

Despite Max's confidence in the driver, he couldn't help but wonder if he was the man who was tasked with killing him after the breach. Or, would it be Mr. Winthrop, himself? Perhaps it was neither of them. Perhaps a firing squad would await Max at some secluded chateau outside the city. They'd drive in, breathless and full of adrenaline after their mission, with good wine and food awaiting Mr. Winthrop and the driver—and a hail of bullets for Max.

More likely, they'll just have one of the snipers shoot me as I'm getting in the car. Other than the mystery of who shot me, it'll give the Parisians a dead perpetrator and everyone will eventually move on with their lives.

Max shrugged away the thoughts—in his mind it didn't matter. They'd absolutely kill him after a successful breach. There was no safe passage to the Bahamas. There was only death. About this, there was no question. All that remained was what Max aimed to do about it.

So now, having breached the mock-up time and time again, there was but one thing to do. Max was going in and he was going to get the briefcase, and get the money. He had no other choice. He simply had to keep his mind open to escape, or maybe some other option that could provide him with the freedom he so desired.

He checked his shotgun, feeling the security of the custom extension tube that held seven rounds. He'd enter with the frangible round already in the chamber, along with seven rubber rounds in the tube. Unlike all his other times, there'd be no steel buckshot as a safe second, nor would Max have his 1911 pistol. He'd only have the shotgun.

"Why can't I take my pistol?" he'd asked Mr. Winthrop.

"You think I'm going to let you come back outside and shoot me after you're done?" Winthrop had countered, shaking his head. "Think again."

"You said you'd have snipers posted. That should give you all the confidence you need."

"No pistol, Max."

That had been the discussion two nights ago. Now, as a bead of sweat gathered on Max's nose, he held out his hand.

"I'd like to load my shotgun now," Max said.

"Not yet," Mr. Winthrop replied, staring out the window at the base of the bridge they'd parked under. In front of him, the driver was silent, smoking a smelly filterless cigarette with his window half-open.

"You wanna tell me who I'm hitting?" Max asked.

Mr. Winthrop looked at his watch. He lifted the two-way radio—it was more compact than any Max had ever seen. Admittedly, he hadn't been around any two-way radios since his time in the Army, but this was surprisingly small and sleek compared to those Max had used. Winthrop held the earpiece into his left ear and made a transmission, laconically asking for a status update. He listened for a moment, his eyes alight before clapping the driver on the shoulder. The driver cranked the Mercedes, flicked his cigarette away and off they went. Winthrop turned to Max.

"Are you ready?"

"I need my ammo."

"You'll get it." The corner of Mr. Winthrop's mouth turned up—a rarity. "Are you prepared to hear?"

"Yes. Tell me."

"You're going to breach a little-known United States Secret Service location."

Max opened his mouth to speak but no sound came out.

"I realize that's probably a bit concerning," Winthrop said. "*Don't*—be—concerned. Just do your job and wear your mask and disappear when this is over with your pile of cash."

"Are you fucking crazy?" Max stammered as the driver roared into the evening Montrouge traffic on Paris' south side.

"No, because our country needs what's in that briefcase. I've set all this up for you, Max. No one knows who you are. You're not killing anyone, nor are you stealing the country's money. Every dollar you take is counterfeit. The counterfeits are why the office was originally set up. Counterfeiting our currency abroad is *huge* business—hundreds of millions annually."

"What's in the briefcase?" Max demanded, thinking Mr. Winthrop might finally tell him now that the hour was nigh.

"You can't know that, Max. Just understand that there's been an extreme lack of cooperation between branches of our government. Believe it or not, what you're doing tonight is a service to your country."

Mr. Winthrop produced a brown paper bag from his leather briefcase. "Load your weapon and keep it pointed away from me." When Max had loaded all the less-than-lethal rounds, Winthrop handed him the single frangible round for the chamber. "Make that one count."

"I wish you'd give me a back up."

"No." Mr. Winthrop reached inside his coat and brandished a shiny silver Walther PPK. He aimed it at Max and cocked the hammer for emphasis.

Sweat springing from numerous zones of his body, Max checked his weapon several times. That done, he placed his mask in his lap.

"We're gonna be early," the driver said, the first words Max had ever heard him speak. He sounded American.

"Linger," Winthrop instructed tightly, keeping his eyes on Max. "I want us pulling up at 1930 hours to the second."

On they drove, as Max tried to reconcile that he was about to punch Uncle Sam squarely in the face.

"Max," Mr. Winthrop whispered. "I know you, and I know what you're capable of. There will be eyes on you the entire time. Don't consider taking a weapon from an agent and trying to use it on me. When you come out, you'll hand me the shotgun, butt first. If you don't, you'll be shot by a sniper and we will have our briefcase and your cash. Do you understand?"

"Yes."

"Say it back to me."

Max did. Then he asked what would happen after he was back in the Mercedes.

"We'll drive back to the farm. You'll stay there for a few days and then depart for the Bahamas with all your money."

"How will I get the money to the Bahamas?"

"Don't think about that right now. It's all planned out. You focus on what you're about to do." Mr. Winthrop almost sounded genuine when he said "*bonne chance*," in a Parisian accent.

On they drove, in the noise and congestion of the 9th Arrondissement, near the famed Moulin Rouge. The citizenry was out and about, barreling into their Friday evening with bliss. The holidays would soon be here. Times were good.

None of them had any idea of the cataclysmic event that would soon occur.

It was now 7:24 P.M. Central Europe Time. The date was November 22nd.

The year was 1963.

Part Two

La criminalité

Chapter Five

The United States Secret Service station in Paris, France was located on the south side of the traffic circle at the Place de Clichy. A bustling roundabout with a busy metro stop, *"Place Clichy,"* as it is known to Parisians, is one of only a few locations in Paris where four arrondissements intersect—in this case, the 8th, 9th, 17th and 18th. In the center of the lively traffic circle was a 6 meter-high monument to Jannot de Moncey, a prominent soldier from the Revolutionary and Napoleonic wars known for, among other things, his refusal to cooperate with King Louis the XVIII. Surrounded by hotels, brasseries, and shops, Place de Clichy couldn't have been more different than any location Max had hit before.

He only had a few moments to ponder this distinction as the Mercedes screeched to a halt on the traffic circle's south side. To Max's right was the black gate and fence, and behind it the low granite building where he would perform his breach.

The mock up had been built exactly to scale. Though it shouldn't have startled Max, it did. The mock up he'd practiced on looked exactly like what he viewed at this very moment, even down to the lighting. The only difference to the naked eye was the surrounding area.

"Go to it," Mr. Winthrop commanded.

Max lurched from the car, his nose assaulted with the mingled scents of exhaust and baking bread. He hesitated inside the pass-through gate's "tunnel", created by thick black fencing on his right and the guard building to his left. There was even a section of fencing overhead, spiked on top. Just as Winthrop predicted, the gate was open, held that way by a piece of thick cardboard between the lock and the fence. Since his shotgun was still in his bag, Max appeared no different than a visitor entering the facility. Looking like an average businessman, he wore a gray blazer with a white shirt and wine tie along with dark gray slacks and comfortable shoes. Topping off his businesslike appearance was a gray fedora that he wore low and cocked. Max paused at the safety glass, peering inside the guardhouse. Both men were on the floor. There was a cigarette burning in the ashtray. Max adjusted his vision so he could view through the talking hole in the glass—thanks to the overhead light, he could see the guards were breathing. He also smelled a chemical odor coming from the guardhouse, similar to chlorine. Max correctly deduced the two guards had been gassed. Winthrop had assured Max that the men would be unconscious for at least 15 minutes—plenty of time to breach and leave.

At this point, everything looked good. The guards weren't a threat and the gate was unlocked. Mr. Winthrop's promises were thus far bona fide. Max stepped inside the gate and replaced the cardboard to keep the gate from locking. He eyed the nook at the back of the guardhouse, confirming Mr. Winthrop couldn't see it from his vantage point on the street. Max shifted his gaze upward, peering at the roofline on the nearest building. The views to the guardhouse were partially obstructed. Committing those facts to memory, Max paused and peered into the shadows of the nook.

There was heavy steel grate there, secured by a padlock.

That's why the nook is there. The grate is either for drainage or ventilation.

Setting his thoughts aside, he hurried across the courtyard, bounding up the steps and into the building. Once inside, he jerked the shotgun from the black bag, replacing it with his hat. He covered his face in the black mask.

Once masked, he listened quietly as his breathing calmed. He heard nothing at all, even when he put his ear to the door he would soon enter.

The anteroom was exactly as it had been replicated in the mock-up—same size, same color, same steel door that presumably led to the prizes. To the left were several sitting chairs and a stack of tattered magazines next to a telephone. Max eyed the steel door, examining the electric locking mechanism. Yes, it was precisely like the one he'd practiced on dozens of times. Max briefly wondered if Mr. Winthrop, or someone else from his organization, had visited with the Secret Service in order to reconnoiter their facility.

Refocusing on the resistance he should encounter behind the door—he'd been told there were two or three agents inside—Max inhaled a deep breath and aimed the shotgun at an angle between the pull handle and the electronic bolt.

Boom!

The frangible round smelled different than normal buckshot—probably due to the powder mingling with the copper shot. Regardless, there was a mangled hole where he'd aimed. Max pumped the Ithaca and yanked the door open, startled to see a man in a white shirt and tie in the hallway, coming Max's direction. The man lifted his pistol. Max drilled him in his chest with the rubber buckshot, watching as he skittered backward while a smattering of crimson stained his shirt.

The masked intruder again pumped the Ithaca. The breach was now full speed ahead.

Pushing forward, Max picked up the agent's pistol, un-cocked it and tucked it under his belt. Max then cleared the first room to the right, the meeting room. To his left, the first office was clear—probably where the agent had come from. At the second and last office, Max halted when he saw a woman standing behind a desk. She was rather tall and attractive, and there were dark mascara lines down both cheeks of her face. She held her hand over her mouth and stared at Max in horror.

Max tensed the shotgun but couldn't quite pull the trigger.

"Come here!" he roared in French. The woman nearly fell, the result of a heel tangling under her foot. She kicked the shoe off and limped around the desk to him. He turned her around, seeing no weapons. He told her to stand flat against the door to the secure room, face first, hands above her head. As she stood there, Max checked the fallen agent's pistol. It was a Colt Detective Special, loaded with .38 Special ammunition. Max rolled the agent to his stomach. Keeping a watchful eye on the woman, Max used his trademark Ty-Rap to bind the fallen agent's hands and ankles. Thankfully, he was still breathing.

After again sliding the revolver into his belt at his back, Max handed the woman the circular key to the strong room.

"Please don't hurt me," she said in English.

"Open it," Max commanded, sticking with his French.

When she hesitated he barked his next question, asking her if she spoke French. She nodded, paralyzed by fear. He repeated his command that she open the door, but this time he spoke the words in a calm voice, finishing with, "*Je ne vous blesserai pas si vous coopérez.*"

Translated, it meant, "I won't hurt you *if* you cooperate."

The woman seemed to calm down a bit. She opened the door with his key and eyed him though her jade eyes, still full with tears. Max told her to go in first. She did. He then used Ty-Rap on her wrists and secured her to the vertical support of the thick shelving to the left. Max hurriedly cleared the space one more time just in case there was someone else in hiding.

There was no one else in the space. It was just Max, the bound agent on the floor and the woman. The agent on the floor was conscious again, but dazed. He was moaning and babbling about being shot.

Max began raking the stacks of bills into his bag, sticking to the money on the right as he'd been told. They were American dollars. Most of the bills appeared to be used, just as Mr. Winthrop predicted, all in large denominations. As Max worked, he turned and viewed the items on the center shelf. At the bottom, exactly where he'd been told it would be, was the briefcase.

The woman cried quietly while Max worked. In all, he'd spent about 90 seconds in the room. His bag full, weighing at least 25 pounds, Max knelt and yanked the heavy briefcase from its spot on the bottom shelf. Just as Winthrop had indicated, the briefcase was abnormally heavy. Several binders that had been stacked on the briefcase tumbled to the ground. Max eyed their contents, realizing they were 35 MM slides. He held a sleeve of them up to the light. They appeared to be mug shots. Leaving the slides, Max stood and prepared to leave. He turned to the woman. She'd buried her face into her bound wrists and shuddered quietly.

Wait a minute…

Despite his urgency, a peculiar notion occurred to Max. When he'd first arrived, she'd *already* had mascara trails down her face. But she couldn't have begun crying so quickly that her makeup had run. He'd seen her within mere seconds of breaching the door.

So, why had she been crying? Something had happened *before* he'd ever breached the Secret Service station. Did she and the man have something going on? Perhaps one of them was married, and Max had walked in on the end of the affair?

No way. Too convenient.

Maybe she'd somehow found out about the two guards at the gatehouse. It was entirely possible that she panicked and began to cry.

Possible, but not likely.

The source of her tears suddenly seemed of great importance to Max.

He touched her arm. She flinched at his touch and eyed him warily, one jade eye peeking above her blouse.

Sticking with his French, he asked her why she'd been crying.

"What?"

He repeated his question.

She lifted her head. "Because I thought you were here to do the same," the woman said in American-accented French.

"Do the same?" Max asked. "Do the same what? What are you talking about?"

Despite her grief, the woman blinked her fresh tears away. She cocked her head, as if she were amazed. "You don't know, do you?"

"Know what?" Max demanded. His mouth was suddenly parched. "Tell me what you're talking about."

"Just before you came in and *shot* Agent Lang," she hissed, "we were told that President Kennedy had been shot in Dallas."

Max's eyes searched the woman's face. She was telling the truth. "Shot?"

"Yes, in his motorcade. Someone shot him."

The entire world spun off its axis. Forests blazed. Earthquakes rumbled. Tsunamis surged. Cyclones raged. Max struggled to maintain his composure.

"Is Kennedy dead?" he asked, realizing his query came out as a whisper.

She began crying again as her face contorted with grief and fear. "They don't know but Agent Lang said it sounded very bad. Please don't kill me."

"Are you an agent?"

She shook her head. "No…I work here."

Mind whirring, Max told the woman to count to sixty. He hurried from the secure room and viewed Agent Lang. He was still breathing but wasn't writhing anymore. Max knelt and pulled the agent's hair, lifting his head. The man was conscious.

"Can you hear me?" Max asked in English.

The agent nodded.

"I didn't want to do this. I was coerced by a man named Mister Winthrop. He's American and he took me to an Army post in what I think was Germany where all this was set up. You got that?"

Agent Lang didn't respond.

"Got it?" Max demanded.

"Yeah...Mr. Winthrop...coercion...Army post probably in Germany. I got it."

"You *have* to tell your superiors."

"I will."

Max dropped Lang's head and hurried down the hallway, emerging into the anteroom. Eyes searching out the one-way window, Max noticed the sniper on the roof across the traffic circle, above the Boulevard des Batignolles. Despite the darkness, the man's silhouette was betrayed by the lighted sign marquee of the Montmartre Hotel. Given the level of preparation for this job, Max didn't think that was the only sniper. On more than one occasion, Mr. Winthrop promised snipers. Plural.

Searching the buildings, Max calculated the angles.

Recalling the nook and its grate, Max reached behind him and gripped the Colt Detective Special.

Maybe, just maybe...

***

Max had confirmed that at least one sniper was perched on the roof of the Hotel Montmartre. Max was intelligent enough to surmise that the sniper was not alone. Max was correct. But unknown to Max was the staggering blanket of protection that existed *around* his high crime at Place de Clichy. It wasn't only protection for Mr. Winthrop—it was protection from the host country's authorities. The tentacles of this operation went far beyond Max's circle of 20/15 vision. Not only was it a highly coordinated breach, the machinations of the takedown had been planned for more than a year.

The outside guards were, indeed, gassed—just as Max had thought. On top of the guardhouse, the heating vent had been partially removed by a member of Winthrop's team. He had climbed there in the early morning darkness, more than 14 hours before. The man had used a ladder, hurriedly placed there at the same time a loud fender bender occurred across the Place de Clichy.

When the wreck had occurred, two men slid from the back of a separate truck with the 3-meter ladder. The rooftop man, wearing a black jumpsuit, had scurried up the ladder to the roof, where he would hide over the course of the entire day. The roof itself was covered in tar, the blackness blending with his jumpsuit in the event anyone from the nearby hotels gazed down at the guardhouse. The man had to be quiet so the guards wouldn't hear him thumping around above them. There was also a sizeable false front surrounding the small roof of the guardhouse, probably built to conceal the ductwork and to make the building blend in with its centuries old surroundings. The false front shielded the man's presence and activities from pedestrians. Once situated, he carefully positioned a tube into the intake of the heating system. The tube led to an aerosol can he controlled.

From that point, it was simple. He made sure he was able to manually switch the small heating unit on. Once the terminal was on and the man depressed the aerosol can's nozzle, heated air would flow into the guardhouse, carrying with it a steady stream of 3-Quinuclidinyl benzilate. After being depressed, the nozzle of the aerosol would stay on, and would spray for 7 minutes. The volume of the spray was metered. After it stopped spraying, the guards' period of unconsciousness—and subsequent torpor—would last for ten to fifteen additional minutes.

Several minutes before Max arrived with Mr. Winthrop, a quasi-legitimate visitor was sent to the pass-through gate, his primary goal being one of distraction. He spoke with the guards through the hole in the glass, polite at first, then demanding he be admitted. The guards patiently explained he was at the wrong address. Within 15 seconds, both men fell to the floor, unconscious from the gas. The man at the pass through gate used a special telescoping rod to press the green button on the opposite side of the small room. When he did, the gate buzzed. He opened it and slid the cardboard between the gate and the fence before quickly departing, leaving only the man on the guardhouse roof.

As soon as Max had begun shooting inside, the rooftop man had dropped onto the sidewalk and walked away to the east. Still wearing black, he timed his exit when there were no pedestrians nearby. No one took notice of him.

Elsewhere in the general area, also during the breach, two separate diversions had been created to ensure that no wayward police would randomly happen by the Place de Clichy courtyard and interrupt Max's efforts.

A half a kilometer to the west, just above the Rome Metro stop, a road-clogging traffic accident had occurred. Each driver sustained injuries that seemed serious, especially given the copious amount of blood. The police and paramedics would later report that, while initially triaged as critical by bystanders, both wounds were easily closed by a dozen combined stitches. Other than a few bumps and bruises, the cuts were the only injuries.

And to the south, adjacent to the nearby Liège Metro station, two different citizens called the police and reported what appeared to be a violent mugging. One caller told the police that the mugger was a savage-looking, white-haired, bearded man who had run to the south. Another citizen reported the mugger's victim as a "striking woman" who, for whatever reason, had somehow become topless, and *braless*, and was last seen streaking to the east on the short Rue de Milan.

This call, of course, resulted in an exuberant response from the nearby police—as well as several police who weren't nearby.

None of the reports were made up. The actual situations might have been choreographed—but it would have been a true miscalculation on Mr. Winthrop's part not to provide the police with actual human beings to seek during their responses. The wreck, of course, was real but staged. It involved an older Citroen and a shiny new Renault Floride convertible, both driven by trusted members of Mr. Winthrop's organization. The drivers' resulting injuries were self-inflicted just before the wreck, but this wasn't suspected by any of the first responders. One man gashed his scalp; the other sustained a deep laceration on his forearm. Both cuts were done in such a way to provide a large amount of blood. Several hours before the accident, both drivers had taken aspirin in an effort to thin their blood. In all, there was enough blood at that accident that a person might have thought a fattened pig had been slaughtered.

In addition to the wreck itself, a number of locals stood about, arguing over who was at fault. This, in itself, was a major distraction to the police and medics on the scene. All in all, the situation that had seemed bad at first turned out to simply be an innocuous pain in the ass.

Regarding the alleged mugging: A white-haired man was briefly detained after being apprehended just south of the Parc Monceau. None of the responding officers described him as savage—just drunk, stinking of wine and hashish. Looking every bit the part of a Bohemian, he claimed he didn't remember what had happened five minutes before. He had no weapons on him and his papers were spotless. He also had no criminal record. The police tried to find a witness to the mugging but could not. They had no way of knowing who called in the threat so, after a period of time, they released the man.

And, of course, numerous officers questioned—and paid a significant amount of attention to—the Moroccan beauty found lingering in front of a known brothel in the Pigalle area east of where she'd first been spotted. She was indeed topless, boasting rather impressive breasts that "jutted out like 155 mm artillery rounds," according to the ranking officer's written report. She claimed to know nothing about a mugging. She told anyone who would listen that she removed her top and brassiere to "feel free" and accepted her warning ticket with a wink and a hug for each of the officers present. There were smiles all around, and perhaps several offers for a private meal.

The two distractions close to the Place de Clichy had succeeded. All nearby police were sidetracked by the events, along with the news that was spreading like wildfire through the city regarding what had happened across the Atlantic, in Dallas, Texas.

A number of precious minutes would pass before the police were even clued in to the strong-armed theft that occurred right under their noses at the Place de Clichy.

***

Though Max had been inside for perhaps a minute longer than Mr. Winthrop would have liked, there was no reason yet to be concerned. After the breach, Winthrop had heard at least one muffled shotgun blast. He surveyed the traffic circle and surrounding pedestrians, seeing no one in the Place de Clichy that had taken notice of their Mercedes parked up on the curb. A moment ago, he watched with satisfaction as his black clad guardhouse rooftop man dropped down to the sidewalk. He hit and rolled before brushing himself off and walking away. Mr. Winthrop didn't see a soul who saw him, much less cared.

Nearby, a member of Mr. Winthrop's team monitored the police radio. He would call if there were any distress signals from the Secret Service station at Place de Clichy. For the moment, the local police were busy with the two nearby incidents. There'd been no mention of Max's breach. The remainder of the nearby pedestrians paid no heed to the two men parked illegally on the sidewalk of the Place de Clichy. This was Paris, after all. The streets were a veritable zoo. One quick glance evidenced six other vehicles stopped in no parking zones, all around the large circle.

Winthrop checked his watch again. Another thirty seconds and he would begin to grow uneasy.

Finally, light spilled from the door as Max emerged. There was enough ambient light in the courtyard that Winthrop could see the heavy black bag over Max's back, and the briefcase in his left hand. The case was heavy enough that it altered Max's gait, making him lean as he quick-stepped.

"Be ready," Mr. Winthrop said to the driver, whose family name was Edge—a fact that had remained hidden from Max. Winthrop opened the door slightly before leaning back in the seat, taking a series of chest-expanding breaths as the reality struck him.

We did it. We really did it. No one will ever forget November 22nd, 1963, and I played a key role. A huge role, actually, when the contents of that briefcase finally get put to use. In time, it will overshadow even the killing of Kennedy.

It will overshadow everything, save for wars and Holocaust, in recent memory.

And I triggered it. I did.

Me.

Edge slid the car in gear, depressed the clutch and goosed the engine.

Due to the large granite columns outside the courtyard, Mr. Winthrop briefly lost sight of Max as he passed through the smaller gate beside the guardhouse. Then, nothing. Winthrop frowned and leaned forward. Max should have emerged by now.

"Where is he?" Winthrop demanded on the radio.

"I lost him after he came through the courtyard," the sniper on the north side of the street answered.

"Shit!" Winthrop hissed. "Did that dumbass go into the guardhouse?"

"Negative. He must have gone behind it."

Mr. Winthrop whipped his head to the guardhouse. If Max had walked behind it, he couldn't go anywhere. On that side of the courtyard was a 4-story building. Winthrop turned the dial again, asking the same question of the second sniper. Perhaps he had a better vantage point. As Winthrop was speaking, the cracking reports of gunfire could be heard. This was matched by a flash of orange light next to the guardhouse.

Winthrop lurched forward. Had the gate guards woken up prematurely? Why was Max shooting out in the open?

And that didn't sound like a shotgun.

"Can you see him?" Winthrop demanded of his two snipers.

"Negative."

"Then alter your position, dammit!"

This is bad. This is so bad. What the fuck is he doing?

Small-arms fire cracked again, this time from elsewhere. Mr. Winthrop whipped his head back to the right, seeing the door to the Secret Service station open again, backlit by light from the anteroom. An agent was crouched down in the doorway, firing a pistol. Each shot brought a spear of orange from the muzzle of the man's pistol.

"Where is he?" Winthrop boomed into the radio, feeling this operation slipping from his grasp. As he waited on an answer, he propped his own pistol on the door window and prepared to return fire through the bars of the heavy gate.

"I just saw him," Sniper One said. "He dropped down into a hole."

"What hole?" Winthrop demanded.

"I watched him when he first came out and hurried to the guardhouse," the sniper said. "I had him in my sight the entire time. Then, at the guardhouse, he stepped out of my vision, around on the other side. There were some flashes from gunfire. After you told me to move, right when the guy from inside started shooting, I saw your guy throw something aside and jump down into a hole right beside the guardhouse."

"What hole?" Winthrop roared.

"It's right by the guardhouse. He might have just dropped down into it for cover."

The second sniper spoke. "He threw aside a rectangular grate. It's on the ground next to the hole."

"The locked grate by the guardhouse," Winthrop hissed. "Dammit all to hell!" He knew about the grate and knew it was padlocked shut. They'd deliberately left it out of the mock-up. Had Max blown the lock away with a pistol he'd taken from inside? Without letting himself go too far down his fatalistic line of thinking, he turned his eyes to the agent who'd been at the door. He was now moving warily into the courtyard, his pistol outstretched. Winthrop licked his lips as his mind raced.

"Sir?" Sniper One asked. "That guy's heading to the hole."

Mr. Winthrop gritted his teeth, silently cursing all mankind and especially that French-American bastard who'd just disappeared into the hole.

"Sir?" the sniper demanded.

Winthrop made his voice clear. "Green light on the courtyard target."

The sniper didn't even question the command. Though suppressed, the .308 round was still supersonic, and it cracked loudly as the agent crumpled to the courtyard, unmoving while a steaming crimson pool slowly spread around him.

Winthrop grabbed his flashlight and popped Edge on his shoulder. "Stay here."

Hurtling from the rear of the Mercedes, Mr. Winthrop walked with his head down to the guardhouse. Once he reached the pass through, he brandished his Walther openly. With a quick glance into the lighted guardhouse, he saw the two gate guards were still out cold. They weren't moving at all, other than their breathing. Having no desire to leave fingerprints, Winthrop used his shoulder to push through the still open gate and, just as soon as he passed through, he realized exactly what had happened.

That sneaky, criminal sonofabitch.

Just past the guardhouse, tucked into the nook on the left, the ventilation shaft was wide open. The grate was on the concrete beside the hole. Winthrop flipped the grate over. Max had known better than shoot the lock—something reserved for movies. Instead, he'd fired several shots at the rivets on the hasp, disabling it. And because the grate was situated in the protected nook, Max had been largely in both snipers' blind spot. He'd nestled himself into the corner and fired at the hasp. He'd yanked the grate aside before leaping into the darkness below, just as the agent from inside had started shooting.

The concrete opening was plenty large, approximately 2 feet by 3 feet. Wanting a better look, Mr. Winthrop extended his pistol and edged forward, aiming the flashlight with his left hand. The rectangular shaft was similar to what one might see on a big city sidewalk. It was deep, lined on four straight sides by concrete. At the base were a number of various sized pipes and conduits, and in three directions, large drainpipe openings—all of them easily large enough for a man.

Max was nowhere to be seen. He'd escaped through one of the drainpipes.

This was a complete and utter disaster.

Mr. Winthrop knew every square inch of this Secret Service station—because of that, he'd been confident that Max had no escape route. He'd known about this access shaft but had never considered that Max would be able to utilize it.

The building itself had offered no chance of escape. In spite of modern fire regulations, the old structure had been grandfathered in. Unknown to the Parisians, it had been gutted five years before, all of the work happening indoors, inside a shell of steel plating. There was only one way in and one way out. This was by strict design. And the vault where the cash and the briefcase had been held were of the latest technology. This was why Mr. Winthrop knew they had to rob the facility via the front door. Because there was no "back door exit," Winthrop had felt Max's only methods of possible escape were limited.

Months before, when he'd pondered Max's only available options, he'd come up with a few scenarios.

First, Max might have been tempted to simply stay inside of the Secret Service station. He could plead with the agents on duty. He could spill his guts about his capture, his imprisonment, and this crazy scheme. No one would have believed him and Max would have gone to jail for a very long time, especially given his criminal record. Max hadn't spoken a word to anyone outside of this operation. He wouldn't know where to tell the Secret Service to start, not that they'd have even cared. Winthrop hadn't thought for a second that this would have been an option to Max. He was smart enough to know that such a scheme was fraught with problems, especially given his history.

But the second scheme was the one Winthrop had worried about. He was concerned that Max might either try to break and run upon exiting the courtyard. Or, he might come out shooting, only to go down in a blaze of glory, especially if used his rubber rounds. But he could always come out with an agent's weapon. Regardless, Winthrop had countered both versions of this scheme by placing experienced snipers on the rooftops, both armed with suppressed .308 rifles. Despite the nighttime darkness, the area around the guardhouse was well lit. If Max tried to run, he'd be weighted down by the money and the briefcase—which was all Winthrop cared about. The snipers would simply shoot Max, and Winthrop would have his prize. Voila. Yes, there'd be a corpse in the street, but who gave a shit about that?

Mr. Winthrop's final poison pill, in case all else failed, was framing Max for the murders in Marseilles. The Algerians who Max thought he'd left alive were indeed now dead. If Mr. Winthrop were to leak Max's identity through several key channels, Max would be fingered for the Marseilles hit, along with a string of other hits that had occurred all across Paris. A manhunt would ensue, and Max wouldn't survive.

Until now, every conceivable detail had been accounted for.

Until now...

The grate had been considered, but not in tremendous detail. No one in the room had seen any possibility that Max would have had the gumption to identify it, get a pistol, blow it open, and descend into the Paris underground unmolested.

When it had been discussed, all involved believed the snipers could have picked Max off as he tampered with the grate. The snipers' line of fire had been reconnoitered ahead of time and, yes, the slight blind spot behind the guardhouse had been noted. One sniper could have easily readjusted position to cover the nook, but doing so would have put the sniper in a bad spot for the remainder of the plaza. Had Winthrop known this might happen, he'd have posted three snipers. In the end, no one anticipated Max working so quickly. Much like a plane crash, not a single person had predicted the three failures working in tandem with one another: the pilfered pistol, the ventilation grate, and the blind spot.

Every plan has a weakness. And somehow, the scant weakness in this plan had been exposed. In the end, despite collective failures, it was all Mr. Winthrop's fault.

The worst had happened. Max was gone.

As was the briefcase.

Even with so many permutations in his mind, only 20 seconds had passed since Mr. Winthrop had exited the car. He peered downward, deliberating over whether or not he should follow his wayward charge. Despite the two proximate diversions, Winthrop wasn't deluded enough to think that someone nearby hadn't reported a man being shot in a courtyard at the Place de Clichy. At bare minimum, gunfire would have been reported.

I've got to go down there. Hell, he could be ten feet inside one of those pipes, stuck.

Winthrop's head turned as light spilled from the Secret Service station door once again. A woman stepped several feet outside, holding the door open. Winthrop lifted his radio.

"At the door, green light. *Now.*"

The woman had to have seen the agent on the ground because she hurriedly rushed back inside. Just as she did, the bullet sparked on the pavement where she'd stood, followed a fraction of a second later by the supersonic crack.

She'd seen him—she'd seen Mr. Winthrop.

Dammit!

This quandary had gone to hell very quickly—and Mr. Winthrop would be blamed for every bit of it. Not only had his man escaped, now he had a dead Secret Service agent laying out in the open, and a woman who'd almost certainly seen enough of his own face to provide a basic description.

From quandary to catastrophe.

Damning the torpedoes, Winthrop dropped down into the rectangular hole, yelling out in pain when he reached the bottom. Because of the pipes and conduits inside the standing water, he'd been unable to judge where exactly to land. His right foot landed sideways on a pipe, thereby twisting his ankle to the right at an extreme angle, making him feel as if he'd broken it. Pushing the pain from his mind, Winthrop held the pistol and flashlight up, peering into all three drainpipes.

It only took one glance for him to see the marks in the grimy pipe that ran to the north—directly under the center of Place de Clichy. The pipe wasn't long at all and, judging by the amber light ahead, appeared to dump into the cavernous underground network of Paris's staggering subterranean system of sewers, pipes and Metro tunnels.

Knowing better than to chase Max, Mr. Winthrop climbed out of the hole via the rebar rungs, limping away with his injured ankle. At least it wasn't broken.

He tumbled back into the Mercedes and told Edge to haul ass. Then Winthrop put out a radio call, sending the advance team in an expanding search around the Place de Clichy. Max had to surface somewhere, and he wasn't going to let go of the bag or briefcase. Winthrop then told his personal team to head for a rendezvous at their predetermined Site 1. It was the same place where Max would have been taken—and killed—following the heist. As the Mercedes screeched through northwestern Paris, Mr. Winthrop rubbed his ankle and lamented.

Max Warfield, a known criminal with a high degree of intelligence and the ability to speak native French, was on the run in Paris with probably a half-million dollars in high quality counterfeit money. Worse still was the fact that, in his left hand dangled a briefcase containing what might have been the world's most damning secret.

Chapter Six

At 12:30 P.M. Central Standard Time, the President of the United States, John F. Kennedy, was shot while traveling in his motorcade in Dallas, Texas. Hit multiple times, the president was rushed to nearby Parkland Hospital where he was pronounced dead a half hour later. A short time later, in Paris, France, Mr. Winthrop closed himself in the front room of a quiet neoclassical home off of Rue Saint-Joseph. He collapsed into a soft leather chair, removing his glasses and vigorously massaging his face. He longed for a glass of cold vodka but knew better than to dull his senses at a critical moment like this. Instead, he rubbed his ankle for a moment before taking a series of deep breaths. When he'd prepared himself for what he faced, he attempted to make a long distance call to Austria.

"I'm sorry, sir," the French operator said. "I can't get a line right now. There's been an incident in the—"

Mr. Winthrop hung up the phone and muttered a curse word. He touched the military radio, quickly deciding against using it. Given the Kennedy assassination, every listening post in Europe would be ears-up. The phone was far more secure. As he waited on a line, he beckoned his people to the front room. There were nine men in all, including his driver, Edge. They stood there quietly. The tension in the room was thick.

"I take it there've been no sightings or contact from the field?" Mr. Winthrop snapped, wiping his glasses with a clean handkerchief.

Edge shook his head.

"Nothing at all?" Mr. Winthrop demanded.

"No sightings," Edge replied.

"You're keeping your transmissions clean?"

Edge nodded. "If anyone heard us, they'd think we're looking for a lost teenager, just as we planned."

"Then get your asses out there and coordinate with the field team. Consider how far Max could have traveled while underground, especially given his load. Also, take into account that he could have surfaced nearby. I estimate he was carrying seventy or eighty pounds. Having to negotiate the maze of tunnels, he won't have gone far. Leave no stone unturned and don't assume a damned thing. I wouldn't put it past him to hide under a pile of garbage. He's patient enough that he might stay below ground until tomorrow." Winthrop shot a glance at his watch. "We keep the hammer down on the search until noon tomorrow, maybe beyond. No one stops to eat, drink, piss...nothing."

There were a few grumbles from the group. Winthrop slowly stood, leaning on his good ankle. He eyed the assemblage for a moment before he went on an uncharacteristic, viciously vulgar tirade that ended in a series of calm threats. As he made each threat, he poked the table for emphasis. No one doubted the legitimacy of the threats. Afterward, at his direction, the men departed.

Mr. Winthrop sat back down and popped a peppermint into his mouth. As he again tried to get a long distance call through, he folded the wrapper into a variety of shapes while his mind ran scenarios that reached in every conceivable direction.

At 9:55 P.M., Winthrop finally got a line to Vienna, Austria. He crunched his fourth peppermint as the line purred with an Austrian ringtone.

"This is Vickers," was the abrupt answer, in English.

"We had a problem," Winthrop declared without preamble.

"Yeah, I know you had a problem. There was a dead agent in the plaza at the Place de Clichy, and based on what I've heard, he was shot by a high-powered rifle. I'd call that a serious fucking problem. This was supposed to be a soft touch."

Mr. Winthrop twirled the most recent cellophane shape he'd created—it was an isosceles triangle—dreading the words he would utter next.

"You there?" Vickers asked.

"Yes."

"So? Was it all there?"

"I don't know."

"It's been hours. You haven't checked yet?"

"I don't have the package."

The directive was eerily calm. "Explain that."

Winthrop told Vickers everything. The retelling took ten minutes and ended with Max's diving into the shaft that led to the Paris underground. "I determined he cleared the sewage pipe along with his likely direction. Knowing that, we've put on a full scale search."

All that followed was the familiar electrical hum of an inter-Europe long distance connection. Finally, Vickers broke the silence. "And there's no sign of him?"

"Not yet. I've got every asset in our command out looking."

"Did anyone other than the dead agent realize there was more than one infiltrator?"

"Some woman. I don't who she was."

"Was she in the building?"

"Yes."

"With the agent who was shot?"

"Yes."

"How did she know he wasn't alone?"

"She saw me," Winthrop replied.

"She saw *you*?"

"Yes, when I dropped into the ventilation shaft."

"Did she get a *good* look at you?"

"When I speak to her, I'll ask her."

Just as Winthrop had before, Vickers unleashed a torrent of curse words. After, neither man spoke for a moment.

"Use one of your false identities and fly out of Orly," Vickers commanded. "I want you here, in Vienna, tonight or in the morning at the very latest."

"What about the train?"

"That'll take too long. Leave the team to do the searching. Make sure they're properly briefed." Vickers was quiet for a few seconds. "And you'd better hope to God they find him."

"You don't want us to leak his identity? We could also tip the French that he's the author of the Marseilles murders."

"Not yet. If I decide to, I can handle that from here."

"I'm on it."

"Wait…"

"What?" Winthrop asked.

"Unless she's in protective custody, have someone kill that witness."

"Understood."

The line went dead.

Mr. Winthrop radioed Edge, calling him back. He briefed him and sent him on his way.

Alone again, Winthrop retrieved a bowl of ice and broke the seal on a bottle of vodka, pouring a tall glass over thick ice cubes with a squeeze of lemon. He usually drank his vodka straight, but occasionally preferred to alter the flavor depending on his mood. As he drank, he finally managed to get another phone line, booking the earliest flight available on KLM out of Orly. He'd fly direct to Vienna, posing under a well-used passport as American businessman Ralph Rowland, of Cincinnati, Ohio. That done, Mr. Winthrop extinguished the light and sat there in the dark, listening to the sounds of the city as he drank.

He attempted to envision what Max Warfield might have done, beginning with the moments after his escape. After applying some critical thought, Winthrop theorized that Max knew better than to remain close and hide. He'd want to put as much distance as possible between himself and the site of his escape. Would he consider jettisoning the briefcase in an effort to increase his speed? Winthrop reminded himself to have the team go underground and scour hiding locations in case Max stashed the heavy item.

If he somehow escaped Paris clean—and that was a big "if"—Winthrop had trouble reconciling what future actions Max would take. The man was peculiar to begin with. He'd successfully lived an underground life for a number of years. Hopefully, he'd be satisfied with his counterfeit money and live quietly for the balance of his days.

Winthrop also made a mental note to find out how easily Max's counterfeit money could be traced. He'd told Max the bills weren't marked, but that was a lie. Winthrop actually had no idea, but assumed the Secret Service could identify the counterfeits.

Given the resources at his disposal, he was confident they'd eventually recapture Max. But deep in the pit of Mr. Winthrop's gut, he was concerned that Max would strike out in retaliation, especially once he'd learned the immense value of the secret he'd stolen.

But, would Max's revealing of the briefcase's contents be the worst thing? Other than a host of logistical issues Winthrop and Vickers would need to hash out, Max's letting it out might be a unique way of exposing the entire affair to the public. No, it wouldn't give Winthrop's organization the leverage they desired; but the revelation, especially after Kennedy's assassination, could still have the desired effect.

Winthrop was nearly done with his drink. A prostitute would be just the salve he needed tonight. No. He needed to maintain discipline. Instead of cheap sex, he washed his face, brushed his teeth, and finished with powerful mouthwash. As his team prowled the cold nighttime streets of Paris, Winthrop wore silk pajamas and slid between the starchy sheets of a warm bed. He managed five hours of alcohol-aided sleep before being whisked by hired car to Orly Airport the following morning.

To a Vienna rendezvous he dreaded.

Dreaded, because he'd failed.

***

As news of the assassination blazed like wildfire across the world, Max Warfield had moved just about as far as his body could carry him after the incident in the Place de Clichy courtyard. He knew Mr. Winthrop would release the false tip that Max had killed the Algerians in Marseilles. Winthrop would also somehow finger Max for the shooting of the Secret Service agent. After Winthrop leaked that information to the French, the official manhunt would be on. At this point, what other move did Mr. Winthrop have? None. Max had to assume that every police and federal force in Paris would soon be searching for him. Because of that, when he crawled into the first tunnel under the Place de Clichy, he'd given himself thirty minutes to move before he went into hiding.

Upon dropping into the vertical shaft after the breach, he'd shoved his items ahead and crawled northward, into a large tunnel that ran east and west under the Place de Clichy. The tunnel was adjacent to the Metro tunnel. Max knew that the Place de Clichy was near the center of Paris, but on the northwestern side. Therefore, heading west would be the quickest route to take him away from the center of the city. Before he'd gone far, he attempted to open the briefcase. Due to its extreme weight, extracting the contents would lighten Max's load considerably. But Max couldn't defeat the locks and there was certainly no time now for an extended effort. So, with his bulging bag of money and even heavier briefcase, and with his Ithaca shotgun slung over his torso, Max had loped to the west as fast as he could.

Varying in size and design on what seemed like every city block, the large tunnel Max navigated was thankfully mostly flat at its base. With a dusty concrete surface below, the tunnel was arched overhead, the apex of the curve nearly coming to a point. Branch tunnels were marked by archways, many of them brick. Overhead, a massive pipe ran the length, just off the center of Max's tunnel. Miles of conduit in various sizes were affixed to the walls of the tunnel and down to the right was a channel with foul smelling liquid running slowly to the east. Occasional lights threw just enough amber light to prevent complete darkness. The Metro trains could be felt nearby, rumbling as they sped through the catacombs under the City of Lights. Every so often, Max passed massive pumps that worked at a deafening level. The staggering infrastructure underneath the city amazed him.

Twice during the first part of his escape, Max saw people in the tunnel. The first time, he saw two men working on some sort of electrical box at one of the branch passageways. Neither man noticed Max go by. A short time afterward, Max encountered a grimy man who looked as if he might spend a great deal of his time in the underground. His clothes were tattered and his eyes were sunken in their sockets. He babbled upon seeing Max. The man continued to yell queries at Max as he continued westward.

The labored, heavily weighted jog was grueling, made worse by his predicament. But at least he'd escaped Mr. Winthrop. Yes, the weight of the world would probably be brought to bear on him. Yes, he'd erroneously be wanted for the murder of three Algerians and probably for killing a United States government agent. Still, Max was convinced, had he not escaped, he'd be dead by now. He knew it. Therefore, being a wanted man was better than being dead.

In the steamy, stinky, rat-infested underground of western Paris, Max Warfield was covered from head to toe in sweat and grunge. He felt this could be a potential problem when he surfaced, but he'd rather deal with being conspicuous in a safe place than coming up in an area where the police were actively seeking him.

Although heading west had been his best tactical option, he'd come this direction for another reason. During his training, Max had wracked his brain to determine whether or not Mr. Winthrop and his people knew about Ludivine. Of course, Mr. Winthrop had discovered Max's previously buried go-box from Cimetière Saint-Vincent, which threw their long-term surveillance into Max's face. He'd buried it way back in the summer, a point Mr. Winthrop had bragged about.

But on the occasions Max had stayed at Ludivine's, he'd taken extreme precautions beforehand, making certain he wasn't leaving a trail. He'd been cautious because he was occasionally suspicious he was being followed. But his greatest concern was for Ludivine's safety. He'd always been vigilant when making his way to her, having no desire to endanger her due to his hidden profession.

Still—did they know about her?

They'd known about the go-box. Because of that, Max assumed Mr. Winthrop and his people also had knowledge of his illegal warehouse flat at the end of Rue Nacionale, overlooking the Seine. There were a number of places nearby to watch him, and reacquire him.

But if they knew about Ludivine, Winthrop would have mentioned her and levied threats against her in order to make Max do as he wanted.

Yes, Max was sure of it. Mr. Winthrop would have used Ludivine as leverage, but he didn't.

Meaning, Mr. Winthrop knew nothing of Ludivine.

So, should I involve her?

According to his Rolex, there were six minutes remaining before he needed to go into hiding. Further movement would put him in great jeopardy. He pressed on, violently shaking his head as he unsuccessfully attempted to forget the horrors he'd seen tonight.

Burned into his mind was the puff of pink blood he'd seen in the courtyard as the sniper shot the Secret Service agent who'd only been doing his job. Seconds before, Max had talked to the agent. Now the man was dead, all thanks to Mr. Winthrop. Max thought back to his own imprisonment, and the strings Mr. Winthrop had pulled to orchestrate his deadly scheme.

Though it seemed crazy to even consider, Max couldn't help but wonder if the killing of John F. Kennedy was somehow related to tonight's events. Hoisting the heavy briefcase, his greatest physical burden, Max viewed it through gun-slit eyes.

Was it possible that the shooting of Kennedy was a diversion just so Max could steal this briefcase? No, Max decided. Not possible. There was only one agent on duty. Why shoot a sitting president to distract a lone Secret Service agent who was on another continent? Such a notion bordered on ridiculous. No matter what was in this briefcase, it wouldn't come close to the killing of a sitting U.S. president.

Even so, while maybe the assassination attempt wasn't a diversion, what if it was somehow related? What if the attacks were coordinated? What if there were dozens of other attacks that had occurred around the globe, all intended to cripple the United States?

Max kept moving. He couldn't afford to ruminate over this right now. In fact, for all he knew, Kennedy was alive and well. The only proof Max had was the woman he'd encountered. It wasn't out of the realm of possibility that she'd been fed false information by Winthrop's assets in order to distract her and the agent. Max recalled from his training with Mr. Winthrop that the "workers" at the breach site would be "distracted."

Therefore, it was conceivable that the Kennedy assassination was an elaborate hoax played on the workers of the U.S. Secret Service station in Paris.

None of that mattered at this moment. For now, Max was faced with a much greater decision. If he involved Ludivine in this situation, it might eventually lead to her imprisonment or her death. Should he do that to her, and would she even accept him? By going to Ludivine, she might turn him in.

On he charged, desiring a glass of water worse than anything he'd ever wanted in his life. At the next tunnel intersection, Max saw a beaten marker for Les Sablons, a western Paris Metro station that Max knew to be less than a kilometer from Ludivine's flat. He searched the area for an exit point, seeing a column across the tunnel that led to what appeared to be an access shaft and a manhole cover. Metal rungs led upward to freedom.

As Max prepared to cross the sludgy river of excrement, he caught sight of movement from his left. He turned just before the muzzle flash.

Backward Max lurched, flailing and scrabbling into the much smaller cross tunnel that ran underneath the Rue d'Orléans.

He tugged the money bag and briefcase with him.

∗∗∗

I'm not hit.

For the moment, it was the most important conclusion. Max's happiness lasted about a quarter second.

Clutching the Colt Detective Special in his sweaty hands, he waited, applying every bit of focus he could to the situation. The shooter was just around the corner.

Of concern to Max was *who* the shooter was, and why he had taken a shot at him.

Most concerning to Max was exactly where the shooter was now. Though the view hadn't been clear, Max was almost certain it had been one man—one very large man—and he was alone.

Risking a fast glance backward, Max saw the tunnel he was in ran on and on. It was just smaller in diameter. Regardless, if the man who was pursuing him was concerned about Max fleeing, he'd have to come around that corner soon.

When he did, Max would shoot him.

But…

What if he's a cop?

What if he's a Secret Service agent?

Doesn't matter.

It's kill or be killed at this stage, Max. You didn't put yourself into this predicament—Mr. Winthrop did.

True, but it was your criminal career that made you a target to begin with.

Despite the internal philosophical argument, Max aimed the Colt at the corner of the tunnel intersection at a height of approximately 4 feet. His aim and the Colt's positioning was as steady as if on a mount. He'd adjust accordingly if and when the person came—

There!

Max saw the barrel and chassis of a black semi-automatic pistol. The shooter had edged forward, making Max slide backward due to the old soldier's adage: If you can see them—they can see you.

That wasn't exactly the case here—there weren't eyes on the shooter's pistol. But another few inches and he'd be able to see. Because of that, Max continued his backward movement while continuing to aim.

Something hard halted Max's rearward progress.

He again chanced a fast backward glance, finding a narrow wall of mortared bricks. It was built up to the ceiling of the tunnel as a support. The only way around would be to cross the sludge, something Max couldn't do right now because of the shooter's angle. And of course, to Max's right was the two-foot drop down into the moving filth. To Max's left, between him and the wall, was a pipe that was hot to the touch.

As Max aimed, he quickly became aware of a burning sensation along his beltline on his left side. It was right at his kidney. Because he could barely hear after the thundering gunshot, he didn't pick up on the hissing sound of the steam. But now that he was aware of it, he could hear it.

He could absolutely feel it.

A jet of searing steam spewed from the hot pipe, shooting into his side. Max's leather belt had provided a shield for a few seconds, but now it felt like someone had jabbed his side with a red-hot poker and left it there.

The pain was otherworldly and made it difficult to breathe. If Max moved forward, the shooter would see him. If Max moved right, he'd expose himself while falling into the river of shit and piss. And he couldn't move backward without standing to go around the wall. If he did that, he'd get shot.

So, he was stuck. Stuck in place while a geyser of steam cooked his left flank.

Eyes watering, Max summoned every bit of concentration he could. Now the shooter's pistol was almost completely forward of the corner. If Max wasn't holding such a short-barreled pistol—which leads to gross inaccuracy—he might attempt to shoot the pistol from the man's hands.

Argh...the pain could be felt beyond his skin, on his insides. His intestines felt as if they were being boiled.

Wait...

Deal with it.

Deal with it.

You've dealt with worse.

Five more seconds.

I lied...five more seconds.

Lied again! Just five more...

Finally, mercifully, the shooter made his move. Just in time, too. Max was ready to kill. Max was fine with being killed. At that moment, he truly didn't care which.

The shooter burst past the opening and began making the turn. Max fired once, catching the man in his abdomen. Due to his momentum, the large man kept coming.

Max caught him in the face with the next round.

That shot left the man graveyard dead. He face-planted forward in a mess of blood and guts, his body resting just where Max had been only a minute before.

In considerable agony, Max struggled to his feet. He desperately wanted to touch his side, but didn't. In a painful crouch, Max carefully passed over the dead shooter and rushed around the corner with the pistol outstretched.

Clear. No more shooters.

At this point, despite his willpower, Max turned his attention to his side. His jacket was wet—nothing more. He lifted the jacket and un-tucked the left side of his shirt. The fabric tugging against his skin felt as if someone applied a belt sander to his side. It was all he could do not to scream.

In a triangle of light from overhead, he viewed his wound. The exposed skin above Max's belt was a spectrum of red. The center of the burn—almost certainly where the jet of steam had been aimed—was right at his waistline and bloody red, although no blood dripped from the wound. Outward, stretching about three inches in all directions, the red faded to pink and had bubbled his skin.

Max gingerly pulled his shirt and jacket down. No sense in looking at it.

He rolled the shooter over, ignoring the wound to his face. Max performed a rapid search for identification, finding none. He took the shooter's money—there wasn't much—and his pistol, a MAB Model D. He slid the pistol into his bag and shoved the corpse into the river of sludge. In moments, the man's body was enveloped by filth. Someone would have to be looking closely to even notice it.

The shooter wasn't a cop—that much Max knew. So, if he wasn't a cop, he had to be one of Winthrop's men. And if Winthrop had one down here, he probably had two dozen elsewhere. It was time to find cover.

Straightening once again, Max noticed that his side seemed to be numb. From experience, he knew that often happened with severe burns. But it wouldn't last. The numbness would go away, and then the real pain would begin.

Back in the main tunnel, he moved west to a wooden plank footbridge, crossing and coming back to the rebar ladder that led to Les Sablons.

Once he'd broken the shotgun and concealed it in the money bag, Max ascended the rebar rungs on a vertical shaft. Above was a heavy manhole cover that he carefully slid aside. He had to time his emergence with the steady nighttime traffic, bursting onto the Rue Charles Laffitte to a hail of horns from the evening rush.

Covered in sweat and filth, he stopped traffic as he slid the manhole cover back into place before rushing south into a nearby alley. Hopefully, no one would see the need to report a man emerging grimy from the sewer with a large black bag and briefcase.

This was Paris, after all.

Chapter Seven

Max was correct about the dead shooter being one of Winthrop's men. For now, Winthrop's men were the only pursuers. For now. More would come later, once the Parisian police were finally granted access to the Secret Service station. Max had to assume he was hunted by everyone—while incorrect, he was wise to be so cautious.

Because he'd negotiated so much of the city in the sewer, he now only had six blocks to cover before he'd arrive at Ludivine's. Rather than stop somewhere and clean himself, he stuck to dark alleys and narrow passageways between buildings. He managed to lug his cargo across roads during periods of low traffic. From what he could tell, no one took notice of him.

As he waited in the mouth of an alley, Max heard a number of people reacting to the shooting of President Kennedy. In fact, that's all anyone on the street talked about. So, it was confirmed. The killing wasn't some ruse Mr. Winthrop had created. It was real. A sitting American president, murdered.

Who was the last president who was assassinated? McKinley?

Occupy your mind with more important things. For now, find cover.

The six blocks to Ludivine's seemed an eternity; in actuality, they took 15 minutes. Due to his fatigue and stress level, each second was a minute, each minute an hour. Once Max arrived at her apartment building, he peered through a window and saw no one in the unswept foyer. He pulled open the heavy wooden door and trudged up the worn spiral stairwell to Ludivine's flat.

Peering upward, he couldn't help but wonder if Winthrop's people knew. Were they waiting? They'd have probably killed her—they'd be waiting inside.

One way to find out.

Ludivine's building was tall and narrow, with two apartments on each floor. It was probably 80 years old. All of the requisite sounds of a low-end, rent controlled building could be heard. There were babies crying. People arguing. Loud radios. Someone upstairs, a man and a woman, seemed to be in the middle of an amorous moment. Covered in grimy perspiration, he eventually reached her landing.

Max could smell himself. Not in his chain of concern at the moment.

He lowered the briefcase to the floor and moved the money bag to his left shoulder.

Pistol behind his back—ready to fire, finger on the trigger—Max tapped quietly with his fingernail. Then he increased the sound of his tapping, finally hearing footfalls.

This was it. He tensed.

The door opened to the length of the security chain.

A woman's face.

Not Ludivine's. What the hell was this?

Max managed to stammer a question in French, asking if Ludivine was home.

The woman's eyes narrowed as she took in Max's filthy appearance. "Who are you?"

"I'm Maxime. Is she here?"

There was a flicker of recognition upon the mention of his name, followed by a smile. "Wait here, please." The door shut and the bolts clicked home. Max got a brief whiff of the aroma of food coming from Ludivine's flat. Whatever it happened to be was heavy on the garlic—it smelled delicious. After a moment, he heard more footfalls before the bolt snapped again and the door was yanked open. This time it was Ludivine. She was breathless and her eyes widened.

What a sight she was. Max nearly crumbled in his relief.

Ludivine was shorter than average, just a hair over five feet tall. She was built sturdily, with muscular legs and large expressive features. Her short, dark brown hair matched her coffee eyes. But it was her full, sensuous lips that always put Max into orbit. Ludivine wore a black sweater and a knee length skirt. She was barefoot, holding a cooking spoon in her hand as she surveyed Max.

"Hello, my pretty lady." He deftly tucked the pistol behind his back, chafing the outer edge of his steam burn. The grunt he uttered was unavoidable.

"What happened?" she asked, taking in his appearance.

In the light that spilled from her fragrant apartment, Max looked down at himself, seeing the sooty nastiness that he was certain also covered his face. "I'm fine and I'll explain."

"I wish I'd have known you were coming," she said, glancing backward. "I'd have been prepared."

"I'm sorry. I should have called you. May I come inside?"

"*Bien sûr*," she answered, beaming as she stepped aside from the doorway.

Max entered, seeing the other woman peering with curiosity from Ludivine's kitchen. The woman was stirring a sauce of some sort. The smell inside the confines of the apartment was heavenly. Max hadn't realized the magnitude of his hunger until the cooking aromas touched his nose.

Ludivine leaned close and spoke in a low voice. "Why are you so filthy? Why do you look like that? Is everything okay?"

"Everything's fine. Again, I'm sorry for showing up unannounced."

Once again, she looked him up and down, an expression of grave concern blanketing her face. "You're so thin! Have you been eating?"

Well…I ate a rat. He was my cellmate. We were imprisoned by a man named Mr. Winthrop. He'd love to meet you, I'm sure.

"I had the flu," Max lied, hating himself for it. "I finally got better a few days ago."

"You poor man. Please, put your things down."

After relieving himself of his heavy burden, Max rotated his cramped neck and shoulders before he asked for water. He drank three glasses in quick succession and stood in the kitchen with Ludivine as he gave a brief, and false, story about all that had happened. More lies. He expanded on his tale of the flu. Then, Max claimed his motorcycle had broken down this afternoon in Sarcelles, about 15 kilometers away. The yarn came to him as he spoke.

"I tried to hitchhike but no one would pick me up," he lied. "I got frustrated and just started walking. When I was on the outskirts of the city, I took a stupid shortcut through a coal yard. There were dogs and they chased me. That's how I got so filthy." He looked down at himself and shook his head. "I'm sorry for showing up like this and looking this way. I was hoping to surprise you. Bad idea."

Ludivine laughed. "It's a good surprise. I would hug you, but…"

"Later."

"Indeed, later," Ludivine replied, giving him a look that made his heart race. She turned. "This is my friend, Aveline. She started working with me about…"

"Three weeks ago," Aveline finished for her.

"Yes. Three weeks ago," Ludivine replied. "We have a lot in common and thankfully she's been keeping me company while you've been gone."

Max washed his hands in the kitchen sink and shook Aveline's hand. She had a firm handshake and didn't seem to view him with any type of suspicion at all.

"I've been traveling for work for a number of weeks," Max explained.

Aveline sipped her red wine, smirking. "Oh…I've heard *all* about you."

"Are you hungry?" Ludivine asked. "We have plenty of food."

"I'm definitely hungry," Max said. "What have you been doing?"

"Tonight? Just cooking and talking."

The radio wasn't on.

They have no idea about President Kennedy.

He didn't mention it. Instead, he asked, "Would you mind if I cleaned up in your bathroom?"

"Why don't you have a bath? There's time. You've got clothes in there, don't you?" Ludivine asked, pointing to his duffel bag.

"Yeah, I've got some clothes," he said, hesitating slightly. He actually didn't have clothes, but he needed the bath. After devouring a piece of buttered bread, he carried his items to the bathroom and shut the door. Max turned on the water and let the tub fill. As the water ran, he undressed.

Ludivine's mirror was small and rectangular, covering the medicine cabinet. Max eyed his sooty face, recognizing the hollowness around his eyes from the malnourishment during his imprisonment. Since then, despite being well fed, he'd probably burned more calories than he'd consumed. With the weight loss and stress he looked ten years older.

The toothbrush and toothpaste he'd left here were still in the medicine cabinet. As he vigorously cleaned the inside of his mouth, he viewed his side. The steam burn was crimson at its center. Unfortunately, the feeling was beginning to return. Max could only imagine what the bath would feel like. He'd have to deal with it. Such a wound could become infected. When he finished brushing his teeth, he stowed his toothbrush and located a nearly full bottle of Merthiolate on the same shelf in the medicine cabinet.

That'll feel really good.

As a child, he and his friends had called Merthiolate "monkey blood." Whenever Max came home with bloody knees or elbows, his annoyed mother would roughly rub his wounds with a cotton ball soaked in Merthiolate. By the time he was 8 years old, Max refused to cry over the wounds or his mother's lack of empathy.

He continued to poke around in the cabinet.

Though there were no dressings, Ludivine had a tattered elastic bandage that looked plenty long enough. To the right of the cabinet was a wicker shelf with two towels and two washcloths. He chose a dark blue washcloth that was tattered but smelled clean. It would do. He put the bandage, the washcloth and the Merthiolate by the tub. He grabbed a towel and threw the other washcloth into the bathwater.

Then, just before he climbed into the warm water, he stopped and stared at the briefcase, resting there like a coiled snake.

Mr. Winthrop's briefcase…

Actually, no. Instead, it was the briefcase Mr. Winthrop so desperately desired.

The briefcase that belonged to the United States Secret Service.

The briefcase that, for a year, Max was shadowed for.

The briefcase Max was hit in the head over.

The briefcase that Max was imprisoned because of.

The briefcase that caused Max to eat a rat.

The briefcase that resulted in many nights of intense urban assault training.

The briefcase that might somehow be connected to the killing of President Kennedy.

Max laid his hand upon the briefcase. Did he want to attempt to open it? Should he?

Yes. But…

Not now.

Instead, he climbed into the bath, defeating the urge to hiss as the warm water enveloped his burn.

Agony.

Overcome the pain. Pretend it feels good. Trick your mind. Free it…

Max thoroughly cleaned himself, paying special attention to his burn. When he was done, he toweled off and dressed his wound in Merthiolate. The antiseptic hurt nearly as badly as the initial burn and took him back to his childhood.

Max forced an ironic laugh. It beat crying.

Afterward, he covered the burn with the washcloth and wrapped his midsection in the bandage. Then he called out to Ludivine. He whispered to her through the crack in the barely opened door, hiding the bandage.

"Do you have a robe I can wear?"

"What about your clothes?" she asked, puzzled. "You have your bag."

He made his expression apologetic. "I just opened my bag. Everything is soaked and filthy."

"Oh, okay. No problem."

"You sure you don't mind?"

"Of course not. I hope you don't."

She retrieved the robe and brought it to him. With the door still cracked, Max held the robe between thumb and index finger.

Ludivine smiled. "Think it'll fit?"

He forced another ironic laugh.

It beat crying.

***

Five minutes later, Max sat at the small table, waiting on the two women. When Aveline had first seen him in Ludivine's robe, she'd not been able to contain her chuckling.

Max had closed his eyes and nodded, even opening his arms to encourage it.

"Go ahead and get it out," he'd said. In reality, he appreciated the humor. It was excellent medicine. Certainly better than Merthiolate.

The two women laughed and giggled—their collective amusement was certainly in good spirit.

Max seated himself at the table, making sure the robe was closed. He had no underwear on underneath. He looked down, studying the rose pattern against the dark hairs of his legs.

Very sexy.

"Can I help you with the food?" he asked.

"No," Ludivine answered, still smiling as she poked her head around the cupboard. "How hungry are you?"

67

"Famished."

He could hear them plating the food. He could hear his stomach. Now that his side was patched, his hunger outweighed his pain.

While the women worked, Max allowed his eyes to gaze the small apartment. He'd thought of it so many times when he'd been locked in the concrete cell. Typical of a low rent Paris flat, the apartment consisted of three rooms, all of which were cramped, made worse by low ceilings. At the rear was the bedroom, barely large enough for a twin bed and a narrow wardrobe. That's where the money and briefcase were.

Between the bedroom and the main room was the bathroom he'd just bathed in. On his last visit, Max reasoned that the tub had to have been in place before the bathroom was walled in. Otherwise, there would have been no way to get it through the door or the small window.

The room where he currently sat was the main room. The kitchen was nothing more than a stove, a noisy icebox, and a rectangular section of cracked tile floor below the two appliances. Ludivine had partitioned the kitchen off with a cupboard she'd found behind a building. She'd painted it white with yellow flowers. That's where she kept her dry goods and spices. On the opposite side of the cupboard was a long folding table where she stored her plates and utensils. In front of the cupboard and table was an old sofa covered in a quilt, along with another chair. She didn't have a television, but instead had an old Sonora radio in brown Bakelite finish. It was at least 20 years old and had to warm up for a minute before it would even receive.

Again he thought about the Kennedy assassination. After dinner perhaps he could convince them to turn on the radio. They needed to know the momentous news.

And at some point, Max would have to tell Ludivine what had really happened.

Not now. Eat your supper. Be a good guest.

"We made spaghetti," Ludivine said, sliding his plate in front of him. "I had some leftover beef from last night so we chopped it up and made the sauce by taste. We used real tomatoes. I hope it tastes okay."

"I'm sure it's wonderful," Max dutifully replied.

"Ludivine's being modest," Aveline added. "The sauce tastes very good and she did all the work."

"Nonsense," Ludivine answered as the two women settled into their seats.

"How long have you two been cooking tonight?" Max asked, again wondering if they had any inkling about President Kennedy.

Ludivine shrugged. "Aveline came home from work with me. We talked for a bit and listened to a show, then we started cooking."

They definitely don't know.

Despite his current state, Max ate two plates of spaghetti. Aveline was correct, the sauce was quite good. Rich and strong. He also had three more large pieces of buttered bread. The savory meal settled his nerves a bit.

"How much weight have you lost?" Ludivine asked, still concerned.

"I don't know. I wasn't eating much to begin with, because I was so busy. Then that flu knocked me for a loop."

"Did you see a doctor?"

"No. I worked through most of it," he lied. He then deftly steered the discussion away from himself.

Most of the conversation was light, centering around the ladies' work. Ludivine worked as a typist at the nearby textile plant. Aveline had gotten a job in the same department. She was the secretary for one of the senior managers.

"What type of work are you in, Max?" Aveline eventually asked. "Traveling around France on a motorcycle certainly sounds like an adventure."

"My job's actually pretty boring. My partner drives the work truck and I meet him at the work sites."

"What exactly do you do?"

"We work on crematories."

"What are those?" Aveline asked.

"It's where they burn bodies," Ludivine added.

Aveline made a face.

Max shrugged as he explained the cover he'd invented months before. "It's nothing more than a gas oven that's capable of getting extremely hot."

"Just a tube in which a human body is turned to a pile of ash," Ludivine said with a shrug. "No big deal."

She touched Max's hand, rubbing it as the threesome laughed at the morbid joke.

Aveline had a few follow-up questions but thankfully seemed to take everything about Max at face value. After dinner, Max and Aveline smoked at the table while Ludivine had another glass of wine. Max took a brief inventory of his current state. He was pleased that he felt almost completely relaxed. Each time the night's events crept back in, he pushed them aside and looked at Ludivine.

Despite all the horrors of what had happened, he was here, and free.

For now.

Enjoy this moment, Max. Winthrop obviously doesn't know about Ludivine. If he did, he and his men would've already busted down the door. Your precautions surrounding her and the location of her flat were excellent. Too bad you didn't take other precautions...

That's over and done. You're free, Max. Now, you have to be clever enough to determine how to stay that way.

Just before 10 P.M., Ludivine popped from her chair. "I want to hear the weather. If it's supposed to be nice, maybe we can go to the Saturday market tomorrow?" she asked Max.

"Yeah...maybe." Max tensed as the old radio warmed. It hummed at first as the internal capacitors and tubes came up to their operating temperature.

When the radio eventually crackled to life, they heard the crisp voice of French journalist Jacques Chancel. He typically wouldn't be broadcasting at this time of night. Normally, there would be a top-of-the-hour news brief followed by the show *Les Aventures de Poivre* at 10:05 P.M.

Chancel was in the middle of an unclear statement about conflicting reports. This was just before he tersely called the top of the hour in France. Papers could be heard rustling as he cleared his throat.

"To recap the tumultuous news out of the United States," he said, his voice sharp but clearly disappointed. "In Dallas, Texas: American President John Kennedy was killed today as he rode in his motorcade. The governor of the state of Texas was also hit by a bullet but is expected to survive. Dallas police have arrested a man named Lee Oswald and charged him with the killing of President Kennedy and the shooting of the governor. In addition, Oswald has been charged with the killing of a Dallas policeman, who authorities claim Oswald killed during his attempted escape. American Vice President Lyndon Johnson has been sworn in and is the new president of the United States. We're getting reports every few minutes and doing our best to keep you updated with the latest."

When she first heard the news, Ludivine made a sharp sound as her hand flew to her mouth. Aveline had taken the news without reaction, at first, but had now begun to softly cry. Max didn't quite know what to do so, in his best effort to be normal, he cursed.

"What's wrong with this world?" Ludivine asked, beginning to cry herself. "He was so young and full of hope."

"His wife..." Aveline said, unable to go on.

Ludivine hugged her friend and Max just sat there, the news having brought back the events of his evening. The three of them were numb, although Max's numbness was certainly of a much different variety. After a few minutes, Ludivine opened a new bottle of wine and they toasted the American president's memory as they listened to a solid hour of news, gleaning small details about this blackest of days.

During that fateful hour, his mind lubricated by two glasses of rough table wine, Max decided, after Aveline left, he would tell Ludivine everything.

Every bit of it.

She deserved to know.

And if she wanted him gone, he'd leave.

From the wine, another sensation began to mushroom inside of him. It was anger.

Anger at Mr. Winthrop, the sonofabitch who'd upended his life.

As the two women talked, Max excused himself. In the bathroom, he eyed his hollow face, staring into his own eyes as he whispered, "What are you willing to do about it?"

Chapter Eight

For as long as the world's current inhabitants would live, most would be able to relay where they were and what they were doing when they learned of John F. Kennedy's assassination. It was a seminal moment that would still spark a hot debate 50 years later. Countless books, movies, television shows and even plays were eventually built around the drama of the gruesome killing. Careers were ended. Careers were made. In the United States, life halted until its president was laid to rest on the following Monday—after another shocking event occurred over the weekend, when Lee Harvey Oswald was killed by Dallas nightclub owner Jack Ruby.

Because the assassination and surrounding events were such headline dominating news, few people took note of the American Secret Service agent who was killed on the same day as the American president, at almost the same moment, in Paris, France. The Secret Service had not yet publicized that they even had an office in Paris. In their limited press release, they claimed the agent was there "on assignment" and had been killed in the course of a strong-arm robbery. Back in the United States, in the special edition of the November 23rd Washington Post, the story appeared on page 7. It consisted of only 6 column inches, buried at the bottom of the page, hardly a footnote, regarded by few after the vital and tumultuous assassination news that ruled the edition.

But one man did take note of the murder, although he'd heard the news a short time after the killing occurred. He'd been at the bureau late on that Friday, paralyzed like everyone else over the breaking news out of the United States. Gaspard Lacroix was a police detective in Paris. A war veteran, like so many of his contemporaries, Gaspard had taken a bit of a circuitous route to his respectable position of senior homicide detective. In his youth, Gaspard had no designs on becoming a policeman. In fact, when the Germans had invaded France in 1940, Gaspard had been the youthful proprietor of a burgeoning printing company on Paris' east side, in the suburb of Montreuil. After the invasion, the Nazis appropriated his business, demanding he print their propaganda signs in order to keep his business afloat. When Gaspard resisted, he was beaten to within a breath of his life and subsequently imprisoned. It was a miracle he didn't die in jail. A thick scar ran across his scalp and forehead, a visible reminder of the truncheon that the Gestapo had used on him.

In jail, Gaspard slowly recovered and, upon his solemn promise to ply his trade for the Nazis, he was released many months later. He did resume his operation, only to escape two weeks later to Vichy, France while a blizzard raged. It was in Vichy that a badly frostbitten Gaspard located his uncle, an influential former member of the *Deuxième Bureau de l'État-major general,* the external intelligence agency that had met its end with the German occupation. But Gaspard's uncle was still active, and he soon deployed his highly motivated young nephew back into occupied France as a reporting member of the resistance.

Before long, Gaspard had made his way to northwest France, where he would remain until the end of the war. He developed an underground network to aid and assist allied service members—typically pilots or airmen who had been shot down. In 1943, his efforts turned to espionage as he created reports that made their way back to England in preparation for the Allied Invasion that would come in 1944. The senior officials of the OSS grew to rely on the economical but hyper-accurate communiqués from the quiet resistance Frenchman across the Channel.

After the war, Gaspard was awarded the French Resistance Medal. He'd enjoyed the chance to ply his intelligence for the greater good, giving what was left of his printing business to his younger brother. In 1946, Gaspard accepted a position with the *Préfecture de police de Paris.* Following a steady rise up the ranks, Gaspard now worked as a member of the Direction Régionale de Police Judiciaire de Paris, also known simply as "36" because of the riverside address where the detectives and investigators were housed.

Unknown to almost everyone were Gaspard's maladies, all of them thanks to his resistance and subsequent imprisonment. After being beaten and left for dead, Gaspard had suffered severe frostbite and had nearly lost the use of his left hand and left foot. The frostbite had returned with a vengeance during his escape to Vichy. Now, though his extremities functioned and appeared normal, they suffered under extreme nerve pain that came and went without warning. The bottom of his left foot was the worst, spiking with phantom pain that sometimes made him yell out in his sleep.

During his wakefulness, Gaspard didn't complain. He soldiered on, quietly going about his business. Unfortunately, his police work was sometimes too consuming, and it had claimed his marriage five years before. He was the father of two children, boys, but they lived with their mother and her new husband. Gaspard saw his sons as often as possible, which wasn't nearly enough. He passed his time by working, but did allow himself to be sidetracked by good food and drink, two things that Paris provided in great measure. A tall, handsome, brooding fellow, he didn't have a difficult time finding regular female companionship, either.

Tonight, however, Gaspard's mind wasn't on food; wasn't on wine; wasn't on women. It was on the body of the man that lay inside the Place de Clichy courtyard, covered with a white sheet while flashbulbs popped and cracked from outside the iron fence. Finally, after four hours of bureaucratic bullshit involving two embassies and a host of elected officeholders; a captain, who was perched several rungs above Gaspard, gave him a preemptive ass-chewing over the sensitivity of what had happened here.

"I finally got us access and I laid my career on the line to do it," the captain growled, stinking of wine and garlic. He hitched his thumb to the clutch of suit-wearing agents standing on the landing by the door to the building. "They just lost their president to a bullet. Remember that." The captain poked Gaspard's thin tie. "I'm not going to have my own ass reamed out because you come dancing in here and create a shit storm where there isn't one, got it? This was a strong-armed robbery and the dickhead perp made off with a bag of counterfeit money." The captain pointed outside the gate. "His partner blasted this poor sonofabitch when he came out, and that's where it *ends*." The captain made a cutting gesture with his right hand. "It *ends* there. We can go nab the culprits, but we're not digging in on the victim side, here. Not at all. I know trouble when I see it."

Gaspard didn't respond, he simply tilted his head at this political animal who might have once been a policeman.

"You got it, Lacroix?" the captain rumbled. "You've got a reputation of being a badgering prick. I'll replace your skinny ass right now if you don't give me your word."

"I'll be in and out, captain," Gaspard said with a polite smile, tugging on the brim of his tobacco brown trilby. "These people have been through enough. The shooters are who we seek."

The captain seemed mollified but lifted a warning finger. "Don't let me find out otherwise." He stalked away in the light rain, climbing into the back of the black Peugeot 404, probably heading back to his wine and Friday night mistress.

The captain's top lieutenant, a man named Dimon, had listened to all this without emotion. He clapped Gaspard on the back. "You now know what I deal with all day, every day."

"I don't know how you stand it."

"Tonight he was in a good mood," Dimon said with a chuckle. "You need anything?"

"Just time and space."

"Then, you shall have it." They shook hands and the lieutenant departed.

Gaspard shrugged off the encounter with the captain and walked to the body, nodding to the forensics technician who was carefully probing the entry wound just below the left shoulder.

"The captain's such a warm man, isn't he?" the forensics tech asked. "I need to find out the date of his birthday so I can buy him some hemorrhoid cream."

Gaspard grinned indulgently. "Anything yet?"

"High-powered rifle is my guess." The technician stood, cracking his knees. He pointed toward the guardhouse with the small steel prod. "You might want to look at that grate over there. Looks like the inside man shot the hasp off. But he didn't use the same type of round he shot the inside door with. Maybe he only had one."

Gaspard turned his head in both directions. "And what type of round is that?"

"They're called frangible rounds. I've only seen the evidence of one in my fourteen years. Military started using them a few years back. The round employs a powdery metal that, at speed, will blow apart other metal. Unlike a bullet, it won't ricochet but it has to be fired from point blank range. They're made specifically for breaching."

"What else?"

"Interestingly enough, it seems the same shooter used rubber buckshot when he was inside, on this gent." The technician pointed to the torn area of the dead man's bloody shirt. "Our inside shooter also bound this agent's hands and ankles, and the woman's hands too. My guess is he'd hoped to avoid killing anyone so he knocked down the agent with the rubber bullets."

Gaspard surveyed the courtyard. "So, the perp comes back out and shoots open the grate. While he's doing that, this agent gets free and comes out shooting. But he gets it from the inside man's partner, who's walking around Paris with a hunting rifle?" Gaspard screwed up his face. "Am I correct?"

The technician mussed his own hair and shrugged. "That's what it looks like, detective. Maybe the outside shooter was concealed somewhere—a sniper."

Frowning, Gaspard viewed the body, the grate and the front door. He did this twice, scratching his chin afterward.

"What is it?" the technician asked.

"Can you tell where the rifle round came from?"

"Not with certainty." The technician pointed to his own body. "It went in here," he said, pointing to his own upper left pectoral, just above his heart. "And came out near the middle of his back. Might have severed his spine, too. We'll know later."

"So, the bullet was fired from above?" Gaspard asked, pointing to the numerous rooftops surrounding the Place de Clichy.

"I haven't had a chance to search for the bullet or to see if it ricocheted off the concrete but, yes, it would seem that way. Unless the agent was bent forward for some reason, but it would've had to have been a helluva angle."

Gaspard lifted the technician's flashlight from his toolbox and searched the ground near the corpse. It only took a moment to see the blemish. About the size of a fingernail, it appeared that the concrete had been scooped out to a depth of nearly a centimeter.

"That it?" Gaspard asked, aiming the light.

The technician eyed the mark. "I'd say so. I'll have to test it. But that sure looks like a ricochet. What's left of the bullet is probably around here somewhere. They usually bounce. After going through this man then hitting the concrete nearly head on, I doubt it went too far."

Gaspard eyed the rooftops on the western side of the courtyard. The one that would provide the best vantage point, and also create an angle such as the one the technician demonstrated, was brightly lit by the marquee sign from the Hotel Montmartre. Using his finger, Gaspard drew a line from the rooftop, through where he assumed the man had stood, down to the ricochet mark.

"I'd say that's a good guess," the technician agreed.

Gaspard frowned again. "So, let me ask you a question. Are we reasonably certain the inside shooter didn't kill this agent?"

"Reasonably, yes."

"Good." Gaspard paused for a moment, ordering his thoughts.

Something was wrong, here. Something made no sense.

He eyed each of the significant locations.

"Question: Why would our inside shooter stop to blow out this grate leading to the sewer shaft? If he had a partner on the outside, wouldn't they escape together?" Gaspard halted the technician's reply with a raised finger. "Furthermore, why have the sniper up on a rooftop? Why not have him here, at ground level, so their joint escape is quick and easy?"

After opening his mouth to respond, the technician closed it and shook his head. "Doesn't make sense."

"If they wanted to escape via that shaft, why not have your shooter down in there, ready to pop up?"

"We looked at it. The shooter didn't come in that way, but he definitely left that way. The drag marks in the pipe are telling."

"Maybe all this does make sense," Gaspard breathed. "Maybe there was enough money inside that the job was worth having multiple escapes? Maybe there were more than two men? Maybe there were a dozen? Maybe it was mayhem out here? Maybe they purposefully created a bizarre plan in order to confound us?"

The technician shrugged. "You lost me there, detective. All I've got is probable evidence of one inside man, and a shooter who was elsewhere."

"I know, and you're correct to stick with the facts. Be right back." Gaspard exited the courtyard and spoke to two other investigators, deploying them to the Hotel Montmartre to ask about anyone who might have been on the rooftop.

He lit a cigarette and walked the perimeter of the courtyard, eyeing the scene, his mind focusing on the puzzling escape through the steel grate. One of Gaspard's younger detectives emerged from the building—he'd been questioning the female employee inside.

"Who is she?" Gaspard asked.

"Clerical. Her official title is translator. Apparently, she helps with the locals, with paperwork, et cetera. She's American, parents both first-generation French. Her French is excellent. She said the shooter wore a mask and seemed to be a pro at what he does."

"Was the shooter French?"

"Yeah, Parisian accent."

"Good. Go on."

"She said, in the middle of the robbery, he stopped what he was doing and asked her why she'd been crying when he first came in."

"She'd been crying?" Gaspard asked.

"Before the perp blasted his way in, they'd just gotten off the phone with their people in the United States."

"The shooting of Kennedy?"

"Right," the junior detective said, his pencil tapping his notepad. "She said the dead agent knew several people on Kennedy's security detail. So, as they're both dealing with the shock of their president being shot—and they didn't know Kennedy was dead at that moment—the perp comes in shooting."

"And he bound the agent's hands?"

"And ankles. *Her* hands, too. Used something called Ty-Rap." The junior detective hitched his thumb to the building. "It's in there if you want to see it. The perp tied her to a shelf. She got free by sliding the Ty-Rap over the sharp support of the shelf, then freed the agent. His pistol had been taken by the shooter, so he grabbed a spare and went out shooting. Then he got shot by whoever had the rifle."

"Did she see any of it?"

"No. When she came out, the dead agent—his name was Lang, by the way—was on the ground where he is now. She said there was a man in a suit standing over the hole where we think the inside shooter escaped. Then the sniper, or whatever we're calling him, took a shot at her. There's a ricochet mark on the landing where she'd have been standing."

Gaspard showed his palm. "Wait. A man in a suit?"

The junior detective nodded. "She said he wore a suit. She said he was trim and wore shiny horn rimmed glasses."

"But he wasn't the perp who'd been inside?"

"Definitely not."

"What else?"

"She said she felt like the man in the suit was around fifty years old, but judged all that based solely on posture and shape. I really pressed her to get that, so don't put too much stock in it."

"How do we know the shooter went down that shaft?"

"Two civilians who were walking by hid behind one of the columns after the gunshots. They saw it. He shot the grate, slid it aside, and jumped in. He had a duffel bag, a briefcase and the shotgun."

"What else did they see?"

"Nothing. They ran away right after."

"If they ran away, how did we find them?"

"They came back."

"We have their information?"

The junior detective tapped his pad again. "I've got it."

There was a bit of silence as Gaspard processed all this. "Them," he said pointing to the two guards, now covered in warming blankets and sipping paper cups of coffee.

"They were incapacitated. Didn't see anything." Before Gaspard could ask, the junior detective continued. "There was an aerosol can on top of their guard house, with a tube running into the ventilation duct. The can seems to contain some sort of gas that knocked them out."

Gaspard's eyes widened. "Do we have anything from that?"

"We're checking."

"Did they see anyone?"

"They said a visitor arrived right before they blacked out."

"Who?"

"Neither man can remember."

"Do we know anything about the visitor?"

"A man. That's it."

"So, it could have been the perp?"

"Maybe. Maybe not."

Gaspard muttered a curse word. He'd worked some strange ones through the years. Though he only had a few of the facts, and they were sketchy at best, this one was setting up to be a humdinger. Professionals for sure. They didn't expect the agent to come out into the courtyard, and that's where it all went bad.

Gaspard spent the next two hours walking the scene of the crime. The detectives at the Hotel Montmartre found nothing—no witnesses, no evidence. All rooftops were subsequently searched with the same result. No casings. No obvious evidence.

Several civilians recalled a sedan being parked near the entrance to the courtyard, but that's all. No make. No tag. No faces remembered. One remembered the sedan as being dark in color: probably blue or black. There was no useful physical evidence left anywhere. The shotgun casings were common. They'd be checked by forensics but Gaspard was counting on nothing.

All Gaspard had was the woman.

He walked inside, finding her alone in the meeting room. She was smoking a cigarette. In front of her was an ashtray with a small pile of cigarettes, each with a faint lipstick ring.

He introduced himself. "Are you okay?" he asked.

"No, sir, I'm not." She crushed out her cigarette and looked up at him, her green eyes glistening. She was sitting at the end of the table, a rather unique and arresting woman, probably in her late twenties. Her hair was pulled back and woven, held together by two emerald clasps. She wore a simple white blouse and dark gray skirt. The blouse had a gray smudge—probably from cigarette ash. He could tell she was trim, and her high cheekbones and jade eyes suggested Nordic ancestry, despite her parents being French.

"I have some additional questions," Gaspard said. "Do you feel like answering them?"

"I'd really like to get some sleep."

"That's understandable. Will tomorrow suit you?"

"That would be better."

Gaspard explained that he couldn't allow her to go home. He said he could have someone retrieve her things, and that he'd arrange for her stay in a nice hotel for the evening.

"Am I in danger?" she asked, alarmed.

"Not that I'm aware of," Gaspard replied, doing his best to soothe her. "But let's just play it safe until we can figure out who did this. Why don't I get you taken care of and we can speak tomorrow?" He consulted his notepad. "How about two in the afternoon? That will give you enough time to get a good night of sleep."

"That'd be fine, thank you." She lurched and touched his arm. "Sir?"

"Yes?"

"Is there any way you can get me a sleeping pill of some sort? I can't stop thinking about—" She began to cry.

Gaspard typically made it a point not to touch strange women other than a handshake. But this woman needed a hug. He gave her a polite and reassuring embrace and handed her a tissue. "I will make sure one of the medics provides you with something to help you sleep, good enough? If they don't, I'll go home and get you one of my pills. I often cannot sleep."

"Thank you."

"You're going to be okay. I'll see to it."

Eyes glistening, she nodded.

He bade her farewell and spoke to his junior detective, giving him full instructions. They would have to inform the U.S. Secret Service of what they were doing, as a courtesy. Gaspard could think of no reason why they would object. The junior detective found two sleeping pills for the woman, and arranged for her to stay at the sumptuous Le Meurice on Rue de Rivoli.

When Gaspard finally departed, it was after midnight. He went home and drank a half a bottle of Chinon as he watched the appalling news of the assassination on his small television. The American president had been pronounced dead a short time after he'd arrived at the hospital. It was almost too much to digest. Soon after the president was shot, a Dallas police officer was killed. This led the police to a man whose name was Lee Harvey Oswald. He was arrested in a movie theater, of all places. Information on Oswald, at this point, was sketchy. But the news organizations were already digging into his supposed ties to the Soviet Union.

Gaspard slept very little that night. He continued to be harangued by all that had happened, and one question that continued to assault his senses.

Was it purely coincidence that a little known United States Secret Service station in Paris, France was robbed minutes after the American president had been shot in Dallas?

Mere minutes…

Gaspard had no idea how many dozens of times he would ask himself this question in the days leading up to his being shot.

Twice.

***

Late in the evening, Aveline stood and stretched as she prepared to go home. She apologized for staying too long. Ludivine told her she was welcome anytime. As Aveline used the restroom and gathered her things, Ludivine held Max's hand. He turned to her, getting a tepid smile underneath glassy eyes. She still seemed numb over the news of John Kennedy's assassination. They all did.

Max then said his goodbyes to Aveline and told her he hoped to see her again soon. After she had gone, Ludivine embraced him, holding him tightly. At first Max thought she was crying, but she wasn't, she was simply holding him, enjoying the moment. He couldn't decide when, or how, to tell her the truth.

"Ludivine…"

"No more talking. I want you."

As Ludivine brushed her teeth, Max leaned into the bathroom.

"I need to tell you something before we go to bed."

"Is it bad?"

"It's not good."

"Tell me later," she said, rinsing her mouth and drying her face. "My mood is so down after hearing about President Kennedy that I can't take anything else. I just want to be close to you tonight," she said. Her words weren't intentionally seductive, like they'd been on his last visit. This time, they were tinged by sadness over the horrific news from the United States. Perhaps Max's touch would rebalance her.

Max was concerned about his injury. He rubbed his heavy beard as he contemplated how to tell her. "I need to brush my teeth again. And do you care about the beard?"

"I like it. I'll get the bed ready."

When he finished brushing, he thought about the rat. He brushed his teeth again. Then he used Ludivine's mouthwash.

Still wearing the rose-patterned robe, he crept into the darkness of her room. The dormer window was open, a cool breeze fluttering in. The room was bathed in indigo light. He heard the sheets rustle.

"Come to me," Ludivine said.

"I don't have any nightclothes."

"You don't need any. Drop that robe and get in bed."

Max stood there. "Before we go too far, there's something I really *must* tell you."

"Not tonight, Max. Please, just be with me."

"I have an injury."

"What kind of injury?"

"I got burned."

"Where?"

"On my side."

"Are you okay?"

"It hurts, but I'll be okay."

"We don't have to do anything. We can just lay here."

"I'd like to try—I really would. I just don't know if I can."

"Do what you feel comfortable doing."

While his side might have hurt, the rest of Max was ready, evidenced when he let the robe slide to the floor. He slid into the bed, feeling her silky warmth.

"Is your burn the 'not good' thing you wanted to tell me about?"

"No. What I need to tell you could affect us. That's why I keep insisting."

She grew still. "Are you seeing someone else?"

"No…God, no."

"Then just lay here with me, Max. Everything else can wait. *Everything.*"

Ludivine smelled good and pressed her sweet tongue into his mouth.

He rested on his back and moved her on top of him. His side hurt but it wasn't unbearable. The benefits outweighed the negatives by a large margin.

"Sure you're okay?"

He answered her with a kiss.

Ludivine moved gently on top of Max as his mouth remained joined with hers. Max began to move with her and, because it had been so long since their last time, the moment didn't last very long. Afterward, Max dipped his head in disappointment.

"I'm sorry…that was too quick."

As he kissed her again, he could feel her smiling.

"It was perfect, and I now know you missed me."

"I wish I had the words to express how much I missed you."

Ludivine slid off and lay with her rear end pressed up against him. She tugged his arm over her stomach and clasped it there, whispering to Max that she would now be able to sleep, now that he was safely with her.

If she only knew all he'd gone through to get back to her.

Fifteen minutes later, as the rhythmic sounds of her sleeping occurred, Max's mind lurched uncontrollably back into gear. He thought about the events of the evening, and of the past week. Would there be a manhunt? Was there already one occurring? And who was Mr. Winthrop and what branch of the U.S. government was he working for? He had to be a government man, correct? How else could he have managed a private prison on a military installation in Germany? How would he have known all about the Secret Service station at the Place de Clichy? He'd even mentioned it earlier—Max clearly recalled him saying something about branches of *our* government not working together.

Suddenly, the same notion he'd had earlier halted before his mind's eye, beaming as brightly as the marquee for the Hotel Montmartre.

The briefcase. Whatever is inside that case was worth many months of surveillance; was worth my imprisonment and all that went with it; was worth building a mock-up of the Secret Service station; was worth allowing me to steal thousands of counterfeit dollars; was worth deadly snipers killing a Secret Service agent.

And it might have been worth simultaneously assassinating the president of the United States.

No…

Max couldn't—or *wouldn't*—yet allow himself to believe that the timing of the two events were intentional.

Just ponder it…

Okay…could the assassination have been performed as a diversion? There'd only been one agent, and a woman, to divert. *No…not a diversion*, he decided.

But, perhaps an adjunction.

It was the only possibility Max would allow that related his breach to the assassination. Certainly the killing of Kennedy was not done as a diversion. But Max now admitted to himself that—perhaps—the two events were related. And, just as he thought earlier, there might have been other coordinated breaches and activities he wasn't yet aware of.

There weren't—but he didn't know that.

As he lay there, willing his mind to come back to neutral, the touch of Ludivine's backside reawakened a different portion of Max's being. She awoke, too, and their second union on this evening was much better than the first. More creative and, dare he think it, fun. Afterward, truly exhausted, his side aching wonderfully, Max actually slept.

His sleep was deep and dark and dreamless.

Chapter Nine

Although he awoke early, Max willed himself back to sleep. His mind and body needed the rest. He managed another hour. When he awoke the second time, his brain lurched into action over what happened, and what loomed. Ludivine finally stirred around 9 A.M. humming with delight as she settled against him, skin on skin. He allowed her enough time to fall back asleep. When she didn't, when she finally sat up and rubbed her face, Max told her he had to speak with her now.

"It's urgent," he added, hating that word. Hating to press.

But she had to know.

"Do you mind if I make coffee first?"

"No," he breathed. He sat on the side of the bed, smoking a cigarette as she worked in the kitchen. He wasn't frustrated with her; it was the situation that bothered him. If Mr. Winthrop, or the authorities, were to find out she helped him—he shook his head, clearing the fatalistic thoughts from his brain. Max held the cold glass ashtray in his left hand, trying to get his mind around the correct phrasing of words he'd use.

A pigeon landed on the windowsill, fluttering and cooing. Max slowly turned, watching as the pigeon's mate landed. They sidled close to one another.

Two is better than one.

Sometimes.

When the birds flew away, Max crushed out his cigarette, laying back, shutting his eyes, preparing...

After ten minutes, Ludivine returned with a tray holding two large mugs of coffee, the darkness of the liquid cut by whole milk in true French style. Beside the coffee rested two small pieces of chocolate. Though sweets weren't his thing, Max ate his dutifully. The milk had cooled the coffee enough that he was able to swill his, drinking half of the strong brew in one gulp.

Out with it, Max. Just get it out there and deal with the fallout later.

"Ludivine, after I tell you this, I'll leave if you want me to."

Her dark eyebrows lowered. "That scares me."

"I know, and what I'll tell you will probably scare you even more." He finished the majority of the coffee and lifted the pack of cigarettes Mr. Winthrop had provided. There were only two remaining—now was certainly the time for one. He fingered the cigarette and joined eyes with her. "I don't repair crematories. And I'm American…not French." He spoke a few lines of American English.

Her lips parted as though she might respond. But she didn't. She blinked. Once.

"A number of years ago, I was accused of murder in San Francisco. The man did die at my hands, but I didn't murder him. It was self-defense. Since then, I've been on the run." He let that sink in.

"I can tell there's more," she said, lifting her chin. Her lips drew tightly against her teeth. "Go ahead. Tell it all, Max, or whatever your name is."

"It's Max."

"How nice."

"Since I was a fugitive, I couldn't let anyone know who I was, which meant I couldn't have a regular job. So, after I got away from San Francisco, I started performing robberies. In time, I learned how to do it so no one died and I could take enough that would allow me to live for weeks or months between hits."

"You rob people." It wasn't a question.

"I rob *criminals*."

"Criminals?"

"Yes."

"In the United States?"

"Yes, for many years. I nearly got caught. So, I had a false passport made, and came here, and this is where I've been ever since."

"Is that why you showed up at my house on a Friday night, covered in filth?"

Max lit the cigarette, supporting his head in his hand. "Sort of."

Her lip trembled. "Did you rob someone last night?"

"Yes, I did."

"Who?"

"Ludivine, when I left here nearly a month ago, I went south, to Marseilles. I spent a full week casing drug dealers until I learned where their cash hoard was. When I knocked them over, everything went to plan. But afterward, when I got back to my motel, I was captured."

"By the police?"

He dragged on the cigarette and shook his head. "Not the police. I don't know for sure. Americans, I think."

Ludivine shook her head. "I'm confused."

"I am, too," he breathed. "These people captured me and put me into a jail. But the jail was just for me. They held me until I agreed to do what I did last night."

"Is this why you lost so much weight?"

He nodded.

"How long were you there?"

"A few weeks."

"And who did you rob last night?"

"At 'Place Clichy,' I robbed an American Secret Service office." Max pointed the cigarette at the bag. "That's why I didn't have any clothes to put on last night. They weren't filthy. I was lying. In that bag are thousands of dollars and my shotgun."

She turned to look. "And the briefcase?"

"I don't know what's in there, but that's what they wanted."

"Who wanted?"

"The people who coerced me into stealing."

"You robbed the American Secret Service?"

"Yeah."

"They guard the president, don't they?"

"Yes."

"But you said the people who captured you were American?"

"Yeah, and I'm pretty sure they're with the government."

She shook her head, clearly confused. "So, if they're government, then why would they steal from their own government?"

"The government has many layers—and, believe me, there are plenty of villains lurking within those layers."

Ludivine was quiet for a moment. She took the first sip of her coffee. "Why are you telling me this now?" Her next words had more heat. "And why have you been lying to me for so long?"

"I'm sorry. I just...I didn't want to lose you." He paused. "By being here, I'm endangering you. The men who captured me don't care about liberties or citizens' rights. They don't care about you, or me, or Aveline, or anyone else. They'll kill either of us and never blink." He eyed her intently. "Now you think about that. Think long and hard." Again, he paused. "Do you want me to leave?"

Ludivine's face twisted. "Of course not."

"I'm serious, and you should think it through. I'm causing you a great deal of exposure by being here."

"No, Max. I believe everything you've told me."

"It goes beyond believing me, Ludivine. Aside from these men, I'm wanted for murder. The police can charge you with all manner of things if they even suspect that you've helped me."

"Do they know about me?"

"If they did, we wouldn't be talking."

"Then they can't find out."

After tapping the long ash from his cigarette, Max puffed it one last time before crushing it out. He drained the last few drops of his coffee. "By now, I'm quite certain the police, and who knows who else, are scouring Paris for me. People could have seen me near here, or even in the building."

"Wait…I thought this group from the government was after you. Why are the police involved?"

"Because, I may be wanted for murder."

"You told me that."

"Not the murder in San Francisco…murder *here*."

"Of whom?"

"Someone shot a Secret Service agent last night, after I'd robbed them." Max explained the entirety of what happened, finishing with his escape through the sewer and underground.

"And *you* didn't shoot him?"

"I did shoot him, non-fatally." Max explained about the rubber rounds.

"And when he came outside, *they* shot him?"

"Gunned him down, just like they'll do to me or you."

It began to rain outside and they sat there in silence for quite some time. Ludivine refilled their coffees and afterward they rested beside one another on the bed.

Facing away from him, Ludivine said, "If you turned yourself in and told the truth…"

"I can't do that."

"Why?"

"I can't put it into words. But I won't do that."

"Why?"

"It's just not who I am."

"Would you rather die?"

"I'd rather not die. But, yes, I'd choose death over surrender."

They grew silent again.

"Do you have a plan?" she asked.

"Not yet. And again, if you want me to leave, I will."

"Stop saying that." She lifted up and turned. "How much money is in the bag?"

"A lot," Max said. "But it's counterfeit."

"So, it's no good?"

"No, that money has use. I just have to be smart about it."

"We."

"We?"

"*We* have to be smart about it."

Max eyed Ludivine. Her expression said everything.

The pigeons…two is better than one.

Sometimes.

"What about the briefcase?" she asked.

"That, Ludivine, just might be the key to everything."

"And you don't know what's in it?"

"I have no earthly idea."

"Have you tried to open it?"

"It's locked."

"May I try?"

"Go ahead," he said.

She tried, unsuccessfully. The locks weren't standard briefcase locks. They were riveted on and very sturdy. Max watched her from the bed.

Eventually, she gave up and placed the briefcase by the bed. She plopped down next to him. "You're really American?"

"Yes."

"Where are you from?"

"Chicago."

"The Windy City, correct?"

"That's the place."

"Will you take me there?"

"I'd like that."

"Let's make a plan."

"We can try."

After an hour's worth of discussion, they decided not to confide anything in Aveline. Ludivine believed, even if Aveline saw a picture of Max as a wanted man, she would keep it to herself. Besides, Max's appearance had markedly changed since he'd last had a photo taken. Regardless, he and Ludivine agreed it was best to leave town as soon as possible.

Once their basic plan was formulated, using what little cash she had, Ludivine went shopping. She bought Max two very inexpensive changes of casual clothes from a thrift store. Both sets of clothes would make him appear impoverished and common. At another discount store, she purchased his undergarments and a few other items. Ludivine also bought two newspapers and watched several channels of television in a department store. When the news update aired, there was no mention of the robbery at the Secret Service station, and certainly no sketches or photos of Max. Everything involved the killing of American President John F. Kennedy, especially the reaction from the French leaders.

While she was gone, Max cleaned and polished his filthy shoes. He also counted the money and was unable to discern anything resembling a marking pattern. The money looked and felt genuine.

When Max finally turned his attention to the briefcase, like Ludivine before him, he was unable to defeat the twin locks. He pondered shooting the rivets with a pistol, just as he'd done with the hasp. But he certainly couldn't do that here, in the city.

It would have to wait.

***

Detective Gaspard Lacroix sat motionless, not wanting to influence his witness in any way. Her name was Evelyn Durand. She was American, from Florida, and had attended the University of Miami. She'd explained that, during her formal schooling, she'd spent a semester in France. It was then her love for the country was borne. Evelyn had worked for the U.S. government since graduating university, managing to get posted in France two years before. Evelyn had only been at the Parisian Secret Service station for two months. Based on several comments she'd made, she struggled to make ends meet and was unwilling to ask her parents for support. Such was her love for France, however, that she was willing to scrimp just to be here.

Gaspard couldn't help but immediately like her. And her flawless French with a decided American accent only made her more attractive to him. In his experience, it was rare to find an American who spoke French so well.

She'd spoken with him for the better part of two hours. Though he'd gleaned several useful items from Evelyn's testimony, he'd categorize this session as fairly unproductive, thus far. Nothing she'd given him was going to provide an early break to this case. Following a short breather, Gaspard asked her if she could recall any other details than what she'd told him, even if they were unclear. Her hand moved to her mouth as she gnawed on a fingernail.

"I did hear something," she said, after considerable deliberation. "But it was muddled and I don't know if I heard it correctly. I wouldn't want to steer you the wrong way—that's why I haven't mentioned it."

"It's okay if you didn't hear everything clearly. Even if you heard just bits and pieces, I need to know. Please, tell me."

She sipped her water. "I was in the secure room and that…cord…whatever the thing was he'd tightened around my wrist…it held me to the steel rack. I couldn't move closer to hear better. Plus, I was scared. The guy, the thief, he'd just left."

"Left the vault?"

"Yes, it is a vault but we call it the secure room, for whatever reason."

Gaspard made a notation.

Evelyn continued. "With all he was carrying, it was noisy when he moved, you know? That's why I was being still, because I could hear him. Then, I heard him stop in the hallway…he talked to Agent Lang."

"Agent Lang was awake at this time?"

"He'd been moaning. I could hear him mumble something to the thief. They talked for a few seconds and then the thief left. I heard the outside door click shut. That's when I rubbed my wrists up and down to get loose. I used a pair of scissors to cut Agent Lang free." Evelyn began to cry again. "If I'd have just stayed in that secure room, he'd be alive." She sobbed and dipped her head. "He'd be alive."

Gaspard slid the tissues to her. This had happened several times over the questioning. It was clear to see this woman was carrying a burden of guilt for the agent's death. He couldn't help but wonder if she were involved with him.

Rather than reassure her again, which he'd already done, he remained quiet. She cried for about a minute.

"What do you think the perpetrator said to Agent Lang?"

"He said…" She shook her head. "I'm just…I'm not sure I heard it correctly."

"Please, just tell me what you *think* you heard."

"It was something like, 'I was forced to do this.' There was something about him being imprisoned—I think he said on an Army base in Germany—and forced to do this by someone named Mister Winthrop."

Gaspard struggled not to overreact. He wrote every word on his yellow notepad and underlined *Mr. Winthrop*. "Anything else?" he asked, after swallowing with difficulty.

"It was hard to hear."

"Germany?"

"Yes, I think he said the prison was at an Army base in Germany, and Winthrop was an American. He insisted Agent Lang tell his superiors about this."

The clock ticked. Gaspard's frenzied scrawling sounded like rocks being dragged over pavement. He looked up.

"So, Agent Lang understood the perpetrator's French?"

She narrowed her eyes. "No, actually the thief spoke English."

"But you said he spoke Parisian French?"

"He did. Sounded like anyone on the street."

"But he spoke English?"

"I'm sorry…I should have said that first. Yes, this was in English. In fact, he sounded American."

As alarms sounded in his mind, Gaspard forced himself to appear calm. He placed his pencil on his notepad and laced his fingers over it. "American English?"

She nodded.

"Evelyn, are you certain? You told me you didn't hear him clearly. How can you be so sure he spoke American English?"

Evelyn cut her eyes away. "I guess I heard a lot more than I said. It's just…"

"Just what?"

"It was the content of what he said. It was crazy. I couldn't believe my ears." She turned her gaze back to Gaspard. "But it *was* American English."

"And did his American accent have a regional dialect?"

"Northern."

"How can you be sure?"

"I'm from Florida, detective. We have a number of northerners there. I know their accents compared to my own. It's like you hearing someone speaking French in a *Gascon* dialect."

90

"I understand. From his accent, are you able to be more specific about where he might have come from?"

"Now you're really making me grasp."

He shrugged in a French manner. "Act as if you're having a conversation at a party. The result is meaningless."

"Upper-Midwest, maybe? Like people sound who are from the Great Lakes area."

"Is this a strict guess, or do you have any certainty?"

"You just told me to take a wild shot at it. No, I'm not certain."

"But, in guessing, you believe—"

"Forced to guess," she interrupted. "The thief sounded like an Upper-Midwest American when he spoke English."

He nodded as he wrote. "This is very helpful."

Mon Dieu! Gaspard did all he could to hide his excitement.

"Mademoiselle Durand, do you have an opinion, or even another guess, as to whether the perpetrator was American or French *by birth*?"

Again, she chewed her fingernail. After a moment's deliberation, she shook her head. "He sounded like a native in both languages. I heard the French much more clearly, but I can't guess."

"And did his mask conceal everything about his face?"

She shrugged. "I told you what I remember. He had a short beard and dark eyes."

"And he was neither big nor small?"

"Correct. His hands were really big with large knuckles. I noticed that when he tied me up."

"Was he rough with you?"

"No. He told me he didn't want to hurt me. Before he left the vault, when he asked me why I was crying, I could tell he didn't know that President Kennedy had been shot."

"Yes, you mentioned this."

"It upset him. He was jolted and could barely whisper after that."

Gaspard grew quiet and eyed the woman.

She looked away for a moment before bringing her green eyes back to Gaspard. "That man I saw outside, with the glasses. I think that was Mister Winthrop, the man the thief mentioned. The thief...the perpetrator...I believe him. He said 'I didn't want to do this.' There was some sort of decency about the thief."

"A decency?"

"Yes. He was vicious at first, but gentle with me." She looked away for a moment. "Something happened when he left the building, and that's why that man was out there, staring down in that hole. That's why they shot Agent Lang. That's why they shot at me."

"Who is *they*?"

She shook her head back and forth. "I have no idea."

Gaspard waited until she was silent for a few beats. He said, "I have one last question, and it's personal."

"What could be more personal than all of this?"

He nodded his agreement. "Were you and Agent Lang romantically involved?"

She placed her hands in her lap and stared at them.

"Ma'am?"

"If I tell you, will you promise to keep it to yourself?"

"I can't promise that, but I can promise to be discreet."

She seemed satisfied. "No, we weren't involved, but he was an instant friend to me. You know, when you meet someone, and you automatically connect?"

"Of course. But, may I ask why that's sensitive?"

"Agent Lang didn't like women, detective." She arched her narrow eyebrows, as if saying, "Do I need to go on?"

"Oh," Gaspard replied. "I understand your discretion. Have no fear, there's no need for me to pass that information on to anyone."

Following a brief summation, Gaspard provided Evelyn Durand with a cigarette and led her through the labyrinthine corridors of headquarters. Standing inside the lobby, he asked her if she'd been comfortable in the hotel room he'd arranged.

"Yes, it was quite nice. If the circumstances had been different, I might have enjoyed it," she said, doling out a tight smile.

"We'd actually like for you to stay there for the time being, as would your American employer. I can have an officer take you to your apartment so you can gather—"

"Excuse me, but I'm planning to stay in my home."

"We don't believe you're in danger, but we'd rather you remain in the hotel."

"Can you force me to do that?"

Gaspard stuttered. "Well, no."

"Then I'm going to my home. I have a cat. She needs me."

He shrugged. "Will you allow me to give you a ride?"

"I'll walk. The fresh air will do me good."

"I'll probably need to speak with you again."

A tremor went through her cheek and lips. "I'll be around."

With that, Evelyn Durand exited the building and descended the steps. Gaspard stepped outside, watching her go under the fluffy ceiling of gray clouds. It was cool and windy as Evelyn strode to the southeast on Quai des Orfèvres, her lithe silhouette made prominent by the Seine behind her.

Although she'd been extremely helpful, Gaspard was now more confused than he had been before. Perhaps American—perhaps French. Imprisoned in

Germany on an Army installation. Forced to perform a robbery by a Mr. Winthrop…

And Evelyn Durand…my, my, my…

Gaspard shook away the flash attraction he'd had to the young woman and concentrated on what he'd learned. As he walked back inside to rewrite and categorize his notes, he muttered the words, "*Deux pas en avant un pas en arrière.*"

Two steps forward, one step back.

***

By the time evening rolled around on Saturday, reality had begun to set in for Max. If he were to survive, his first step was to come up with a short-term plan. Nothing more than a strategy to get him through the next 72 hours. At that point, he'd probably need another short-term plan. Then, another. Hopefully, if he could put a week or two behind him, he might have a chance to somehow persist over the long-term. But for now, he was thinking three days down the road—no more. He surveyed the food in Ludivine's sideboard and icebox—there wasn't enough for two people to make it through the weekend. Although he felt miserable for doing so, Max asked Ludivine how much money she had. She told him.

"Do you have that here?" he asked.

"Yes."

"Any in the bank?"

She shook her head. "Only enough to keep the account open."

Max stared at the duffel bag of American money. He had a few thoughts about how to use it, but that wasn't in his current short-term plan. For now, he needed enough money to keep them afloat without having to constantly be in and out of the apartment. If Max could stockpile enough food to lay low, he might just ride this out. Ludivine might have to talk to Aveline, but he wasn't ready to worry about that yet. That could wait till Monday. For now, he needed money—French money.

An idea occurred to Max. It was risky, but given his predicament, risks would have to be taken. And a risk like the one he was envisioning could provide him with enough untraceable cash to spring them from the city. It would also be a way to get cash without alerting the authorities.

Max decided to act. Right now was not the time to stop and think.

"I need to go out for a bit."

"Are you coming back?" Ludivine asked, alarmed.

He walked to her, cupping her face in his hands. "Of course, I'll be back. Would you mind making us something to eat? I shouldn't be gone more than an hour."

"Where are you going?"

"Not far."

"But where?"

"I'm going to Chaillot," he said, referencing the posh area south of the Arc de Triomphe, only about two kilometers from her flat.

"Why are you going to Chaillot?"

"Because that's where the money is."

Max stood in front of the mirror in her bathroom. He touched his side, satisfied with how it felt. For good measure, he opened his shirt and tightened the bandage.

Next, he used a bit of her eyeliner under each eye, darkening the sockets. A bit of rouge around the base of his nose, followed by several sniffs of her perfume gave him a genuine runny nose and the appearance of someone with a cold—or an addiction. With no beard, his new clothes, and his hat pulled tightly over his hair, Max felt he'd pass a cursory street inspection. He didn't look anything like he'd looked yesterday.

Ludivine gave him her small handful of money, which he folded into a neat wad and slipped into his pocket. He tucked the Secret Service agent's compact pistol under his jacket and headed out into the early evening, making his way to the broad Avenue de la Grande Armée with the majestic Arc towering in the near distance. Tonight was cool and crisp, and a Saturday, resulting in heavy crowds on the wide sidewalk. Max passed two policemen who were chatting with one another while scanning the crowd. Neither seemed to take notice of him.

After passing by the Arc, where he overheard snippets of several conversations revolving around the death of President Kennedy, Max continued onto the Champs-Élysées for a short distance, peeling to the right at the famed eatery, Fouquet's, known for its traditional French cuisine and overuse of crushed red velvet. He navigated through the line of limousines and waiting cars, following the sound of music coming from an area several blocks behind the restaurant.

As he walked past the rear of Fouquet's, the smell of fine food touched his nose, making him hungry. After tonight, Max needed to fortify himself with good food at least three times a day. With the loss of weight he'd experienced, he was quite certain he'd lost strength, too. The lack of muscle made what he planned to do tonight all the more risky. He continued on, finally arriving at his destination area.

In the tony hotel and club area of Chaillot, Max smoked a cigarette and walked slowly on the Rue Francois, keeping an eye out for an early evening entrepreneur. Given the narcotics explosion of the last decade, he knew there'd be at least one dealer nearby. Being an upscale street, the dealer would certainly be protected, probably by the neighborhood beat cop he paid the bribes to. Violence in this area was rare, especially at an early hour. That's why he'd chosen Chaillot. Max also assumed there would be more than one dealer—maybe two or three—all of them working for the same crime boss. They'd all watch each other's backs, but their guard should be down given the locale and the time.

How many times have I done this? First, find the scumbag street dealer. Then, follow the money, grubby hand to grubby hand, until you eventually find the strong room. Not tonight, though. All I need is the scumbag street dealer...

Yes, what Max had planned was extremely risky. But he'd mitigated what risks he could, and he and Ludivine needed money—money they could actually use. More than anything, he needed to acquire it from someone who wouldn't file an official police report.

After nearly a half-hour of walking up and down the busy street, Max believed he'd identified his target. The man was tall and handsome, in a sleazy sort of way. He wore a tweed waistcoat and a derby hat. His three-day beard was nicely manicured and, when he smiled at his customers, Max could see the glint of silver behind his canines. He reminded Max of the alpha alley cat—possibly dangerous when cornered, but probably just a lot of hissing and spitting.

Max had watched as the man led four different pedestrians from the sidewalk. During each encounter, Max saw the following: there was a brief conversation on the sidewalk; then the sleazy-handsome man showed his customer through the rows of cars to an unseen location in the shadows. Within a minute, the customer and the dealer would reemerge. The dealer would be all smiles and the customer would hurry away for his fix.

He's the one.

Max stepped into an alley and moved the pistol to his right coat pocket. He shut his eyes, focusing his mind. After all that had gone on last night, this was the last thing Max thought he'd be doing tonight.

Hunching over as if he were cold, his hands deep in his coat pockets, Max walked to the dealer. While chilly tonight, it wasn't nearly as cold as Max made it seem. His teeth were chattering. The man, his eyebrow cocked in amusement, acquired Max when he was 10 meters away. A skilled dealer, he knew a junkie when he saw one.

"Hero?" Max asked, referring to heroin.

The man shook his head. "No hero, not this month. I could possibly help you find some *Bleu Mollies*. A nice substitute to tide you over. I can probably get some other things, too, for the right person."

"*Bleus* work," Max said pulling out the small wad of francs.

"Not here," the dealer admonished, cursing. He led Max through the adjacent parking lot. They walked to the far rear corner, to a blue sedan, a Renault. The corner of the lot was dark due to the angle of the buildings. There was a light fixture overhead, but the bulb was out. Max assumed the dealer had knocked out the light for privacy. The parking lot backed up to the row of buildings from an adjacent street. Max stood with his back to the wall; the summer's now dead weeds had grown up from the corner of the building and tickled his hands.

"You don't look like you belong here," the dealer said, suspicion in his voice.

"I live up in Saint-Denis. *Les keufs* are complete pricks up there, bringing down the weight of the world on the working man just for buying a simple petard."

The dealer shrugged. It seemed as if he knew this wouldn't be a large transaction and now he was ready to take Max's pittance and get on with his night. "How many *bleus*?"

"How much are they?"

"Two francs each."

"What if I buy a bunch? Can I get a discount?"

The dealer arched his eyebrow again. Perhaps he'd underestimated this red-nosed junkie from Saint-Denis. "Discounts begin at twenty bleus," he said offhandedly. "Can you manage that?"

"Okay, how much for a hundred bleus?"

After a moment's rumination, the dealer said, "One-seventy-five."

"One-fifty," Max replied.

The dealer's chest hitched with amusement. "Only because it's early." He dug into his pocket and removed a small set of keys, opening his trunk. The man took his time as he came out with foil sheets containing the amphetamine pills.

"Twenty per sheet. Here are five sheets," the dealer said, straightening. He spoke as he turned. "Give me the money and then you can count—"

Despite the relative darkness, there was definitely enough light to discern the revolver aimed at his face. The dealer froze.

"Do not make a loud sound," Max warned.

"Do you have any idea who you're fucking with?"

"I'll shoot you," Max said, his voice just above a whisper. "Don't try me."

The dealer simmered.

"Drop those pills in the trunk."

The dealer obeyed.

"Slowly...and I mean slowly...remove the cash from your pocket with your right hand."

The dealer went inside his jacket, causing Max to tense the pistol. Then, just as he'd been instructed to do, the dealer came out with a large wad of cash in a neat bundle. He turned his palm so Max could see it.

"Keep that in your right hand and use your left hand to get your cash stash from the trunk."

"I don't keep a stash in my trunk," the dealer countered. "Just those pills."

Max cocked the hammer.

"Alright, alright…hang on."

"Get it with your left hand only. Keep that right hand up where I can see it."

Grousing, the dealer rummaged in the trunk. He flipped open what was probably a shoebox before coming out with a similar sized bundle in his left hand.

"That's it?"

"It's early, man…I haven't taken in much yet."

"If I go in there and find more…"

"Search it if you want," the dealer said.

Max believed him.

"Keep the money in your two hands while you quietly close the trunk. Do it with the cash *still in your hands.*"

His frustration obvious, the dealer obliged.

"Now put the money on the trunk, then put your hands behind your head, and walk over here and face the wall."

The dealer set the two wads of francs on the trunk, placed his hands behind his head, and walked to the wall. He turned slightly. "Don't do this, man. Please. I'm begging you."

"Shut up. Get on your knees," Max said, using his own left hand to stuff the dealer's money in his jacket pocket.

A voice behind Max got his attention. It sounded like someone out by the road. Whoever it was yelled, *"C'est quoi ce bordel?"* A colloquial phrase, roughly translated, it meant, "What the hell is going on?"

Whether or not the phrase was directed at Max, he knew time was of the essence. He swung the pistol in an arc, striking the drug dealer at the base of his neck and crumpling him. Turning, Max watched as a man came forward from the light of the road with a switchblade in his hand. The knife-wielding man was dressed similarly to the dealer—probably his partner. He was six cars away, moving forward with caution. Despite the darkness, he'd obviously seen enough to realize a robbery was taking place.

Max knelt behind the drug dealer's car and waited. He couldn't shoot—not right here in the middle of Paris. Who knew how many people were already searching for him? Firing the pistol was Max's absolute last resort. Behind him, the unconscious dealer softly moaned. The stun to his vagus nerve had knocked him out of commission, but for how long?

Looking to his left and right, Max saw no avenue for escape. There was an alley to the left, but it was blocked by a high fence with razor wire at the top. If Max moved to the right, he would expose himself and end up in a foot chase through Chaillot—another poor option. This wasn't some poor section of town. This was an exclusive street, and drug dealers chasing junkies would be frowned upon by the police. Besides, due to his weakened state and injured side, Max wouldn't have much endurance.

There were few choices.

As the second man continued forward with his straight razor leading the way, Max remained crouched behind the car.

He un-cocked the hammer of the pistol, gripping it securely.

Chapter Ten

Vienna, Austria

The drum brakes of the silver rental Opel chirped as Mr. Winthrop eased to a stop in front of the large, three-story home in Vienna's quiet Margareten neighborhood. The street was well lit. He eyed the house and the two cars in the driveway, seeing no activity. Mr. Winthrop turned the rearview mirror to check his tie, then he checked his teeth. He'd eaten while driving from the airport and wanted to appear his best for his superior. He twisted open a peppermint and popped it into his mouth, quickly flattening the cellophane before leaving it on the seat in a neat square. His hand dug into the newspaper to his right, grasping the pistol. He slid the loaded Walther into his shoulder harness and contorted himself to don his jacket in the car. That done, he exited, again looking at his reflection in the door glass as the peppermint clicked in his mouth.

Satisfied, Mr. Winthrop walked the cobblestone path to the slate gray home. While his ankle still hurt, his limp was much better. He noted the cheery mulberry chrysanthemums in the planters surrounding the imposing stone porch. The flowers made him wonder why Vickers had chosen this domestic home as his temporary headquarters. Skipping the doorbell, Winthrop rapped loudly on the door and waited.

A tall, imposing man he didn't know answered the door. With nary a word, the man pulled the door all the way back, motioning for Winthrop to come in. The tall man, who was perhaps 35 years old, might have been handsome other than the extreme acne scarring on his face. Once the door was closed, the man told Mr. Winthrop to lift his arms. Mr. Winthrop saw Vickers sitting on a sofa in the room to the left. Vickers nodded. At that point, Mr. Winthrop lifted his arms and allowed the tall man to disarm him. The man opened a drawer and dropped the Walther in with a clunk, sliding the drawer shut as he motioned Winthrop into the sitting room.

Vickers removed his reading glasses and set his newspaper, The Guardian, on the coffee table in front of him. "Drink?" he asked, lifting his own libation.

"Coffee," Winthrop replied.

Vickers turned to the tall man. "Go make a pot of strong coffee. And before you do, call Timmons and tell him to head this way."

The tall man nodded and exited to the rear of the house.

"Nice place," Winthrop remarked.

"Was that a limp?"

"Twisted my ankle. I'm fine."

Mr. Winthrop sat in the chair opposite from Vickers. They were in the living room of the stately home. The room had an interior fireplace surrounded by shiny black tile. It looked as if it had never been used. Next to the fireplace was an electric organ. Beside the front window was a small bar with various bottles of liquor and a bucket of ice. The remainder of the room was rather formal, with another chair to Winthrop's left and the sofa Vickers sat on. The two chairs were patterned and the sofa was upholstered in shimmering green fabric. Several oil paintings adorned the walls, each showing springtime farm scenes. The coffee table between them was mahogany, inlaid with gold accents. Next to Vickers' newspaper was a slim manila folder.

Vickers was in his early 60s. A short man, he was rather stocky and had probably been athletic in his youth judging by his retained musculature. He had a full head of gray hair and his skin was rather pale. His pug nose was crooked. He was the type of man few would remember if they'd not spent time with him. Though he was a man of few words, Vickers was known for his quick and bold decisions.

"What took you so long?" he asked.

"Long delay leaving Paris. I guess due to Kennedy. They weren't saying much. I should've taken the train." Winthrop crossed one leg over the other. "Any updates?"

"Wallace is missing."

"Wallace? He was on the alpha team. I put him in the sewer."

"And no one's heard from him since."

Winthrop looked away for a moment. "Max killed him."

"Agreed. But we haven't found the body, nor have we gotten report of one. Wallace was compartmentalized, wasn't he?"

Winthrop nodded. "If Max somehow snatched him, he'd get nothing. A fool's errand."

"That's it. No other news," Vickers answered, his dissatisfaction obvious.

"What about this fellow, Oswald?"

"We're not here to talk about Oswald. We're here to talk about you and Maxime Warfield, the man *you* lost."

"It's not that simple."

"The net result *is* that simple: you lost him."

Winthrop sat stone still.

"Admit it," Vickers commanded.

"I lost him. Mistakes were made."

"There, was that so difficult? No one is infallible. What matters is what happens now." Vickers sat forward. "In full detail, tell me again exactly what happened. Describe everything from the moment you stopped at the Place de Clichy until you phoned me afterward."

Mr. Winthrop crunched his peppermint and swallowed the remains. He then took his time telling the entire story, going through the full mission, not leaving anything out. Such debriefings are often a good practice, especially when recounting a moment of high stress. Additional details often emerge, even though none did on this occasion. As Winthrop spoke, the tall man with the acne scars brought in a tray with an urn of coffee. Mr. Winthrop drank two cups as he recounted the tale, taking almost a half-hour. The coffee was good and rich, clashing with the peppermint until the taste had been washed away.

Just as Winthrop was finishing his detailed retelling, the doorbell rang. The tall man admitted Major General Ronald Timmons, dressed in a plain gray suit. Winthrop knew him quite well.

And despised him.

Timmons had recently retired from the U.S. Marines and still looked the part. An average sized man, he walked ramrod straight with his shoulders back. The general was 53 years old and didn't appear a day over 45. His deep tan contrasted with his salt-and-pepper flattop, both of which looked quite out of place in Vienna. Timmons had received numerous citations and medals, including the Navy Cross for heroic actions during the Battle of the Tenaru at Guadalcanal. After being frisked he requested a whiskey, neat, from the tall acne-scarred man. Then, the retired Marine walked into the room and took a seat on the sofa without a word. He glared at Mr. Winthrop as he finished his story.

The acne-scarred man poured a drink from the bar and placed Timmons' drink on the coffee table in front of him. The group was quiet until the man left again.

"And given all that time you, and your team, watched Max Warfield, you can't come up with any possible place he might be hiding?" Vickers asked Mr. Winthrop, opening his hands plaintively.

Winthrop shook his head. "No. We've checked every location we knew about."

"He's obviously gone to ground somewhere," General Timmons said, his first words since arriving.

"Oh, that's profound," Mr. Winthrop mocked. "What other proverbs do you have for us, general?"

Timmons sipped his whiskey. "I'm not the man who lost a weakened prisoner in the middle of a walled-in, barred-in courtyard, am I?"

Winthrop spoke to Vickers as if Timmons wasn't in the room. "Some people are only effective with the underpinnings of a war machine behind them."

"And others are simply ineffective—period," Timmons countered.

As silence enveloped the room, Mr. Winthrop poured a third cup of coffee. He finally spoke. "General, our file on you is two, maybe three inches thick. I read every bit of it. You were chosen by this organization because of your prior military position as well as your connections within the Department of Defense." Winthrop sipped his coffee. "But there were some who were opposed to bringing you into the inner circle."

Timmons sat and stared. Mr. Winthrop continued.

"We had a report, general, that you earned your Navy Cross by hiding in a foxhole, whimpering, while the Japs tore your Marines to shreds." Long pause. "I'll get you a copy. It was well written, penned by a major serving in the unit that rescued you. The real Marines died bravely that day, but you veiled yourself under their dead bodies, earning your precious decoration through their blood."

"That's enough," Vickers warned.

"It's okay," Timmons replied, his voice calm. "If I respected this man—if he was capable—if he were *qualified* to judge me—I might care about his opinion. I *know* why I was chosen and I'm quite confident in who I am. He's deflecting because he knows I was called here today due to *his* failure," Timmons said, leveling a finger at Mr. Winthrop, "not mine."

"Gentlemen…you've lobbed your volleys," Vickers muttered, massaging the bridge of his nose. "Please refocus."

Timmons sipped his drink. "Refocus. Fine. I'll refocus." He eyed Mr. Winthrop. "How could anyone lose a debilitated man, who was laden with a hundred pounds, in the middle of Paris?"

The query must have touched a nerve.

Winthrop's retorts came with machine-gun force. "Were you there, general? Do you have any idea about what *actually* happened, or are you out of your depth as usual? And have you ever commanded anyone as skilled as Max Warfield? Have you read his file? Do you know what he did during his time in the Army? Do you realize what he's pulled off in the past few years?" Winthrop appraised Timmons. "He'd break you in minutes."

"Stop it, both of you," Vickers snapped. "This is unproductive and you're both risking discipline." He let that sink in for a moment. "We have to take action, soon, and we also need to consider what our exposure is." He looked at Mr. Winthrop. "Brass tacks: what do you believe Warfield will do with the evidence?"

Mr. Winthrop took a few deep breaths, calming himself. "Assuming he still has the briefcase and discovers its contents, it's difficult to say. Warfield is intelligent and resourceful." Winthrop halted for a moment and looked away, deep in thought. "I believe he'll reveal the evidence, but I can't say how. Common sense tells me he'll use it to somehow save himself."

It was clear that General Timmons wanted to lash out again, but didn't. The mere mention of "discipline" had its desired effect on both belligerents.

Instead, Timmons spoke directly to Vickers. "What do the French and the Secret Service have so far?"

"As you might imagine, the information I've gotten from a source inside the Secret Service has been spotty, at best. They just suffered the worst black eye in their history and now have to deal with the aftermath. If they're looking into the killing in Paris, it's being done so far down the line that I'm unable to pick up anything of substance."

"And the locals?"

"From what one source in Paris tells me, they're treating the murder like an armed robbery gone bad." Vickers looked at Mr. Winthrop. "The female interpreter saw you, but couldn't tell them much."

"What else do they have?" General Timmons persisted.

Vickers shook his head. "Hardly anything. They believe the courtyard bullets came from a rooftop. They know the very basics. The way we ran the op will provide them with nothing but dead ends…unless we decide to feed them something."

"We can give them the Marseilles killings," Winthrop offered.

"When we set that up, we never envisioned he'd have the briefcase. It's no good," Vickers countered. "If the French grab him, he's going to tell them everything about the background of the mission *and* give them the briefcase."

"Is their having the briefcase the worst thing?" Winthrop asked.

"They may not use it," Vickers answered. "The French have never been predictable, especially in a situation such as this. They might just give it back. It would ruin everything."

"Just to play out the string, let's suppose the French do apprehend him," Timmons said. "Would they find credibility in his story about the background of the mission?"

"They'll have the testimony of the woman who saw me," Winthrop replied. "They'll add that to the agent being shot by a high powered rifle from a rooftop. All of this runs counter to Max's modus operandi—it'll be enough to get their attention. They'll share everything with the Secret Service. Added to all that, the intel in the briefcase."

"*Possibly* making them suspect a conspiracy," noted General Timmons. "Combine all that with the situation in Dallas and—"

"Dallas is *clean*," Vickers interrupted. "There are compartmentalized wheels in motion that will make certain all eyes remain on Oswald."

"Such as?" Mr. Winthrop asked.

Vickers stood and refreshed his drink, dropping several cubes of ice in afterward. He sipped the drink loudly. "Lee Harvey Oswald, a United States Marine, killed President Kennedy." Vickers turned to General Timmons. "What was Oswald's IQ score, general?"

"One-oh-three."

"And how often was he in trouble?"

"He remained in trouble."

"A dense, miscreant communist killed the president of the United States of America," Vickers replied smugly. "The narrative has been set. There's nothing else to discuss about the tragedy in Dallas."

Mr. Winthrop eyed General Timmons. Though the two men detested one another, in this instance they shared the frustration that they weren't going to be made privy to any further intelligence. Both men rotated their eyes to the floor.

"Before either of you got here," Vickers stated. "I made a decision that I believe will bear fruit."

"And that is?" Winthrop asked.

"I'm sending you two to France—*together*."

Timmons didn't react. Winthrop leaned back in his chair, clearly displeased.

Vickers opened his hands, then symbolically joined them. "You'll work together to find Max Warfield. We don't release anything on him unless the three of us agree. Understood?"

"Pardon me, but was I summoned all the way to Vienna for a chat?" Winthrop asked. "We could've done this via phone or radio."

"No," Vickers answered. "I called you here for much more than a chat."

"I don't follow," Winthrop replied.

Vickers drained his fresh drink, wincing at the alcohol burn. Then he said, "Thanks to General Timmons, we're going to interrogate a man who knows Max Warfield better than anybody."

"When?"

Vickers eyed his watch. "Any minute, now."

Chapter Eleven

Twelve minutes later, a shiny blue BMW 1500 pulled to a stop under the streetlight out front. A man exited the car, donning his jacket and hat before walking to the front door. He was dressed casually, in slacks and a cream button down with an off-the-rack tweed blazer. His casual cordovan lace-up shoes were polished to a high sheen. Under the brim of his hat, it was clear to see his hair was cut to the scalp. He had the look of a military man. Lean. Hard. The civvies he wore almost seemed a costume.

Break glass in the event of war.

Mr. Winthrop peered out the window at Max Warfield's longest serving commander in the infamous Devil's Brigade.

"That's Ortega," Winthrop said, recalling the man's extensive profile from the initial research and mission planning. "How did you manage to get him here?"

"Well, he's stationed in *Germany*," General Timmons answered, as if Winthrop's question were elementary.

"Bad Tölz," Vickers added. "He's with the 1st Battalion, 10th Special Forces Group."

"He's a major. His rank doesn't seem all that impressive considering his time in service, but he joined as an enlisted man and didn't go to OCS until after Korea."

"What did you tell him to get him here?" Winthrop asked.

"I lied out my ass," Timmons explained. "And while he's here, I'm Lieutenant Colonel Robert Sides, Marine Corps Intelligence."

"Does such a man exist?" Winthrop asked.

"Sure does. Figured he'd probably check so I used a real identity. Got the credentials in my pocket."

There was a rap at the door and the same procedures were followed as before. The tall, acne-scarred man appeared from the back of the house, only he didn't search Ortega. He greeted him perfunctorily and showed him in.

"Thanks for coming all this way, major," General Timmons said, introducing himself as Lieutenant Colonel Robert Sides, "but call me Bob." He chatted a bit about the sensitive nature of the meeting and confirmed that Ortega had told no one about it.

Ortega was obviously of Hispanic heritage, but he spoke with no trace of an accent. "All due respect, but I'd sure as hell like to know what this is all about. Driving way over here to Vienna on the simple promise of aiding our national security? You'll forgive me, colonel, but I'd like some answers right away."

Vickers greeted Ortega warmly. "You deserve answers, and you'll have them. Please, have a seat, major."

"Please the colonel, but I'd prefer you call me Ortega, or Phil."

"Fine, Phil," Vickers replied. "Would you like something to drink?"

Ortega shook his head.

"Restroom?"

"Stopped on my way in."

Vickers produced an envelope. "Here's travel money for your drive down and back. We had to keep it quiet, so it's in cash."

Ortega accepted the envelope and placed it on the table.

General Timmons—Robert, "call me Bob," Sides—handled the introductions, insincere as he explained who each person was and what they did for the government—explaining that both Mr. Winthrop and Mr. Vickers worked for the CIA. Everything he said was a lie. As Timmons spoke, Ortega's brow lowered.

"Problem?" Mr. Winthrop asked him.

"I thought this was a military inquiry," Ortega said. "When no one knows where I am, and I meet with a roomful of spooks, I tend to get a little uneasy."

Vickers nodded his understanding. "Don't be uneasy. After all that happened yesterday, we're forced to tread lightly."

"And not everyone here is a spook," Timmons added in a poor attempt at humor.

"Do you have your military identification?" Ortega asked Timmons.

Timmons passed the identification over. It was genuine, but with Timmons' photo. Ortega studied it for a moment before handing it back.

"Let's get on with it, please," Ortega said. "My wife and children are distressed by what happened yesterday. I need to be at home."

"They're in Germany?" Winthrop asked.

"Yes, they're regular dependents," Ortega replied.

"You sound as if you were a fan of President Kennedy?" Vickers asked.

Ortega appeared mildly offended at the question. "To be frank, I wasn't crazy about all of his views, but I voted for him. I wanted a Roman Catholic in office and, to be even more frank, I didn't care too much for *any* of the candidates. Kennedy sure as hell grew on me once he was in office." Ortega crossed his arms.

As General Timmons lit a cigarette, Vickers leaned forward, resting his elbows on his knees as he spoke. "We think one of your former soldiers has close ties to Lee Harvey Oswald. We think they were both recruited and misled by a nefarious group of criminals and operatives who wanted to see President Kennedy dead. We need your help in trying to understand more about your former soldier, because we believe it will help us paint a better picture of Oswald."

Ortega's eyes narrowed. "Which former soldier?"

"Maxime Warfield," Mr. Winthrop said.

Ortega took the name without emotion. "Warfield? Why do you think that?"

"We have several reliable sources pointing us in that direction," Mr. Winthrop answered, popping a peppermint candy into his mouth. He went to work on the wrapper.

With a quick shake of his head, Ortega said, "Warfield's too smart to be taken in. He's not a patsy and he's not the type to get involved in the killing of a sitting president. No way. Your sources are wrong. Either that, or you guys aren't telling me the truth."

The acne-scarred man appeared from the left. "Anyone need anything?"

"Privacy," Vickers snapped.

The man disappeared. Winthrop rolled his eyes.

"Max *is* extremely intelligent," Vickers agreed, getting back on track. "And his intelligence is why we believe they put Oswald out front. Oswald isn't all that smart."

"I don't buy it," Ortega said. He shook his head. "Not the part about Max."

"Simply because he's intelligent?" Mr. Winthrop asked.

"Goes beyond that. You serve with a man for years…you eat with 'em…train with 'em…sleep beside 'em…you watch your brothers die…save one another…you do all these things together, and you get to know them as well as you know yourself. Sometimes even better."

"So, no matter what we say, you're disagreeing?" General Timmons asked.

"Unless you demonstrate some *proof* that Warfield is connected, then I ain't believin' it. Not for a second."

The three hosts grew quiet. General Timmons smoked his cigarette. Outside, two teenagers passed noisily by. Winthrop finished squaring his cellophane wrapper. He leaned forward, placing it on the coffee table, carefully aligning its corners with that of the table.

"We can't give you any proof," Vickers replied. "Not right now. This angle of the investigation has tentacles that reach deep into our fabric as a nation."

"And right now, our nation is in peril," Timmons added.

"He's right," Winthrop agreed.

"What *can* you give me?" Ortega asked.

Vickers sank back into his chair and swirled his glass of ice. "Max is on the run."

"He's been on the run," Ortega said with a shrug.

"Not like this. Now there's a manhunt," Timmons replied.

"That's bad for you, because you won't catch him," Ortega said flatly.

"Why do you say that?" Mr. Winthrop asked.

"It's simple: Maxime Warfield was the best soldier I ever served with. If he knows you're after him…knows anyone is after him…then, you won't catch him—unless he wants you to. He's been on the run now how many years? No one's even gotten close."

"That's not true," Mr. Winthrop replied. His expression was smug.

"What?" Ortega asked.

Vickers shook his head at Mr. Winthrop.

Ignoring him, Mr. Winthrop crunched his peppermint and sat forward. "I caught his ass less than a month ago. Wasn't difficult at all."

Timmons cut his eyes at Vickers, who lowered his face into his hand.

***

In Paris, Max heard the slow scrape of the oncoming knife-wielding man's shoes. He was approaching with extreme caution. He'd seen the other dealer being robbed, but now could see nothing. He had to know Max was hiding and perhaps waiting on him.

Max recalled the blade, glinting in the scant light. It was a switchblade, probably razor sharp. The dealer had probably used it before. Street violence is common in the drug trade.

From underneath the car, Max glimpsed the movement of a shadow. The knife-wielding man was close.

Here we go.

Max wiped the sweat from his hands. He was prepared to strike.

***

"What do you mean you caught him?" Ortega asked.

"Hang on," Vickers interjected, smiling politely before shooting a glare at Mr. Winthrop. "Rather than us run off down a rabbit trail about whether or not close surveillance counts as being caught, will you please tell us what you recall about Max?"

"I'd like to hear more from him," Ortega said, gesturing to Winthrop.

"Phil, please, tell us about Warfield," Timmons soothed.

Ortega shrugged. "There's very little I can tell you that you'll find useful."

"And why's that?" Timmons asked.

"It's not that Max was the biggest, or the fastest, or the strongest. None of that crap you see in the movies. What made Max superior was his instinct." Ortega tapped his temple, then his heart. "And that's something none of us taught him. Max always knew when to move; knew when to go silent; knew when to shoot. He should have died years ago."

"But his instinct kept him alive?" Vickers asked.

"That…and the fact that he never gives up."

"So, he has boundless energy?" Timmons asked.

"Max is intelligent. Max is resourceful. Max has instincts that go beyond description. *And*, as I said, he doesn't give up. That's very, very rare."

"Anything else?" Vickers asked.

Ortega thought about it for a moment. "He's ferocious when cornered. You give him no options, and he'll die before he relents," Ortega replied.

"Will you please give us an example of how Max operated?" Timmons asked.

Major Ortega looked at his watch. He unclasped it, handing it to Mr. Winthrop, who happened to be closest. "Read the back," Ortega said.

***

Max waited, knowing better than to strike too early. There was another scratching sound and suddenly the man lurched around the trunk of the car, the blade held high as he prepared to slash downward.

Coiled from his squatting position, Max sprang upward, simultaneously thrusting his pistol-loaded right hand in an uppercut. He aimed for the knife-wielding man's jaw.

Max's aim was true. His hand smashed home with a satisfying crunch.

But the knife-wielding man's right hand had slashed downward at the same moment, gashing Max's scalp above his left ear. The cut began to the left of the crown of his head, moving diagonally down Max's skull, terminating at his cheekbone. Max had no choice but to ignore it.

No choice if he hoped to survive.

As Max began to brawl, he felt his own warm blood flowing down his left side. It was on his neck, shoulder and chest.

Slick.

Warm.

Precious.

Pouring.

***

"Linda and Jeanie," Mr. Winthrop read, peering downward through his bifocal lenses. He shrugged, handing the watch back to Ortega. "So, you have an engraved Rolex watch. Congratulations."

"Max has one, too," Ortega replied.

"Good for Max," Winthrop answered. He turned to Vickers. "I know all about the watch. Let's move on."

"Wait. What's the significance of the watch and engraving?" Vickers asked Ortega.

"Six men were given identical Rolexes by Hiram Schultz," Ortega answered, emphasizing the man's name.

"The multi-millionaire?" Vickers asked.

Waving this off, Winthrop spoke before Ortega could. "I read *all* about this in Max's file. Ortega and Max and a few others happened to be nearby when a couple of kidnappers snatched Schultz's girls from their yacht. Ortega and his men did their jobs," Winthrop said with a dismissive twirl of his hand. "They killed the kidnappers, got the girls back." Winthrop nodded perfunctorily at Ortega. "Nice work, but that's really not the kind of intel on Max we're after."

Ortega eyed Winthrop neutrally. "May I speak now?"

"Please," Vickers said, glowering at Winthrop before nodding at Ortega. "Tell us what's on your mind."

"Yes, the Schultz girls *were* kidnapped. A parent's worst nightmare. But the situation itself, once we found them, was extremely grave." Ortega looked at the three men. "Twin girls, aged three: beautiful, precious, innocent. They were kidnapped off the coast of Thailand, right off the deck of their yacht. The parents had taken the yacht's launch onto shore and their nanny was watching the girls on the deck. The kidnappers' boat slid in unseen, well under the beam. They boarded with a rope ladder to seize the girls before the nanny could react."

"Didn't this Schultz fellow have security on his yacht?" Timmons asked.

"He did. They didn't see the kidnappers coming because they were grossly inattentive when Schultz wasn't around," Ortega answered. He shook his head. "It was a bad deal, all around."

Winthrop studied his fingernails and let out an exasperated breath. He rattled the coffee pot and yelled for more.

From the other room, water could be heard running.

"Who were the kidnappers?" Vickers asked.

"They were Thai. Pros, definitely not their first rodeo. Preyed on the wealthy. They marked the yacht first, then the little girls who liked to play hopscotch on the deck. They waited a day or two for the patriarch to head to shore and that's when they struck." Ortega looked away for a moment. "All anyone heard were the girls' screams as the kidnappers roared away in their long-tail boat."

Vickers and Timmons were rapt. "What then?" Timmons demanded.

"Thailand is a military dictatorship and it was hard to get things done quickly. Our State Department and Schultz's own people went to work. Schultz, thankfully, had the money for bribes and the like. Inside of a day he got a ransom request from the kidnappers. From what I heard, a decent Russian KGB man who lived in Thailand worked through back channels to give our people the identities of the kidnappers. He'd supposedly utilized them before. He gave them up to curry favor with the locals. In a few days, while Schultz's people continued to negotiate on the front end, his hired locals were able to track the kidnappers to a swamp in a place called Tha Pom, in south Thailand, on the isthmus."

"And you all can guess what happened next. Ortega and his men saved the kids and got shiny Rolex watches," Winthrop said monotone. "Nice work, major, but we really don't need you polishing your laurels on our time."

His face beet red, Vickers turned and held up his rigid index finger. "Not one more word till I speak to you."

Mr. Winthrop poured the last drops from the coffee urn. It wasn't enough to drink.

"We'd been TDY in Vietnam in an advisory capacity for a few months," Ortega added, looking only at Timmons and Vickers. "The French had pulled out completely. It created a vacuum. There was significant American interest in helping the Vietnamese repel communism. Before I knew it, I had a full colonel in my face telling me about a crisis. He put me and a small team on a military airplane bound for Thailand. All we knew was that we might have to help several American citizens who were being held by armed men."

"That was all they told you?" Timmons asked.

"That was it. We assumed the prisoners were political or maybe from an embassy. By the time we got there, the locals had tracked the kidnappers to the swamp I mentioned in Tha Pom. It might've been a Louisiana bayou or the thickest area of the Everglades. Except they had crocodiles, not gators. Much more aggressive. And more snakes than I'd ever had nightmares about."

"Where were they holed up?" Vickers asked.

"These two sickos had built a little shack in the middle of a swamp. They'd strung telephone wire in and operated a phone and a few other items by car batteries." Ortega crossed his leg, the difficult memories showing on his face. "The shack was on stilts on an island in the swamp. There were mangroves and a few trees, but none near the shack. The only thing near their hideout was a foot or two of muddy water in every direction." Ortega made a circle with his hand. "In other words, they had a clear line of sight in all directions."

Timmons frowned. "This is interesting, but I have to ask how this is relevant? Just because Max was in on the takedown?"

"It was more than him just being there, colonel," Ortega answered. "Remember, the kidnappers had three-hundred-sixty degrees of clear view around their shack. At night, they used searchlights run by those car batteries.

And all over that open water, in some places hanging as low as just a few inches, they'd strung bells."

"Bells?" Vickers asked, screwing up his face.

"Everywhere, hanging by fishing line. They did it so they might hear someone approaching. We couldn't risk taking a team through the swamp without making a racket. You'd have to use a light to see the bells, and if you used a light, they'd see you."

"Didn't birds and crocodiles trigger the bells?" Vickers asked.

"Yes. And shotgun blasts immediately followed," Ortega replied. "If you could see the setup, you'd know what I mean about it being too difficult to approach with a team."

"Why didn't you just sniper their asses?" Timmons asked.

"That was our first idea, but the kidnappers held the kids in their arms whenever they moved around in the shack. There was too much distance to risk an errant shot. Plus, it wasn't my call." Ortega made eye contact with Vickers and Timmons. Mr. Winthrop appeared to be napping. Ortega continued. "On the second night, once we got approval, Max Warfield put a small gear bag on his back. He took a snorkel and swam and slithered through a foot of muddy crocodile water to the base of that shack. It took him six hours to get there silently. He stayed at the base of the shack until sunup."

"Bet that was pleasant," Timmons remarked.

"How did he avoid the bells?" Vickers asked.

"To this day, I don't know," Ortega replied. "I guess by staying so low in the mud."

"What was the plan from there?" Timmons asked.

"We had several contingency plans based on what Max found. When he got there, he managed to use a handheld periscope to look inside the shack."

"And?" Vickers asked.

"After sunup, Max communicated by using a small slate and chalk and holding up what he'd written. The sniper would read it through his scope. After Max looked inside the shack, what he wrote changed our plans completely."

"What did he write?" Timmons demanded.

Ortega's expression was grim. "He wrote, 'both girls are wired with explosives'."

***

As the second dealer crumpled to the ground behind the Renault, Max glanced to his right, watching as the first dealer, the sleazy handsome man, attempted to come to his hands and knees. Max was prepared to turn and deal with him before the dealer he'd just felled recovered remarkably fast. He went for Max's throat, missing but raking open Max's head wound with his fingernails.

Lightning sparked through Max's brain.

Finding a renewed burst of adrenaline, he swung the pistol in a wild arc, hitting the second dealer again. Whatever damage had been done by the first blow to the jaw might have been completed by this strike. Bone could be heard grinding and cracking as the dealer fell again, this time unmoving, facedown on the asphalt.

Feeling the slick hot blood now soaking his left side, Max whirled to his right. The first dealer was up on his knees, reaching behind his back with his right arm. Max swung the pistol but missed. He knew he could shoot and end the current threat, but shooting would create a whole host of new problems for Max.

As the murine-faced dealer brought a long knife around from his back, Max knew he was in trouble. He was bleeding profusely and the dealer had long arms. Unless he fired the pistol, he couldn't think of any way he could end this quickly.

***

"What do you mean they were wired with explosives?" Timmons asked.

"They looked like suicide vests. Both girls had dynamite crudely wrapped around their little bodies. The dynamite was attached to a blasting device run by a battery. The blasting device was activated by a switch," Ortega explained.

"You'd think the kids might accidentally set them off," Vickers remarked.

"They'd covered the switches," Ortega replied. "Again, I don't think this was the kidnappers' first time doing this. But they were as dead set against getting caught as anyone I'd ever seen. It was truly a real life nightmare."

"Were you able to communicate back to Max?" Timmons asked.

"He had a scope in his bag, so we used the slate and chalk method. After considerable back and forth, we decided to let him take the shots. The windows were nothing more than open spaces on all sides of the shack. He'd have to pop up and shoot both men, doable since he was at point blank range."

"With two little girls wired to blow, also at point blank range," Vickers added.

"Yes," Ortega agreed.

"Sorry to ruin this exciting little Saturday matinee, but Max shot both kidnappers," Winthrop interjected.

Vickers opened his mouth but didn't say anything. He simply wagged his finger.

Glaring at Winthrop, Ortega nodded. "He did. Max had a pistol. He dried it and watched with the periscope. Around mid-morning, one of the kidnappers was on the phone talking about the ransom. The other one was eating what we later learned was a piece of raw meat. Animals. The two girls were sitting on the floor, playing a game of some sort. Max stood on one of the stilt supports, put that pistol through the window and fired two shots. He got them both off in about one total second. Result: both kidnappers dead."

Vickers and Timmons looked at one another. While impressed with such a successful tale, it was clear they expected more.

Ortega read their expressions. He smiled thinly.

"What?" Vickers asked.

"Once the explosives were removed and the medics looked after the girls, they checked on Max," Ortega replied.

"What about him?"

"Six snake bites," Ortega said. "Plus, a host of spider bites and who knows what else. He damn near went into a coma. Took him six weeks to get better." Ortega eyed each man, ending with Winthrop. "Max didn't even flinch when he was being bitten. Never made a sound. He knew any reaction might spook the kidnappers. Then, when Hiram Schultz insisted upon giving us these watches, Max never allowed me to tell Schultz exactly what happened. He wanted all of us to get equal credit."

Everyone was silent. Finally Timmons said, "I'm surprised you took the watches, major."

"It had nothing to do with the value of the watches. It's about a remembrance. Remembering the team, and the men who made up the team." He touched the watch. "Along with the two young girls who were saved."

"And they're okay?" Vickers asked.

"Last I heard, alive and well and living in San Francisco," Ortega replied. He again eyed Winthrop. "You're not chasing an ordinary man. And I don't give a damn what you tell me, he had nothing to do with killing President Kennedy."

"I can't blame you for being proud of Max," General Timmons commented, "but let's don't forget, he killed a man in a bar fight. That's not debatable."

"Yes, he did," Ortega answered. "And I've not spoken to Max since then, but I was briefed on the man who died. He was trouble, by *all* accounts. From what I heard from the military investigator, Max acted in self-defense. The other man started it. Since Max ran, they threw the book at him."

"But if it was self defense, why did he run?" Winthrop asked, his tone badgering.

"Max has suffered the effects of shell-shock ever since the Second World War. You have no—absolute *no*—idea of all he's been through. By the time that scumbag died at Max's hands, he couldn't separate a bar fight from the battlefield."

114

"Oh, poor Max," Winthrop mocked, poking his bottom lip out in a juvenile manner. "Can't deal with the war like millions of other men have no choice but to do."

"I'm here because *you* can't find him. It seems obvious, especially where you're concerned," Ortega said to Winthrop, "that you're underestimating him. When most men would give up from pain or exhaustion, Max just gets better. You won't catch him."

"I thought he was shell-shocked," Winthrop countered.

"He was. Maybe he still is." Ortega eyed each man. "Ask the man who Max killed in that bar fight, or those two kidnappers, if his being shell-shocked made him any less dangerous."

***

Realizing he had to do something unexpected, Max went for broke by pulling back his arm and slinging the pistol as hard as he could. He flung it the way a baseball pitcher hurls a fastball. The heavy steel pistol caught the surprised dealer in his throat, squarely on his Adam's apple. The dealer fell again, gasping for air as his knife and Max's pistol clattered to the ground.

The second dealer, with the shattered jaw, was still unmoving.

Max mounted the first dealer and grasped the pistol. Blood leaking everywhere from his own head, he pounded the man's pointy face with the handgun. Max watched as his own blood mingled with that of the dealer, dribbling down into the grime of the parking lot.

He halted himself before he killed the man. Max then dragged the two dealers into the weeds by the building. He went into the murine-faced dealer's pocket, finding his keys. After pulling the man's sport coat off his back, Max wiped the side of his own head and face and entered the car, a Renault Frégate sedan. He cranked it and exited the parking lot, holding the jacket over the side of his head.

Max was woozy but managed to make his way to the northwest, back toward Ludivine's flat. Each time he released the jacket from his head, blood poured from his open wound.

"Stay awake," Max urged himself. "Stay the hell awake."

He looked down into the seat, aided by the passing streetlights. There was so much blood it was pooling between his legs.

***

"Would it surprise you to know that Max has been supporting himself as a thief since he went on the run after killing that man in the bar?" Vickers asked.

The revelation seemed to send a slight jolt through Ortega. "Yes, it would."

"Well, he has," Vickers answered. "In fact, he's wanted in connection with several recent murders surrounding a robbery he performed."

Ortega crossed his arms and said nothing.

Mr. Winthrop leaned forward and steepled his fingers. "Max is still in Europe, almost assuredly. We strongly suspect he's in France, although he could have made his way out by now. Do you have any idea where he could be hiding? Any place your unit operated? Any old friends? Anything that comes to mind?"

"I have absolutely no idea."

"You didn't even stop to think," Winthrop replied.

"Don't have to."

"Has he called you?" Vickers asked.

"Haven't heard from him in years," Ortega replied.

"Phil," Timmons said soothingly, "let's just say you were us, and you were tasked with looking for Max in France, near Paris…where would you begin?"

Ortega struggled with the question. Finally he straightened and crossed one leg over the other, spiriting a piece of lint from his trousers. "As I said, he'll probably do what you least expect. If pressed into a wild guess, I'd make the assumption that he's with a woman, or headed to see a woman."

"What makes you say that?" Timmons asked.

"I'm guessing, but I know Max. He likes women—they like him."

***

Max parked the Renault in the alleyway behind Ludivine's building. As his head soaked the jacket, he staggered into the building and climbed the stairs, using his bloody right hand for support. On the second landing, Max passed an older woman who appeared horrified at his appearance.

"Is that real blood?" she asked, struggling to process what she was seeing.

"Afraid so, madame," Max replied. "Too much wine and fell down. It's just a scalp wound but boy did it bleed. My friend upstairs will drive me to the clinic."

The old woman seemed to accept this answer. "Are you sure your friend is home? Can I call the *ambulanciers* for you?"

"He's home and I'll be fine. Thank you for your concern."

She reluctantly entered her flat.

Gripping the handrail, Max continued upward.

"Can't stop," he whispered to himself, wanting so badly to lie down and close his eyes. "Can't ever stop."

***

"So, Max likes women? Well, that's a profound tip, Ortega," Winthrop replied, sarcasm dripping. "But checking with every woman in France could be a time consuming process. What can you tell us that might actually be helpful?"

"Won't matter," Ortega answered.

"Why?"

"You won't find him," Ortega replied. "And even if you do, you'll never take him."

"Again, he *can* be taken," Mr. Winthrop countered, unable to contain his ego. "I know this, because I've captured him *before*...and I broke him, *myself.*"

Vickers cleared his throat.

"You broke him?" Ortega asked, arching his eyebrows.

"Damn right, I did."

"If you broke him, why's he out there now, evading you?" Ortega asked, a thin smile forming on his mouth.

Mr. Winthrop flared his nostrils.

General Timmons couldn't conceal a smug expression as he sipped his drink.

"So, I guess you *thought* you broke him," Ortega continued.

"Sure appears that way," Timmons quipped, earning a glare from Vickers.

"So, you caught him once," Ortega said. "I'm guessing you caught him by surprise, correct?"

Mr. Winthrop's silence provided the answer.

"He had no idea you were after him." Ortega nodded knowingly. "I can see I'm correct. That would be the only way to catch Max. But, unfortunately for you, you won't catch him again. Perhaps before he didn't realize you were even his enemy. But now he knows." Ortega wagged his finger. "He'll stop at nothing to evade you."

"We'll see about that," Winthrop answered.

"There is one possibility that could potentially work in your favor," Ortega added. "Well, kind of..."

"What's that?" Timmons asked.

Major Ortega pointed his same finger at Mr. Winthrop. "Rather than running, Max might just come after you."

***

Max opened the door to Ludivine's flat. She turned and nearly shrieked before he silenced her by holding his finger to his mouth. Max closed the door and hurriedly sat on one of the chintzy vinyl chairs from the kitchen table.

"Please don't scream," Max said, holding the blood-soaked jacket to his head. "I'm okay, just very weak."

"*Mon Dieu*, you're covered in blood," she said, tears flowing.

"Before I waste time on what happened, I need your help. Do you have a needle and thread?"

"What?"

"A needle and thread."

"I have a sewing box."

"Get it, and bring your towels. You can also get one of my new undershirts. And would you please get me several large glasses of water? Mix in plenty of salt. I've got to get my blood pressure up."

He removed the jacket from his wound, causing Ludivine to hiss in horror.

"Are you going to sew that up?" she asked, her face contorting as she viewed the ghastly injury.

"No." He smiled weakly. "You are."

Max lay back on the hard floor, elevating his feet to the chair where he'd just sat. He urged her to hurry as he fought to keep his eyes open.

***

"Max won't dare come after me," Winthrop said with a chuckle. "I wish he were that stupid."

"I've said all I have to say. I'm done here," Ortega said. He stood.

Vickers also stood and politely cajoled Phillip Ortega to sit and stay for a few more minutes. Vickers apologized for the lack of information and admitted that they could be wrong about Max's involvement in this entire affair.

Lies.

Vickers was doing all he could to wring out any shred of information that might be helpful. Ortega sat but he didn't look happy about it.

"Phil, were you ever in France with Max?" Vickers asked.

"Yes, but not for long."

"Where were you?"

"In the south. We came in as part of Operation Dragoon."

"Would he have met someone then who he might go to now?"

"No, Max wouldn't have met anyone during that time," Ortega replied. "It was hell—I can assure you we weren't cavorting."

"Was there anyone else during your time in Europe?" Vickers asked. "Think carefully, please…anyplace he might go, anyone he might see?"

"We were all over Italy and France," Ortega said with another shrug. "But I can't think of anyplace he'd have grown fond of. Ours was a true fighting unit. We stayed on the move."

"Are you aware of any of your soldiers who may have settled in Europe *after* the war? Perhaps someone close to Max married a French or Italian girl?"

"You three should have better access to that type of information than I do."

"Answer the question, major," Timmons commanded.

Ortega turned. "I'm the only one I know of, because I'm stationed here. I have *not* heard from him. That's the truth."

After Vickers thanked Ortega warmly, he tried without success to get more information. It was evident the well had gone dry. Ortega was ready to leave.

"Again, Phil, thanks for coming all this way."

Ortega nodded perfunctorily.

"Wait, one moment," Vickers said, holding up his index finger. He turned and nodded at General Timmons.

"I'm ready to go," Ortega said.

"Just one more quick thing," Vickers replied.

Timmons grinned nastily as he allowed the moment to draw out. Finally, he yelled one single strange word. It sounded foreign.

Footsteps could be heard from the rear of the house.

Within a few seconds, the man with the acne-scarred face appeared. From his left hand dangled a stark white, braided garrote. At each end were dark wooden handles. He looked at Vickers who nodded one time.

Ortega was no idiot. His head whipped to each man as he cursed them for the lack of paternal heritage. Then he was on the move.

A brief scuffle ensued, one in which Ortega acquitted himself nicely. In short order, the acne-scarred man was flat on his back. Although he was supine and bleeding from his nose, he was now firmly in control. On top of him, facing the ceiling, was Phillip Ortega—a man who yielded at least 50 pounds to the powerful man beneath him. Ortega's flow of oxygen was severely restricted, but he had managed to get three fingers from his right hand under the garrote. The fingers only served to slow his rapidly approaching death.

Winthrop and Timmons had both sat, watching the show as they might a program on television. Vickers looked away, as if the sight disturbed him.

At one point, Ortega's eyeballs bulged halfway out of their sockets.

Winthrop poured a fresh cup of coffee.

Before the gurgling and gasping Ortega lost consciousness, Mr. Winthrop spoke to him from the comfort of the couch. He informed Major Ortega that he'd soon be reunited with Max Warfield.

In hell.

***

119

Max vomited out nearly all of the water he'd guzzled. Before he'd allow Ludivine to sew up his head, he had her refill the two water glasses, this time without quite as much salt. He held a towel to his head and drank both large glasses, asking for two more. He swilled these as well, fighting the urge to vomit again. When the reflex seemed to have passed, Max laid his head backward, keeping his feet elevated on the chair. Though he knew his next action would go against his furious efforts to increase his blood pressure, he smoked a heavenly cigarette and asked Ludivine to sew him up with her strongest thread.

"I can't," she cried.

"You can."

This went on for several minutes. Max finally convinced her. Ludivine had a spool of strong black satchel thread. Though it was labeled "thread," it wasn't fibrous at all. It felt more like fishing line but much thicker. She'd used it to mend a purse.

"Use that and don't worry about me," he said, urging her to begin.

At his direction, she sterilized the needle with a match, then wiped a meter of the satchel thread with peroxide. Max struggled mightily not to flinch when Ludivine pierced his wounded scalp on the upper end of the gash.

"Does that hurt?"

"Not at all," Max fake-smiled. "Just pinch the skin together and go to it. Doesn't have to be pretty."

The next 27 minutes were grueling. After several stitches were in, each of them resulting with the needle scraping across Max's skull, he bent the needle for her in a curve. This helped the rest of the procedure go much faster. Max urged Ludivine to make his stitches tight. When she was nearly done, she began to relax.

"I think it's working," she said. "The first stitches at the top are only oozing now. But it's ripping your skin."

"It's okay. It'll clot and start to heal."

Max urged her to finish up. When she was done, Ludivine had given Max 37 stitches over the length of his laceration. She tied the last stitch off and expressed concern that the wound might get infected.

"It's fine," he answered, closing his eyes. He began to drift.

"Do you want to clean up and sleep?"

His eyes sprang open. "No. I need to clean up and leave."

"Leave?"

"For good. People saw me."

"I don't want you to leave." Her anxiety boiling over, Ludivine rested her face in her bloody hands, shuddering.

"Ludivine," Max said, tugging her hands away from her face. "I'm hoping you'll come with me."

That helped. They faced one another.

"Where could we go?"

"I don't know. But we have to get away from here." He shut his eyes for a moment. "We need to go somewhere that we can open that briefcase. It's our only hope."

They were silent for a moment.

"Will you come with me?" he asked.

"I don't want to be apart from you ever again."

***

Once all the life had departed Phillip Ortega's body, the acne-scarred man hoisted him in a fireman's carry and carried him upstairs to a bathroom. There, Ortega's body would be drained of blood in the bathtub before being parsed into manageable pieces. A trail of odorous urine dispersed the front room's three remaining occupants. They made their way to the courtyard behind the house. It was private, surrounded by an ivy-covered wall. Dry leaves whirled in a corner of the patio during a gust of wind. Vickers checked his watch as Timmons lit a long cigar.

"Don't touch anything outside," Vickers commanded. "Fingerprints."

"What about inside?" Winthrop asked.

"Everything inside will be dealt with, but I don't know about this furniture out here. Just don't touch it." Vickers tapped his watch. "You two need to get going."

Timmons spun the cigar and puffed. "How are we getting there? I doubt we can catch a flight now—not direct."

"I've arranged for a private airplane." Vickers drained his drink and eyed the two men. "You both know as well as I do who you're up against. Hell, Ortega couldn't say enough flattering things about this man. I doubt the pursuit will be over quickly. Warfield will likely stay buried for days, maybe even weeks. And even then he'll be ultra-cautious when he finally surfaces."

"Can we get more assets in France?" Mr. Winthrop asked.

"It's your team and the general. That's it. Where else do you expect me to bring assets from?"

"What about the ones from Dallas?" Winthrop asked.

Vickers shook his head. "You think you know what went on in Dallas, but you have no idea. Just remind yourself, the substantiation you're after is *greater* than President Kennedy lying dead on a cold slab. You have to find it. Go on, now. I need you there, working...*together.*"

Mr. Winthrop cocked his eyebrow at General Timmons. The general stared back at him.

Reluctantly, the two men nodded at one another.

After a bit more planning, the trio walked through the house as the hacking chop of a meat cleaver could be heard from upstairs. Per best practices, Ortega's feet were chopped off at the ankles. Then his lifeless body was sat up in the tub. Because of the mild slope, much of the blood would drain out in the next half hour. Then he would be fully butchered and packaged.

At the front door, Vickers sent the two men on their way.

After Mr. Winthrop reclaimed his pistol from the drawer, the two Paris-bound men departed together and rode in complete silence to *Flughafen Wien*. On the way there, Mr. Winthrop snatched the cigar from the general's hand and threw it out the window. Though the general grumbled, they still didn't speak.

Within five minutes of their arrival at the airport's private aviation terminal on the northwestern corner, they were speeding east/southeast down runway 11 in a peculiar looking Italian aircraft made by Piaggio. Thankfully, the P.166 model was rather roomy, designed for 13 passengers. This one, however, was outfitted for cargo and flown by a pilot who'd only spoken a few words to them prior to their departure. In seconds, nighttime Vienna could be seen, along with the dark ribbon ringed by lights that was the famed Danube.

After the aircraft had begun to level off and some of the noise abated, General Timmons moved beside Mr. Winthrop and switched on an overhead light. Timmons leaned close to speak. "By the time we land, you and I are going to have every contingency covered. Vickers might be thinking in terms of a week or more, but I want that sneaky sonofabitch Warfield dead within seventy-two hours of us touching down. I think he's still in Paris, somewhere."

"How do you know he's in Paris?" Winthrop asked, dubious.

"Why would he run? You know how many millions of people live there?"

"Two-point-seven million in the city proper."

"Exactly. Why run? He'll just blend in."

Winthrop said little as Timmons outlined his plan. It was long on words, short on substance. Once the plan had been fully explained, Winthrop massaged his eyes.

"What?"

"Your plan is shit."

"I'm the one here who understands tactics," Timmons replied evenly. "We start at ground zero and work our way out. And we *stay* in Paris."

"We already did that. He was headed west," Winthrop insisted. "He's not anywhere near ground zero. He could have hit the outer perimeter, gotten in a car or on a train, and be hundreds of kilometers away by now."

"You *think* he headed west," Timmons countered. "Remember what that shit-bag Ortega said. Warfield'll do what you least expect."

"West," Winthrop maintained. "One of my men who was tasked with searching in the western quadrant went missing."

"Your men might just be poorly trained. What if he went AWOL?"

"These aren't Marine privates with weekend hard-ons. These are highly trained professionals."

"If they were, I don't think we'd be planning this manhunt."

"Fine. Keep talking," Winthrop said.

The general continued to arrogantly shape their plan, insisting he was correct at every critical juncture. Eventually, Mr. Winthrop ceased arguing. He sucked on a peppermint, largely ignoring the general's prattling. Instead, Mr. Winthrop relished visions of how he might kill the general.

Scratch that—how he *would* kill the general.

Of course, he would only eliminate him when the time was right—once Winthrop had the briefcase's contents firmly in hand. After that, in his opinion, the general would be expendable.

Hopefully, soon.

"So, whadya think?" the general asked.

Winthrop fake smiled, imagining dragging a razor across Timmons' throat.

Chapter Twelve

Late in the Paris evening, Detective Gaspard Lacroix hovered somewhere between highly buzzed and piss-drunk. He was at his favorite bar, which doubled as a cozy café by day, staring at the remnants of a bottle of '59 Musigny. It was good wine now, but would certainly be better in a few years. Musignys gained most of their value with time. He topped off his glass and tossed the heavy bottle into the trashcan behind the bar, earning a frown from his bartender friend. Her name was Amelie, but everyone called her "Al." Despite her gruff nature, calling her Al never seemed an insult—though she took, and doled out, insults quite well.

"What's your problem?" Al asked. "You've been moping and pouting all night."

"Kiss my ass," Gaspard replied, avoiding eye contact.

This was how they communicated—in good times.

Al took one of his cigarettes. He lit it for her. She blew the smoke in his face.

"Seriously, what is it?" she persisted.

Gaspard lit a cigarette of his own and sipped his wine. "Al, how wrong would it be for me to show up at the home of a young lady who is emotionally fragile over something horrific she experienced?"

Al leaned on her elbows. "When you say 'show up?'"

"Show up with the irrational hopes of bedding her," he clarified.

"I'll forgo the smart-ass answer, Gaspard, because I have several." She narrowed her eyes. "You do realize, we're not as fragile as you narcissistic men believe us to be."

"I never said women are fragile."

"Does she know you?"

"Of course she knows me."

"Attracted to you?"

"Maybe."

"That means no."

"Thanks."

"But there's still hope."

"Oh yeah?" he asked.

"Sure. Men don't have to only be good looking or rich for us to desire them."

"What else?"

"Power. Charm. Wit." She narrowed her eyes at Gaspard. "You're not powerful. Definitely aren't charming. And you have no money. But you're occasionally witty, so at least you've got a chance."

He stared into his glass.

"Go over there if you're attracted to her. Let her know. The worst that might happen is she slaps you in the face."

"Or, maybe she has a boyfriend who beats me up. Or, maybe she complains about harassment, and I lose my job."

Al shook her head as she said, "*Vous chatte.*"

Such a strong insult, even from Al, got Gaspard's attention. He straightened.

"I am not."

"Right now you are. Do you know where she lives?"

"Yeah."

"What's her name?"

"Evelyn."

"Who is she?"

"The only witness in my only case, and it's an important one."

"Is sleeping with her against the rules?"

"Most definitely."

Al shrugged. "I break rules all the time. Especially if they don't hurt anyone. Would her banging you jeopardize the case?"

"Not that I can see."

"You're so hammered you probably can't see."

"Exactly."

"Go give it a try." Al leaned forward and crushed out Gaspard's cigarette. She dumped the last two swallows of his wine and kept the glass. Then she slid three mints to him. "Haul ass. I expect a full report tomorrow, and you know I'm a perv. If you score, I want to know all the sordid details."

"Screw it," he muttered. Without giving himself a chance to change his mind, he threw money and a generous tip on the bar, took the mints and left. Gaspard rode the Metro east, all the way to the eastern end of the 11th Arrondissement. He checked his watch, realizing he was on one of the last trains.

"Burning my ships," he mumbled, stumbling from the Metro and hoping the chill air might sober him up a bit.

It was nearly midnight in the 11th. Had Gaspard not had his Manurhin revolver snugly under his left arm, he'd have not felt safe walking in this neighborhood a minute after sunset. He wondered if Evelyn often encountered problems. The 11th Arrondissement was probably 1st when it came to violent crime, and certainly in the top-5 when it came to sexual crime against women. It made him admire her even more that she lived here, a foreigner, surviving in this district of Paris known for vice and violence.

Up ahead, a group of men spilled from a bar, yelling insults at one another. Though they spoke French, it was heavily accented. Punches were thrown—few connected. Thankfully, the drunk are usually too uncoordinated to seriously hurt one another. Gaspard ignored them and continued on.

As he neared Evelyn's building, a gang of malevolent-looking youths who were gathered under a streetlight stopped pitching coins and stood in Gaspard's way. He didn't miss a beat, turning his shoulders to walk between them. After he'd passed, he turned and eyed them—primarily to make sure no one hit him over the head from behind. They obviously sensed his street smarts as they wisely went back to their game.

Gaspard dipped his head as he climbed the stoop to Evelyn's apartment building. Sandwiched between two much larger, equally dilapidated buildings, Evelyn's tenement had been divided into four flats, bisected by a rickety stairway that looked like it might give way at any moment. Gaspard remembered she lived in apartment-C. In fact, he memorized her address the second he learned it, though at the time he wasn't conscious as to why.

Now he knew. Getting here was the easy part. He wondered how this next bit would play out.

Gaspard winced as the stairs groaned under his weight. It was now a few ticks past midnight. Would she be home? Would she be awake? Would she be offended?

Was she with another man? A man who might take umbrage at a drunk detective stopping by with a tent pole in his trousers.

At the top landing, sticking with his sense of urgency to avoid chickening out, he knocked lightly on her door and waited. In that period of silence, he felt the pang of desperate loneliness, along with a slice of self-loathing. He knew this young woman was scared, and probably forlorn. By coming here, he was taking advantage of the situation.

But, he reminded himself, had I met her in a cafe or on the street, I would have still desired her.

Would you? Or are you attracted to the vulnerability? Do her doe eyes and babe-in-the-woods countenance awaken something in you? Like a tiger sensing fear, do you smell her vulnerability, knowing you can take advantage of it?

It was of no matter. She hadn't answered the door. Hopefully the traumatized young woman was getting some rest.

Or maybe she has a boyfriend, and she's at *his* flat, in his bed this very moment.

Ignoring the stab of jealousy, Gaspard donned his hat and eased back onto the stairs, trying not to wake the other residents.

"Hey," came a sibilant voice behind him. He turned. It was Evelyn. He hadn't heard her open the door.

"What are you doing here?" she asked, brow lowered.

"I hope I didn't wake you," Gaspard said, removing his hat and reversing his course. He climbed back to the landing, viewing her through the narrow opening of the door. She hadn't unhooked the security chain, which, in his opinion, was useless against anyone older than 12.

"I didn't realize you'd have more questions for me so soon," she said, cocking her head. "And at this hour."

It was clear she believed his visit was on the up-and-up.

Gaspard took a moment to make sure he said this the right way. In the manner of a gentleman caller, he held his fedora over his heart and spoke in his best *Rive Gauche* accent. "I apologize for the hour and the unannounced visit, but I didn't come here to speak to you about the case."

"Why did you come here?"

"You'll pardon me for saying it so bluntly, but I'd very much like to spend time with you tonight."

There was a long pause. "Are you drunk?"

"I've been drinking."

Evelyn shut the door.

The chain could be heard clicking. The door opened.

She stood aside as he entered. He drank in Evelyn's image, her flowing gown covered by a light satin robe. The house smelled of burning candles and hair products. Most pleasing was the overarching scent of a woman.

Evelyn shut the door and locked it. They stood there, in the studio apartment, facing one another. "You came all the way here to see me?" she asked, her voice trembling.

"From the moment I saw you, Evelyn, I was attracted to you. But I don't want to be here if I'm taking advantage of your vulnerability."

"I'm an adult."

"Yes, you are."

"So, I'll make my own decisions."

"Excellent."

"You can stay." She walked to the cupboard, returning with a bottle of brandy and two glasses. "But you'll have to sleep on the sofa."

They talked for two hours. Eventually, she slept in the chair, and he on the sofa. While Gaspard didn't get what he wanted, he fell asleep satisfied nonetheless.

***

As the detective in charge of the investigation spent the evening with his star witness, and as the mastermind of the Place de Clichy Secret Service heist approached France with a retired Marine general at 8,000 feet AGL, the perpetrator of the heist drove south, away from Paris, in a drug dealer's blood-soaked Renault. Beside the perpetrator was his girlfriend, Ludivine—

she smoked nervously, eyeing her man, making sure he remained conscious. Her eye sockets were dark, as if she'd been awake for days. Her man, of course, was Max Warfield. He'd cleaned himself and changed clothes. Afterward, he wrapped a scarf tightly around his head, satisfied as the cloth absorbed what little blood oozed through his rudimentary stitches. It looked like a fluffy turban with a carmine blot on the left side.

As the kilometers had passed, he'd begun to feel slightly better, but more fatigued. It was probably nothing more than the abatement of his shock. Max knew enough to know that he needed rest, and soon. Preferably, he needed blood or, at minimum, nourishment and hydration.

They passed through Clamart and now zoomed along the edge of the ink black Verrières Forest. Neither had spoken in many minutes, and Max began to worry that Ludivine was having second thoughts.

"Are you okay?" he asked.

"I should ask the same of you."

"I'll be fine. How are you?"

"I don't know."

"What does that mean?"

"I don't know," she replied, tears flowing.

"Talk to me, please," Max said.

She pitched the cigarette out the window and rolled it up, creating relative quiet in the cabin. "You nearly died, and I just walked away from my life, Max."

"I can take you back."

"I don't *want* to go back."

From experience, Max knew better than to let her know she was contradicting herself. Instead, he placed his right hand on her leg, massaging it. He could feel her tension ease at his touch.

After a moment, she continued. "I'm just scared. I'm more scared for you than for me. I don't see a way out of this."

"I'm scared, too, Ludivine. Before we do anything, I just need to get us far away from Paris. If we can find someplace to hide for a few days, then I think I can come up with something."

"Will they know where we are?"

"No. As long as we distance ourselves from this car, and we don't use your name, we'll be okay."

"What about my work?" she asked.

"What will they do when you don't show up on Monday?"

"Fire me."

"That quick?"

"Unless I call, and I think that's a bad idea."

"Will Aveline tell everyone about your mysterious friend who showed up Friday night?"

"Only if they're looking for me."

"They'll get suspicious after a day or two, and that's when they'll search your house. It won't take them long to figure out that your friend is the man wanted for the robbery at the Place de Clichy."

Ludivine stared at him in horror.

"This is important, Ludivine, but I want you to remain calm," he said, digging a cigarette from her dwindling pack. "Times like this call for a cool head."

"I'm trying."

"Can I keep talking it through?" he asked.

"Yes."

"They'll know I was the one who took down Place de Clichy. They'll probably know what happened to those Chaillot drug dealers and they'll start looking for this car." He paused for a moment, deciding to go on. In the respite, he lit the cigarette with the car's lighter, speaking with smoke coming from his mouth. "And if I had to guess, they'll be split about whether they think you're with me, or…"

"Or what?"

"Or if I killed you."

"My God."

"They'll have to consider all possibilities."

"What do we do, Max? And I don't mean tomorrow, or the next day, or next month…what do we do *tonight?* And I'm asking because I'm worried about you."

"I know you're worried, but we're together, so don't worry about my health. I'll be okay." He allowed a few moments to pass. "We need a place to stay, and food, and we need to secure these things without leaving a trail—meaning, without identification."

"Is that possible?"

"Not at a hotel. They cracked down on unnamed guests after the De Gaulle assassination attempts."

"What about a house?"

"You mean, break in?"

"If that's what it takes," she said.

He eyed her, admiring her spirit. "That's a possibility, but the problem of finding one that's unoccupied might be too hard to overcome. That would take time and effort, and I'm not sure I have the energy."

"Where else?" she asked.

"We'll think of something."

They rode on in silence until they passed a sign for Orléans, 68 kilometers away. Soon thereafter, as they sped through a small farming town on the two-lane road, Max saw the familiar sign for a school crossing.

He was struck with an idea and began considering the risks. There weren't many, not this weekend, anyway.

"What do you want, Max?"

"What do you mean?" he asked, recalling his mind to the here and now.

"From life. You've been living this way for years, on the run. Did you have a goal?"

"My goals were only in months," he breathed. "I never had the luxury of thinking farther forward than that."

"Try, for me."

"I'm not sure what you're asking."

"I'm running with you, Max. I've taken a leap of faith that will change my life, correct?"

"Probably."

"Then, please, give me some idea of what you'd like life to be."

He grew silent as the radial tires hummed. "I guess…"

"What?"

He wringed his hands on the wheel. "I guess I'd like to have peace. It sounds silly, but if I could be somewhere, with you, that doesn't require running…or worrying…or stealing to live, then I'd be happy."

"Where?"

"I don't care. It could be hot or cold or beautiful or gloomy. Wouldn't matter. I'd like to be with you in such a way that neither of us are concerned about who to knock over next, or whether or not there's danger lurking around the next corner."

Ludivine's left hand slid across the bench seat and took Max's right.

***

The building was typical of the schools built during the reconstruction period after the Second World War. Boxy and sparse, and only one story, it looked similar to hundreds of others just like it, constructed with efficiency in mind, not looks. Gone were the days of the three-story, institutional building near the center of town, built from marble and granite with imposing architecture. No, this one was basic and plain, probably thrown up in a month or two during the summer by Vietnamese and Algerian immigrants. It was situated on the outskirts of the city and served elementary age children. They'd found it after driving around Orléans, once again locating it from the familiar school crossing sign.

Nestled between residential and commercial areas, the school was set back off the road, screened by a light copse of trees and bushes. Across the street was a row of old homes that had been converted to professional offices. They were all dark. Max turned his attention back to the school.

Getting in wasn't his chief concern—his worry revolved around the police or perhaps a caretaker. Max doubted there was a live-in caretaker: those days were long gone, too. But there could be a custodian living in a cottage on the property. He made a full loop around the school, surrounded by a field of dead grass where the kids probably played *le foot*. There was no caretaker's cottage and no evidence of anyone nearby.

"How will you get in?" she asked.

"Window," he said absently, eyeing the facility. His mind was now on the car, and what to do with it. He turned off the lights and drove up on the sidewalk, pulling around to the side of the school in the darkest of the nighttime shadows. There, he offloaded the briefcase and money, his and Ludivine's things, as well as the drug dealer's items from the trunk. It was quite a pile of riff-raff.

"Stay here," he said. "I'll park across the street."

Max drove away, only turning on his lights once he was back on the road. The professional offices were obviously closed. He was afraid if he parked there, the car might get the attention of a gendarme doing a nighttime drive-by and checking doorknobs. He cruised on up the road, finally parking the car on the street at the edge of the residential neighborhood. Max wanted to remove the license plates, but doing so would probably create more suspicion than a car parked just like so many others. He shoved his hands deep inside his pockets and walked back to the school, the journey taking him 15 minutes due to his slowed pace.

"I'm so cold," Ludivine said when he arrived. "Listen to me complaining after all you've been through."

"It *is* cold. I'm sorry that took so long," Max answered. The activity had made him woozy but he said nothing about it.

He began walking the darkened side of the school. The windows were the newer, tilt-out variety built in long, horizontal sections. There was just enough light for Max to see the handles on the inside, and by his fourth window he located a handle that was only partially shut. Max jiggled the window from the outside, finally able to get a grip on it. As he used his strength to push upward, the steel frame flexed just enough that Max was able to pull the tilt window open, all thanks to some student who hadn't securely locked it.

"Philipe, you are not leaving this classroom until you close each of those windows and clap every eraser."

"Think you can fit through there?" Max asked.

And fit she did. Though it was snug, he boosted Ludivine up and watched as she supported herself on the radiator while he helped manipulate her rear end and hips through the narrow opening. She made a joke about it that made them both laugh, a welcome break from the looming tension. Once inside, she walked to the side door and opened it. They carried all their items inside and Ludivine waited while Max removed his shoes and walked around inside the building. When he returned, he pronounced the building empty.

They located an inner room, the music room, which had no windows. It had doors on both sides and raised levels from the front of the room to the back. Max found a wide roll of masking tape along with dark construction paper that he used to make gaskets around the two doors. He made them so that the doors could still be open and closed, but the gaskets would prevent light from bleeding from the room.

"Just in case someone shows up," he said.

"Do you think someone will walk through?" she asked.

"No, I don't. Not tonight. Tomorrow is Sunday, so somebody could possibly come here to do extra work, or there could be a janitorial crew—we'll have to consider that later." He pointed to the back of the room. "On that end of the building, all the way at the end, is the cafeteria. Do you mind getting us whatever food you can? I'm going to see if they have a nurse's office where I can find some supplies."

He was back first, having found children's analgesic, bandages, gauze and some sort of antibiotic salve. He'd also brought 4 large paper cups, which he filled with water in the nearby bathroom. After taking four of the analgesics, he was on his third cup of water when Ludivine arrived from the cafeteria.

On a pale blue tray, she'd loaded cheese, bruised apples, grapes, cartons of milk, bread and several pastries. "They have meat, too, but it would require me to turn on their warming oven."

"No, this is plenty," Max said, pecking her on the lips. They gorged themselves, only able to eat half of what she'd brought.

When they were done eating, Ludivine asked if they were going to sleep there.

"We're going to have to," Max said, his mood surging from the calories. "In my experience, one of us should stay awake on guard. But I think we'll have to risk sleeping at the same time. We need the rest. If we can somehow stay here through tomorrow and leave early in the morning on Monday, before sunup, then we should be well rested for whatever comes next."

"Sleeping in here won't be very comfortable," she said.

Max had a solution from something he'd seen during his initial reconnaissance. Together, they carried two thin mattresses from the nurse's office, replete with pillows and a starchy sheet and military style blanket for each. Then, Max did something that gave him far greater peace of mind—he located a number of rubber wedges used to hold doors open. After removing a piece of the door gasket, he kicked a wedge under the door and tested it. It would require a powerful person and a whole lot of noise to get the door open. That would allow Max to hear anyone coming. He wedged both doors.

Before they slept, he decided to do a quick inventory of their items. Other than the scant personal items they'd brought, they had the weapons and bag of counterfeit money. Of course, Max also had the heavy briefcase that had been the object of Mr. Winthrop's desire. From the dealer's trunk, Max had taken the box with the two wads of money and all the amphetamine pills. He counted the new francs, pleased that they now had over 300 francs to work with. That would certainly keep them going for a time.

But sooner rather than later, Max was going to have to do something about all these American dollars.

And perhaps tomorrow he could find the janitor's room. There, maybe there would be a crowbar that could grant him access to the mysterious briefcase.

He continued to believe that whatever it held might be the solution to their problem.

For now, it was time to sleep. It was after 2 A.M. when they both used the nearby hallway restroom before he again wedged the door shut and checked the other. After Ludivine coated the side of his head with the antibiotic salve, they lay down side by side for rest in the blackened room. Max didn't even complete his silent prayer before he fell fast asleep.

His stitches held; no one disturbed them; and neither of them awoke until it was nearly noon on Sunday.

Chapter Thirteen

On Sunday, around the time Max and Ludivine were beginning to stir in Orléans, the activities in the Secret Service annex of the United States Treasury Building were still akin to that of a fire drill. Since the president's assassination on Friday, approximately 43 hours before, most of the senior staff had remained with only the brief restoring benefit of a catnap here and there. The public demanded answers, as did Frederick Lynch, the long-serving head of the Secret Service. He was a man who was so respected that he ultimately survived Kennedy's assassination and would go on to serve as director for another decade. For now, he wasn't concerned with his own survival, but that of the people he was charged to protect.

Following a short snooze on his office sofa, Director Lynch had just showered and now watched as Julie Hedstrom, his long-time trusted assistant, arrived with a steaming hot carafe of strong coffee. He attempted to inspect the liquid—he had a rule that coffee should not bleed light. If it did, it was far too weak. Julie knocked his eager hand away as she poured his first cup of the day, mixing two minuscule drops of milk to cut the bitterness, just the way he preferred it.

"After all this time, don't you trust me to make it the way you like it?" she asked. "And I still don't know why you drink your coffee this way, chief," she said, attempting to bring a dose of humor to the grave situation. "All that fuss about it being dark, then you go and put milk in it."

"Why are you even here?" he groused. "I told you last night when you left that I wanted you to come back on Monday."

"I'm here because *we* have a job to do, and I have the utmost confidence in myself that I bring value." She pursed her lips. "And I also believe I can do any job in this organization, including *yours*."

Julie was 36 years old and unmarried. The fifth child of first-generation Swedish immigrants, she'd grown up in Minnesota before moving to Washington D.C. to get away from the family farm. Both of her parents passed away in the same year, leaving Julie to deal with her four bickering brothers. Coming to D.C. with little money and no job had been far more appealing than the mess back in Minnesota. Within a week she'd been hired as a pool typist by the Treasury Department and in relatively short order she worked her way up to the Secret Service Director's personal secretary and assistant. Though he'd never admit it, she was invaluable to him.

A tall, well-built woman, Julie was blessed with a winning smile and a bright face. Her hair was naturally blonde, which went nicely with her blue eyes. Most men found her attractive and magnetic, although she rarely dated. She enjoyed the solitude of living alone but wasn't closed off to the idea of someday marrying. Whoever he was, he'd have to be the *right* man. She would not settle. In her opinion, dating was a tremendous waste of time, especially if she didn't feel that initial spark, which she rarely did.

There had been one man who'd captured her heart—a captain in the Army who'd been posted in D.C. after the War. Sadly, he was killed in Korea a year after they'd met. Just before he'd deployed, they'd gotten engaged. Although his death crushed Julie, she credited it with being the fulcrum for her ascension in the Secret Service. Immediately after his funeral, she'd focused all her efforts on her career—and her efforts had paid off.

She tapped a painted fingernail on the director's desk. "Did you hear me, chief? I can do any job in the Secret Service, including *yours*."

The director rolled his eyes at her oft-repeated maxim. "I heard you...again." He took a sip of the coffee and nodded with satisfaction.

A true Irishman, Director Lynch was compact and sturdy, with a broad chest and back. He had a face to match, distinguished but not handsome, with a lantern jaw that suggested his bulldog nature. His hair was mostly gray and combed straight back. Everything about him, right down to his simple suit, indicated efficiency and a lack of personal ego.

"It's the truth, and you know it," she said.

Julie Hedstrom was the only employee in the entire United States Secret Service organization who could talk to Director Lynch in this manner. Of course, she would only dare do it in private, and because he respected her in so many ways, he allowed it and, privately, he enjoyed it. The only other people on earth who spoke to him with such impertinence were his two daughters, both of whom were now at Dartmouth. Director Lynch's wife had also been rather acerbic until she'd passed away due to cancer two years before.

Since that time, Julie had grown even more invaluable, handling everything from the director's dry cleaning to his schedule with senior cabinet members. When he purchased a new home, she handled everything. Taxes—Julie took care of it. Checkbook—balanced by Julie. Extended family—she returned all correspondence. It was rumored that President Kennedy noticed her efficiency and tried to poach her, but was rebuffed by Julie herself. It was also rumored that President Kennedy had suggested she be much more than a secretary, again rebuffed by the tall blonde Minnesotan. Now that he was dead, only Julie knew the truth; and if it was true, she'd never breathed a word of it to anyone.

Despite a few unknowing whispers, Julie and the director had always carried on an appropriate relationship. Though she was more than a decade younger, she doted on him as if he were her younger brother.

Julie arranged the director's newspapers on his desk, along with a security briefing prepared by the FBI. "Don't forget, you're due at the White House at eleven. You're meeting with President Johnson."

He snorted. "Don't remind me. I've got so much to do by then. I shouldn't have slept."

"You slept only a half-hour and you still look like hell."

"Thanks," he muttered.

"Imagine what you'd have looked like had you not slept," she sang.

He lifted the Washington Post, eyeing the headlines.

"Chief?" she asked.

"Yeah?" he breathed without looking up.

"Look at me, please," Julie requested. When he did, she continued. She waved a folder in front of her. It had color-coded bars along the open edge, signifying distribution. It was a top-secret folder, similar to several others on his desk.

"Which one's that?"

"It's the latest roll-up of agency reports regarding the robbery and killing of Agent Lang in Paris."

"Put it over here—I'll get to it."

"Chief?"

"Yes?" he snapped, clearly irritated.

"You don't have time for this. You *know* you don't have time for this. And, you've tasked everyone who can fog a mirror to the assassination, as you should."

"Is that a criticism?"

"No, chief…it's a fact."

"I'll call in some help from Treasury."

"They don't have time, either. And you know as well as I do that they don't do this type of thing very well."

He crossed his arms. "What exactly is your point?"

"I want to work on this, and I want to use your authority as I do it."

He shook his head to the stops. "Absolutely not. I should have never let you dabble in the past, but you'll note I've never allowed you to work anything sensitive. On this, which *is* sensitive, there can be no debate." He shot a look at his watch. "You're wasting my time."

She stood still and didn't hand over the file. "I'd like you to tell me why I can't work on something sensitive," she demanded. "I've got a top secret clearance, the same as any other person in this section of the building."

"You're *not* an agent."

"I have the exact same clearance an agent does. In fact, my clearance is deeper than two-thirds of your agents because I see everything you see."

"*Nearly* everything. And a clearance doesn't make you an agent."

"I'm not an agent for two reasons," she said. "I know I didn't finish college, but I lost both my parents in short order. I had very high marks before I dropped out. If you want to send me back to school, I *will* graduate at the top of my class. If you'd like to compete with me in an IQ test, I'd *welcome* the challenge." She took a few steps forward and stabbed her plum colored fingernail into his pecan desk. "But the other reason—the big one—is because I'm a woman, and *you* won't allow female agents."

He averted his eyes back to his blotter and shook his head. "Julie, it's not just that."

"What, then?"

The director lifted his rapidly cooling coffee and sat back in his chair, crossing his leg as he took a long sip. He looked at her. "If it's discovered that I tasked you with something as sensitive as this, then I'll—"

"What, lose your job?" She didn't go on, but she knew she could remind him that he lost a president two days earlier. What could top that?

"Allowing you to work on a case is a clear violation of law, Julie."

"I'm not *working* a case. I'm aiding you." Before he could respond, she continued. "If I turn something up, I'll come straight to you. And I won't leak it to anyone—why would I?" She tapped her temple. "Do you realize what I have in this brain of mine? Things I've never even told *you*. I know something about the former president that would make even you blush."

He cocked his head. "Really? What is it?"

"No. I don't work that way. When I'm in someone's confidence, it remains that way. Now, may I spend the day working on this, for you, because you won't touch it, and you know you won't? It's already been shuttled down to the dregs at State and FBI."

Director Lynch finished his coffee in one slug. He placed the cup back on his desk and watched as she expertly prepared him another. He massaged his eyes and nodded resignedly. "You handle it as if you're making the inquiries for me, because I'm buried."

"Are you not?"

"You get anything I need to know, then you ring me."

She crossed her arms. "But I am free to pursue my own avenues, correct?"

"Just don't trample anyone."

She allowed herself a prim smile. "Question one and only, then I will leave you…"

"What?"

"According to my calculations, the robbery of the Place de Clichy station occurred minutes after the assassination. Do you think there's any chance that the two are related?"

"I don't care for phrases such as 'any chance.' But, I feel the probabilities are extremely slim. This was a robbery that was planned for after-hours on a

Friday in Paris, France. I think you'll find that the time the perp chose was one of the few times when we only had one agent on duty. It's certainly not the first attempted robbery on a field office."

"Very well," she said. "Do you require anything of me at the moment?"

"Nothing."

She nodded, then turned and walked to the door. With her hand on the doorknob, she turned and eyed him. "Thank you, chief."

He cradled his coffee. "Julie…was there ever any question in your mind that you'd spend your day working on that case?"

"No, chief, there wasn't."

With a resigned countenance, the director nodded. Julie departed and pulled the door shut.

***

Before taking any other action, Julie sat at her small desk outside the director's office and read every word from the top-secret case folder. No one interrupted her and the silence was excellent for concentration. She started with the briefs from the two off-duty agents in Paris. They'd called in their reports approximately six hours after the incident. Even though the transcribed reports had been cleaned up a bit, they were far from polished. Julie could glean that both men were shaken after the loss of their colleague—on top of the loss of the president.

The next brief she read was from the State Department, but probably written by someone from the CIA. It wasn't helpful at all—bland and without any information other than facts she already knew.

Finally, Julie read a report from the Paris Police, penned by Detective Gaspard Lacroix and translated by someone at the embassy. Though this report wasn't much more helpful than the other two, it seemed to contain a bit more opinion about what might have happened. Lacroix went on about the second shooter—the sniper—and also about the man who wore horn-rimmed glasses, spotted soon after the robbery by the only living witness: a clerical worker named Evelyn Durand.

Julie made a note to learn more about Ms. Durand. In fact, to speed things along, she called down to Records and told the duty clerk that the director wanted Evelyn Durand's employment file. They were short-staffed in Records to begin with, and with all of the work surrounding the assassination, Julie knew she might not get the file today. At least she was now in the queue.

Once she had a decent mental picture of what happened, Julie reread the reports a second time, then a third. On her third reading, she began to think of alternative theories. By this time, the director departed for his meeting with the president. As she helped him with his overcoat, he asked her if she'd solved the case yet, his sarcasm quite obvious.

Julie handed him his briefcase and his hat, politely informing him that she hadn't solved it—*yet*. His expression wasn't unlike that of a father who was frustrated but secretly proud of his clever but cheeky child.

The director would be gone for several hours, meaning Julie could jump in with both feet. Following her third reading, she had a number of questions revolving around the following subjects: the second shooter, the man with horn-rimmed glasses possibly named Winthrop, the briefcase, the Army post in Germany, the hypothetical coercion of the perpetrator.

According to Ms. Durand, she'd heard the perpetrator confessing about a man named Winthrop. She also heard him say he'd been imprisoned at an Army post. He said each of these things to Agent Lang. Lang had been shot by rubber bullets from a shotgun blast and was immobilized by something called Ty-Rap on his hands and feet. Julie went to the rear of the report, reading the medical examiner's translated notes. The initial injury to Lang was blunt force from the shotgun blast, leaving him heavily bruised but with only superficial contusions. So, presumably, he was only dazed when Ms. Durand heard the perpetrator speaking to him.

After the perpetrator had left, Ms. Durand freed herself along with Agent Lang. By the time she saw Lang again, outside, he'd been shot dead. She also saw a man with horn-rimmed glasses in the courtyard, staring down into a ventilation shaft. The French detective wrote that he believed the assailant shot the lock on the shaft and escaped into the cavernous underground Paris sewer system.

If Ms. Durand was telling the truth—and that wasn't a given—then the presence of the character in the courtyard—who might have been the so-called Mr. Winthrop—and the second shooter, key-holed nicely with Julie's leading theory that the entire robbery was a much larger conspiracy.

Julie put on her coat and took a walk outside. It was blustery, the clouds and blue skies warring overhead. Hands deep in her coat pockets, she walked to the café down the street at the corner of 15th and Ives where she purchased a cake doughnut and a paper cup of coffee.

"Kinda tough workin' today, knowing the president was killed and all," the proprietor said to Julie. To her knowledge, he had no idea where she worked.

"I'm sure President Kennedy would want you to go on with your life," Julie answered, sliding the fifteen cents change back to the man.

Rather than go straight back, she ambled through Congressional Cemetery, working on the hypothesis in her mind.

In this particular supposition, she would assume the assailant had been telling the truth when he spoke to Agent Lang. Therefore, she envisioned this Mr. Winthrop character coercing the assailant to rob the Secret Service outpost at the Place de Clichy. The assailant had been held at an Army post in Germany, which was where Julie assumed he prepared for the robbery. Then, on the night in question, the robbery had gone as planned—initially. She recalled the details...

A common gas was used to disable the two guards in the gatehouse. It's possible the assailant could have done this himself, but that was doubtful. The way they'd been gassed was rather sophisticated. Whoever did it had to gain access to the roof of the gatehouse to access the heating system.

Regardless of who gassed the gate guards, the perpetrator then had unabated access to the facility. She pictured the scene...

He storms across the courtyard and into the building, blowing open the reinforced inner door with a special shotgun round.

But he used plain bullets a short time later on the ventilation shaft. Why? Why wouldn't he stick with the same type of round that's designed to defeat locks?

Back to the breach...

He used rubber bullets inside. Grouse hunting with her father and brothers, Julie had fired many shotguns in her youth. She knew the assailant would have probably sequenced his rounds in his shotgun. And if he were using a shotgun loaded with non-lethal rubber rounds, why didn't he shoot Evelyn Durand, also?

As Julie walked west through the cemetery, heading back to the office, she recalled the section about Ms. Durand from the detective's report. Durand claimed that Agent Lang had greeted the perpetrator with his pistol drawn, thereby earning a shot to his chest. Durand hadn't been armed. The perpetrator threatened her but never harmed her.

Julie paused her hypothesis to recall Ms. Durand's assertion that the assailant had appeared to be shaken upon hearing the news about the shooting of President Kennedy. The detective had noted that the assailant had been tipped off by her tears.

It seemed to Julie that if the assailant had been coerced and under duress, then he might stop and talk.

Which he did...

Otherwise, a man with the guts to knock off the Secret Service wouldn't stop and talk. He'd be all business. He'd probably shoot Evelyn Durand, as well. Probably. After all, they were merely rubber bullets.

So, Julie envisioned the perpetrator tying Lang's hands and feet, then doing the same to Evelyn Durand. Then, as he stuffs his bag with counterfeit money, he turns to her and asks why she's crying. She tells him the president was just shot in Dallas, and the news surprises the perpetrator. After he gets his money, he rushes out and that's when she hears him speaking to Agent Lang. A bit sexist, but Lang *was* the agent, and Durand *was* the secretary.

Julie knew all too well how things worked.

So, Durand rubs her wrists up and down, freeing herself.

The woman saves the day, as usual.

She cuts Lang free and he grabs another pistol and runs out of the building, getting himself shot in the process. The shot comes from what appears to be a high angle, meaning a shooter on a rooftop. Evelyn Durand hears the shot and runs outside, spotting a suit-wearing man with horn-rimmed glasses peering down into a ventilation shaft that leads to the sewer.

Julie thought back to the detailed report from the Parisian detective. In his questioning of Ms. Durand, she said the man in glasses lifted a radio and spoke a few words. Fearing for her safety, Durand rushed back inside, just before a bullet struck the porch. According to Detective Lacroix, preliminary forensics supported this—a ricochet mark was found just outside the door. The deflection angle indicated a shooter above, probably on the roof of the Hotel Montmartre.

Effectively, this ended the sequence of events. The assailant escaped into the sewer. The man with glasses, perhaps Mr. Winthrop, was gone. The shooter, who might have been on the roof of the Hotel Montmartre, left no evidence of his presence. Agent Oscar Lang, a nine-year veteran of the Secret Service, lay dead in the courtyard. And Evelyn Durand, a translator and clerical worker, huddled in the rear of the outpost, fearful for her life.

The assailant used the pistol to shoot the ventilation lock because his coercer, Winthrop, only gave him one of the special rounds for the breach. That has to be correct.

The French detective suggested several possible diversions that had occurred near the Place de Clichy. They were only possible diversions—the police were attempting to determine if the incidents had merit but there was no proof as of yet. Julie didn't plan to focus on this unless she was given more information.

She finished her coffee and threw the cup into a trash receptacle at the cemetery's edge while a chilly wind pushed dead leaves around her feet. She came to several early crossroads in her mind. Each took radically different paths.

First, based on what she knew, she certainly didn't believe the assailant acted alone. Discounting all evidence from Evelyn Durand, Julie placed great weight on the preliminary forensics from the French regarding the bullet that killed Agent Lang. It had come from above. Now, perhaps the assailant simply had a partner, but why would the assailant blow open the ventilation shaft to escape? If he'd been thorough enough to gas the gate guards, he'd have also made sure his escape route was clear before he went inside.

So, that led her to her two paths. The first tracked with her gut instinct: The perpetrator had been coerced by the Mr. Winthrop character, just as Durand claimed. If that were the case, why? Was it simply for a bag of counterfeit money? Julie's instinct told her there was more.

The second path would create all sorts of problems: Could Evelyn Durand somehow be in on it?

Julie paused at the main steps to the headquarters building. As the brisk wind scuttled a bank of clouds away from the sun, a brief moment of sunshine beamed down, warming her cold face. She tilted her head backward.

Which path, Julie?

She held her breath, thinking.

Take the first path.

So, it was settled, for now.

Then what was it that Mr. Winthrop wanted? She thought back to what the perpetrator had taken...a bagful of counterfeit money and, from the bottom shelf...

A briefcase.

Ding. Ding. Ding.

Julie hurried back inside.

***

At that same moment, across the Atlantic and in the Orléans primary school, a better rested Max and Ludivine were determined to discover what was in the briefcase. They'd located a janitor's room that had a whole host of tools. Max had clamped the heavy briefcase in the workbench vise and drilled the two locks with increasingly larger bits from the janitor's electric drill. There were sharp metal filings everywhere. It was obvious the briefcase was constructed to withstand fire, as well as a bomb blast. Ludivine smoked a cigarette as she watched Max work. Every now and then, he had to stop due to the heat he was generating. He couldn't afford to pour oil over the bit, which he would have normally done, because he didn't want to risk spoiling the contents.

Finally, after nearly an hour of drilling, one side of the briefcase gave way. Max was able to pry it open with a large screwdriver, eventually popping the other side open with the noise of a gunshot. Ludivine used a rag to wipe away the shards of metal.

Max placed the briefcase flat and lifted one side. He had no idea what to expect, his expectation delayed by some sort of fabric sack around the contents. The sack was long and flat, similar to an expandable envelope. The fabric was unlike anything he'd ever touched, shiny slick, and strong. He held the sack in his hands, guessing its weight as two or three pounds.

This is it. This is what Mr. Winthrop wanted. All the torture and misery, just for whatever is in this sack.

He tried to tear the sack open with his hands but couldn't. The janitor's box cutter did the trick, neatly slicing the bag open. Max carefully removed the contents, holding the items in his two hands. There were three tape reels and a large manila envelope. Max viewed the tape reels for a moment before Ludivine identified them as audiotape.

"We use the same type at work for the manager meetings," she said. "It's my job to set up the recorder and change the reels."

He slid each reel back into the fabric sack. Max then slit the manila envelope open, finding a stack of 8" x 10" photographs that were slightly yellowed at the corners. At first glance, there seemed to be around ten photos.

The top photo displayed a rather striking woman ascending a ramp. The ramp appeared to be the gangway to a ship. Due to the high-vantage point, the photo seemed to have been taken without her knowing. She was dressed conservatively with a pleated, knee-length skirt and a fitted suit jacket with squared shoulders. Her two-tone Mary Jane shoes and peaked hat prompted Ludivine to estimate the photo was at least 20 years old.

At the bottom of the gangway were two men in dark suits and hats. They were facing away and fuzzy, since the camera was focused on her.

Ludivine flipped to the next photograph. It displayed the same woman, seated on a leather sofa in what appeared to be a stateroom. Behind her, several round portholes were surrounded by stained wood. She sat primly with her hands on her knees. Again, the photos seemed so natural that it would indicate they were taken with a hidden camera.

Several more photos followed, all of her on the sofa. Judging by her brow line and mouth, she was speaking much of the time and doing so with fervor.

Following that photo were three in a series taken from another angle. These photos displayed two people—the woman, and none other than Reginald Stuyvesant Whitestone, the 32nd president of the United States. Wearing a trademark tweed suit, he sat across from her in a leather club chair. Each of the three photos was similar. Based on his smiles, they were having a pleasant conversation.

"What in the world?" Ludivine asked. "That's the man who was President of the United States, isn't it?"

Max whispered his confirmation. He had a feeling something powerful was yet to be revealed. He lifted the last photograph of the woman and the president, revealing the one behind it.

The photo made Ludivine gasp.

The very same woman was shown slumped on the sofa, a bullet hole in the exact center of her forehead. Her eyes were open—dead eyes. Max had seen the same dull stare too many times. Though it pained him to view the photo clinically, he couldn't help himself. He saw the etching of the powder marks, meaning the bullet had been fired from close range. It had been a rather large caliber bullet.

Following that photo was another that was far more gruesome. Someone had turned the woman to display the carnage at the back of her head, along with the shiny slickness on the sofa's leather, and the lumps of brain.

Whoever had fired the shot had aimed downward, so the bullet would take out her brain stem—the mark of a skilled assassin.

Ludivine covered her mouth with her hand. "Why?" she asked, repeating the question several times.

Max spread each of the photos out. He had no idea who the woman was. There were no other people in any of the photos, except for the out-of-focus men in the gangway picture. Max tried to glean something else from the photos but couldn't.

When she'd calmed down, Ludivine remarked that the woman's clothes were high quality and appeared to be winter clothes. That was it. That was all they learned: the photos were probably at least 20 years old; they were taken in the fall or winter; and the woman's clothes were expensive.

And, of course, the woman had met with President Reginald S. Whitestone.

Before she'd met with a bullet.

Maybe.

"The pictures seem to be in order," Max said.

"Her boarding the ship. Her sitting and talking. Her meeting with the American president. Then her dead," Ludivine said.

"That's what it looks like."

"I wonder if she was talking to him in the first photos?"

"No way to tell," Max replied.

"Did the president order her killed?"

"I don't know," Max muttered. "I can't imagine a president doing such a thing."

Ludivine touched one of the pictures. "Do you have any idea who she is?"

"No."

"So this is what the man…Mister Winthrop…was after?"

"Had to be. Something vital must have been discussed between this woman and the president."

"Vital enough to have her killed?"

"It seems that way." Max lifted the three reel-to-reel tapes. "We need to hear what's recorded on these."

***

Julie searched for any indication of what might have been in the briefcase but couldn't even come up with a suitable place to start. There was nothing anywhere about the briefcase. In the vault inventory that had been provided by the two remaining agents in Paris, no briefcase was listed. So, had the perpetrator brought the briefcase with him? That made no sense. He'd brought a duffel bag for the money—that made sense. But to bring a briefcase?

Perhaps the briefcase was part of his cover during entry. But why carry it when leaving? Why not just discard it? Perhaps it had weapons inside?

Without giving herself much time to think, she flipped open her directory and called the first of the two remaining Paris agents. His name was John Humphries. She knew him by face and recalled he was from the south. He had an excellent reputation, but his occasional hotheadedness with the general public had gotten him removed from security detail.

Julie smirked as she recalled the most famous response from his internal questioning after his last incident. "I just don't have much patience with dumb-asses," he'd said with a shrug. Though Agent Humphries didn't know it, Director Lynch quoted his line on a weekly basis.

Perhaps we needed a few hotheads like Agent Humphries in Dallas, she mused as the international line buzzed.

When he answered his phone, Julie greeted him briefly before giving her rote spiel that she was calling for Director Lynch. There was a brief authentication they both provided from the daily pad before she asked him about the briefcase.

"I'm confused," she said. "Evelyn Durand claims the perpetrator took a briefcase along with the counterfeit money."

"That's correct. He took it from the vault."

"I don't see a briefcase listed in inventories performed by you, Agent Dorsey or Agent Lang."

"That's correct, ma'am. It was stored in the vault but it deliberately wasn't listed."

"Why?"

"I can't really say. When I first got to Clichy…that's what we call it…I did an inventory in my first few months and I was told to leave the briefcase off."

"By whom?" she asked, a bit more sharply than she desired.

"By Agent Lang, ma'am."

"Why?"

"He said that was the way it had always been. He said Agent Jackson told him that. I recall this because he was very deliberate about it, and he said Agent Jackson was very deliberate with him about it."

"Jackson…Jackson…*Danny* Jackson?" she asked, searching her memory.

"Yes, ma'am."

"Do you know Agent Jackson?"

"Not personally, no."

"Do you have any idea what was in the briefcase?"

"No, ma'am. I moved it once. It was abnormally heavy. I guess I always assumed it had something to do with our anti-counterfeit mission; perhaps it was engraving plates. I dunno…after some of the…er, troubles I've had, I didn't concern myself with it."

"Thank you, Agent Humphries."

"Yes, ma'am. Is there anything else?"

She thought about it. "There is, in fact. What's your general opinion on Evelyn Durand?"

"Do you mean, could she be in on it?"

"The director wanted me to ask."

"No, ma'am. That's the first place we would have looked. I can state unequivocally that I do not think she's in on the robbery. She's a fine person and strikes me as completely honest and upright. I think I can speak for Agent Dorsey on that because we discussed it."

"Thank you. I'll reach back out if I need something."

After the call, Julie was tempted to cross out Evelyn Durand's name, but couldn't bring herself to do it. However, Agent John Humphries' testimony went a long way with her. Despite his losing his temper a time or two, his reputation and character were excellent. She trusted his instinct.

Her next call was to Agent Mickey Dorsey—it was nearly word for word as her call with Agent Humphries. Dead ends, but at least confirmation of an off-the-radar briefcase and a solid character reference for Evelyn Durand.

And, of course, references to old instructions from retired Secret Service Agent Danny Jackson.

It was now late-morning on Sunday. Julie knew Danny fairly well, and she seriously doubted he was in church. Danny was a former Texas Ranger and a decorated veteran of the Second World War. He'd transitioned to the Secret Service after the War and served on the presidential detail for a number of years. If Julie was correct, he was currently on his fourth wife—or perhaps it was his fifth. In a service that had a reputation for robot-like agents, Danny certainly broke the mold. He picked up on the second ring.

"Yello?"

"Danny Jackson?"

"This is a long distance call, isn't it? I can tell by the two clicks."

"Yes, it is."

"Knew it. Now, say, 'Danny Jackson is the greatest man I know,' in your normal voice."

Julie rolled her eyes. "Danny Jackson is the greatest—"

"Julie Hedstrom," he interrupted. "I always knew you had a thing for me, Julie. When you wanna come on down to Abilene for a week? The wind is hell through the winter but we don't need to go outside to have fun, now, do we?"

Julie couldn't help but smile. "I'm not making a social call, Danny. And aren't you married?" She almost said "again" but bit off her words before it escaped.

"Nah, not married," he breathed. "She left back in September. I was too much for her…always am."

"Was that four?"

"Five. You need to catch up. I'm currently lookin' hard for six and I'd be lyin' if I said I wasn't keepin' a keen eye out for seven. At some point, I gotta add a redhead to my collection. You believe that? I ain't never had a redhead. Well…I've *had* plenty, just never *married* one."

This was how Danny flirted. He convinced women—some women—that he was such a cad that they dropped their defenses. He was probably in his late 50s by this time. Julie assumed he was still handsome and rugged, overcoming his age with charm and charisma.

"Do you have a minute to talk?" she asked.

"Sure do. Just got in from huntin' and now I'm brewin' up a pot of coffee."

"You just got in? It's morning. When did you go out?"

"'Bout four. White tail season. Didn't get a damn thing, neither. They was all laughin' at me."

"Danny, I need to ask you a few questions on behalf of the director."

"Sent you, did he? Guess I ain't important 'nuff for him no more. Not that I'm complainin'. I'd much rather talk to you, sweetheart."

"Thank you, Danny."

"Tell him that."

"I will."

"I'm serious."

"I know you're serious," she said. "Now, back to the business at hand."

"Damn shame about what happened," he lamented. "Damn shame."

"I'm actually not calling about the assassination. I'm calling about an incident in Paris."

"That's what I'm referring to," he clarified. "You thought I was talking about Dallas? Shit…that's been comin' for a while, Jules. I knew the director wouldn't send you to talk to me 'bout that."

"You always were a bright bulb."

"Still am. By the way, that Oswald character is a patsy, sure as hell. He didn't shoot Kennedy but once, the one that hit him in the back. That shot took some skill, for sure. But a body is a pretty large target at that range, 'specially to a Marine. The other bullet was fired from Kennedy's two o'clock. I got that on good authority, but I can tell they're already shapin' the single-shooter story. You watch—no matter what comes out, our people will stand by the fact that there was a lone shooter."

Julie had heard all the talk over the weekend from the director and various agents. She wanted to ignore this and move on, but couldn't help but make a few comments. "Have you told anyone what you've heard?"

"What I've heard? Shit, Jules, I got that straight from fellas on the president's detail. They've been getting debriefed all weekend."

"And they said that there was more than one shooter?"

"One of 'em told me that that's what they *believe*. And more than one agent heard shots from two distinct locations. Forensics is tryin' to say it was echoes. Shee-att. Damn near everyone on that detail has combat time in Dubya-Dubya Two or Korea. They know what gunfire echoes sound like. A gunshot echo loses its punch. It doesn't crack. They said they didn't hear no damn echoes."

"Well, if you know anything pertinent, I can have the director call you."

"Nah, he knows where I am. The boys on the detail know all there is to know."

"Fine...back to Paris. I don't have much time, Danny, but I do have an important question."

"Shoot," he said, chuckling afterward.

"Do you recall a heavy briefcase that was stored in the vault at Place de Clichy?"

"*Bien sur que oui,*" Danny replied in the affirmative. It was funny to hear French in a Texas accent. Danny was fluent in French and Italian, and could get by in German and Russian. Oddly enough, Julie recalled that he claimed he couldn't speak Spanish—despite the fact that he'd been a Texas Ranger. The rumor had always been that he spoke native Spanish, but hated doing it because it reminded him of his first wife, the only one who'd died—the only one who hadn't divorced him.

"What was in the briefcase, Danny?"

"I have no earthly idea," he said.

"Why was it there?"

"Clayton Fairchild put it there."

"Clayton Fairchild?" Julie answered, remembering him by name only. "He's been dead since..."

"May of Forty-nine. Damn shame that was. Despite bein' a fancy Ivy Leaguer and all, he taught me a lot once I got past his blue blood and clinical case of lockjaw."

"Why did he store a briefcase in that vault?"

"I dunno. But he did. Told me to leave it be, no matter what. He never drew hard lines like that, so I knew it was serious."

"How long before he died did he store the briefcase?"

"Let's see...we opened Clichy in forty-seven, right when all the French and Belgian bootleggers went to work making counterfeit fives and tens. It was like the Wild West over there at that time, Jules. Counterfeit money coming from fifty sources. Cigarettes as currency. Normal women turned to hooking to feed their kids. People were desperate, and of course, wolves prey on the desperate."

Julie shut her eyes. "*When* did he store the briefcase, Danny?"

"Sorry…those memories are cold—and warm—all at the same time. Clay stored that briefcase in there right after we opened, so it would'a been forty-seven or maybe early forty-eight. He read me the riot act about screwin' with it. After Clay got killed, I carried on the tradition with the new agents, and I assume the agents there now still—"

Danny stopped cold. "Holy crap. It was stolen, wasn't it?"

"Yes, it was."

"I'll be damned, Jules. I'm gettin' old and I've lost my touch. I didn't even think about the briefcase gettin' swiped till just now. Damn, Danny…time to hang 'em up," he lamented.

"Danny, what could be in the briefcase?"

There was a significant pause. "I dunno, Jules. I only saw Clayton Fairchild get emotional one time, and it was when he talked about that briefcase. I 'member him sayin' what was in it was personal to him. He got teary and angry all at the same time. Said he loved our country even more than he loved what was in that briefcase."

"My goodness, what could it have been?"

"Beats me, and that's the truth."

"Did he say anything else about it?"

"No. I'd remember because that briefcase, and the way he acted about it, was so against type for him."

"Danny, do you think someone would have knocked over the Place de Clichy outpost *just* for the briefcase?"

"It's possible. Did they take money, too?"

"Yes. A large duffel bag of used counterfeits."

There was nothing but the light static of the long distance connection for a protracted moment. Finally, Danny broke the silence. "During the war, Clayton Fairchild was a key operative in the OSS, part of the X-2 group."

"X-2?"

"Counterintelligence. He touched all sorts of sensitive things, Jules."

"Do you think it was something related to that?"

Another pause. "Yeah, Jules, I do. He was a patriot, through and through, but he always talked about how subversive some of his contemporaries were. Men who were charged with protecting the nation, who exploited it instead."

"Like who?"

"He never said. But I could see in his eyes he knew things."

"Danny, can you even make a guess about the briefcase?"

"No, Jules. I've got no idea."

"Do you remember what it looked like?"

"Metal…dull metal, with ribs, and heavy. Really heavy. I obeyed Clayton but I did have to move it a time or two."

"Will you please call me if you remember anything else?"

"You know I will. Julie?"

"Yes?"

"Did you really call me for the director, or are *you* working the case?"

"You won't tell anyone?"

"Jules...why would I share you with anyone? I won't tell a soul."

"I'm working it. How'd you know?"

"'Cause ol' Lynch knows you're more talented than any of his agents," Danny remarked, his tone indicating that he meant it. "You need anything, Julie...any-damn-thing at all, you call me."

"I will Danny, and thank you."

When Julie hung up, she phoned Records again and told the clerk the director wanted everything on Clayton Fairchild, including his military personnel records.

After scribbling two pages of notes, she stood and walked down the hallway of the annex. Once she'd departed the executive wing, she turned left, past an empty meeting room, finding a roomful of agents working the phones. The room was a zoo of noise and activity, and stunk of cigarettes, coffee and cheap cologne—probably covering up a lack of bathing since Friday.

Julie crossed the room, waiting for the senior-most agent, Ken Grebel, to finish his phone call. Grebel was a large man, with white hair and a face that could have been chiseled from marble. He looked quizzically at her as he placed the receiver back into its cradle.

"Julie Hedstrom, to what do I owe this high honor? Wait...don't tell me...the director is calling me on the carpet?" He showed his hands in mock surrender. "It was a mistake, I promise. She took her ring off before I met her...how was I to know?"

Julie rolled her eyes. "I don't know what you're referring to, nor do I *want* to know what you're referring to."

He was satisfied with his joke.

"Ken, search your memory for a moment. How did Clayton Fairchild die?"

"Car accident outside of Paris. Bad."

"Single car?"

"Hit and run. Someone swiped him and sent him off an embankment. He didn't die from the impact. He burned. Like I said...bad."

"Did anyone suspect foul play?"

"Nah. The frogs claimed that spot was awful for speeders and what not. There'd been a dozen accidents there in the years before."

"Thank you, Ken."

"Hang on, hang on." He put his feet up. "Our investigators thought the fire outweighed the gasoline."

"What does that mean?"

"Clay's tank held about fifteen gallons but several experts claimed the fire indicated twice that."

"So, what was done about it?"

"Nothing. There was no evidence anywhere to be found. The fire just seemed worse than it should have been." Agent Grebel cocked a silver eyebrow. "What's this about, Julie? You helping on that Paris thing?"

"Yes."

He looked around and beckoned her close. "I honestly don't know anything about it, but some of the old guys used to talk about Fairchild. They said he had a Hiroshima-grade secret in his brain. Took it to his grave."

"Did they know what it was?"

"No one did. That was the kicker. There were whispers…"

"About?"

"A few guys thought maybe he was eliminated, especially after that inferno he died in."

"Who suggested that?"

"I don't remember."

She stared at Agent Grebel. "You're not going to give me names, are you?"

"I don't know what you're talking about. And they were only whispers. But maybe that'll help you a little bit."

Looking like a man who realized he'd said too much, Agent Grebel spun back to his desk and lifted his phone again.

Knowing she'd get no more, Julie thanked him and walked back to her desk to continue her work.

Part Three

Le révéler

Chapter Fourteen

The search of the school had taken over an hour. As it turned out, the Magnetophon-style tape player had been right under Max and Ludivine's noses the entire time. They found it in a closet in the music room, just a few yards from where they'd slept. This particular model was rather new, manufactured by the German company Telefunken. Max plugged it into the wall and Ludivine tested the playback with the tape that was currently mounted. They were greeted with the sounds of what was almost certainly the school band: a cacophony of missed notes that made both of them wince. Satisfied the machine worked, Ludivine rewound the band reel and removed the tape. She threaded the tape reel from the briefcase marked "1" through the machine and put her finger on the play button. Max nodded and the two refugees listened closely.

Static for 20 seconds. Several loud clicks. Finally, a man's voice.

"She's here. She's coming up the gangway. Like we discussed, I'll do most of the talking. Based on what she already told us, I don't think we'll have to ask too many questions."

The man spoke American English. His accent was crisp and northeastern—like someone from eastern Pennsylvania or New York. Max stopped the tape.

"Were you able to follow along?"

"Yes," Ludivine answered in English. "I'll tell you if he speaks too quickly."

Max pressed play.

"Look at those gams, will ya? I'd love to climb up on her back and take a ride."

"Can't blame old Hermann, can you?" This was another man's voice.

"Not a bit. Nobody said he's stupid. Alright...she's coming through. Here we go."

There were several indistinct murmurs followed by the sound of a door opening and the first voice greeting someone. He began introducing her before the tape was obscured by a loud squelching sound. It went on for at least 20 seconds before the normal recording resumed. Someone had deliberately obscured that portion of the recording.

Obscured the names.

"There's no reason at all to be nervous," the man said. "Please, sit there on the sofa. Can I get you anything?"

"No, I'm fine, thank you." A woman's voice. American.

154

"Was your trip over here pleasant?"

"I've never had an entire airplane to myself."

"First time in Newfoundland?"

"Yes," she laughed.

"Excuse me. Are we picking that up?" the first man's voice asked. He must have gotten an affirmative answer because he said, "Fine. Lucy, just so you know, we're recording. Please speak your answers clearly. State your name, your age and your outward occupation."

Cleared her throat. "Pardon me. I'm still nervous."

"It's fine. Deep breaths. Try to relax."

"My name is Lucy Thaler. I'm thirty years old. I live in Berlin, Germany, as I have since I left university. I work at the Residenz Berlin Hotel as a hostess and planner for all special events."

"You're American?"

"Yes. I have dual citizenship. My mother was from Berlin."

"Thank you, Lucy. Are you currently involved in a love affair with a member of Adolf Hitler's Reich cabinet?"

Silence.

"Go on. No secrets here, and we have limited recording capacity so we have to get right down to it," the man replied academically.

"Yes, I'm involved in an affair."

"He's a married man, isn't he?"

"Yes."

"Who is he?"

"His name is Hermann Goering."

"Fine. We all know who Herr Goering is. How long has the affair been going on?"

"About a year and a half. It began not long after his child was born."

"How often do you see Herr Goering?"

"Anywhere from one to three times a week, if he's in town."

"Does he confide in you?"

"About some things, yes. But what I've come here today to tell, I learned by overhearing him."

"Where was this?"

"At my place of business, at the hotel."

"Where?"

"In a guest room."

"Please describe when this was, and what the circumstances were."

"I don't feel I should have to go into too much detail about this," she said. "I understand my job but some details aren't important and could be misinterpreted later."

"Your concerns have been noted," the man said. "Tell us in general terms the circumstances."

"We'd taken a suite. It was early evening. We ordered room service."

"Had you made love to him?"

There was nothing but light static for a moment.

"Go on," the man urged. "Tell us."

"Yes. He has a...significant appetite for that. We did that as soon as we occupied the room. He was agitated beforehand. It relaxes him."

"When was this?"

"Eight days ago."

"Why was he was agitated?"

"He was taking a great deal of criticism from his colleagues over the Luftwaffe's defeat at the hands of the Royal Air Force."

"Did he talk about it to you?"

"Only in general terms. He was very angry and felt betrayed by men he thought were his friends. He cursed them, especially Martin Bormann. He was recently promoted, but I'm sure you know that."

"We do."

"Hermann seemed calmer...afterward. We talked a bit before he ordered food, and then he made a phone call. The phone call was what prompted me to respond with urgency to come in."

"Before we get to that, about your traveling here...are you certain the reason you gave for your absence won't cause problems later?"

"My reason for leaving was perfectly fine. I can resume my position without any problems." She went into detail about her reason to travel to England to see her sister. The OSS provided her with several letters, with all the correct stamps and postmarks, to leave as evidence in the event he had her quarters searched.

"Back to the phone call Goering made," the man said.

"Yes, he was on a call, ranting over being stabbed in the back by Bormann. Hermann cursed a great deal; he was very upset. He then began to discuss an attack on the United States forces."

Murmurs could be heard on the recording.

"Did Goering know you were listening?"

"Of course not. The suite consisted of two rooms. I'd run a bath in the tub and he was in the sitting room. He thought I was in the bath. He had his back to me and was drinking, which was typical. I knew he wouldn't get up. He's also quite loud, so I could hear him clearly."

"Who was he speaking to?"

"No idea."

"Could you guess?"

"I won't. It was a confidant, of some sort. Someone in the know. But other than that, I have no earthly idea."

"Fine. Tell us about the attack he spoke of."

"At first, it was difficult to get the full context since I was hearing only his side. But after he lost his temper about Bormann, he talked openly about the attack."

"Go on."

"From what I could understand, whoever he was speaking with knew of communications between an Abwehr agent and Japanese intelligence in Honolulu. According to the Abwehr agent, the Japanese are planning a surprise air attack on our navy in Hawaii."

"When is this attack on Hawaii?"

"It's months away. That's all I know."

"Where is the Abwehr agent based?"

"Honolulu."

"Do you know the person's identity?"

"No."

"Any details?"

"Hermann seemed to indicate that the agent has been there for years."

"How do you know that?"

"He said something about the agent's pinpoint accuracy over the past decade."

"You didn't say that before," the man replied sharply. "Every detail is critical."

"My apologies."

"What else?"

"Goering was extremely insulted that he wasn't contacted directly for his advice, by the Japanese. Much of his diatribe revolved around his own personal irritation at being slighted, especially with the Reich sharing intelligence."

"Were there any details about the attack?"

"All I could tell is that the attack will be significant, and aimed at crippling the entire Pacific Fleet prior to full scale war against the United States."

"Damn. I'd say that's—"

The tape ended. Ludivine frowned at Max.

"Did you understand all of that?" he asked, realizing his voice was shaking.

"Yes."

Max swallowed thickly. "Do you get the significance?"

"I think so, because the U.S. wasn't ready." She gestured to the tape player. "But clearly they knew."

"I'm sure that's the point of why this was saved," Max said regretfully. "And why Mister Winthrop wanted it."

"History isn't my strongest subject," Ludivine said. "So, answer something for me…did the Germans know about the coming attack at Pearl Harbor?"

"Obviously, some of them did."

"Wait…what I mean is…before today, was anyone aware that the Germans knew?"

"I've never heard that. No one has—not to my knowledge. The attack on Pearl Harbor cost thousands of lives and sucked us into the war. If they were in cahoots, I believe it would be common knowledge by now."

"Is it possible whoever she's speaking with aren't really Americans?"

"Good thought, Ludivine. This could all be a setup."

"But what about the pictures of her and the president?"

"Photos can be faked. You might be onto something. This could all be some elaborate hoax created by intelligence types just to cause problems."

But Max didn't really believe that. Not yet, anyway.

He handed Ludivine the tape reel marked "2." She carefully unwound the first reel before storing it in its container. Then she set about threading the second tape through the player.

Each second seemed an hour.

***

Less than a kilometer from where Max and Ludivine prepared to listen to the second reel's recordings, a local gendarme cruised the streets of Orléans. Only, to him, this particular street wasn't just any old street—the police officer's mother lived here. The policeman was headed there for a bite of Sunday dinner—his shift had ended twenty minutes before. A faithful son to his rapidly declining *maman*, he visited her at least 4 times per week. Therefore, he'd come to know the cars that normally parked on her street. This afternoon, a strange car happened to be parked in the spot where the gendarme typically parked, the spot that had been vacated a year before when old lady Nieves had passed away.

The gendarme eyed the car. It was a Renault Frégate, blue in color. The car had Parisian plates—most likely belonging to an out-of-towner staying with relatives. The officer circled around the block and had to park a bit farther from his mother's house than usual.

As he walked to his childhood home, he whistled. He'd only had a bit of bread that morning, building his appetite in anticipation of his mother's famous *backoeffe*—a hearty stew with plenty of meat and potatoes. It had been cooking since this time yesterday. His mouth began to water, putting a halt to his whistling.

Passing by the Renault, he glanced inside, noting its tattered interior. He halted because something had caught his eye. The gendarme leaned close, seeing the significant rust colored stains around the driver's seat. He passed around to that side of the car, eyeing the deep brown drops just below the window and also on the back of the seat.

Those were drops of dried blood.

The doors were locked. He whipped out his notepad and scribbled the license plate before knocking on the doors of the three nearby houses, asking if anyone knew whose car it was. Two of the residents were home and told him the Renault had been there when they woke up this morning.

The officer arrived at his mother's house, inhaling the aroma of her rich *backoeffe*, his hunger roaring back with vigor. As she prepared his meal, he phoned the shift supervisor and relayed the number of the plate along with his report of what was almost certainly dried blood around the driver's seat. He suggested they phone Paris to check if there was any sort of flag on the license place. The shift supervisor agreed, and the Orléans officer relieved his mind of his duty.

Now unencumbered, the famished gendarme ate three large portions of Sunday dinner—a fact that sat well with his doting mother. An hour after arriving, he was snoozing on his mother's sofa, a nearly empty glass of Burgundy dangling precariously from his right hand. The gendarme was blissfully unaware of the chain of deadly events he'd set off, all because he'd noticed a blemished car from out of town.

***

One of Mr. Winthrop's numerous assets in Paris was a police sergeant in Dispatch. His last name was Patten. Sergeant Patten had no idea who he was actually working for. A week before, he'd been hired by a coquettish woman who approached him as he left work. The proposition was quite simple and seemed harmless enough—especially for the money. While on duty, Patten was to immediately relay all calls regarding a variety of subjects to one specific Parisian phone number. In exchange, he would receive 20 francs per day, cash. Once he determined he wasn't being set up, Sergeant Patten readily agreed to the proposal. This had been going on for a week, and each night when he departed, the cash was hidden exactly where he'd been told it would be.

Every time he called, the same woman answered. She listened to his information, answered with a simple "*oui*," and hung up the phone. The sergeant had no idea he was one of four men in the Parisian police providing a similar service, nor did he care. He was currently embroiled in what *had* been a waning affair with the insatiable wife of a younger policeman. The wife enjoyed fine dinners and gourmet chocolates. Before being approached by the flirty woman on the street, Patten had been nearly tapped out. The new money came in handy and, since the proposition, the affair had roared back to life.

This late afternoon, Sergeant Patten listened to the radio and heard the call from the dispatcher as it was relayed to several divisions. The call concerned a Parisian-registered Renault with possible blood on the seat. It had been found parked on the western side of Orléans, on a residential street. Within minutes, a detective from the auto theft unit relayed that the car had been reported stolen just that morning. The owner of the automobile was a known narcotics dealer who claimed he'd been mugged and robbed of the vehicle.

This news certainly fit within the parameters of what Patten was being paid for, so he scrawled the details and phoned the Parisian number he'd called so many times. He relayed the specifics, including the street address where the stolen car had been spotted in Orléans. Thinking nothing more of it, he went back to his work, waiting patiently until his paramour's husband arrived for the night shift. Sergeant Patten would use today's earnings to take the young vixen out for a sumptuous meal before making love well into the evening.

While he awaited the cuckolded husband, Patten called his own wife with grave news, informing her that he would be working late tonight.

"Again?" she asked.

"*Oui, mon chou.* I'm tracking a very important suspect."

"But you've worked seven days straight and have stayed late on all but one."

"And that may continue. Crime is up. I'm needed. If I don't stay, I could lose my job."

Sergeant Patten finished his shift early and departed 36 Quai des Orfèvres, tingling with anticipation as he thought of something new he'd like to try tonight with his limber and willing mistress.

***

Mr. Winthrop and General Timmons had been at it all day. Upon arriving in Paris, they'd immediately been briefed by key members of Mr. Winthrop's Parisian team. The alpha team member, Wallace—a man with a distinguished military background as a commando—had been found dead. His decomposed and partially eaten body was located in the sewer, devoid of identification. Though the French didn't know who he was, they suspected he'd been killed by the man who'd taken down the Secret Service location at Place de Clichy. According to two sources, the French were split over whether the corpse was that of a hobo, or someone who'd pursued the assailant. Without identification, they were forced to work other leads until the body was identified.

Winthrop's remaining team had worked several other tips, none of which had borne fruit. Then, despite the team having already searched there, Mr. Winthrop and the general accompanied nearly every team member into the Paris underground. Wearing workers' uniforms, the team was charged with searching kilometer after kilometer of underground space.

"He may have stashed the briefcase somewhere," Mr. Winthrop had warned. "Check every nook and cranny. And I wouldn't put it past him to still be hiding in the underground. The man ate a rat—hiding in the sewer shouldn't bother him."

When, after six hours, nothing was found in the underground, Mr. Winthrop and the general had retraced all of Max's steps from when he was under surveillance. Since the incident at the Place de Clichy, he'd not gone back to his flat, nor had he been spotted at any of the other locations where he'd been seen before his capture.

Max Warfield was nowhere to be found.

In the early evening, Mr. Winthrop and General Timmons hurriedly ate a meal in a café on Rue Saint-Ferdinand, in Paris' Ternes neighborhood. They had no earthly idea how close they were to Ludivine's flat.

The same driver from the heist at the Place de Clichy, Edge, walked into the café and handed Mr. Winthrop the most recent brief from the Paris Police. Winthrop shoved the last bite of *jambon persillé* into his mouth, chewing as he scanned the brief. It being a weekend, the brief was chock full of stabbings, robberies, muggings and the like.

Mr. Winthrop and General Timmons discussed two listed crimes but dismissed both of them after reading the descriptions of the suspects. One suspect was tall and thin, verified by four witnesses, and the other had pale skin and light blue eyes. He'd also lost his shirt in the skirmish and possessed no identifying tattoos or scars.

On the final page was a handwritten notation in the middle of several rote reports. The handwritten portion involved a stolen automobile with bloodstains inside.

"This one," Winthrop said, tapping the paper. "The stolen car. Where is Orléans?"

"South of here," Edge replied.

"But the car was stolen in Paris?"

"Yes."

"When?"

"See my notes? Last night."

"Where?"

"Near the Arc."

Winthrop whipped his head around to Timmons and pointed. "The Arc is in *west* Paris. Max went west." Winthrop eyed Edge. "And the police claim the car's owner is a known drug dealer?"

"They were sure of it. High-end stuff. No current arrest warrants but he has a rap sheet."

"Max needed money and wheels," Winthrop said knowingly. "Sonofabitch. He could be anywhere."

"Explain," Timmons commanded.

"Think of his M.O.," Winthrop said. "He knows drug dealers have cash, so he knocks one off—a high end dealer probably in an effort to avoid violence—and steals his car."

"But he already had cash," Timmons objected.

Winthrop closed his eyes and shook his head, as if he were an impatient kindergarten teacher with a class full of dolts. "He has counterfeit *dollars*...dollars...American. Try to keep up."

Reddening, Timmons sat back and crossed his arms.

"How far is Orléans?" Winthrop asked Edge.

"About 120 kilometers."

"Everything in the trunk?"

"Yes."

Winthrop tossed some money on the table. "Let's go. I want to be there in an hour. If he moves again we're fucked."

"I think we should radio a few men from the team," General Timmons said, unmoving.

"No. We're going to do this ourselves."

"Why?"

"If he's holed up, I don't want to spook him."

"What if it's not him?"

"It's him. Wait and see. Max is in Orléans. Maybe he knows someone near where he parked. Remember what Ortega said about him being with a woman?" Winthrop stood. "Come on."

Ten minutes later, the car raced from south Paris. Edge settled into the left lane of A10, known as L'Aquitaine, and flashed his lights at slow-moving cars.

Rubbing his healing ankle, Winthrop watched as the speedometer needle disappeared on the right side of the gauge, past the 120 mark. Satisfied, he inserted a peppermint into his mouth and began to flatten the wrapper.

"What if it's not him?" Timmons asked.

"Do you have a better lead?"

"But do you think he's stupid enough to remain near a blood soaked car?"

"Think about it. If he's bleeding, perhaps he's mortally wounded. Hell, he could be dead for all we know. Or maybe his bleeding got so bad he had to stop."

The general took the police brief and studied it with the help of his lighter. He directed his query at Edge. "Are the Orléans police searching the car?"

"One of our assets slowed the Parisian response. A detective is going down in the morning to meet a detective from Orléans. They'll go over the car together and bring in forensics."

"I'm surprised they're not in more of a hurry."

"They don't suspect this is related to the heist," Edge answered. "And they're not breaking their necks to help a drug dealer get his car back."

"What if Max gets back in the car and leaves?" Timmons asked.

"One of the Orléans police popped the hood and removed the coil wire," Edge answered. "That car's not moving."

"There," Winthrop replied, satisfied, nestling back into the seat. "Maybe we'll catch a break. Maybe the briefcase is in the car. Maybe Max is somewhere nearby, dead, bled out from his injuries."

General Timmons seemed unimpressed but said nothing.

Mr. Winthrop didn't believe Max was dead. In fact, he was confident he'd get one more chance at him.

He was confident, and correct.

***

There had been a minor problem with the tape reel. Ludivine told Max she could fix it. After finding a pair of scissors, she expertly trimmed a few centimeters off the lead before threading it through once again. As she worked, Max thought about what they'd already heard. He made the natural assumption that the woman in the photos was the woman, Lucy, on the tape. He wondered if her death had been recorded and whether or not it was on the second reel.

"Are you ready?" Ludivine asked.

"Are you?"

"Hearing it won't change what happened," she said.

"No, but it might be disturbing."

"I want to know."

"Do it."

She flipped the switch. After a few moments of static, the conversation resumed with the man's voice again.

"Lucy, how will Goering react if you question him about what you heard regarding the Hawaii attack?"

"That's hard to predict."

"Try."

There was an extended pause. "Well, he'll be angry with me for eavesdropping. Very angry. I'm afraid something so bold might cause him to end our relationship. Or worse."

"You don't feel you have a strong enough hold on him?" another man's voice asked. This was the other voice they'd heard at the beginning. It was spoken with a southern American accent.

Lucy replied. "His ego is wounded, and if I ask him about something that's caused him personal embarrassment, he'll feel he's diminished in my eyes. It wouldn't be a good idea. I'm in a desirable spot from an intelligence viewpoint. He could replace me with any number of women."

"We understand," the first man replied.

"Does he ever share critical information with you?" the southern man asked.

"No."

"Ever?"

"Not directly."

"Explain that."

"Just like his grousing over this incident, he'll sometimes complain about little things that clue me in to the bigger picture. But he doesn't share important facts about the Reich with me."

"You told your contact in Frankfurt that you fear Goering might move on from you soon?"

"It's a concern, yes," she answered. There was a long delay before she spoke again. "In thinking about it, he hasn't been as...ravenous...lately. It could mean he's taken another lover."

"That's not what you indicated earlier, about what happened at your hotel on the night in question."

"Please allow me to be the judge of such," Lucy replied with an edge to her voice. "It's not about any single interlude, but rather the frequency. Unless he's overindulging on food and drink, he could be getting his romantic satisfaction elsewhere."

"Anything you can do to bring him back with greater frequency?" the southern man asked.

"Such as?"

"You're the woman. You tell me."

"Perhaps. I'd have to think on it a bit."

"Please do. Excuse us for a moment."

The door could be heard opening and closing again. There was near silence for two full minutes. Max eyed the tape reel. It was nearly finished. There'd been many quiet pauses on this reel. Finally, the door was heard opening...

The first man spoke. "We're going to let you meet President Whitestone."

"Excuse me?"

"President Whitestone…he's onboard. He wants to meet you."

"Are you pulling my leg?" Lucy asked.

"Not at all. We wanted to discuss things with you first."

"President Whitestone is here, on this ship?" She was clearly incredulous.

"He's out there waiting."

"I don't believe it. Why would he be here?"

"We wouldn't lie about it, Lucy. And I can't really go into why he's here. As you might imagine, his presence, and that of those who are coming, is highly classified. This is one of the main reasons we went to such lengths to get you here today."

Lucy was silent for a moment. "I still can't believe it."

"You're critical to the security of our country. I hope this proves it."

"Just be honest about anything he asks about," the southern man said.

"Anything?"

"No secrets with the President."

"Is his being here why there was so much security coming into the port?"

"Yes'm."

"Are you ready?" the first man asked.

"My goodness, I guess so."

"Just be natural. Be yourself."

"I will," she replied.

"I'm going to step out and brief the president on what you've told us," the first man said.

"I'll stay here with you, doll," the southern man said.

The door opened and closed once again.

"While he's out there, I'll switch over to the larger reel so—"

The end of the second reel flapped round and round.

Max turned his eyes to Ludivine.

"What is it?" she asked.

"If Whitestone knew about Pearl Harbor, why didn't he stop it?"

"We don't know that he knew."

Max pointed to the third reel. "She's about to tell him."

"My papa used to call the government '*la machine de guerre*.'"

"The war machine," Max said in English.

"He claimed government, at its core, wants war." She hefted the third reel. It was twice the size of the other two. "I can't wait. I've got to hear this."

"I'm still thinking about your notion that this might have been faked."

"Maybe we'll know after we hear this one."

Max watched as Ludivine stored the second reel and loaded the third one. This time, she didn't ask. She played the tape once it was threaded. Both people leaned forward, hanging on each sound…

"Tape's rolling," the southern man whispered. *"Here they come. Just be your delicious self."* There was an extended period of silence, followed by a knock, an answer, and footsteps. Finally...

"Lucy Thaler, please meet the President of the United States."

"This is such a wonderful surprise," she said. Hurried footsteps. "My goodness, Mister President, it is a pleasure to meet you. I'm sorry for my astonishment but...well...I had no idea you'd be here until a few moments ago."

"Thank you, my dear. May I sit here?" President Whitestone said, his Minnesotan accent distinct.

"You sit anywhere you like, Mister President."

"We'll step out and give you two some privacy," the first man said.

Shuffling and a door clicking shut before the president spoke again. "Lucy, we appreciate your putting yourself in the middle of so many things there in Berlin."

"It's my distinct honor, sir."

"So, you know Hermann Goering?"

"I do, sir."

"In a nutshell, what's he like?"

"He's not the typical German, sir. He overindulges in nearly everything he enjoys. Food. Drink. Power. He's a gluttonous man. Despite that, he still possesses a great deal of charisma and even charm."

President Whitestone wasted no time with his next question. *"Would he work for us?"*

"In what way, sir?"

"Could you turn him? Would he remain in place but feed us information? Would he do as we ask, within reason if we make him promises for after the war?"

"I...I don't think so, sir. If the outlook was worse for the Reich, then possibly."

"They told me you said he was upset over the Luftwaffe being bested by the Royal Air Force? And now the Bormann promotion is a slap to him, too."

"Indeed, sir, but he's still bolstered by Hitler's naming him as his successor if something were to happen to him. It's an enormous source of pride for Hermann."

"But Hitler's not close to death," the president countered.

"True. Mister President, I hate to be so stubborn about something with you, but I can't see Hermann turning on the Reich. Not now."

"I'd rather you be stubborn as long as you're being honest."

"I am, sir."

President Whitestone paused for a moment. *"Lucy, what does Goering covet the most?"*

"Well...he covets many things, but I'd say it's fame, sir."

"Not power?"

"He adores his power, but he prefers the adulation that comes with it. I feel it's his ultimate intoxication."

"So, if we wanted to flip him, that's what we'd have to promise him? Fame."

"Yes, sir," she breathed. "But I don't see how we could possibly ever provide him with more fame than he has now."

"Yes, yes, I s'pose you're correct. Do you personally know Adolf Hitler?"

"No, sir, I don't."

"Have you met him?"

"Oh, yes. Several times at functions. But it was just a quick hello. He wouldn't remember me."

"Know anything useful about him? Any obscure facts that might be helpful?"

She hesitated for a moment. "The only item of significance I can think of is his relationship with his personal physician, a man named Theodor Morrell. Hermann has no use for the doctor, and calls him by a number of derogatory names including 'Der Reichsspritzenmeister,' which means Injection Master of the Reich."

"Ah, yes," the president replied, chuckling politely. "We've heard of Adolf's reliance on medicines and narcotics. Anything else?"

"No, not that I can think of. However, I'm confident I can deliver more in the coming months."

"Fine. I'm sure you will." Slight pause. "So, am I to understand you brought us significant news?"

"I believe it is, sir."

"I haven't heard the specifics—please, the floor is yours."

"Mister President, I overheard Hermann talking about an attack."

"Oh?"

"Yes, sir. The Japanese are planning an attack on Hawaii." Lucy retold the story exactly as she had to the two other men. The president asked several excellent questions, but she had no other information than what she'd already relayed.

"This is momentous intelligence, Lucy. You've served your country well."

"Thank you, Mister President. While I don't enjoy the day-to-day in Berlin, I'm thrilled to serve our country."

"We may call on you to approach Goering with an offer. But for now, please resume your activities as your handlers direct you."

"Thank you, sir. I'm so glad to have met you."

"As am I."

There was some shuffling and murmured compliments.

"Should I stay here?" she asked.

"Yes, please. The others will come back in. You do know I'm onboard for an important summit with Prime Minister Churchill?"

"Prime Minister Churchill? Goodness, me. No, sir, I didn't know that. Is he here, yet?"

"No, but he'll be here in a few hours."

"Well, Mister President, I'm sure your meetings will bear fruit. Thank you for taking time for me."

"Good to know you, my dear. Be well."

Footsteps, the door opening. Then…

The tape squelched, just like the earlier one. It only lasted for a few seconds. As it ended, the president was speaking. He said goodbye again.

The southern man spoke next.

"Nice work, Lucy. That was excellent. Have a seat on the sofa again, please."

The first man spoke. "President's clear now; he's on the other end of the passageway." The door clicked shut.

"I think he liked you," the southern man said.

"I'm still stunned. That's one of the greatest surprises I've ever experienced. He was very kind."

First man. "He was impressed, indicative of the importance of your good work, Lucy."

"Prime Minister Churchill is coming here, too?"

"No one knows about that," the southern man replied. "This meeting is likely the prelude to war."

"I won't speak of it."

The first man spoke after a brief pause. "Lucy, exactly how will you renew your relationship with Goering?"

"I'll do anything I have to. He has several…desires…that I've resisted. I'll acquiesce, or tantalize him with the prospects. That should do the trick."

"Good. We want you to go back to Berlin and resume your affair with Goering. As you do, I want you to pay close attention—"

She interrupted. "Excuse me. What is he doing with that—"

PFFT.

Max and Ludivine heard a wet, sucking sound similar to that of a drain swallowing its last bit of water. It was followed by a solid thump.

"Dammit! Why'd you use a jacketed round? Now we've got brain everywhere."

"It's all I had with me," the man with the southern accent replied. "Hated doing that, too. I'd have loved to tap this gal before that fatso spoiled her. Bet she could throw it on you, too." A rustling sound. "Look at that, will you? It's beautiful, even on a dead woman."

"You're a cold fish," the first man said, chuckling.

"Didn't you hear what she was getting at about Goering? She was gonna take it up the rear for him, or maybe bring another gal to the bed. I got no use for those Nazis, but damn if they don't have things rolling at the moment."

"Look at this crap. We're gonna have to clean all this up," the first man lamented. "Get the stains out, too."

"Won't be the first brain I've cleaned up. And it won't stain the leather if we hurry. The stuff's coated for spills."

"Hang on. Let me get some snaps of this." A sharp squelch. "...is gonna shit himself when he finds out."

"He's not gonna find out. Just like old RSW in there, they're going to think she's gone back to Berlin and then, eventually, she goes missing. No one's going to see or hear any of this if we don't want them to."

A camera's flash could be heard along with the clicking of the shutter.

"What about the tapes and photos?"

The southern man answered in a low voice. "We save 'em, just in case. You think about the leverage we'll have."

"Yeah, I guess we'll forge her reports for a bit, then she'll just go dark and we'll assume she was compromised?"

"Either that, or fake her death in Berlin by some method deemed natural."

"We won't clue the president in about us eliminating her."

"Hell no, we won't. He walked outta here with a hard-on. Good thing he's got Churchill coming, or he'd probably want her tonight."

There was a bit more banter, most of it revolving around the cleaning up of brain, bone and blood. The tape was almost done.

Then, the southern man spoke again.

"What do we do with the intel on the Hawaii attack?"

"President Whitestone said no one can know," the first man replied. "To me, that means no one. Me. You. Him."

"I'm good with that."

"If the Krauts don't spill the beans between now and then, we'll be in a war as soon as the attack happens."

"And get filthy rich," the southern man agreed.

"How up to date is the file of all the companies the contracts are going to?"

"It's current. I've got it broken down by—"

The tape ended.

Ludivine's face was streaked with tears. Max's face was markedly different.

His was one of sheer rage. His fists were balled. His entire body trembled.

A woman was killed because she'd done her job well. It seemed President Whitestone didn't know about her murder, but he damn sure had forewarning of the attack at Pearl Harbor.

Before Max and Ludivine could speak, they were halted by a thunderous crash out in the hallway.

Chapter Fifteen

It had taken 59 minutes to get to Orléans. After viewing the car that had been reported stolen, Edge used a payphone to call one of Mr. Winthrop's moles inside the Paris Police. Through that conversation, Edge confirmed that the Parisian and Orléans police wouldn't examine the stolen car until tomorrow. It obviously wasn't a high priority, especially on a Sunday night, and especially since it belonged to a drug pusher. Edge, who was fluent even though he wasn't French, went door to door at each of the six nearby houses. It being a Sunday evening, all but one of the residents were at home and answered their doors. At the third house, Edge spoke with the sleepy policeman who'd phoned in the out of place license plates. Winthrop and Timmons watched from the Mercedes. Once he'd been to all six houses, Edge returned to the car.

"You spoke to a cop?" Winthrop hissed.

"He's the one who called the car in. Don't worry about it."

"What did you tell him?"

"Told him I was a detective from Paris. Showed him the badge I carried during the Clichy heist. He's obviously not very bright, just a beat cop. He bought my entire story—didn't even ask how I got here so fast. I think he's drunk. Anyway, your boy isn't at any of these houses."

Winthrop crossed his arms.

"You can't know he's not in one of those houses," Timmons added, jumping into the fray. "He could be hiding. And that house right there is dark. He could've broken in."

"Relax. He's *not* in that house," Edge said, his tone snarky as he glared at Timmons in the rearview mirror.

"How do you know?"

"The cop told me who lives there—a family of six. They retire early. Stick to the USA, general. Europe is my territory."

"I don't like your attitude, son."

"I don't care, *branleur*, if you like my attitude or not. I'm not one of your Marines."

Winthrop couldn't help but chuckle.

Without warning, General Timmons swiftly looped his left arm around Edge's throat and seized, pulling his wrist with his right hand. Edge kicked his feet in the floorboard and gripped Timmons' forearm with both hands. Despite Mr. Winthrop's objections, the flailing driver fell unconscious within ten seconds. The general held the choke for just a moment more before releasing Edge, who slumped forward.

"What the hell are you doing?" Winthrop shouted, grabbing Edge before his weight depressed the horn.

"Little sparrowfart talks to me like that again, next time he won't wake up."

Edge came to slowly. His eyes were glazed as he turned to Mr. Winthrop.

"The general put you under," Winthrop explained, hitching his thumb backward.

"Don't try me again, son," Timmons warned, sitting back and jabbing an unlit cigar in his mouth.

Edge said nothing. It was clear he was just getting his wits about him. He vigorously shook his head to clear the cobwebs.

Mr. Winthrop eyed the neighborhood. Across the street was a stretch of woods, followed by a wide field with a few grazing goats. Beyond the field, partially obscured by trees, was a long building of some sort.

"Can you drive?" Winthrop asked.

"Huh?"

"Drive. Can you drive?" he snapped.

"Yeah," Edge muttered.

"Then head over there," Winthrop said, pointing. "And keep the lights off."

As they drew closer, they recognized they were looking at a primary school. It was rather new, very long and built on one rambling floor. Each classroom had outer facing doors that led to several fields and playgrounds. At the front of the school, two flagpoles were unadorned, their pulleys clicking lightly in the evening breeze.

"Today's Sunday," Winthrop pronounced.

"So?" Timmons replied.

"No school on Sunday. No school yesterday, either." Mr. Winthrop unwrapped a peppermint, popping it into his mouth as he spoke. "A school like this has all sorts of things for a man on the run: food, a place to rest, a place to heal—maybe even basic medicine. It probably has a telephone, too, if the man on the run desires to call someone. Most of all, since it's the weekend, it has all the privacy a person would need."

"What do you want me to do?" Edge asked.

"Keep the lights off. Pull into that parking lot over there. Don't anyone close your door. I don't want Max to know we're here."

"You think he's here?" Timmons asked.

"It's where I'd go," Winthrop answered. He checked his pistol. "We'll go in heavy."

"Before we go, we need a plan," Timmons replied. "You're the one that keeps singing this guy's praises. You give me a day in a building to be ready for three intruders and I'll like my chances."

"Fine. We'll make a plan. May we proceed?"

General Timmons rudely gestured his assent. He slid the cigar back into the case.

They exited the vehicle and Edge quietly opened the trunk. Mr. Winthrop handed out shotguns, black Winchesters. He slid the pistol under his belt and took a shotgun for himself, opening the tubular magazine. Then he placed several boxes of shells on the rear fender.

As Winthrop loaded his shotgun, he eyed Timmons. "How do you want to do this?"

The general spoke for a few minutes, outlining the infiltration and how they would cover one another. Mr. Winthrop had several suggestions, which Timmons agreed to. By the time the plan was settled, General Timmons seemed to have calmed down. He turned to Edge.

"Are you and I okay?"

"I guess," Edge said with a shrug.

"That ain't good enough. If you don't reassure me right now that you and I have no bad blood, we're gonna have another problem."

"English isn't his first language," Winthrop explained.

Timmons continued to glare at Edge. "He spoke it pretty good earlier."

"I shouldn't have said what I said," Edge answered. "I don't have hard feelings that you choked me."

"This is apropos for an elementary school," Winthrop hissed. "Are you two finished making up?"

Mollified, Timmons nodded. Edge nodded as well.

"Good." Winthrop crunched the peppermint and pumped his shotgun. "Once we're inside, kill *anyone* on sight."

***

While Timmons and Edge stood guard, Mr. Winthrop used a snap gun on one of the classroom doors around on the far side of the school. A snap gun is a specialized tool developed for defeating locks. It comes with a variety of rods to be inserted into a pin and tumbler lock. By pulling the trigger, an intruder is able to make all the pins "jump" at the same moment. With just the correct amount of pressure, a lock will turn while the pins have jumped, thus defeating the lock. Mr. Winthrop applied a light amount of tension to the knob, alternating the force as he squeezed the trigger of the snap gun. He tried this for about a minute before switching the rod to a longer and stiffer version. This did the trick after only three pulls. The knob turned. He opened the door and listened.

Silence.

Mr. Winthrop pocketed the snap gun and lifted his Winchester, clicking the safety off. He led the way into a darkened classroom. Because they'd entered the rear of the building, there was hardly any light at all bleeding in from the windows. And due to some high bookshelves between the windows and the inner wall, the far side of the classroom was pitch black. Again he halted and attuned his ears. There were no other sounds.

"We'll get to the hallway and go through the building like we planned," Winthrop whispered.

They eased forward. Just as Mr. Winthrop reached the door, evidenced by scant light from the hallway spilling underneath, Edge bumped a table and sent something crashing with a loud clatter.

Mr. Winthrop turned and glared, though no one could see his expression. Timmons bent down and lifted a piece from an erector set. He twisted the metal connector in the scant light. A child must have built a precarious tower and one light jolt sent it tumbling.

"If Max is here, he heard that. Now he'll be waiting," Winthrop whispered at Edge. "So we switch places. *You* lead the way."

Edge opened the classroom door. He stepped into the hallway, whipping his shotgun in both directions before motioning the two men to follow. There was better ambient light in the hall, allowing Mr. Winthrop to get a solid idea of the layout. The school's four hallways were laid out in a rectangular pattern. The classrooms were on the outer perimeter of the building. The interior of the building also had a series of rooms. The first they came to was an art room, evidenced by numerous paintings swaying from the walls, along with a kiln in the corner.

"Now that we know there are *two* main hallways, I'm afraid Max will slip out the other one," Winthrop whispered.

"Why don't I go around and move up the other hallway?" Edge offered. "If he realizes we're in this one, that's the way he'll leave."

"What if he's in an outer classroom?" Timmons asked. "Then he just opens a classroom door like we just came through and escapes."

"I don't think he'd camp out in a room with windows," Mr. Winthrop replied. "Too risky. He'll be in one of these center rooms."

"Don't you think he heard the crash?" Timmons asked.

Winthrop grasped the door of the classroom they'd just exited. Though he'd said so earlier, now he said, "Maybe not. Thick wood door here. The same thick wood door on those inner rooms. Maybe we got lucky."

"Whether he heard us or not, I'll be in the other hallway in case you flush him," Edge added. "Just clear each room as you go."

"I agree with him," Timmons replied, concurring with the man he'd choked a short while ago—strange bedfellows.

After allowing Edge one minute to make his way to the far hallway, the three men set out in the two long hallways. The art room had already been cleared. Winthrop and Timmons would enter each room and Edge would simply wait in the far hall, watching for Max fleeing. The next room was just ahead.

As they drew close, Mr. Winthrop was able to read the sign on the door: *Chambre de Musique.* He glanced at General Timmons, holding his shotgun at port arms. Tense and ready, the general nodded once.

Mr. Winthrop moved for the door.

***

Seconds before, Max listened with his ear to the door. He watched as Ludivine did as she'd been told, securing the tape reels and photos in the duffel bag with the money. She then pulled the light gaskets from the bottom of the two doors. Max turned off the overhead light, leaving the room illuminated by only the two strips of dull light spilling from the hallways. The light from the western door was much brighter due to the outdoor lights on that side of the school. While it was fairly dark, there was enough light to see one another's silhouette.

They were fairly certain the crashing sound they'd heard had come from the eastern side of the building. As Max listened, he swore he heard a sibilant sound coming through the wooden door.

Someone whispering?

He motioned to the western door. It was time to go. With the pistol tucked into his pants and the shotgun in his hands, Max stood at the ready. He clicked the safety off.

"Open the door and stand back," he whispered to Ludivine. "Then be ready to run."

"Do you really think someone's in the building?"

"Yes, I do."

Ludivine winced. Max shook his head.

"Be brave, Ludivine. Being scared won't help you now."

She nodded and took a series of deep breaths.

"You ready?"

Ludivine nodded.

"Open it as quietly as you can," Max said.

Just before she pulled the door open, he saw a slight shift in the light that bled underneath the door. It was a shadow, but she'd already begun pulling the door open.

Too late.

When the door was open by about a foot, Max saw a short man with a long shotgun in his hands. The opening door startled the man and he began to swing the shotgun in Max's direction.

Max pulled the shotgun's trigger, watching as the rubber pellets caught the man in his throat, sending him skittering backward. The man writhed on the ground, hissing and gurgling as both of his hands clutched his battered neck.

Ludivine's shriek could be heard despite the deafening shotgun blast.

Regardless of his dismay that they'd been tracked here, Max hadn't survived all these years without developing split-second instincts. He yanked Ludivine's hand and they lurched into the hallway, pulling the door shut behind them. She grabbed the man's shotgun.

Once his brain had a moment to catch up, Max realized he knew the man he'd just shot—he was the driver from the theft at the Place de Clichy.

Max had little doubt the driver had come alone.

***

Mr. Winthrop had just placed his hand on the music room's doorknob when he heard the blast. He instinctively jumped back. General Timmons was also startled, but moved forward and carefully opened the door. By the time he found the light, the other door had clicked shut and they saw evidence that Max had been in the room. Both men charged through the room but lost all zest by the time they reached the opposite door.

Max could easily have shot the driver and been waiting outside the opposite door for them. If they dared open the door, Max could kill them both.

"Go ahead," Timmons gestured. "I'll cover you."

"You go," Winthrop urged.

Shaking his head in frustration, the general quietly twisted the doorknob. After shutting his eyes for a moment, he yanked the door open and lifted his shotgun, whipping it side to side.

Edge was writhing on the floor up against the far wall. Mr. Winthrop moved into the hallway, clearing both directions. No sign of Max.

Edge's breathing was ragged and labored. He held both hands to his throat.

"Which way?" Mr. Winthrop asked.

Edge gestured to the nearest classroom door.

Again, Mr. Winthrop approached the door with caution. But this time, he opened the door, able to see clearly in this western classroom that was bathed in purple light from the parking lot.

There was no sign of Max.

Winthrop and Timmons charged through the classroom, barreling out the door with their guns ready.

They heard the screeching of tires, getting outside just in time to see their own Mercedes roaring up the street, back the way they'd come.

Edge had left the keys in the ignition.

Both men slumped, their eyes on the ground. Neither spoke for nearly a minute.

To make matters worse, the classroom door had clicked shut behind them, locking in the process. Mr. Winthrop had to open it with the snap gun, once again, only this time it took five frustrating minutes. Because of his injury, Edge never appeared to open the door.

By the time they got back inside, Mr. Winthrop and General Timmons were in a heated argument. They argued about the snap gun. They argued that they'd lost their car. They argued over who should be notified. And they argued about Edge.

But Mr. Winthrop quelled the argument quickly, decisively.

"Why didn't you come open the damn door?" General Timmons bellowed as they walked back into the hallway.

Edge was now sitting up, massaging his throat with his right hand. "I can barely talk," he said, his voice hoarse. As he worked his jaw, Mr. Winthrop lifted his shotgun.

Eyes wide, Edge stared at the black maw of the Winchester. He issued a partial protest before...

BOOM.

Edge's head exploded backward across the linoleum floor. It looked as if a glass jar of raspberry preserves had been flung and smashed on the floor.

"What the hell?" Timmons yelled, ringing out his ears with his index fingers.

Winthrop ignored him and went back into the music room.

There was all sorts of evidence there. Food wrappers. Empty bottles of milk. There were two mattresses on the floor.

Two.

One of the mattresses had a mostly white pillow on one end. The other mattress and pillow was discolored by rusty stains.

Blood.

So, Max was injured, and he wasn't alone.

But most interesting to Mr. Winthrop was the lead-lined briefcase, splayed open at the front of the room. It was empty, save for metal shavings where it'd been drilled. Next to the briefcase, on the table, was a Magnetophon-style Telefunken reel-to-reel tape player. Winthrop pointed at both items as he eyed General Timmons.

"So, now he knows," Timmons groused.

"They know. *They*. He's with someone. Look at the beds."

Timmons knelt beside the bed without the blood stains. He lifted the pillow, pointing to the faint buff coloring on the pillowcase. "Makeup."

"Ortega was right."

Mr. Winthrop hurried to the front of the school where he made a series of urgent phone calls. After he hung up from the last call, Timmons berated him over the shooting of Edge.

"I lost my temper, but it'll be cleaned up," Winthrop said, his tone reasonable. "May I please be alone?"

Timmons placed his unlit cigar in his mouth and walked outside, wedging the door open.

In the darkness, Mr. Winthrop sat in *la chambre du principal* as his people raced from Paris. He could smell Timmons' cigar wafting in through the poorly sealed windows. When he closed his eyes, he could still see the sharp colors of Edge's cerebrospinal fluid and brain matter. And because of the ringing in his ears, he could still recollect the shotgun blasts.

But what he couldn't do is envision Max Warfield's next move.

Mr. Winthrop dipped his head, resting it in his hands.

The current situation was far worse than he thought possible.

Chapter Sixteen

After meeting with the new president, Lyndon Johnson of Texas, Secret Service Director Lynch returned to his office. He didn't greet Julie as he walked past her desk. Sensing his foul mood, Julie made him a fresh pot of coffee, placing it before him and pouring him a cup. He grunted what might have been an acknowledgment. She knew better than to ask about the meeting, nor did she mention her progress on the Paris murder. Once he was off and running on a telephone call, Julie shut his door and resumed her work. Within minutes, she received a phone call that the files on Clayton Fairchild were ready for the director. She walked down to Records and returned with the stacks of folders, arranging them neatly on her desk. Julie looked at Fairchild's personnel file first, reviewing his history as a government employee.

Fairchild graduated Princeton with dual degrees in mathematics and history in 1930, at which time he accepted a position as an investment banker with a firm in Manhattan. Though Julie didn't have experience with banks and such, she could only envision how difficult the environment must have been at that time, after the Great Crash. He remained with the same firm until 1935, when he joined the United States Army, receiving a commission as a second lieutenant in Army Intelligence. His promotions were swift and he achieved the rank of major by 1940. Soon thereafter, Fairchild worked in a joint capacity among all branches of military in the office that would, in 1941, become known as the Coordinator of Information. It was created to do exactly as it was named, primarily to keep the intelligence branches of each service from stepping on one another and duplicating efforts. Fairchild was listed as having transitioned directly to the Office of Strategic Services upon its creation in 1942, where he remained until he departed the OSS in 1946, at the rank of lieutenant colonel.

Fairchild's decorations were extensive, including glowing citations from Wild Bill Donovan and John Magruder. Most of Fairchild's service descriptions in Europe were without significant detail, as only England and France were listed, along with a few bland points about the collective overall mission. Hundreds of lines of detail had been redacted. Julie held the paper up to the light, disappointed that whomever had done the redacting had used a special chemical pen that left no clue as to the letters that had once filled the pages.

She then studied Fairchild's extensive Secret Service files, finding little useful to her search. She couldn't help but be impressed by further remarks and citations of his distinguished service. Julie then scrutinized his dates of service, noting that he'd been posted in France in late 1946. She recalled Danny Jackson's testimony that Fairchild had safeguarded the briefcase at Place de Clichy soon after the new office was opened. In Julie's opinion, that meant the briefcase could very well be some sort of leftover intelligence from the war.

She reread his pre-war and OSS files. Then she took the time to scrutinize Fairchild's numerous citations. One, penned by Wild Bill Donovan, contained the following passage:

```
Clayton Fairchild risked his life numerous
times in his handling of human assets who
were located behind enemy lines. Time and
time again, he put himself in jeopardy in
order to jealously protect and communicate
with his assets. Despite a number of
setbacks far beyond his control, he always
acted in the best interests of the United
States of America.
```

Jealously protect...

Something strange about the last sentence...

Setbacks? What sort of setbacks?

Julie eyed Fairchild's personal information. He was from Pennsylvania, the middle child of five children. She noticed he'd never taken a wife. Flipping back to the front jacket, she viewed his photo. He'd been rather handsome, in a bookish way. His thin face was intelligent and lively, but distinguished. There was a second photo of him in the file, from his Secret Service days. His hairline had receded a bit and there seemed to be a hollowness under his eyes. In fact, he appeared rather sad. She flipped the photo over, noticing "1946" was typed at the bottom. After studying both photos, Julie was of the opinion many women would have found him attractive.

Narrowing her eyes, Julie allowed her intuition to run wild. What could have happened in his handling of an asset behind enemy lines? What sort of setback? She envisioned him slipping into a war-torn city and meeting with his operative. Long, deep conversations—the type with no filters. He'd been a middle child, able to relate to someone who felt left out, or left all alone in a strange land. He had no wife back home, faithfully waiting, making him rush. Clayton Fairchild never hurried when meeting with his spies. He made them feel important.

Long, deep conversations.

Intimacy.

Julie lifted his Army photo, when he was most handsome.

She suddenly was struck with a strong feeling this entire ordeal had something to do with a woman.

A female operative.

Yes, she was far down a rabbit trail, but this was how she worked. Rabbit trails sometimes led somewhere…

Human assets…female assets…a female spy…Clayton was in love.

Jealously protect…

Hazarding an ass chewing, Julie buzzed the director.

"I just got off the phone," he snapped, clearly irritated. "Who wants me now?"

"I actually have a question, chief. Who here in the building was with the OSS in Europe during the War?"

"Why do you want to know that?"

"Didn't you tell *me* to work the case?"

"Can't you look that kind of thing up?"

"Sure, but it's easier just to ask you."

"Oh, for cryin'—try George Trevaglia."

"Is he here today?"

"Better be."

"Thank you."

Julie flipped open her directory and called Special Agent Trevaglia. He worked in the basement as a statistician and actuary. He hadn't always performed these functions, but he was notoriously difficult to get along with. According to a well-known rumor, Trevaglia had insulted Vice President Barkley's young 2nd wife in 1950. She'd asked him a question about the public perception of her and Trevaglia answered—truthfully, using a rather salacious description of her that had been going around.

Since then, Trevaglia had been in the basement, a place he seemed to enjoy. But he didn't usually take well to guests or calls. Julie, however, had a special way of handling him.

"Trevaglia," he growled, answering his phone.

"Well, well, well…if it isn't my favorite agent."

"Hedstrom, what do you want? I've got more work to do than—"

"I can shake a stick at? I know, George, and you really need some new material."

"*What*—do—you—want?"

"The OSS."

"What about it?"

"You served in the OSS during the war, in Europe?"

"That's no secret."

"How well did you know Clayton Fairchild?"

"Julie...can we talk about this later? I'm breaking down multiplicative inverses on more theories and scenarios than you could—"

"Fathom? That's fascinating, George, but I'm on a mission for the director. Please answer the question."

"I knew Clayton quite well. He was a friend...and I don't have many."

"Did he have a lady friend?"

"A lady friend?"

"Yes...a woman."

"He had several."

"Any that stand out?"

Pause. "Yes."

"Tell me about her."

The phone crackled as Trevaglia exhaled loudly.

"I can't, Julie."

"Shall I patch the director in? He wants to know."

Trevaglia mumbled something—possibly Italian curse words.

"Tell me," she said. "The quicker you do it, the quicker you can go back to your counting of beans."

"I'm not an accountant."

"Lovely...now, c'mon, Georgie. Out with it."

"I never knew too many details. I know she was in Berlin and highly placed. He handled her for years and I think he hoped to marry her once he could bring her out."

"What happened?"

"She went missing."

"What do you mean?"

"She went missing. That's all I know. That's all anyone knew. That's the truth."

"When?"

"Maybe forty-one or forty-two? Those years run together, even for me. It was early in the war."

"Why would an agent go missing?"

He was silent for a moment. "Why do you think?"

"She was compromised?"

"Maybe. But she could have gotten hit by a streetcar. She wouldn't be the first agent to die in a true accident, but in this case we felt something more nefarious was involved. We had other people in Berlin who reported she simply disappeared. The Germans put on a big search, but that could have all been window dressing. I remember several agents reporting that their search was genuine."

"Did Agent Fairchild ever confirm that she died?"

"Not that I'm aware of. She vanished and that was that."

"How did he take the news?"

"Like the professional he was. But I could tell it ate him up on the inside."

"Do you remember her name?"

"You sure this is for the director?"

"I can patch him in, Georgie."

He snorted. "I wish you'd quit saying that, and I wish you'd quit calling me that. Her name was Lucy Thaler." He spelled her last name. "She was German-American and if I get in trouble for this, I'm holding *you* responsible."

Julie quizzed George for a few more minutes before thanking him and letting him get back to his matrices. After she hung up the phone, she wrote the woman's name and information across the top of a fresh sheet of paper.

Lucy Thaler—German-American—agent in Berlin—1941 or '42.

Vanished.

***

It was early Sunday evening. Gaspard Lacroix was still aglow from his dizzying night with Evelyn Durand. No, they hadn't slept together, but the spark had been there, and was still there for Gaspard. He'd walked to "36" after going to his flat for a shower and fresh clothes. He was dressed casually in a sweater and slacks with his favorite pea coat. It wasn't unusual for detectives to stop in at 36 on their weekend off. Crime never sleeps and cases often find a way of mushrooming on Saturdays and Sundays. This time, nothing of note seemed to have happened to any of his investigations. Of course, he was most interested in the case involving his new American fancy, and the dead Secret Service agent from the Place de Clichy.

Gaspard first eyed the preliminary report from the medical examiner. Just as the initial forensics had led them to believe, Special Agent Lang had been first shot by rubber shotgun pellets. There was rubber residue on his clothing and his neck, along with early bruising and damage to his skin. The medical examiner cited the cause of death as a second gunshot from a high-powered rifle. Gaspard recalled the scene vividly, and the examiner's notes seemed to keyhole with Gaspard's memory.

The deadly bullet—preliminary forensics indicated a .308 round—entered the deceased just below his left clavicle. It pierced the left atrium of his heart, his left lung and exited his back after it nicked his spinal column. The medical examiner suggested that the victim was probably dead in seconds. After reading the report three times, Gaspard set it aside.

Next, he studied the blotter, starting with Friday. Very little interested him. There weren't as many crimes as there typically would be on a November weekend. He guessed the lack of activity could be attributed to the stunning news from the United States. Many people had stayed in after hearing of Kennedy's assassination. Even today, there seemed to be half the people out on the streets as there normally would be this time of year.

When Gaspard ran through the reported crimes a second time, he did pause at the details surrounding the theft of an automobile in the 8th Arrondissement. Gaspard knew the area well—it was in the western quadrant of the city, teeming with shops and restaurants. He pulled the daily reports from the ledger underneath the blotter. Each report consisted of the remaining dandelion-yellow third sheet from a standard triplicate carbon form. After flipping through the reports, he finally found the correct one.

Gaspard read the desk officer's report, halting at the notes about the victim—a known narcotics dealer. Like so many other criminals, they often acted indignant when *they* were the actual victims of a crime. The victim reported a "brazen man" who'd robbed him of his cash and car at gunpoint. The armed robber was said to be of average height and a little on the thin side, but extremely strong. The victim had claimed the assailant beat him without warning. The desk officer noted that the victim was "heavily bruised and appeared to have taken quite an ass whipping." The victim claimed that another man—Gaspard correctly assumed it was probably another dealer—had attempted to help the victim stave off the robber, and had slashed the robber's head along his scalp and ear. Gaspard noted that the desk officer planned to send a patrol car to the alleged scene but there was no annotated follow-up.

Gaspard walked to the cubby that doubled as a kitchenette. He poured a cup of coffee and lit a cigarette. Afterward, he sat at his desk, resting his chin in his hand as he envisioned the scene. Could the suspect from the Place de Clichy have robbed this drug dealer in an effort to get French francs and transportation? If so, this would certainly change the scope of Gaspard's investigation.

He scribbled the report number and salient notes on his notepad before closing the blotter and returning the report to the ledger. Then he walked around the corner to Dispatch, asking the two secretaries about the open investigation.

"Do you know if anyone went to the scene?"

Both secretaries shook their heads. "No idea," one said. "First I've heard about it."

"What kind of car?" the second secretary asked.

Glanced at his pad. "A fifty-nine Renault Frégate, blue in color."

"I thought so." The second secretary looked at her own notepad. She ran her finger down the page. "I actually took a call on that same car a few hours ago."

"You did?" Gaspard asked, straightening.

"Sergeant Patten handled it."

"Patten?" Gaspard knew Patten, a lousy police officer who'd purportedly purchased his stripes through bribes and kickbacks. He was slippery, but no one ever seemed to be able to pin anything untoward on him. The current captain, a wise man, had thankfully gotten Patten off the street and tucked him away in Dispatch.

"I gave Sergeant Patten the information personally," the second secretary replied.

"When?"

"I didn't note the time." She shrugged. "An hour ago? Maybe two?"

"Where is Patten?"

"He left early."

"What was in the report?"

The secretary went back to her notes, reading. "An off-duty policeman down in Orléans phoned in a Parisian plate. He said he normally wouldn't have called it in, but the car had what appeared to be dried blood on the seat."

"Dried blood?" Gaspard asked.

"Yes. He said there was quite a bit."

Gaspard recalled the initial report stating that the assailant had been cut on his scalp. The detective leaned forward on the secretary's desk. "Who did Patten send the call to?"

"I don't know," the secretary replied. "But he did ask us who was working the theft of the car. It's Detective Roux."

"Is Roux here?"

"I saw him earlier. He typically works weekends."

"Do you know if Patten told him?"

The secretary shook her head.

"Doesn't matter," Gaspard said.

Though this was urgent news, and he had a particular hunch that this assailant was his man, he took the time to offer his thanks to both women. Despite their jobs not having much authority, he'd long ago learned that the secretaries and assistants were key to him achieving his goals.

He walked down the corridor to the auto theft unit. It was very quiet on a Sunday evening, with only a few officers milling about. Gaspard found Detective Roux packing his things for the evening. They stepped into the meeting room.

"Roux, did you talk to Patten earlier?" Gaspard asked, shutting the door. He knew Roux extremely well and considered him a good friend. Pleasantries weren't necessary.

"Yeah, unfortunately."

"What'd he want?"

"He asked about a Renault that was stolen over near Fouquet." Roux shrugged. "Some dipshit drug dealer got what he deserved."

"And?"

"And what?"

"Did he tell you the car was reported in Orléans, *today*?"

"No. Was it?" Roux asked, his brow furrowing lightly. He didn't seem surprised. Stolen cars popped up all over the place on a daily basis.

"Damn right, by a cop. We got the call an hour ago, maybe two. The cop only called because the car had Parisian plates and...get this...*blood* on the front seat."

"Makes sense. The drug dealer claimed someone...probably the asshole's partner...had helped him and, in the process, cut the assailant's head with a blade. A real Good Samaritan. I know I always slash people on the street when I'm helping others."

Gaspard gripped his friend's shoulder. "Listen, Roux, I think there's more to it than that. I think it could be related to my Place de Clichy investigation. You've heard about it?"

"A little bit. Honestly, I didn't pay it much mind. Like everyone, I've been consumed by the assassination of Kennedy."

Gaspard softened his expression. "I know you're getting ready to leave but I have a big favor to ask. Will you ride down to Orléans with me?"

"When?"

"Now."

"Merde." Roux slumped. "Is it that important?"

"It is."

Roux stared at his friend for a moment. "Let me call Melinda. She's going to be pissed."

"Blame me."

"Oh, don't worry, I plan on it." Roux cocked his head. "Are you going to notify Orléans that we're coming?"

"Nope."

"You'll take the blow-back for that, too?"

"With pleasure," Gaspard replied.

"You may have to buy Melinda and me dinner for this," Roux said, lifting the telephone. "An expensive dinner."

While Detective Roux spoke with his wife, Gaspard phoned Evelyn Durand. She assured him that she was fine.

"Is there a policeman still posted on your landing?"

"He left."

"What?"

"He knocked on the door and told me he was being called back in. Really, it's fine."

Gaspard stifled a curse.

"I'm okay, Gaspard."

"Well, I'm headed out of town but I should be back later tonight," he said. "May I stop by?"

"Sure, I'd like that."

"I hope to be back by midnight," he replied. "It might be later than that."

"Just come whenever you get back. Don't worry if it's too late."

Though he was frustrated that his sentry had been pulled away, Gaspard soared over the prospect of seeing Evelyn.

A short time later, the two detectives sped through the outer suburbs of Paris, headed south on Route Européenne 5. At their current speed, they'd be there in a little more than an hour.

***

With no moon visible, the sky above Orléans was stygian black. Mr. Winthrop stood alone on the front steps of the school. He was internally debating whether or not to sanitize the school of the multiple crimes that had occurred there. By doing so, he'd be losing precious manpower that could help him find Max Warfield, his fugitive on the run in the stolen black Mercedes.

Earlier, General Timmons had slid aside what remained of Edge's head, displaying the scars in the linoleum beside his ear. Even if the crime scene were to be cleaned, there would still be significant evidence that something untoward had occurred at the school—beginning with a blood stained scar on the floor of the western hallway.

However, Mr. Winthrop felt all other traces of Max's presence could be removed. They could move the mattresses back to the nurse's office and change the sheets. The floors could be cleaned, the trashcans emptied. If all people saw tomorrow morning was a gouge in the hallway that smelled of bleach, the last thing they would suspect was a gunshot.

But cleaning the building would require people, and Winthrop couldn't afford to lose a single man tonight. Or could he?

"What's the call?" Timmons asked. He'd been smoking his cigar in the deep shadows around the corner of the building.

Mr. Winthrop wanted to ask his opinion, but he made it a practice to never ask the opinion of anyone he despised—so he didn't. Instead, he removed his eyeglasses and carefully cleaned them with his handkerchief, speaking as he worked.

"They'll be here in less than twenty minutes. I've made my decision. We'll leave behind a team to sanitize the school and remove the body. I want them in and out in no more than an hour."

"I concur. However, I still don't know why you killed your own man."

"I didn't ask your opinion," Winthrop replied evenly. "And Edge was no longer useful to us. Max knew his face. I don't need that sort of risk going forward."

"Could've sent him home, instead."

"But I didn't."

"Max knows your face, too. Ever thought of that?"

Mr. Winthrop put his glasses back on and glared at the general. "Let's get something straight: I'm in charge here. If you have any hope of getting what you first approached us for, then I'd suggest you put all your efforts into *assisting* me."

Despite the darkness, the general gestured to their surroundings. "We're out here on a school porch, waiting on our team. What would you like me to do at this very moment, to assist you?"

"You could shut up."

Timmons drew on his short cigar and offered no response. Mr. Winthrop ambled to the glass windows at the front of the school. He could see the lump of Edge's corpse well down the hallway. He put his hands in his overcoat pockets and spoke in a murmur to himself.

"We get rid of the body and the blood, and clean everything else up. No one will have any idea. This is a big building; hundreds of people go in and out every day during the week. So, there's some floor damage and a few things out of place, but that doesn't mean anyone will suspect a crime."

Timmons, standing within earshot behind Mr. Winthrop, turned his head but remained quiet. Neither man spoke to the other until their associates arrived twenty-three minutes later in a convoy of five cars. In short order, Mr. Winthrop had relayed his plan to the group. They left behind four men tasked with removing the body and cleaning the school. Though they pondered taking the bloodstained Renault from across the street, in the end they decided to leave it alone. Too much risk. Its presence here proved nothing other than the fact that it had been stolen in Paris.

Once the foursome had begun their work in the school, the remainder of the posse, led by Mr. Winthrop and General Timmons, drove a short distance away. In the murkiness of a church parking lot, they made a hasty plan to search for the Mercedes 300SE. Winthrop provided the license plate number and plenty of cash for police and underworld bribes.

"He's wounded. He's scared. He's probably making bad decisions. I want the car found by sundown tomorrow. If not, there *will* be consequences," Mr. Winthrop warned, poking the map laid out on the hood of the Citroen.

When there were no further questions, the four cars raced away from the church. By coincidence, the old church, built in Gothic style, was adorned on each corner by a steeple. The four steeples represented north, south, east and west—because the church founders wanted to symbolize they welcomed people universally. Incidentally, Mr. Winthrop's plan called for each car to race away from Orléans in each direction.

But in their errand, there was no welcoming involved. Their mission was death.

Although General Timmons irritated Mr. Winthrop to no end, he decided it would be better to keep the general with him. The two men departed the church together with a new driver, one who'd served as a gendarme after the war. Mr. Winthrop handpicked him many months before due to his ability to ferret out liars and get to the bottom of a situation.

Because Max had originally come south, Mr. Winthrop chose south as the direction they would continue. They sped from Orléans on A71, headed toward Vierzon.

***

Seventy-eight kilometers ahead of Mr. Winthrop and General Timmons, Max and Ludivine had settled into a brisk pace on the same highway, A71 *autoroute l'Arverne*. They now passed over the long and gradual hills of the rich growing area of the Loire valley. On this moonless night, the forests were inky oceans on both sides of the ribbon of highway. With the darkness and the gentle rising and falling of the elevation, it was as if the rolling black sea had been parted for their safe passage. With no appreciable Sunday night traffic, they'd made excellent time to their first waypoint of Vierzon.

Ludivine smoked nervously. Max could see the shake of her cigarette.

"Was that the man who held you captive?" she asked.

"No. It was his driver."

"How did you know to shoot him so quickly?"

"It's hard to explain, Ludivine."

"Yes, but how? Tell me," she demanded. "Tell me how you can shoot a man so quickly? What if he'd been the janitor, there to empty the trash and mop the floors?"

"I saw this shotgun," Max said, reaching under the seat and tugging it forward. "I saw the gun, and I saw *him*."

"You saw the gun and his face, recognized both, and shot him inside of a second? No one makes decisions that quickly." Her words were accusative, and coming forcefully. Max grew quiet, letting her vent, which she did.

"Do you think the man who held you captive was with him?" she asked.

"I do."

"Where?"

"He probably came up the other hallway. Remember, it was dark."

"How did they find us?"

"Had to be the dope dealer's car. I parked it on a nearby street. I'm sure someone saw the blood in the car and called it in. Mr. Winthrop found out about it, checked the nearby houses and then noticed the school. He isn't stupid."

Eventually she stopped talking. Vierzon passed in a blur. Max floored the accelerator, pushing the Mercedes, trying to create distance.

He knew they weren't far behind.

The engine roared, matched by the rushing wind.

Max attempted to talk to Ludivine about other things. She wanted none of it. He patted her leg. She shoved his hand away.

"Do I disgust you?" he asked.

"Don't be silly. I'm just pissed at life."

"What can I do?"

Nothing.

"Ludivine."

"I don't know, maybe some music?"

He turned on the radio, adjusting the dial for a station. Finally, he settled on Radio Luxembourg, broadcast through Paris via the most powerful transmitter in France.

The kilometers passed slowly as the music played. There was no conversation in the icy cabin of the Mercedes. Then...

"We interrupt tonight's programming to bring you additional breaking news out of the United States. In Texas, Lee Harvey Oswald, the man accused of assassinating American President Kennedy, has been shot. Repeat, Lee Harvey Oswald has been shot while being transported. He was allegedly shot by a man who stepped from a crowd of onlookers." Papers riffling. "There are conflicting reports of Oswald's condition. Nothing has been confirmed as of this moment. However, we must note, several Dallas news agencies are reporting that Oswald has died from his injuries." The announcer could be heard whispering something to someone. "Pardon me. Radio Luxembourg is now confirming that Lee Harvey Oswald is indeed dead. He died as a result of a gunshot from a man who is now in the custody of the Dallas Police. This follows the tumultuous news of Friday when President John Kennedy was killed by gunfire, allegedly from Lee Harvey Oswald. Also shot was Texas governor John Connally. At last report, the governor was in serious but stable condition. We're still gathering details about this latest development. Say tuned to Radio Luxembourg for more information at the bottom of the hour."

Max listened to the report without emotion. When the music resumed, he turned to Ludivine. She was staring at the radio, catatonic, as more tears trailed down her face. Finally, she turned to him and said, "What on earth is going on?"

Unfortunately, Max had no answer. He maintained his high speed as he tried to picture the scene in Dallas.

Pandemonium. Fear. Anger. Bewilderment.

"Is all of this somehow related to our situation?" she asked.

"I don't know. But after hearing that tape, I'm beginning to wonder."

"Will they find us?"

"We have to be smarter than them. It's not the police who are after us. This is someone else."

"What about this car?" she asked.

"It's all we've got."

"Will they be looking for it?"

"Oh yes."

"So what are we going to do?"

"Ludivine, the only thing we can do is to get as much distance between us and Orléans as possible, while it's dark. Then, we hide the car—better this time—and we hole up somewhere."

"Then what?"

"I don't know." He looked at her and shrugged. "I truly don't. But once we're hidden, we can make a new plan."

She was quiet for a moment. "How's your head?"

Max couldn't help but laugh. "Well…it hurts."

Ludivine reached over and grasped his hand. He tugged her to him. The closeness of Ludivine's body emboldened his spirit. An hour later, as Ludivine slept with her head on his shoulder, Max took the exit at Montmarault, driving east in the direction of Moulins, Bourg-en-Bresse and their next destination…

Les Alpes.

Chapter Seventeen

The annex portion of the Treasury Building nearly collapsed on itself when the news of Lee Harvey Oswald's killing came in. Julie fielded no less than 10 calls from other agency heads, each insisting to speak to the director. Rather than spend time on one phone call, the director rushed back to the White House for a joint session with the new president and the heads of numerous other agencies. By this point, the word "conspiracy" was utilized liberally at the Secret Service—an absolute no-no up until today. But with the killing of Oswald, even the most skeptical of agents began to feel they were up against some sort of unstoppable force. The man in custody, Jack Ruby, was a small-time player in Dallas with connections to organized crime. Several agencies were familiar with him, but had never looked at him as anything more than a minor cog in the Dallas underworld. Julie did everything she could for the director before he left. Afterward, in her wing of the building, things calmed down.

With some measure of peace, she forced herself to refocus on her own "conspiracy." Julie eyed her yellow notepad, staring at what she'd written in her own Spencerian script: *Lucy Thaler—German-American—agent in Berlin—1941 or '42. Vanished.*

Realizing she was now overstepping her bounds, Lucy took a series of steady breaths before lifting the phone and dialing Langley, Virginia, where the CIA headquarters was located. She asked for the deputy director, but he wasn't in at the moment. He was probably at the same briefing Julie's director was attending. She could only imagine the accusations flying about the briefing room.

The deputy director's secretary was named Harriet. Julie had spoken with her before on numerous occasions.

"Harriet, would you be willing to do a favor for me?"

"Name it."

"It's a big one, Harriet. You might have to twist a few arms for me."

"On a day like today, it's amazing what a secretary can accomplish. Let me hear it."

"Director Lynch and several agents are looking into a crime unrelated to the assassination. After quite a bit of investigation, it's led them to a rather bizarre lead that reaches pretty far back. One of the people he asked me to learn more about actually worked in some capacity for the OSS. Her name was Lucy Thaler." Julie spelled the last name. "She was German-American and lived in Berlin. Do me a favor and find what you can about her, as quickly as possible? If there's a full file on her, I can have a courier run by. If what you find is minimal, just call me."

"Sure, I'll help." Harriet reconfirmed the spelling.

"You sure you don't mind?"

"Not at all." Harriet paused a beat. "Julie, am I going to get in trouble if I poke around on this?"

"Just keep it quiet, if you can. If someone gets touchy about it, send them my way."

Harriet agreed to help and promised an update within two hours.

It took Harriet 93 minutes.

She phoned Julie.

"No need to send a courier because all I have is a single sheet of paper from the file. Her name was Lucy Evangeline Thaler. She lived in Manhattan until she was sixteen, when she moved to Germany with her father after her parents divorced. Her father was German by birth and moved back during the rise of the National Socialist Party."

"From what I recall, most people tried to get out," Julie remarked. "Not go back."

"That's the way I remember it, too. Okay, you ready?"

Julie flipped to a clean sheet of paper. "Fire away."

"Other than the personal information about her birthdate and address in Manhattan, there are question marks about the other items. First is 'University of Giessen, language studies,' followed by a question mark. Next is 'Potsdam, hotelier's school, followed by a question mark.' Next is 'initial contact made in Berlin, 267,' followed by a question mark. I'm assuming that number is the Julian date. The last paragraph has been redacted, and it was long one."

"Oh my…you're kidding me?"

"No. And they used a burner. I can't see the typing underneath."

"That's it? There's nothing else?"

"There's one last line. Last contact July 1941. Thaler posted as a missing person by Berlin Kripo and Abwehr."

"Do you have any way of knowing who was working with her, Harriet?"

"There's nothing here."

"Anyone who would know?"

"I'll have to think about that. We've got some people here who were around then."

"Harriet, do you remember Clayton Fairchild?"

"Of course, I know he ended up in the Secret Service but I've heard all the stories of him from his time in the OSS."

"Will you see what you have on him? From what we've learned, he was Lucy Thaler's handler. I'm curious if there were other handlers who might still be around?"

Harriet clucked her tongue. "If they even exist, those old records are stored across the street." She hesitated for a moment. "This is for the director?"

"Yes."

"Want me to try?"

"You'll be a Godsend."

"Let me see what I can do."

Julie thanked her and hung up the phone. She stared at her notes, unable to take her eyes away from the last line she'd written.

Last contact with L.T. July 1941.

***

In Orléans, the two Parisian detectives viewed the stolen Renault with flashlights. They saw the bloodstains. The stains were on the driver's seat, down the backrest and at the base of the seat, all consistent with someone bleeding from their head. They confirmed this Renault was indeed the correct car, not only by the license plate, but also by the vehicle identification number, known as a VIN. The VIN was stamped on a plate under the hood, which Detective Roux accessed via a catch latch above the grille.

Gaspard briefly flirted with the idea of calling the Orléans police, not to tell them they were in their jurisdiction, but to find the officer who'd initially spotted the car. But what good would that do? He hadn't reported seeing anyone leave the car, and also said he spot-checked the nearby homes and found no evidence of anything out of order.

"And his mother lives here on this street," Gaspard said to Roux. "Let's at least give him enough credit that he'd know if something was amiss."

"Their forensics might find something in the car that could garner us an identity."

"On Sunday night?" Gaspard countered. "They'll have to cross reference the prints against thousands of others and you know as well as I do, they won't even begin until tomorrow."

Roux nodded his agreement. "Let's wait."

The two detectives left the stolen car and drove around the rural area. They were a few miles outside of the city of Orléans, on the western edge of the small city. Here, while some probably drove into the city for work, most either worked at the nearby textile factory or farmed their land. And that's pretty much all Gaspard and Roux found nearby—farmland. He wondered if the perpetrator might have swapped the stolen car for another car. But, if so, would he have been stupid enough to steal a car near where he dumped the old one? Gaspard didn't think so, and neither did Roux, now that he knew the entire story.

The only other structure nearby was a primary school. It appeared to be rather new. And it was the weekend, meaning the school should be empty—a possible hiding spot. The two officers drove to the school and illuminated the front door with their lights. As they peered through the glass at the front portico, an old flatbed truck rumbled around to the side and slowed. The driver eyed the two detectives.

"Let's see who that is," Gaspard said.

Detective Roux lifted his badge and began walking toward the truck. The driver turned off the engine and opened the door. Someone got out of the passenger side, too. The two people were obscured by darkness on this mostly cloudy, moonless night.

"Careful," Gaspard warned, watching as Detective Roux put his hand on his pistol for safe measure.

They were greeted by the slow sound of an older man speaking French in what is known as *l'accent bourguignon*, with plodding speech and rolled R's. Though not always the case, many in France looked down their noses at this particular accent, associating it with farmers and isolated mountain people. As the two detectives drew closer, they could see both people were indeed older, probably in their 70s. The man asked what the problem was and how could he help.

Gaspard and Detective Roux stepped forward and had a brief conversation with the man, learning that he and his wife were the weekend janitors. They worked for the Orléans-Tours Education Authority and cleaned 6 local schools every weekend. This was always their last, as it was near their home in nearby Bucy-Saint-Liphard.

Without ever telling the older couple that they hailed from Paris, the two detectives explained that they had reason to believe there was a man wanted for questioning nearby.

"He probably never came near the school but, before you and your wife go to work, we'd like to take a look around inside—just in case."

Minutes later, after the janitor unlocked the doors and turned on the lights, the two detectives searched the school, room by room. The search took nearly a half an hour. They found no one. The janitors waited in their truck until Gaspard called them in.

"Would you mind taking a look around to see if anything is out of place?" he asked. "It looks normal to us, but we don't know what normal actually is."

The older woman had wiry gray hair pulled back in a haphazard bun. She was short and hunched with an abnormal amount of wrinkles and leathery skin, probably from decades spent working in the sun. She began pushing a wheeled rubbish container down the hallway, emptying trashcans outside each door as she went. This was a bit frustrating for the detectives as she didn't seem to be following their directive. Instead, they followed her husband down the opposite hallway while he scrutinized the school, doing as they asked.

"Looks like it looks every Sunday," he said, ambling along with his wide-brimmed, sweat-stained hat kicked back on his head. He was very large and bordered on heavy—a giant of a man. Like his wife, his skin was deeply brown. He wore faded blue overalls covered in old stains and dotted with patches. Gaspard noted that the man's old boots might have weighed 20 kilos each, the way the man dragged his feet. He and his wife probably farmed during the week and supplemented their income with this job on the weekends.

Gaspard noted the man's enormous, calloused hands. It seemed as if each step pained him. Gaspard could only imagine all the man had seen and experienced in his lifetime. He and his wife were symbolic of the people who kept France moving despite all it had been through.

"How about that Oswald fellow?" the old man asked.

Both detectives murmured their outrage over the assassination. The old man stopped and joined eyes with each of them.

"Didn't you hear?"

"Hear what?" Roux asked.

"Don't you have a radio?" he asked.

"We haven't been on the air," Gaspard replied. "What are you talking about?"

"Oswald's dead," the old man stated. "Some fella killed him today."

"What?" Roux demanded. "Who killed him?"

"Me and the missus were leaving the last school and heard it on our radio. We like to listen to the radio a'tween jobs. Anyway, they said the police were movin' Oswald and some fella lunged from the crowd and shot him."

Both detectives were dumbfounded. "Is he definitely dead?" Gaspard finally asked.

"Yep. He's dead. Lived for a short bit, it seems, but took a bullet to the gut. Hard to survive that. Seen it many times myself back during *La Premiere Guerre Mondiale.*"

"Did they get the shooter?"

"They did. Don't know who he is but that's all they can talk about on the news."

"Sonofabitch," Detective Roux muttered, turning to Gaspard.

"Yep," the old man agreed. "Our American friends are startin' to get a taste of how we've had it as long as I can 'member."

Just as Gaspard was preparing to respond, they heard the janitor's wife calling out from the other side of the school. The man's name was probably "Vernon" as she steadily yelled for "Vern," her voice shrill and loud.

When the three men arrived, the wife was standing rigidly in the hallway, her hand pointing to a saucer-sized blemish on the linoleum floor. Upon further examination, it was more than a blemish. It was outright damage, because the concrete below the linoleum could be seen. At first glance, it appeared as if someone had hit the area several times with a pickaxe.

"That ain't never been there," Vernon mumbled, removing his hat and wiping his brow with a handkerchief. "This place is only a few years old."

"Smell that?" Roux asked Gaspard.

Gaspard bent down and took a great whiff. He looked up and spoke three words.

"Eau de javel."

Translated, the words meant "bleach."

***

It didn't take very long for the detectives and the janitors to piece things together. The wife discovered that there were no sheets and pillowcases in the laundry sack for cleaning. Part of the janitors' duties were collecting the week's linens and leaving a new set. The school had numerous sets, but at least one—the one that was used that week—was always sent out for cleaning. This week, the laundry sack was empty, meaning someone might have made off with the third set. A close examination of one of the pillows revealed rust-colored bloodstains on both sides of the pillow. This had been concealed by a clean pillowcase.

Gaspard and Detective Roux went back to the damaged area of the hallway floor. They asked the janitors to wait in the nurse's office and to hold off on their cleaning.

"What do you think?" Gaspard asked, kneeling over the spot.

"Shotgun blast," Roux replied. "Look at the concrete."

"Could be."

"And the bleach?"

"To remove blood, or bone, or who knows what else?"

"Gaspard, should we call Thirty-Six and tell them what we've found?"

Gaspard spun his fedora in his hands, shaping the brim. Finally he stood, his knees cracking. He lit a cigarette, squinting his eyes at his friend. "That bleach tells me we'll find nothing helpful, and then you and me will spend the next week answering questions and writing reports and getting our asses gnawed off."

"So, we don't call it in?"

Dragging on his cigarette, Gaspard shook his head. "Come with me."

He walked down the hallway to the older couple. He apologized for the inconvenience and asked them to say nothing of tonight's events. "This is part of a much larger investigation." He produced 30 new francs, handing them to the wife.

"For your inconvenience."

As they departed, Detective Roux peppered Gaspard with questions.

"Do you really think someone died in that school?"

"I do."

"Do you think it was your guy, the one who took down the Secret Service outpost?"

"He was there."

"Is he who died?" Roux asked.

"No idea."

"Where are we going?"

"Back to Paris."

Roux was quiet for a moment before he asked, "How the hell can you afford to give away money like that?"

"I intend to get my money back from who we're going to see."

"Who are we going to see?"

Gaspard flicked his cigarette from the car in a hail of sparks. He eyed his friend. "We're going to see Sergeant Patten. He's who leaked the call about the stolen Renault. He leaked it to someone, and that's who will lead us to the man who took down the Secret Service outpost."

Pressing the accelerator pedal into the carpet, Gaspard watched as the needle disappeared well beyond the 140 kilometers per hour top speed mark.

Chapter Eighteen

As Ludivine slumbered in the seat next to him, Max rested his right hand on her hip and settled deeply into the comfortable seat of the stolen automobile. Unlike he was with almost everything else in his life at the moment, Max was actually pleased with the progress they'd made. With little traffic and a powerful Mercedes, they'd averaged 125 kilometers per hour for several hours straight. Not only were they well south of the school, they were now actually in a completely different region of France. His current challenge was a lack of gasoline, but after keeping his eyes peeled for a bit, he'd eventually located an all night petrol station, just off the autoroute in Moulins. In the event anyone there might provide testimony about the man with the wounded head driving a black Mercedes, Max entered the station from the east, filled up with gasoline, and departed to the west, headed the opposite direction on the autoroute. He then made a U-turn when he was out of sight. Hopefully, no one would ask the attendant. But if they did, they'd think he'd headed off in the opposite direction. A minor bit of subterfuge, but Max knew such tiny details were often the difference between life or death.

"Where are we?" Ludivine mumbled.

"Still driving," Max replied. "Everything's fine. Go back to sleep."

Now that the car was full of gasoline, he pushed his speed even higher, doing better than 150 kilometers per hour, a comfortable speed in the big Mercedes, until he reached the curvy roads of the Jura Mountains in less than an hour. The Juras were the gateway to the western Alps. As they ascended, Max watched the road signs and quickly settled on a destination: the skiing village of La Clusaz. But he didn't decide on La Clusaz due to its charm or the towering slopes that surrounded it. No, he chose it because the town had an abundance of visitors. Two strange faces—even one with a scalp wound—shouldn't peak anyone's interest. Besides, injuries and skiing went hand in hand. Also, due to its high elevation, La Clusaz might have the benefit of snowfall, which would further assist in Max and Ludivine's anonymity.

Luckily, twenty minutes outside of town, as they passed a road sign marking 1,000 meters of elevation, the snow began. By the time they arrived in the village of La Clusaz, half dollar size snowflakes blanketed the sleeping town in a sheet of white.

Max drove the small town for twenty minutes before deciding on the correct spot. He wanted a parking location that would cover the car in snow tonight, but also provide shade tomorrow in the event the day was sunny. He finally located what he was looking for on the outskirts of town in a flat lot cut into the side of a hill. Given the angle to the east and north, the parking spot should be shaded for most of the day tomorrow. Once he'd backed the Mercedes into the space, he awoke Ludivine and moved her to the backseat. He provided her with several pieces of clothing to use as blankets. Once she was asleep, Max stood outside the car and smoked a cigarette as the snow fell around him. There wasn't a trace of wind, which made the air rather comfortable. The snow gave him new hope, despite his crumbling physical condition.

Max felt his scalp wound. It was fully clotted and had perhaps begun to heal. He touched the burn on his side. It was still tender but largely numb at its center. He'd probably suffered nerve damage. The best course of action for all his maladies involved rest and nutrition—for more than 12 hours at a time. Max walked around the parking lot, making sure he stepped only in tire tracks.

As the snow quickly accumulated, even on the warm Mercedes, he pondered their next move. With luck, they'd both get several hours of sleep in the car. Tomorrow, they would be wise to somehow go on the offensive. If Max continued to react to what others were doing, he'd eventually make a wrong move—and it would cost him and Ludivine their lives. In the trunk of the Mercedes was the evidence of Lucy Thaler's death, and a war that could have possibly been prevented.

Along with a half million dollars in American currency.

If this were a game of poker, Max had a mighty large stack of chips—but his hand was weak.

He could fold. Or...

Perhaps he could bluff—and raise.

He eased back into the car and rested on the front bench seat. Despite the chill and all they'd been through, Max slumbered deeply as his body craved the healing that only sleep can provide.

***

Paris Police Sergeant Henri Patten lived in the commune of Aubervilliers, a suburb just northeast of the city. Primarily a low-income area, Aubervilliers was crowded, populated by the working class and immigrants brought in after the war. It was also an area known for violent crime. Gaspard had been here many times, usually when working a case. Judging by the defensive way Detective Roux exited the vehicle, he was also familiar with the area.

Patten lived in a large post-war apartment building, similar to the dozens of others on the north side of Paris. Devoid of any character whatsoever, it was built of concrete to a height of eight stories. With doors at the base and square windows around each floor, there were no other accouterments, other than a few flowerboxes added by residents. Several garish spotlights below shined on the building, making it appear an ugly concrete fortress.

Because France had reversed its population decline after the war with a baby boom, there simply wasn't enough affordable housing to take care of so many burgeoning families. Apartment buildings such as this were hastily, and cheaply, erected to keep pace with the growing population. In a very un-French manner, little thought was given to appearance.

Inside, the lift was broken so the two detectives hastily climbed the stairs to the fifth floor. They were both short of breath after the ascent. In the narrow hallway that reeked of dueling cooking, two shady characters blocked their path and levied threats. The two men probably had no idea they were dealing with police detectives. Roux wasted no time with the punks, slamming one of them to the wall with his forearm at the man's throat. He thrust his badge into the man's face as Gaspard removed his pistol, asking the other punk if there was a problem.

The two men cowered away. There were easier targets elsewhere. Gaspard and Roux continued down the hallway.

Near the end, one apartment's door was open. As they passed, they saw a woman just inside the door. She was thin and wore a tattered red negligee and high stockings. Her face was garishly adorned in makeup, her hair bottle blonde with deep brown roots. She sat in a cheap lawn chair and smiled seductively at the men, licking her scarlet lips before making a ribald suggestion.

Given the economy, such scenes weren't uncommon in Paris. Gaspard would wager she had two or three children sleeping in one bedroom as she worked these extra nighttime hours to clothe and feed them. He tossed 10 new francs at the woman and asked her to close her door for five minutes. Cigarette dangling from her scarlet lips, she readily complied.

"More money?" Roux asked.

"He now owes me forty," Gaspard answered.

"What's your pay rate?"

"We'll talk about it later. Roust him."

Detective Roux rapped on Sergeant Patten's door. His wife answered, a petite woman with olive skin, large brown eyes and black hair. She wore a long conservative robe and slippers. She glanced at both men, taking only a few seconds to mark them as police.

"You're looking for Henri."

Gaspard smiled disarmingly. "And we're sorry to bother you on a Sunday night. We hope we didn't wake anyone."

"We're all still awake. Henri's eating his dinner. He just got home from work."

The two detectives shared a look. They'd been told Patten left in the late afternoon. And because he was assigned to Dispatch—a desk job if there ever was one—all of his work was contained in the building at 36 quai des Orfèvres.

"Something wrong?" the woman asked, picking up on their shared expression.

"No ma'am, we just regret having to disturb you."

"Won't you come in?" Based on her accent and appearance, Gaspard guessed Detective Patten had married a Berber—one of the many that had flooded into France after the war. She smiled politely at the two men, gesturing inside.

"Madame Patten, while we do regret interrupting, will you please ask your husband to step out here for just a moment? We need to discuss a case and the nature of our discussion is rather private."

"Does this involve the important case he's been working on?"

"Uh, possibly. What's he said about it?" Gaspard asked, struggling not to look at Roux again.

"Not much. But he's worked late for the last month, always telling me there's a very important—"

She was interrupted by her husband, Sergeant Patten. He appeared from around the corner, roughly pulling her away from the door. Patten remembered he had a napkin protruding from his collar, which he yanked out. He eyed the two detectives harshly. While he didn't know them personally, he no doubt knew who they were. And he also knew they knew who he was. Based on his stern expression, Patten planned to be a hard egg.

Though chastened by his physicality, his wife remained right behind him.

Gaspard perfunctorily introduced himself and Detective Roux. "Would you mind stepping out here for just a moment?"

"Why?"

"It has to do with the *important* case you've been working on."

Patten murmured something to his wife and stepped into the hallway. He pulled the door shut behind him and spoke with the impertinence of a man comfortable with bucking authority. "Neither of you pricks is in my chain of command, nor are you I.G.P.N.," he said, referencing *Inspection générale de la police nationale*, the French police's internal affairs division. "So, unless you're here on the direct order of my commander, you can both fuck each other as far as I'm—"

Gaspard went for his throat. Patten was a big man, and powerful. He thrust his arms upward, knocking Gaspard's away. Thankfully, Detective Roux was ready and came through with a straight right that caught Patten on his jaw from the side. His knees went weak. Gaspard caught the big man before he crumpled to the ground. He slid him to the side, pressing him against the wall.

"Patten, you either cooperate, or we'll violate your ass, not only to your lieutenant, but also to your wife. I know who you're screwing," Gaspard hissed in a calculated lie. "When I bring you down on that, it'll be the final nail in your dirty coffin."

"Bullshit," Patten growled, working his jaw.

"Try me. Now, you're going to tell me who you've been feeding calls to. You tell me now—and we walk."

Patten seemed genuinely surprised that this was why he was being braced. "What?"

"You heard me. You gave up that stolen Renault from Orléans and I want the details right now." Gaspard glanced at Roux. "Start talking, or we call your pretty wife out here and tell her about your tart. Then I go write your ass up for selling information and for having an affair—which you've been counseled on more times than I can remember. You'll be out of work tomorrow, and you won't qualify for de Gaulle's unemployment. Not after this."

"Or just tell us and we're gone," Roux said, his hand ready to knock on the door.

Patten looked away.

"Tell us," Roux warned.

"All I'm doing is calling a number and giving out calls as they come in," Patten answered, his eyes shut.

"Who?" Gaspard asked.

"I don't know. I was approached by a woman after work one night. She told me they'd pay me if I relayed certain types of calls to them."

Gaspard eased up on his hold. "What types of calls?"

"Petty crime, assaults, murders, thefts. She said she didn't care about accidents, deviancy or major crime. She wanted small stuff. Current stuff."

"How much?" Roux asked.

"Twenty new francs a day."

Roux whistled. "Must be nice."

"Who paid you?" Gaspard demanded.

"There's a rock in Bois de Vincennes she puts the money under. It's been there each day, so I keep calling."

"A rock?" Roux asked.

"Yes, a rock. It's big but it can be lifted."

"Where?"

"On the southernmost edge of the park, under the tallest evergreen by the rock wall."

Roux grunted as if he didn't believe this.

"How long has this been going on?" Gaspard demanded.

"Weeks…maybe a month."

"What number have you been calling?"

Patten slumped. Roux pulled back his hand to knock.

"Alright, alright…N-D-Q-6167."

"Hang on." Roux whipped out his notepad, scribbled the number and confirmed it with Patten.

Gaspard pulled on both sides of Sergeant Patten's collar and spoke through gritted teeth. "You get ideas about revenge, and all of this is coming out. The affair, and the bribes."

"You won't say anything otherwise?"

Gaspard released him and hitched his head to Roux. They walked away.

"You won't say anything?" Patten yelled, still on the floor, his voice echoing down the hallway.

Once they were on the stairwell, Gaspard winked at Roux. "I knew that asshole was having an affair. He denied it at first but didn't deny it at the end. Guilty."

"I can't believe any woman would want him," Roux remarked.

"People rarely change. Very rarely."

"You didn't get your money back?"

"It was the wife that did me in. I can't take their money," Gaspard lamented.

The two policemen made plans to meet at 0800 the following morning. Having no desire to go home, Gaspard headed south to the 11th Arrondissement.

He planned to spend the night with Evelyn Durand, even if all they did was talk. At the very least, he'd be there to protect her.

***

Across the Atlantic Ocean, on Sunday evening just before she planned to leave for the night, Julie Hedstrom built up the courage to make a telephone call. She didn't practice it ahead of time. She planned to be spontaneous and genuine. Most concerning was the sadness her call might generate. Regardless, she felt strongly this was her most logical next step. *If* what she was working on was as big as her instinct told her, then one woman's sadness was a price that had to be paid.

"Hello?" A man.

"Hello, may I please speak with JoAnn?"

"Who's calling?"

"This is Julie Hedstrom. I'm an old friend from her childhood. I hope this is JoAnn's number?"

"Yes, it is…one moment."

Muffled sounds and scratching as the phone was covered by a hand.

Here you are, Julie, lying through your teeth. And you despise liars. How does this make you feel?

Shut up. This is lying with a purpose.

Nice justification.

Finally...

"Hello, this is JoAnn. Did you say your name was Julie?"

"JoAnn, I'm sorry. I made up a story to get you to pick up."

Long pause.

"You lied to my husband?"

"I did it because I actually don't know you. I'm calling about your sister's disappearance."

Instant exasperation. "That's been over twenty years ago. I have no desire to ever speak to another reporter or Nazi-obsessed head case about—"

Julie instantly hated what she'd done. *Why didn't I just tell the truth?*

You can start right now.

"JoAnn, I'm sorry to cut you off, but I'm neither. Please listen for just a moment. My name *is* Julie, it truly is. I work for the United States Secret Service in Washington. And as crazy as it might seem, there could possibly be a connection between your sister's disappearance and a case we are working on *today*. Please, just hear me out."

Silence.

"JoAnn?"

"I'm here."

"Again, I apologize for lying to your husband. I really do. But I need to know a few things about Lucy."

JoAnn's tone changed ever so slightly. "I don't know what else I could possibly tell you that I haven't already told the dozens of investigators before?"

"That's just it, JoAnn. I can't find any good records on your sister, about her life or her disappearance. Though the government has many resources, record-keeping isn't always among our core strengths."

"I see."

"And I'm not aiming to dredge up anything awful. I'm genuinely attempting to help solve a new case, and it may be related to your sister's disappearance. That's the unvarnished truth."

"Excuse me for a moment."

Again, the phone was covered. Julie could hear snippets of JoAnn assuaging her husband's concern. As the phone was uncovered, Julie heard her say, "...go back to the news and I'll be in there in a minute."

A door could be heard shutting.

"Julie?"

"Yes."

"You're with the Secret Service?"

"Yes, I am."

"Are you an agent?" JoAnn asked, puzzled.

"No, I work for the director. He asked me to call."

"*The* director?"

"Yes."

"I can't imagine he's got time to think about my sister. Everyone's been consumed with the news of the assassination and then the shooting of that Oswald psychotic today." JoAnn abruptly stopped. "Wait, don't tell me Lucy's disappearance has something to do with the assassination?"

"That's not what I'm working on. There was another crime on Friday, in Europe. That's what your sister's case might be associated with. Everyone else is working on the incidents in Dallas, which is probably why I'm working on France."

Silence.

"JoAnn, what can you tell me about your sister's final year?"

"She was in Berlin, as I'm sure you know, against our mother's good wishes. She'd been in Germany, off and on, for about eight years at that time."

"She moved there with your father?"

"Yes."

"Why?"

"Lucy wasn't the typical oldest child. She was always restless and daring. Always...even when we were young kids. She'd sneak away and they'd find her miles from the house. When she was thirteen, she went to Philadelphia all by herself. Mama was hard on her but papa always let her get away with bad behavior."

"How much older than you was she?"

"Two years and one day."

"Were you close with her?"

"When we were young. As we grew older, we weren't best friends or anything like that. But we wrote letters and talked when we could."

"JoAnn, do you have any idea what happened to your sister?"

"Of course I do."

Julie straightened. "Would you please share that with me?"

JoAnn snorted. "I told the State Department people this no less than a dozen times. Lucy told me, more than once, that she was having a fling with Hermann Goering. I suspect you know who he is?"

Julie gripped her desk as the world spun. "Yes...yes, I do."

"I'm positive he killed her, or had her killed. That's what they did in that regime. When someone became a problem, they made them disappear. He got what he wanted from her and, I dunno...maybe Lucy got a little jealous of Goering's wife, or something like that...either way, in the end, I believe he killed my sister."

"Do you know this for certain?"

"No. But it's what I suspect. It's logical."

"When did you last talk to your sister?"

"At the very end of July, by letter. I'll never forget it."

"This was in 1941?"

"Yes."

"And what was the nature of her letter?"

"Our meeting in London."

"Excuse me? Meeting in London?"

"If you're really with the Secret Service, I'm surprised you don't know all this. Don't tell me you're some reporter telling me more lies."

"Forgive me, JoAnn, for not knowing these things. I can assure you I work for the United States Secret Service. Things are a bit hectic here and, like I mentioned, getting information and records is difficult with all that's gone on."

"Well...anyway...I was in Plymouth, England for a summer trip and Lucy and I made plans to rendezvous in London and spend a few days together. We'd written back and forth about it for months. At first she planned to come in early August. Then she told me her plans had changed but not drastically. She told me she would arrive on August tenth but she never showed up."

"How soon did you report her missing?"

"I did it while I was in London. I allowed her an extra day to arrive before I went to the embassy. They were wonderful and did their best to help."

"What did they uncover?"

"Not much, but I always found it peculiar that one of her closest friends in Berlin insisted that Lucy flew from Tempelhof. She said she went to see her off and watched her get on the flight."

"There were airline flights from Germany at that time?"

"There *were* passenger flights, but not direct to England. The Luftwaffe controlled every flight leaving Germany. Lucy was booked to Zurich, then to London."

"And her friend saw her board?"

"That's what she claimed. But you remember who was in charge of the Luftwaffe, don't you?"

"Goering."

"Yes."

"When did her friend claim Lucy left Berlin?"

"I don't remember the exact date she left, but it was several days before we were to meet. Lucy told me she had one piece of business to attend to first, hence her original schedule change."

"Business in England?"

"She said it was something for her hotel. She didn't say where. They scrutinized her letters but that was all she mentioned. As I'm sure you know, she had a rather high social position due to her job."

"JoAnn, did she ever mention the name Clayton Fairchild to you?"

A delay. "Are you serious?"

"Yes. Why?"

"Well, he questioned me, of course. Time and time again, he called with dozens of questions. It bordered on obsession."

"When was this?"

"Gosh...I guess in forty-one and definitely on into forty-two. Maybe beyond."

"I see. What do you remember about him?"

"He told me he was with the State Department, or intelligence, or something like that...I always felt like he'd taken her disappearance personally."

"I see."

"Why the question about him?" JoAnn asked, her tone suspicious.

"I have a number of questions about many things."

"Yes, but why him? Were they somehow involved?"

"I honestly don't know, JoAnn."

"Look, Julie Hedstrom of the Secret Service, I've been honest with you tonight, despite your lying to get me on the phone. I'm sitting here in a dark room, giving my time to you while angering my husband. He despises me talking about this because it usually wrecks my sleep for weeks. The least you can do is be honest with me."

"Okay, JoAnn. I'll be completely transparent with you. Ask me anything."

"Was she involved with this Clayton Fairchild?"

"I can't really say for sure but—"

"Hear me out," JoAnn said, cutting Julie off. "I'm the first to admit that Lucy had a large appetite for men. I don't know why. My father loved her—doted on her, in fact. Still, after she turned fifteen, she always enjoyed a good romance—and usually carried on more than one at a time, if you know what I mean. Older men, almost always. She knew I didn't like it, so we didn't talk about her flings too often."

"So, having an affair with Goering didn't surprise you?"

"From the time she went off to college, my sister was permanently involved with at least one married man. In short order, she started going for the ones with power. First it was her professor, then the dean, and before long the university chancellor. He was sixty years old. I believe she enjoyed the thrill of it, and I know she preferred the married ones because she could end it cleanly." JoAnn paused. "You probably think she was a monster."

"I don't judge people, JoAnn."

"Was Clayton Fairchild married?"

"No."

"That doesn't mean she wasn't involved with him. Marriage wasn't her only prerequisite. As I said, she liked power, and intelligence."

"He had power, and he was extremely intelligent," Julie replied.

"Do you think they were involved?"

"Based on some of the things I've learned, I wouldn't be surprised if they had a relationship. But I can't say for sure because I don't know."

"But how? He wouldn't have been in Berlin while she was there, would he? We tried to get Lucy out when everyone else was leaving. I thought the U.S. had pulled all our embassy people out by then."

"He traveled to Berlin to meet Lucy. He went there a number of times."

"When?"

"In the last year or two leading up to her disappearance."

"Why would he have done that?"

"She was working for him, for us."

"For the Secret Service?"

"No. For the United States."

"No, that's wrong. She worked for a hotel, a German hotel."

"That was her cover, JoAnn. The affair Lucy had with Goering—it was planned."

The gulf in the conversation was significant, as reality descended upon JoAnn Thaler Wiley of Darien, Connecticut. She was sitting in the dark, connecting dots that had mystified her for all these years. When she finally spoke, her voice was a whisper.

"Are you saying Lucy was a spy?"

"In essence, yes."

"I don't believe it."

"You asked me to be transparent. You deserve the truth, especially after I lied to get you on the phone."

"How did it start?"

"I don't know yet, JoAnn. Typically, a person is approached after a long period of research and surveillance. Because Lucy was well placed, and I suppose because she was a patriot, they chose her. Was she against the war?"

"Yes. She'd grown to love Germany but she despised the Nazis and their violence."

"Despised the Nazis but carried on an affair with one of the top Nazis?" Julie asked. "Think about that for a moment."

JoAnn's frustration was evident. "You'd have understood if you knew Lucy. Like her affairs, she enjoyed being in the middle of things. Even things she disagreed with. She was a thrill seeker. And in those years, Berlin was the center of so many things."

"I understand. So, JoAnn, you now know what I know."

JoAnn's voice took on a different tone. "And what does any of this have to do with a current investigation?"

"We just came across Lucy's name today. We could be way off base, but there was a theft in Europe on Friday, in France. We believe the object of the theft could be something involving your sister."

"She's not alive is she?"

"No, JoAnn, I don't want to give you any false hope and I'm sorry if I did."

"Then what on earth could be involved that includes my sister? It's been twenty-two years."

"I believe it might be evidence of some sort."

"What kind of evidence?"

"Evidence of her death."

JoAnn was quiet as she digested this news. Julie liked her.

Finally, JoAnn spoke. "I've always believed Goering killed her, or had her killed. Just tell me this—have you found anything that would clue you in on who killed my sister?"

"No, I haven't. The only testimony I've come across involved Clayton Fairchild. It seems rather obvious he cared deeply for Lucy."

"Where is he now?"

"He's dead."

"How?"

"Car accident."

"When?"

"I believe it was about thirteen years ago."

"Tell me what you know about him," JoAnn demanded.

They spoke for five more minutes. When Julie had finished telling JoAnn about Fairchild, they ended the call. JoAnn promised to speak more, if need be, but not until tomorrow. She sounded as if she were crying when she hung up.

Though Julie hadn't learned a great deal, she was now positive that Lucy Thaler, the sexy German-American with an appetite for romance, had become involved with her handler, Clayton Fairchild.

And he'd hidden something about Lucy in a heavy metal briefcase…

At the Secret Service outpost in Paris' Place de Clichy.

That evidence was out there, somewhere, stolen by a man who used rubber bullets, who was accompanied by a man with a high-powered rifle and another man in horn-rimmed glasses. Julie scribbled every fact she could think of on her notepad, underlining several points. She shut her eyes and rubbed her temples, inventorying her mind to make certain she hadn't forgotten anything.

She hadn't.

Julie realized that, like JoAnn, she too was crying. They weren't tears of sadness—although Lucy's story certainly made Julie sad. No, they were tears of hope, and anticipation, and discovery. Julie knew she was close to deciphering this riddle. She wiped her tears and reviewed her notes. She'd done all she could do—today.

Clearing her brain the way a teacher wipes a chalkboard, Julie packed up her things and hurried home. She wanted a few hours of relaxation with a book, along with a good stiff drink.

This would all be here tomorrow, bright and early.

If Julie had any idea about what tomorrow held, she'd have probably stayed home.

Chapter Nineteen

The sliver of vertical light on the otherwise dark landing of Evelyn's apartment stairwell sent a spike of fear through Detective Gaspard Lacroix. The light meant her door was partially open. He knew there was no way in hell her door should be partially open, especially not in this neighborhood. As he drew closer, he could see the door had been broken around the lock, which is why it wouldn't fully close. Gaspard drew his weapon.

Why didn't I insist she stay in a hotel? No...God...please, no.

Easing inside Evelyn's flat, he could hear nothing. The only light came from the small lamp on the far side of the room. Evelyn's bedroom was to the right, overlooking the 11th Arrondissement side street. Gaspard turned, keeping his pistol extended as he moved to the bedroom.

He knew what he would find—Evelyn, dead in her bed, all alone.

All my fault...

Gaspard thought about her parents, thousands of miles away, shrieking in their mourning, cursing the day she first sailed to France, fueled by her Hemingwayesque dreams. And now she probably lay in her own blood, her body cold, a final expression of horror frozen on her face.

The door was partially closed. Gaspard pushed it open, steeling himself.

Evelyn was not in her bed.

Purple light bled in from the street, throwing splashes of color across the unmade bed that held only two pillows and a comfortable knit blanket.

Thank God. Thank God.

Gaspard checked the bathroom, finding it empty. Though relieved she wasn't here, now he feared abduction—or worse. If someone wanted to silence her, they could have taken her from here before killing her.

Maybe she's been taken...or perhaps she's simply gone out for the evening and a burglar robbed her flat. She could be with another man. Perhaps she's been seeing him for weeks. She wouldn't be the first woman you've pursued only to learn she was taken. Remember the Italian woman several years ago? Remember what you learned on that Tuesday night when you surreptitiously followed her?

As Gaspard's mind raced off in the wrong direction, he heard a light sound from the main room. Rather than move, he froze, his pistol aimed at the bedroom door. He felt like someone was coming his way.

Nothing.

He waited a full minute. Finally, carefully, he picked his way back to the front of the apartment as fears of Evelyn's abduction had now overtaken his mind. When he reached the front door, pistol outstretched, he watched as the door across the hall slowly opened. A large older woman in a housecoat peered around the edge of the door, asking Gaspard who he was.

Relieved to have someone to question, Gaspard lowered his weapon and produced his badge. He asked the woman if she'd seen who kicked the door in.

But as soon as Gaspard's name had left his mouth, the door opened wider. The first thing he saw was a white, longhaired cat that bolted from the old woman's apartment and into Evelyn's. The second thing Gaspard saw was Evelyn, herself.

Gaspard nearly went slack with relief.

She wore what must have been the old woman's other housecoat. It swallowed Evelyn's diminutive frame. She rushed from the apartment and into Gaspard's arms, clutching him in the tightest of embraces. He questioned her but she couldn't talk for a moment as she sobbed into his shoulder.

Though it took several minutes, Gaspard eventually learned that Evelyn had been in bed, awake. She'd heard several footfalls on the steps outside her apartment, along with what sounded like someone trying to break the lock on her door. Her cat in hand, and wearing only a chemise, she eased out of her dormer window and perched on the steeply pitched roof on the front of the building. All she'd had to hold onto was a rickety antenna with her bare feet perched precariously on the gutters. When she heard no more noises inside, she slipped back through her apartment and hid with her neighbor.

"Did you see them?" Gaspard asked.

"No. I was out of sight."

Gaspard turned to the neighbor. "Did you?"

"All I heard was the thump when they broke the door. I never saw them."

He turned back to Evelyn. "Could you hear them?"

"Yes."

"What were they saying?"

"I couldn't understand them."

"Was it muffled?"

"No, not really." She walked him through the flat so he could see the dormer. She tapped the thin glass. "When they were in the bedroom, I could hear them clearly. I just couldn't understand their language."

"Not French?"

"No. Not French, and not English."

"Do you have any idea what it was?"

"I couldn't say for sure."

"Guesses?"

"Slavic, maybe?"

"Were they Russian?"

"I don't know. It just had…you know…that deep guttural sound and the hard consonants."

Once Gaspard had asked every question he could think of—and learned nothing else—he thanked the neighbor. After she went back to her flat, he called 36 and ordered in a forensics and security team. Forensics would see if they could find anything useful and the security team would watch over the neighbor and also question the residents to see if anyone got a look at the intruders.

Ninety minutes later, Gaspard helped as Evelyn checked into the Hotel Verneuil, situated in the heart of Paris, just below the Seine. Evelyn's cat accompanied them, smuggled in by Evelyn as Gaspard occupied the night clerk.

In their room, Gaspard made Evelyn comfortable and encouraged her to sleep. She would hear nothing of it. They drank a glass of champagne before sharing their first kiss. Gaspard pulled away, muttering something about not wanting to take advantage of the situation.

"I know what I'm doing," Evelyn said, kissing him again.

The following hour was Gaspard's finest in many, many years. Afterward, they finished the champagne and avoided talk of the case. Instead, they talked about Florida, and the French Riviera, and the war. It was a glorious time. Their talk was followed by more passion.

Gaspard got very little sleep in the comfortable Hotel Verneuil bed.

***

In southeastern France, it was just past 3 A.M. when the gendarme-turned-criminal halted at the self-service all-night petrol station on the autoroute near Moulins. This was their 11th stop and, thus far, none had borne any fruit. No one had seen a dark Mercedes. No one had seen anyone remotely resembling Max Warfield. Mr. Winthrop had grown uncharacteristically despondent as the night had worn on. It seemed they'd had their chance back in Orléans but missed it.

As Mr. Winthrop and General Timmons dozed in the car, the Gendarme topped off the tank before heading inside. He paid for his fuel and provided a few new francs to the sleepy attendant for a cup of coffee from the man's personal percolator behind the counter. The two men had a smoke together, chatting the way two strangers will often do in the wee hours of the morning. It's as if the loneliness of the cold onyx night draws people closer. Once he'd gained a bit of trust, the Gendarme peeled off more bills, holding them seductively in his hand.

"Want to make a little scratch?"

"How?"

"Seen a black Mercedes sedan tonight?"

The attendant eyed the money before his brown eyes flicked back to the Gendarme. He played the ancient game well, as he answered, "Maybe."

The Gendarme peeled off one of the bills and slid it over.

"Yeah, I saw a Mercedes," the attendant answered.

"Who was in it?"

The attendant made a curling motion with his fingers. An expert.

Two more francs.

More curling.

A roll of the eyes. Two more.

"A man filled the tank. Must've been almost empty. I think he took about seventy-something liters. There was someone else in the car, sitting low, probably sleeping. I couldn't see."

"Woman?"

"Couldn't see."

"What'd the man look like?"

"Rough. Huge gash on his head with stitches."

The Gendarme fought to remain neutral. "How long ago?"

"Four hours, maybe. A while."

"Which way did they go?"

The attendant arched his eyebrows and looked down at the money.

Five more new francs.

"They headed west."

"West? You sure?"

"Yeah."

"Which way did he come in from?"

"The east. I noticed him pull in. I've been robbed a few times so I always watch."

"You're certain?"

"Yeah, of course. I've had only five, maybe six customers all night."

The Gendarme slid his cup over to be topped off. They nodded at one another before the Gendarme walked outside. He started the Mercedes and exited the petrol station, driving a half a kilometer west before pulling off to the side of the road. He awoke Mr. Winthrop and General Timmons and relayed the entire story.

"He told you that with no prompting?" Timmons asked.

"Word for word."

"A four-hour head start. We've got to haul ass," the general replied.

Mr. Winthrop said nothing, his gun-slit eyes joined with the driver's in the rearview mirror.

"What are we waiting on?" Timmons demanded. "We need to get to a phone and tell our gal in Paris. Once everyone checks in, we can all at least be heading in the right direction."

Winthrop said nothing so the Gendarme accelerated to the west, toward the entrance ramp to the autoroute.

"Wait," Winthrop said. "Pull over again."

"Why?" Timmons asked.

"Think about this for a minute. Max is trying to trick us."

"Th'hell are you talkin' about?" Timmons bellowed.

"Max would have been going west to east from where we'd last seen him at the school. He *had* to have been. There's little reason to suspect he drove east of the petrol station and then came back."

"You're suggesting he altered his route to throw us off?"

"I'm suggesting Max saw the petrol station from the highway. He drove past, took the next exit, and arrived from the east. Then, to maintain his little deception, he exited the station to the west and then doubled back east right there," Mr. Winthrop said, pointing to the overpass just in front of them. "That way, if the attendant testified that he'd been to the petrol station, at least we'd head off in the wrong direction."

Timmons seemed unconvinced but the Gendarme eyed Mr. Winthrop in awe.

The Gendarme looked at his watch. "If he got here four hours ago, he would have been making incredible time from Orléans. There's no way he could have been coming from the east."

"You see," Winthrop said to Timmons, who didn't argue.

"Max is bright. I'm brighter," Winthrop said. "Go east, and haul ass. I'm willing to bet he didn't go much farther."

"What's east of here?" Timmons asked.

"The mountains," Mr. Winthrop and the Gendarme answered simultaneously.

Chapter Twenty

Max Warfield awoke to cold temperatures and very little light bleeding into the cabin of the Mercedes. He heard the rhythmic breathing from Ludivine as she slumbered in the back seat. It was nearly ten in the morning and the car was blanketed with snow. This was good as far as their concealment went. After pulling on his shoes and jacket, he told Ludivine to go back to sleep as he stepped from the car and surveyed his surroundings.

He might have been in heaven.

The sky was mostly cloudy, touched by random brushstrokes of brilliant blue. In the distance, cottony clouds swirled restlessly between the mountain peaks. There was little wind here in the valley, meaning even the trees were decorated in white. Max turned his attention to the parking lot.

Nearly all of the cars were covered in six inches of snow. He'd parked the Mercedes well after the snow had begun, but there was still plenty to obscure the paint. He eyed the front license plate, wondering if he should swap it with another car. He decided to wait, doubtful that even the most vigilant gendarme would find this car in such a secluded lot. Plus, Max was afraid he might attract attention by swapping plates in the broad daylight. For now, he decided to chance it.

With aching muscles and joints, he tramped through the snow up to the main street, viewing a sidewalk full of vacationers who'd almost certainly hurried to the ski resort for the first major snow of the season. Many of them were carrying snow skis, fully dressed for a day on the slopes. Max remained turned so no one would see his fresh scar.

Inside of a few minutes, Max saw three police cars. He couldn't imagine the police in La Clusaz searching for him. Max doubted they'd have even received a telex about the Parisian crime. But, Max reminded himself, Mr. Winthrop *had* somehow tracked Max to Orléans, and the only way he could have done that was via the dope dealer's Renault. And the easiest way to track down a stolen car was with the help of the police.

So, perhaps the police *were* looking for him. This was an unnerving series of thoughts, but something he couldn't waste time worrying about. He walked back down the hill to the parking lot, where he pulled out his pocketknife.

It was worth the risk.

After removing the two license plates from the Mercedes and concealing them under his jacket, he walked alone through two alleyways before spotting a Citroen with Parisian plates. The car was parked off to the side of a cottage, obscured by snow-covered trees. Acting as natural as possible, Max swapped the plates. No one saw him. He made his way back to the Mercedes, affixing the stolen plates front and back. His last effort was kicking snow around his footprints—especially those in front of the Mercedes.

He then awoke Ludivine, asking if she'd mind going for food, coffee, stocking caps and ski jackets.

"I'd go but I don't want anyone seeing this scar on my head," he explained. Max gave her the last of their French money.

Without a word of complaint, Ludivine stretched outside the car and headed off in the fresh snow. Max remained beside the car, smoking a cigarette, watching as the streets slowly turned to slush. Though it was frigid, especially with the wind, it wasn't quite cold enough to keep the snow from melting. He looked at the Mercedes, seeing no evidence of melting, yet. Perhaps the ground had been warm before the snow arrived.

Forty-five minutes later, Ludivine returned with two large paper cups of coffee. She had a bag of fresh croissants and had purchased jackets and stocking caps.

"It's expensive here. The clothes took nearly half our money," she said.

Max and Ludivine sat in the Mercedes and enjoyed their food and coffee. They discussed options as Max peered out the uncovered glass of his side window. On the mountains surrounding La Clusaz, numerous chalets could be seen, evidenced by wispy smoke emanating from their chimneys.

Such a striking view provided Max with an inspiration.

***

An hour later, a nourished Max was purposefully far out of character in a garish red and blue ski jacket. On his head was a matching stocking cap, deftly concealing his scar. He made sure he walked through plenty of snow to obscure his utility boots. When covered, they might have been ski boots. His costume complete, and with an ash-laden cigarette dangling from his mouth, he burst into the agent's office on Chemin des Riffroids, near the center of La Clusaz. Wearing extra makeup, Ludivine went with him, holding his hand and smacking her chewing gum. Max beamed at the mousy woman behind the counter. He opened his arms wide, as if she were a long lost friend, and bade the woman good morning in loud, obnoxious American English.

"What a day," he pronounced, gesturing outside. "Look at all that snow, will you?" His brassy tone caused the two men in the glass offices behind the attendant to turn and glare at him.

"*Bonjour Monsieur,*" the attendant replied, her smile pinched and unwelcoming. "*Comment puis-je vous aider?*"

"Honey, I don't know what you just said but I need a private chalet, *quickly,* for me and my little croissant here." Max gave Ludivine a salacious squeeze. "I've been slaving away up in Geneva since summer, then last night I heard this storm was coming. And boy, did it ever hit. I hear there's more snow coming, too—hope so, anyways. No matter what, I think I deserve a few days off for some skiing and a little French-style fun, don't you?"

The woman arched her eyebrows and shrugged.

Ludivine spoke next, explaining that her friend was American and spoke no French. "We would like to rent a chalet, one that's rather private," Ludivine explained, batting her eyes coquettishly.

The woman was uninspired. "We've only a few left and the rent is expensive this time of year."

"What'd she say?" Max asked.

"She said the chalets are expensive."

"Good thing I'm loaded," Max countered, winking.

Though the agent volunteered no English, it seemed she understood Max. It also appeared she'd been made to suck on a sour lemon.

"May we see a listing of the available chalets?" Ludivine asked.

The woman lifted a brown leather binder from behind the counter and studied the page that corresponded to the current week, then she wrote the numbers 11, 14, and 23 on a piece of paper. She walked to the shelf behind her and produced another binder, this one thick like a photo album. After opening the binder, she turned to Chalet 11, which displayed several photographs of a cabin that butted right next to three other cabins.

"Nope," Max said, crushing out his cigarette in the ashtray on the counter.

Chalet 14 was better, with seclusion on both sides, but there was a ski slope directly behind the house. "Maybe," Max replied. Ludivine translated but it seemed the prim woman understood his English words.

Chalet 23 was easily the best, situated off the road in a bit of a gully. There were large rocks all around the property, and a line of trees ringing the property line.

"No other houses nearby?" Ludivine asked.

"No," the woman replied.

"Tell me about number twenty-three," Ludivine said.

"It's suitable, but not in the best location. The driveway is difficult to navigate in the snow. I wouldn't recommend it."

Ludivine translated. Max shooed away the concerns. "We'll take it," he said. "How much for a week?"

Ludivine translated, listened, then turned back to Max. "Four hundred new francs."

"How about in dollars?" he asked, removing a stack of bills from his ski jacket.

The woman immediately shook her head upon seeing the dollars, explaining that they could only accept francs. She seemed rather satisfied to finally be able to deny him.

Max was offended. He ripped the band from the bills and asked why dollars couldn't be accepted. Though he grew an octave louder, he made certain to remain polite at this point, never crossing the line as a mild debate ensued with Ludivine the translator.

Eventually, the younger of the two men from the offices behind emerged. He was tall and thin, with spectacles perched on his nose. The man had graying hair that was combed over a burgeoning bald spot. Despite his bad hair, he was dressed rather nattily in a brown wool suit with a brilliant tie and matching pocket square. He peered at his associate.

"Mathilde, what seems to be the problem?" he asked in English.

"She doesn't speak English," Max replied, grinning warmly and shaking the man's hand. Max explained the situation. The man informed Max that he could walk to any of the banks a short distance down the street, all in the central valley, and exchange the dollars for new francs.

Gesturing him off to the side, Max put his arm around the man and spoke in a whisper. "If I do that, they're going to make a record of my name, my address...that kind of thing."

"This is a problem?" the man asked, frowning.

"What's your name?"

"Philipe."

"Look, Philipe, my wife and I aren't on the best of terms right now, if you know what I mean?"

Philipe glanced at Ludivine and maintained his whisper. "She seems quite pleasant."

"Her?" Max asked. He chuckled. "That, Philipe, is *not* my wife."

"Oh, I see. I see, indeed," Philipe replied, allowing a bit of a smile—a true Frenchman.

"See, my real wife's got a team of ex-cops on my ass. It was all I could do to slink out of Geneva without a tail. It's all about money—she wants everything, get it? So, Philipe, do me this favor, please." Max lifted his cash. "And to demonstrate my thanks, I'll pay you double in dollars, plus a generous handling fee, for *you* personally, of two hundred bucks. How 'bout it?"

Philipe straightened, his face suddenly stony.

"I say something wrong?" Max asked, sliding a cigarette from his pack.

"Mathilde, are you listening?" Philipe asked loudly, in French. He continued to maintain his gaze on Max.

"Oui."

"Draw up a contract right now for chalet twenty-three."

"But we can't take dollars," Mathilde protested.

219

Philipe turned and gave her an icy stare. His subordinate slumped in defeat.

After producing a gilded lighter, Philipe ignited Max's cigarette. Max counted out the money in crisp $20 bills. The two men shook hands as the deal was sealed. Keys were provided, along with directions and a brochure containing a list of restaurants and ski rental companies.

Max then asked Philipe if grocery delivery was available. After a brief negotiation, Max provided Philipe with more cash and an extensive hand-written list of grocery items. There was also a list of items needed from the *pharmacie*. In order to maintain his ruse, Max listed two boxes of prophylactics beneath the basic first aid supplies.

"Gonna be a great week," Max chuckled to his new partner in crime. Philipe, quite a bit wealthier than he was minutes before, laughed indulgently.

Forty-three minutes later, Max and Ludivine settled into their new home as more snow pushed into the area.

***

Shortly after noon, while light snow fell outside their secluded chalet, Max and Ludivine discussed their options. Max was quite aware that the photographs and the tape recordings in their possession were explosive. They proved that certain people in the United States government had ample warning of the coming Japanese attack at Pearl Harbor, including President Whitestone. Years before, when he was still in the military, Max had heard rumors that elements of the government ignored the growing Japanese threat in the late 1930s and early 1940s. He'd even heard that some military commanders and politicians had desired war with the Japanese. But Max had never heard a person even suggest that his own government knew almost precisely when and where the attack was coming, but did nothing to stop it.

And while it paled in comparison, the evidence also demonstrated that a woman was murdered in cold blood simply to bury her secret.

It disgusted Max.

But spilling the evidence would be a luxury, and luxuries were something Max simply couldn't afford at the moment. He and Ludivine spoke at length about their current risk level. Max believed Mr. Winthrop would learn that they had used counterfeit money at the rental agency. Then, in rather short order, he'd learn about the chalet they'd rented.

That would be the beginning of the end.

But, this was by Max's design. He wanted Winthrop to find them.

"How will he know?" Ludivine asked.

"I won't underestimate him again," Max answered. "He'll find us. We've got a day, at best. Five, maybe six hours at worst."

"Is there any way to stop him?"

"Oh, there's a way. There's always a way."

"How?"

Max said nothing.

"Tell me," Ludivine said.

"We kill him—him, and his men."

"Me and you?" she asked.

Max smiled a humorless smile. "Not good odds, are they?"

Ludivine stood and walked into the kitchen. On the center of the counter that separated the kitchen from the living room was the large black duffel bag that held the counterfeit money. She hoisted the heavy bag and brought it into the living room, placing it on the roughhewn coffee table in front of Max.

"What if we use this?"

"This guy can't be bought," Max answered, doing his best to keep his tone light even though the stress tempted him to lash out.

"I'm not suggesting we pay *him*."

He eyed her for a moment.

"Who are you suggesting we pay?"

"I don't know. Who could help us?"

Max pondered her question but made no reply.

"Can't you think of anyone who'd help us for this type of money? Surely there must be someone. That's how Mr. Winthrop is getting his help, isn't it? Paying people? Paying cops with bribes? Paying criminals to help him?"

As the snow accumulated outside, blanketing the area in a deafening white shroud, Max was able to hear his pulse in his ears.

Ludivine was correct.

"Do you know someone?" she asked.

Max remained silent.

"Do you?"

"I don't know the man personally, but you've given me an idea."

"It's someone who could help us?"

"Possibly, yes. But…"

"But what?"

Max joined eyes with Ludivine. "He might be more dangerous than Mister Winthrop."

After gnawing on her fingernail for a moment, she said, *"Aux grands maux les grands remédes."* Roughly translated, it meant, "Desperate times call for desperate measures."

The past several days had drawn Max closer to Ludivine than he'd ever been to any other person, even his closest Army friends. He bear-hugged her.

"So?" she asked, pulling her head back.

"Putain ouai."

Chapter Twenty-One

On the island of Corsica, in the rugged hills above the commune of Bastia, Guillermo "Gustav" Casson had finally awoken at 2:20 P.M. This was rather late, even by Gustav's standards, but he hadn't fallen asleep until 6:15 this morning. Before he did anything, he took a headache powder and washed it down with a full glass of water. That was ten minutes ago. Now, Gustav was robed and sat in the corner of his bedroom having his *café au lait* along with a pastry, attempting to wash away the bitter aftertaste of the powder. His *petit déjeuner* had been prepared by the young woman he'd bedded last night. He'd been with her only once before last night's marathon session. Many years before, Gustav had enjoyed a lengthy fling with her mother. And it was actually her mother who'd arranged the current relationship with her pert 19 year-old daughter. Like so many others, the mother hoped to curry favor from Gustav. Although she was still rather attractive in her mid-40s, she knew she was far too old for Gustav. Despite his own age, he'd never been with a woman over the age of 32.

Having gotten Gustav situated, the young lady now sat in bed, having her own coffee as she perused a magazine. She looked up, catching Gustav staring at her. The girl slid the duvet aside and licked her lips.

"Later," he said. "When this hangover's gone."

She fake pouted and went back to her magazine.

Gustav finished the pastry and noisily licked his fingers. He drank some of the coffee, finding it slightly on the weak side. He'd have his housekeeper teach the girl how to make it stronger. Gustav despised tepid coffee. The girl had probably made the mistake of not heaping the grounds in the middle of the press. Or, perhaps she'd been impatient and not waited for the water to come to a full boil. Nevertheless, he could live with it—for today.

In his own mind, Gustav was no tyrant.

He stared out the window at the brilliant late November afternoon. A chill Mediterranean wind whipped and shook the knotty eucalyptus trees. The balminess of the summer was gone, after the warm period they'd enjoyed earlier in the month. From this point until May, the roller coaster of winter temperatures known to all Corsicans would begin. Over the balance of a Corsican winter, the island's inhabitants knew if they didn't like the current weather to simply give it time. Each block of 48 to 72 hours brought something entirely new.

The bedroom telephone rang. Gustav answered, listened for a moment, murmured his assent and hung up.

"Who was that?" the girl asked.

"Cover up and go to the other bedroom," he said.

"Why?"

Gustav closed his eyes. "Because I said."

"But I want to know."

To Gustav, the girl's youth and looks—and skill—absolved her of her impertinence. He hitched his head to the door but bestowed on her the wisp of a smile.

The girl stood from the bed and paraded to him completely nude. She could stand to gain a few kilos, but what she had was tight as a drum. A dancer, she pirouetted in front of him before leaning down and pecking him on his cheek.

"Go on, now," he urged, admiring her ass as she wrapped the duvet tightly around her nubile body. She had pronounced dimples of Venus—a mark of beauty. The girl kept her head bowed as she crossed the hallway in front of Gustav's right hand man, Louis. He, too, kept his head bowed, as he dared not offend Gustav by leering at her.

Louis, faithful servant he was, brought Gustav a fresh cup of coffee. "I made a new pot. The other looked weak."

Gustav readily traded cups and motioned Louis to sit. The right hand man then leaned forward and lit his boss's cigarette, watching as he settled back into his chair with his strong cup of coffee and a smoke. Gustav was the high don of the Unione Corse, known in some circles as the Corsican Mafia. He valued brevity, honesty and loyalty. Louis, an employee of 19 years, readily provided all three.

"I have three things to cover, then I will leave you," Louis said. "Before I begin, you'll please recall, we have dinner tonight at ten with the men from Ajaccio." Ajaccio was the Corsican capital, and the men Louis referenced were governmental puppets looking for bribes and graft opportunities.

Gustav exhaled loudly, nodding in a resigned manner. "Yeah, yeah. Get on with it."

"Indeed. First, the drop from the week was especially good. We thought Kennedy's death might hurt business but, in some peculiar way, it actually seemed to have helped. We're still closing the week but it appears we'll finish up nearly ten percent over last week and six percent over the same week last year."

"How are we year-to-year?"

"Now we're up just a hair over eight percent."

This was an acceptable number. While conservative in relation to their cousins in La Cosa Nostra, the Unione Corse demanded annual growth of at least seven percent. During Gustav's reign as high don, they'd never dipped below that magical number. There were several levers he could pull if the number decreased, almost all of the levers surrounding the heroin trade to the

United States. But he didn't dare do it unless as a last resort. For now, the current growth would be satisfactory to the thirteen men he answered to—men whose names were associated with high government and global big business. Men who were thought to be squeaky clean. Men who secretly scrubbed dried blood from their cash-laden hands after every monthly distribution.

"Do you have any other questions about the numbers?" Louis asked.

Gustav smoked. No reaction usually meant he was pleased with the report he'd been given.

Louis cleared his throat and straightened his tie. "The second item involves our people in Nice. I'm afraid we've a bit of a problem. Without going into too much detail, for your own protection, there was a bit of a confrontation two nights ago between some of our soldiers and several off duty British sailors. One of the sailors was stabbed and later died. Our man is in the custody of the French locals."

"Who is he?"

"You don't know him. He's a *fantassin*, a foot soldier."

"So?"

"Aristide in Nice asked if you might help?"

There was a considerable pause. "I'd like more detail before sticking my beak into this. If it was a fair fight and the sailor died honestly then, yes, we'll lean on the prosecutor's office. But if our man acted cruelly or without honor, then no." Gustav smiled thinly. "I think we can handle a bit of bad press in Nice, don't you?"

"Oui."

"So, you'll get me the details?"

"I will. I'll come back to this at a later date," Louis replied.

"Now, the last thing," Gustav said, twirling his finger. Whenever he moved with this sort of speed, he was anxious to end the meeting.

"This one is rather strange." Louis frowned. "This morning, several telegrams were received in Marseilles, at Le Grand Casino de la Côte d'Azur." Le Grand was widely known as the French mainland headquarters of the Unione Corse. "The telegrams were addressed to you. Oscar received them and called me immediately."

"And?"

"You recall the cash depot robberies? The man who used rubber bullets?"

"The man who killed my men in Marseilles?"

"*En effet.* We believe the telegrams are from him. There was no confession in the telegrams, but the first one named each robbery location. In the second telegram, the sender requested a meeting with you and your representative in La Clusaz, France. The man claims he's willing to refund your stolen money, with significant interest, along with presenting you another business proposition. He awaited a reply, so I replied."

"And?"

"I asked for more. He provided several more details that seem to authenticate him as the marauder."

Brow furrowed, Gustav crushed out his cigarette. "When does he propose to meet?"

"Midnight, tonight."

"Who is he?"

"I don't know."

"Where did the telegrams originate?"

"La Clusaz—where he wants to meet."

Gustav turned up his coffee, draining it and enjoying the gritty residue at the end. At least this cup was strong. He fingered a new Gauloises cigarette for a moment, finally perching it between his lips, allowing his *conseiller* to light it for him. Gustav smoked for a moment, his eyes narrowed as he pondered such a strange request.

"Do you have a recommendation?" Gustav asked.

"I wouldn't meet with him."

"Why?"

"What's there to gain?"

"My money."

"You don't need it. The money he stole was insignificant."

Gustav dragged on his cigarette and spoke with smoke exiting his mouth. "Noted. Now, cancel our dinner and prepare the airplane. We'll depart at five and dine in La Clusaz, before the meeting." He pointed his cigarette upward. "Years ago, you and I ate at a wonderful restaurant there..."

"Le Vieux."

"That's it. Get us their best table. Then, set the meeting with this stealing rat on our terms. Call in our people from Geneva. We will meet with this rat, take everything he owns and torture him as punishment. He *will* die, but not tonight. What are your questions?"

Louis showed his palms. "It will be done. Enjoy your afternoon."

"And send the girl back in." Gustav walked to his bathroom, flicking the cigarette into the toilet and gargling with strong mouthwash. He heard his young flame bouncing on the bed. Eyeing himself in the mirror, he smiled.

Today, and tonight, showed great promise.

***

In Washington D.C., Julie Hedstrom had been at her desk in the Secret Service Annex of the Treasury Building since 6:25 A.M. She'd gotten a little less than four hours of sleep the night before. Julie would have been tired if

225

she weren't working "the Paris case," as she'd come to brand it in her mind. It had energized her and gotten her out of bed earlier than usual. The director hadn't left last night, not after the killing of Lee Harvey Oswald. This morning, after he'd grabbed forty winks, he showered and was just now eating a bite of breakfast. When she'd brought him his food, she told him she wanted to update him on her progress. He asked for ten minutes to eat.

Nine minutes later, the intercom buzzer on Julie's desk sounded. She pressed the gray button. "Yes, chief?"

"You ready?"

"I am."

"Let's get to it. How long do I have?"

"You're meeting with the deputy director of the FBI in twenty-four minutes."

"Where?"

"Here in the building: conference room one."

"C'mon in."

The director was behind his desk, a mostly clean plate in front of him with a few paint streaks of yellow—the remains of the two yolks from his runny eggs. A paper napkin emanated from his neck and rested over his tie.

"You saving that napkin for later?" she asked, sitting across from him.

"Jeez," he lamented, snapping the napkin from his collar. "I swear, Julie, I'm beat to the socks. I really am. Can't remember the last time I was this tired."

"Tonight, you need to go home and actually sleep. You're not doing the country any good in this state."

"Yeah, yeah," he touched his watch. "Alright, Jules, we're skinny on time so let's hear it."

Julie used no notes. She gave Director Lynch a clear, concise summary of the entire case, leaving out no facts and not skipping over the parts he'd already heard. When she neared the end of her summary, and spoke about the revelations from Lucy Thaler's sister, she watched Lynch closely. He hardly reacted but he did gnaw on his tongue a bit—something he did when he was intrigued. She'd dropped all her basic artillery and ended with the hydrogen bombs involving Lucy Thaler's programmed affair with Hermann Goering and her subsequent disappearance. For good measure, she emphasized Clayton Fairchild's words to Danny Jackson about the briefcase, and Fairchild's premature death in a solo automobile accident. When she finished, having taken 13 minutes to summarize her investigation, the only sound was the ticking of Lynch's desk clock.

Julie knew better than to interrupt his cogitation.

"Well, I must say..." He stopped what he was saying and twisted his lips. Julie remained quiet. The director slid the lever of his flip top address book to

"V". He pressed the button—it made the lid pop up. He ran his finger down the page as he lifted his telephone, spun three digits and waited.

Julie had only seen him dial a number on a telephone once before—it amused her. And she'd populated his new address book only a few weeks before. She was proud to see him use it.

"Yeah, this is Lynch. Is Vann here?" The director shut his eyes, as if summoning patience. "Find him now and send him to me, will you? Tell him Julie's in my office and to just come straight in. Thank you." He hung up the phone and eyed Julie. Though his mouth didn't smile, his eyes did.

"Even if you're way down the rabbit trail to end all rabbit trails, I've got to give you credit, Julie. You've done a commendable job of pulling all this together. And your summation was as good as I've ever heard from anyone in these walls. *Anyone*." He sat forward and crossed one hand over the other. "Julie, I'm—"

"Yes?"

"I'm sorry I gave you such a hard time. Truly."

"You didn't, chief. In fact, I feel it was just the opposite."

"Well, it seems that way to me. It seems I've had to push you down more times than you deserve. You're worthy of any job in this building. If I can survive all that's happened on my watch, you have my word that I'll do everything I can to put you into a position with more responsibility."

"Just working on something important is enough for now."

The director leaned back in his chair, crossing his leg over the other. "So, you believe Fairchild stored critical intel in the briefcase in the vault in Paris?"

She lifted her index finger. "He did, chief. Unless Danny Jackson is lying. That part isn't conjecture."

"Fair enough. Jackson wouldn't lie, unless he was misled—which I doubt. So, Clayton Fairchild *did* store a briefcase in the vault in Paris. We're assuming what was in it was valuable. The briefcase is probably one of those bombproof types they made in the late forties. Your research has led you to believe that the intel inside has something to do with the disappearance of an alleged field agent named..."

"Lucy Thaler."

"Yes, Lucy Thaler," he said, scribbling on his yellow legal pad. "And according to what you've learned, Thaler was in Berlin in forty-one and involved in an affair with Hermann Goering. Thaler's sister believes Goering had her killed."

"Yes."

"And from what others have told you, Fairchild went through a rough patch after Lucy went dark, making you suspect he was involved with her?"

"Correct. I believe he was in mourning."

"So, now the $64,000 question is what in the hell was in that briefcase?"

"Indeed."

"Do you believe the briefcase was the reason for the theft? Do you feel as if the money was just a cover?"

"It's a possibility, but I haven't found anything that could help me make that determination."

"Fair enough. Anything on the suspect?"

"No, sir."

"So, we've got a shooter who spoke French and American English. We've got a mystery man in the courtyard and a probable shooter on a nearby roof."

"Yes, sir."

He whistled. "This would be a humdinger if we weren't dealing with the assassination of a president."

The building frown on the director's face told Julie the weight of the situation was sinking in. She remained quiet.

Inside of a minute, Harry Vann stepped into the office, looking as if he'd just walked out of a bandbox. Six feet tall, freshly shaven, wearing an immaculately cut blue suit, crisp white shirt, striped blue tie and highly-polished cordovan brogues, Vann could pass for a middle-aged catalog model. He'd always been a poster boy for youthful, vibrant looks and wore the clothes to match. His wife was a well-known stage actress in D.C. and the rumor was that Vann had been invited for minor onstage roles more than once, based solely on his looks.

Despite his clothes and appearance, he was also known as an excellent agent. He currently worked in D.C. on the vice president's security detail at his home, Les Ormes, up in Spring Valley. Now, however, Vann's life was upended along with everyone else. When this crisis was settled, President Johnson would almost certainly take him to the presidential detail—primarily because Vann was a fellow Texan and Ladybird Johnson adored him.

For now, Vann was working with everyone else on the myriad of problems surrounding all that had taken place in Dallas. He was surely thrown for a loop by Lynch's first question, one that was hurled at him after no pleasantries following his arrival.

"Vann, do you remember Lucy Thaler, a Berlin agent who worked for the OSS in 1941?"

Vann looked at Julie before turning back to the director.

"She's cleared for this," Lynch said, waving Vann's concern away. "Dispense."

"Yessir, I do."

"Tell me about her. Facts. Go."

"That was all compartmentalized. I don't know many facts. I wasn't in that chain of concern."

"Tell me what you do know."

"She'd initiated an affair with Goering. She provided good intel for a period of time. She disappeared and nearly everyone felt she'd been compromised, and eliminated."

"Was Clayton Fairchild involved with her?"

Vann shook his head. "Fairchild was a gentlemen's gentleman. I truly don't know, nor would he have talked about it. There was a rumor that they'd been involved, but that's all it was. I remember he never admitted it, even through weeks of debriefings."

"Any more facts?"

"None that I recall."

"Then, tell me more rumors."

Clearly uncomfortable, Vann shifted his posture. "Fairchild was upset after Lucy disappeared. Very upset. He went to Berlin and learned that the Germans were treating her as a missing person. Could've been window dressing. Of course, the State Department got involved but the lines of communication and diplomacy had deteriorated badly by that time." Vann glanced at Julie before he turned back to the director. "In my opinion, something else happened other than the Nazis simply eliminating her. I don't know if we hung her out to dry accidentally, or if someone made a grave mistake and blew her cover. After she went missing, Fairchild actually had to be put under surveillance for a time. But after a few months, he got himself together and performed as well as anyone did during the war."

"What else?" the director asked.

Vann opened his hands. "That's pretty much all I remember, rumor or fact."

"There has to be more. Who else was involved with her handling?"

Though he'd been standing at the position of attention, Vann pressed on his closed eyes with his thumb and index finger. "It's been so long. Obviously, Fairchild. He was her handler and, if I remember correctly, he recruited her. I also recall Eddie English and Vic Roach being involved. Only because Fairchild reported to their group."

Lynch grunted upon hearing their names. "Eddie English is dead, isn't he?"

"Not yet, but he's close." Vann tapped his chest as he turned to Julie. "Lung cancer."

She nodded, but had never heard of him before. She then spoke, asking, "You also mentioned Vic Roach. Is he *the* Victor Roach?"

"Yep," the director answered, looking none too happy about it. "He's *that* Victor Roach."

"I didn't know he was OSS during the war," she remarked.

Lynch nodded as his phone rang. He lifted it and spoke tersely. "Our meeting time isn't for a few more minutes." He listened a bit more before his tone changed. "Something's come up. Tell them I need a half-hour." He snorted. "Well he can just be pissed off, and so can Hoover. What the hell are they going to do to me that hasn't already been done?" Lynch went to slam the receiver down but halted an inch above the cradle. He replaced the phone softly and uttered a particularly vile word used to describe a group of unpleasant people.

Vann suppressed a smirk.

Trying not to smile, Julie said, "Chief, if you need me to go handle the deputy, I can."

"Apparently, Hoover came, too. Let 'em wait." The director looked up at Vann. "Sit. Keep talking."

Vann continued. "The group that handled the deep agents in Germany was small and tight. I can't remember anyone other than Fairchild, Roach and English working with Lucy Thaler."

The director twirled a pencil. "Normally, I'd call Roach but…"

"But what?" Julie asked.

"He's about as prickly as a person can get. Hates the government, now, especially the federal branch. Only associates with his inner circle of yes men."

"How'd you hear of him, Julie?" Vann asked.

"I read a magazine article about him from a few years back. It stuck with me because I've always wanted to go to Hawaii. They printed a picture of his plantation." She stacked her hands over her heart. "It looked like heaven on earth."

"He's top-thirty wealthiest…in the world," Lynch said. "If I remember correctly, when they printed that article, he'd just jumped into that one-hundred to two-hundred million bracket."

"Did he make all his money since the war?" Julie asked. "Or did he inherit?"

"That's the kicker," Lynch replied, cocking his eyebrow. "Julie, you're cleared, but what I'm about to say goes beyond much of what you've ever been exposed to."

She gave him a disappointed expression. "Chief…"

"I know, I know," the director said. "Victor Roach didn't have two nickels to rub together. His dad was a farmer who lost everything in the crash. Victor was smart as a whip, and clever, too. Started out at Northwestern, if I'm not mistaken. Ended up at one of the Ivy League schools. Got scholarships. Tough times back then so he joined the Army and got accepted to officer candidate school. Tested off the charts." He turned to Vann. "What was his first job?"

"He was Army SIS but did all manner of things. We all did. Before the war, most of us were handling communications, decryption, all that. Roach was very good." Vann eyed Julie. "But there was always something about him that made me uneasy. And I wasn't the only one."

"None of that tripped any official alarms?" Lynch asked.

"No, because it was simply my gut feeling. The man was squeaky clean and, believe me, he was checked thoroughly. We all were."

There was a bout of silence. Julie broke it.

"Where are you two leading with this?" Julie turned to the director. "What were you about to tell me about Roach?"

"Him and Eddie English were on a submarine that got sunk in forty-two, or maybe forty-three. They'd been in Germany and the sub successfully extracted them but got hit near the English Channel by a U-boat. They were able to surface. Bunch of survivors. Vic and Eddie both got medical releases." The director arched his eyebrows. "They *both* got rich after that."

"Eddie got rich," Vann clarified. "Vic Roach got wealthy."

"How'd they make their money?" Julie asked.

"Brilliant, savant-style investing," the director replied. "The thing is, it was later discovered that they'd taken out loans *before* the U.S. entered the war. They used everything they could to get the loans, including promissory notes that carried illegally high interest rates. They conned relatives into mortgaging land. Borrowed money from loan sharks. You name it. Both men were in debt out their ears."

"Isn't that how people end up on skid row?" Julie asked.

Vann nodded. "Sure is, unless you're smart enough to take that borrowed money and make spectacular investments. I'm referring to the type of investments that give you returns in the thousands of percentiles."

The director spoke up. "So, naturally, a number of people believed that English and Roach used illicitly gained intelligence to profit from the war."

"Did they?"

"Doesn't matter if they did or didn't," Vann replied. "Because they both passed muster of a damned thorough investigation. They were checked through and through and no one was able to pin anything on either of them."

"Joe Kennedy was no longer SEC chairman by then, but plenty of people whispered that even he stuck his big Irish nose into the investigation," Lynch remarked with a touch of irony, since he was of Irish ancestry. "Supposedly, Kennedy was pissed off that one of Vic Roach's best investments—a California naval petroleum enterprise—knocked out one of Kennedy's portfolio investments. Put it under at pennies on the dollar."

Julie sat forward in her chair. "But Roach and English were involved with an unbelievably well-placed agent in the Third Reich. They might have learned that Goering told Lucy of Hitler's war plans. They might have used that information to make those investments that made them wealthy."

The director tossed the pencil to his desk. "You're a brilliant lady, Julie. It took you a few minutes to come to a conclusion that it took bright men months to come to."

"There was one thing that was peculiar about their investments," Vann said, lifting his finger for emphasis.

"Yes?" Julie asked.

"None of them had *anything* to do with the war in Europe."

"It's true. Their investments dealt with American companies who primarily serviced the Pacific," the director added.

"And neither Roach nor English were privy to a scrap of intel about the Pacific," Vann finished. "As I mentioned, our department was incredibly compartmentalized."

"And at the time, we had no idea the Japs were going to hit Pearl Harbor," the director said.

"Could they have possibly learned that from the Germans?" she asked.

"The Germans didn't know," the director replied. "There've been whispers for years that they knew, but we've never found a single piece of evidence that they did, and that includes hundreds of debriefings of Nazis who wanted to work with us. They would have told us. It's just one of many so-called fringe theories that happen after a war."

Vann agreed.

Julie deflated. The three of them sat there in the quiet, listening to the desk clock.

"Your meeting?" Julie asked.

"Hoover can wait," the director answered.

Vann stood. "Use your guest phone?"

The director nodded his assent.

They listened as Vann made two telephone calls at the rear of the office. When finished, he said, "Eddie English is at Thomas Jefferson University Hospital in downtown Philadelphia. He's only expected to live for a few more days."

Director Lynch asked Vann how busy he was.

"I'm just doing as I'm told. Right now, I'm working on Oswald's service in the Marines."

"How many are on that?" Lynch asked.

"Four of us."

"You're off for now." The director briefed Vann for five minutes, giving him the high points of Julie's investigation. When he was finished, he placed both palms on his blotter and joined eyes with Julie.

"Are you comfortable with an overnight trip to Philadelphia with Agent Vann?"

Her lips parted. This was certainly unprecedented. She blinked, then nodded.

"Then you two be smart about it. Get up there as fast you can and see what Eddie English remembers, if he can even talk." The director pointed at Vann, then at Julie. "Dying men tell tales. Be bold. Ask him."

***

In La Clusaz, Mathilde, the rental company's mousy clerk, tramped through the slushy remains of last night's snow, eyeing the grocery list in her hands. Her eyes slid to the bottom of the list—the pharmacy portion. Antiseptic. Bandages. Surgical tape.

Prophylactics! Utterly disgusting.

Mathilde had never been married, and had certainly never gone beyond a few basic smooches with a boy. The kisses had been 11 long years before, during the last year of her schooling when she was 17 years old. She didn't know much about what women and men did together, nor could she even envision exactly what a prophylactic was used for. She'd heard several stories from people she no longer associated with. Horrid, vile stories involving bodily fluids, strange sensations and even peculiar smells. She pinched her lips together as her mind wandered back to that obnoxious American man from earlier. This was *his* list. She thought of him, unclothed with that young French woman, both of them grunting and moaning like two dogs in heat.

Because the pharmacy was on her way, she stopped there first, buying the requested items. Mathilde made sure she showed the list to the pharmacist, informing him that the list was for a vacationing couple and in no way were the items for her. The pharmacist helped her and thankfully did nothing to add to her embarrassment.

That unpleasantness taken care of, Mathilde headed to the bank. On the way there, out of sheer curiosity, she sat on a bench and opened the bag from the pharmacy. There, in a plain orange and white box that could be opened without fear of tampering, were the packages of prophylactics. She removed one, hiding it in her lap. It was in its own pouch, round and rather hard, like a key ring. Doubting that the man and woman would miss one, Mathilde secretly ripped open the pouch. Concealing the item in her lap, she carefully unrolled the oily piece of thin rubber, gasping as the covering slowly extended in front of her.

It's shaped just like a—

Mathilde could hardly breathe. She'd never seen one on a grown man. When she was young, there were several boys who insisted on showing theirs with regularity. And she'd been to enough farms that she'd seen several on livestock. But this prophylactic, aimed at catching whatever emanated from a man, was quite a bit larger than she might have imagined. It made her insides feel strange, as if she'd just drank a glass of carbonated Orangina too quickly.

This is just scandalous, including your own curiosity. You should be ashamed.

Balling the items up in her hand, she threw them in the first receptacle and closed the box and bag tightly before continuing on to the bank.

I'm very upset with you, Mathilde inwardly scolded herself. You've always managed to resist temptation, even when alone. Such curiosity. Where did it come from? Why would you want to know anything about the size of a man's—

She shook the thoughts from her head and hurried to the bank. The door jingled as she went inside. The bank was warm and hushed. A thick, wine colored carpet runner beneath her feet welcomed her. As she unbuttoned her coat, Mathilde saw *him*—Simon, the young assistant manager who always made her feel special. She'd be lying if she said his presence didn't make her flush and tingle, all at the same time. Simon was thin and bookish with a residual of adolescent acne, and he always reserved the brightest of smiles just for her. He placed his pencil in the center of his ledger and stood, walking to the counter and leaning over, clasping his hands in a prayerful pose as he awaited her.

Imagine that oily prophylactic glistening on his rigid...STOP IT!

"And how does today find the lovely Mademoiselle Mathilde?" he asked, his voice singsong.

Mathilde's throat felt as if it were closing up, the way it had when she'd first tried shrimp as a teenager. She finally managed to swallow and broke off eye contact, turning her gaze down to her handbag. Mathilde removed the money pouch from her purse and did her best to conceal the shake from her voice.

"Good afternoon, Simon, I'm very well but in quite a hurry." She placed the money pouch on the counter. "There are two deposit slips in the pouch, one for francs and the other for American dollars."

"American dollars?" he asked, feigning shock. "You've never brought me American dollars before. I didn't know your agency accepted them." He peered over his spectacles. "You know, Mathilde, there is a standard fee for conversion. But, because you're so special, perhaps I can speak to the manager about waiving it, just this once—and only for *you*, because you're such a valued client of *mine*."

"That would be quite nice, thank you," she answered, looking up, only to see him staring at her with unconcealed interest.

"You look very nice today," he said, lingering.

"Thank you...I..."

Just for a moment, allow yourself to fancy what it would feel like, down there, with Simon. The prophylactic is oiled to make it easier to slip ins—

Mathilde faked a sneeze and turned away, digging into her bag for a tissue.

"My goodness, I hope you're not sick," Simon said, taking the money pouch from her. He unzipped the bag, removing the two stacks of money. First, he counted the francs and wrote out a receipt, sliding it to her, allowing his fingers to touch hers. He then went to the stack of American money, carefully counting and recounting. Several times while he counted the money, his eyes cut to hers followed by a knowing grin.

"…deux quarante, deux soixante…"

As he worked, Mathilde recalled some of the decade-old talk with her cribbage friends, from back when they'd attended clerical school together. The girls would drink too much wine. Then the heavy one, Norma, always bragged about the older Italian man she worked for on Saturdays. He would close his shop early and take her into the back room where he liked to put his head down between her legs, using his tongue on her nether regions. She loved to tell how the man's actions made her giggle and scream. It put her into such a state that she would do anything with him. Though the other girls roared with laughter, such talk frightened Mathilde. She eventually stopped playing cribbage with them and, since then, had given up drink altogether.

But now, with a man she cared for, things seemed markedly different. While Simon concentrated on the money in front of him, Mathilde allowed her mind to wander as she imagined him with no clothes on. He'd be thin and pale. Judging by his boyish face and smooth forearms, she believed he'd have little hair on his body. She wondered how his manhood would look. Would it hang limp, or stand erect, the way her aunt's billy goats used to get in the springtime. A tremor passed through her body, making Simon look up.

"You alright?"

Unable to speak, she nodded. Her neck and upper chest were aflame, along with another area of her body. She carefully crossed her legs and squeezed her thighs together.

Again, Simon leaned over the counter. "Why don't we have dinner some night, Mathilde? Perhaps a movie afterward?"

"I…I…don't know."

"Why not? You're not married, are you?"

"Oh no, nothing like that."

"Boyfriend?"

Making no eye contact, she shook her head.

He placed his hand over hers, allowing his thumb to dig to the underside of her palm, where it rubbed seductively. "There aren't many of us here in La Clusaz, Mathilde…unmarried people. Sure, there are plenty of people on holiday, but few like us who live and work here." His eyes roamed her face, down over her ample bosom before coming back up. "I think you and I could grow very close."

Mathilde nearly perished on the spot.

Flushed, tingling, on the verge of passing out—she nodded and couldn't believe the words escaping her own mouth. "I'd really enjoy a date with you, Simon."

"Good," he replied. "Tonight, then?"

"So soon?"

"I don't think I can wait."

Another spastic nod, as wispy breaths escaped her mouth.

"Perfect," he replied. Again his eyes roamed. "Let me finish up here."

"Take your time," she replied, a five-piece brass band blaring in her mind as she pondered what might happen on this evening.

As they'd spoken about their date, he'd held the American bills in his hand. "I'll be right back. We have to check all American money for counterfeits. Give me just a moment, please."

He walked smartly to the rear of the bank and was gone nearly five minutes. At one point, Mathilde watched as a man in a suit was summoned to the back room. When Simon returned, he wore a concerned expression on his face. "Mathilde," he said, gesturing her close. She thought he was preparing for another suggestion.

He wasn't.

He whispered, "Mathilde, the American money you gave me might be counterfeit."

"What?" she hissed.

"*Might* be. You shouldn't worry. Did you get it from a renter?"

"Yes, a vile American who I had to stop and buy…"

"Buy what?"

"Groceries…I have to buy him groceries. That's where I'll go next."

"Well, it may be nothing, so please, do nothing—and *don't* warn the American. I'll let you know. The manager has called a specialist. How long is the renter staying in La Clusaz?"

"A week."

"Very well. Buy him his groceries and act normal, please."

"I will."

Simon offered his hand and she shook it. This time, he used his index finger to tickle her palm. "Tonight, seven P.M. Meet in front of your office?"

Eyes down, she nodded.

"Dinner?"

Another nod.

"A movie?"

Another.

"May I make a suggestion?" he asked.

After a difficult swallow, she said, "Of course."

"We can skip the movie, if you prefer. My boarding house has a back entrance. I'm positive I can get you upstairs. I have my own television. It's small, but on cold nights it gets good reception. We could watch a show there."

Mathilde's jaw ceased working. She continued to stare at the floor but managed to nod several times and mutter something about seeing how she felt after dinner.

"So, that's a maybe?" he asked.

Another nod.

"Why not six o'clock, then? Cuts down on the wait. Gives me more time to convince you I'm not a murderer."

"That's f-f-fine."

"That was a joke, Mathilde."

"Oh. Yes, that was funny," she said.

Simon's smile was smug and simpering and full of knowing. "Very good, indeed. I will be counting the minutes."

Mathilde exited the bank, hurrying toward the grocery. Once she'd gathered herself, all she could think about was tonight, her first date in 28 years of life. And though it made her loathe herself, she couldn't help but wonder what Simon had planned for their rendezvous in his boarding house room.

While she was shopping, Mathilde halted in the produce department, concealed behind a pyramid of melons. She opened the pharmacy bag and the prophylactic box, removing two more of the small packages. She thrust the packages deep into her handbag, making a mental note to transfer them to the clutch she would carry on her date tonight.

Mathilde had already forgotten all about the possibility that she might have deposited counterfeit money, and was preparing to use more in the grocery. Her mind was far more consumed with leaving early so she could get home and bathe properly before her date with Simon.

Simon, the 23 year-old banker, who made her feel so special.

Chapter Twenty-Two

At 0830 on Monday morning, Detectives Lacroix and Roux had stood before Roux's lieutenant. They'd entered his office and stood beside one another, having reported to the lieutenant in a military style manner. In the closet-like room filled with blue smoke, the two detectives had successfully petitioned the lieutenant to loan Roux to Detective Lacroix for three days—and three days only. The lieutenant had agreed, but only if Gaspard agreed to provide future assistance—off the clock—to the auto theft division. This was a common ask for rising officers in the Paris Police, as many divisions judged their leadership on conviction rate and successful case closures. In essence, Gaspard would have to pay the lieutenant back in spades, something he was more than willing to do. Because, if he were to share his own case with anyone from Homicide, he risked losing it due to its high profile.

And there was no way he was letting it go.

Their petition had occurred six hours before. That done, Gaspard phoned Evelyn, safe in the hotel where she was a guest staying under a pseudonym. She was able to order meals from room service and her cat was with her. Evelyn assured Gaspard they'd both be fine. She made a kissing sound and asked Gaspard to call her later.

Satisfied that his new flame was secure, Gaspard dispatched two plainclothes policemen to Bois de Vincennes to spy on the rock where Patten's illicit employer left his daily payments. Neither detective placed much hope in nabbing anyone at the rock. First, Patten may have warned his payer. Second, even if he hadn't, whoever was paying him probably used a blind courier to place the money. They'd have to be incredibly stupid to place it under the rock themselves.

There was one thing that genuinely surprised the two detectives: the phone number Patten had provided was genuine. Utilizing the technical assistance of the *Direction Générale des Télécommunications*, the two detectives were disappointed to learn that the phone number in question worked in a blind relay. Neither man could understand why the phone company couldn't pinpoint where the relay was. The area they were able to nail down was associated with a local exchange, and was made up of approximately 4 square blocks. In that area, there were more than 12,000 phone lines—far too many for them to check.

"And all you'd likely find, even if you did find the relay, is a junction box with a shitload of wires," the bored technician told them. "Typically, these types of things are located in the basement of a building, and the residents of the building are unaware."

"How hard is it to put one in?" Gaspard asked.

The technician shrugged. "Simple. No training required. That's why crooks do it all the time, and in a crowded city like Paris, it's like finding a needle in a haystack."

When the technician had departed, Gaspard tried the number from his desk. It was picked up on the third ring, although the person said nothing.

"Fifi?" he asked.

The person immediately hung up. Whenever he called, Patten probably spoke the information and that was all. It really was a nice setup. But without being able to pinpoint the source of the call, the number and the silent person on the other end were useless to them.

While both detectives believed a crime had occurred at the school in Orléans, they continued to be convinced that there was little to be gained by sending in forensics. They believed that the potential benefit was far outweighed by the red tape they'd both have to cut through, especially after having traveled there and entering the school without authorization.

"What happened there is done and gone," Roux said. "If your man stole the Renault in Paris, and then shot someone in that school, then I believe he's being chased. And with the sort of money he took from the Secret Service, he's not being chased by only one man. He's being chased by many. The key is finding him before they do, or you'll have another dead body on your hands."

"But that will close my case."

"Will it?"

"If I can prove it was him."

"Someone scrubbed that school clean. I suspect they'll do the same if they find your man."

"What if my man died in that school?" Gaspard asked.

"Do you think that's what happened?"

"It could have."

"But is that what your gut tells you?"

"No," Gaspard answered. "I think he's still on the run."

"Why?"

After a pause, Gaspard said, "The phone number Patten used here is still active. If my man had been found, they'd have shut it down."

"Good point."

They'd gone through a number of case files and perused numerous suspects for pattern behavior such as the shooter at the Place de Clichy displayed. They spoke to several individuals across multiple departments at 36. They discovered nothing of interest.

After a quick lunch at a nearby café, the two detectives now sipped coffee in the main Homicide meeting room. Both men had notepads before them, writing down ideas when a thunderbolt arrived in the form of a letter.

A secretary from Homicide knocked and entered. She handed Gaspard a sealed envelope bearing the return address of his Homicide lieutenant. The lieutenant had a reputation as a renegade officer. He also reported to the captain who'd given Gaspard so many preemptive warnings at the Place de Clichy. Gaspard thanked the secretary and sent her away.

When he turned the envelope over, he saw it was marked with a purple wax seal and, above the seal, the words *"Très Confidential."*

Eyeing Roux, Gaspard slid his finger underneath the flap and ripped open the envelope. He flattened the plain piece of *tellière papier* on the table and read:

G.

Just received word from Sûreté that possible American counterfeit bills were passed <u>today</u> at the Auvergne-Rhône-Alpes Banque in La Clusaz. The call came in to the special inspector at 14:12 hours. He's expecting the bills to arrive late tonight via Air France for inspection.

The man who passed the bills was reportedly American. He was of average height, with blue eyes and a short dark beard. He was with a younger woman. The man wore a stocking cap that covered his head. He never removed the stocking cap. I remember your man was allegedly wounded on his scalp.

The man and woman rented a chalet, although the specifics haven't been gathered yet as the bank isn't certain the bills were counterfeit. The rental company is in La Clusaz, as is the bank. The rental company is called L'Agence Chalet de Montagne.

The Americans are hammering us for information. I will
try to contain this until morning. If the Sûreté inspector
stays and checks the bills tonight, I expect he will notify
the Americans.

I will attempt to get the address of the rented chalet.
Check with me later.

D.

His pulse sounding in his ears, Gaspard slid the note to Roux. Roux read
it silently before turning to his short-term partner.

"Holy shit."

"Indeed," Gaspard whispered.

"We need to get to La Clusaz."

"Yes, we do."

Roux shook his head, lamenting. "That'll take six, seven, maybe eight
hours. And I heard they had snow down there."

Gaspard walked to his desk and retrieved his checkbook. He opened the
register, viewing the most recent subtotal. He flipped to the rear, staring at
the amount in his savings account before turning to his partner.

"Get your coat."

"Are we going to La Clusaz?" Roux asked.

"One way, or another."

***

Mr. Winthrop threw cold water on his face and eyed his reflection in the
mirror of the roadside motel in Bonneville, France. Late last night, after
downing three fast vodkas, he'd managed 4 hours of restless sleep on the thin
mattress. Speaking of where he'd slept, he now viewed the bed in the daylight.
The blankets were pulled back. On the bed sheet—yellow stains everywhere.
Not large yellow stains, either. Small and splotchy.

Disgusting.

He went back to the mirror, examining his face. Bags under the
bloodshot eyes. His mouth drawn downward. Pale skin. This chase might be
the death of him. If Mr. Winthrop only knew he was less than a half-hour
away from Max Warfield. Forty-three kilometers, to be precise, the way the
crow flies. Sixty-four kilometers on a curvy but easily passable mountain road.

But Mr. Winthrop had no idea he was so close, and had uncharacteristically
begun to doubt himself. What if Max had gone west from that petrol station?
What if he'd doubled back on purpose? What if he'd done something entirely

different? Once Max got far enough away, he was gone forever—no doubt about it. The man was a worthy adversary.

Wearing his slacks and undershirt, Winthrop turned on the television and waited for the tubes to warm up. Sitting at the foot of the bed, he watched a bit of the news about Kennedy, Oswald and Jack Ruby before switching the set back off. The rectangular picture vacuumed into a tiny silver dot in the middle of the screen before disappearing.

Mr. Winthrop had already shaved and brushed his teeth but he didn't feel like eating. He popped in a peppermint, checking his stock afterward. He had only five left in his briefcase, along with his emergency peppermint in his jacket pocket. He'd need to get more today.

Once he'd neatly squared the wrapper, he made the bed, covering the nastiness. Then he tugged the curtain back and viewed the parking lot. There were only a few cars parked among the quickly melting snow. From what he'd heard from the night manager, the higher elevations had gotten much more snowfall. General Timmons and the Gendarme were in nearby rooms, just down the breezeway. Winthrop knew he should roust them and create a plan, but his lack of confidence made him resist the urge to do what he knew was right. Plus, he just couldn't stomach Timmons yet. Every second away from the military man was a small victory.

Touching his pistol, several murderous thoughts flitted through Mr. Winthrop's mind.

No, this isn't the place, isn't the time.

Put away your personal dislikes—for now. You got your rest; it's time to go. Every hour matters.

Winthrop pulled on his soiled white shirt without buttoning it and slid into the simple chair next to the bedside table. Lifting the phone, Winthrop jiggled the hook until the man in the office picked up.

"Outside line," Winthrop said in French. Once he had a line, he dialed the operator and placed a collect call to Paris. The phone rang four times before it was picked up by woman.

"*À quelle heure fermez-vous aujourd'hui?*" Mr. Winthrop asked, giving the correct code that would sound innocuous to anyone who happened to be listening.

"Is this line secure or shall we arrange for another?" the woman asked. Her voice was tense.

Winthrop straightened. Something must have happened. "It's secure enough. Tell me."

"First, the female witness from Clichy has been moved."

"Did you go in?"

"We did. She's under protection somewhere."

"And she saw me?"

"Yes. But they have nothing concrete on you. But that's not what's important."

"Speak."

"There's a ski village called La Clusaz in Auvergne-Rhône-Alpes. Just this morning, a man matching the description of your target passed a significant number of possible American counterfeit bills at a vacation rental business."

Winthrop's voice was a blade. "Who told you this?"

"The contact from Sûreté."

"Shit. Are they on it?" he demanded.

"They're typical feds. Right now, they're awaiting the bills in Paris. Once they examine them, then they'll respond."

"Then we've got time."

"Indeed. Nothing follows." The line clicked dead.

Mr. Winthrop slapped the bedside table and fought the urge to let out a victory cry. His hope soaring above the nearby peaks, he quickly pulled on his shoes and hurried down the chilly breezeway, rapping on the doors belonging to Timmons and the Gendarme. Each man opened his respective door—the general was showered and shaved and ready—the Gendarme appeared straight from the bed, his hair matted up one side, red sleep lines on his face. Mr. Winthrop told them to be in the car in five minutes. As he waited, Winthrop studied the map on the hood of the car.

Rather than rush straight to La Clusaz, Mr. Winthrop made the decision to stop at a café for coffee, food and the creation of a plan. He couldn't afford to materialize in La Clusaz half-baked. Besides, if Max had rented a chalet, he wasn't leaving anytime soon.

The plan they made was solid. It covered all contingencies.

Or, perhaps not.

Mr. Winthrop had no idea he'd just made an error that would result in the loss of lives of men on his side.

Not that he cared.

***

There were approximately 30 minutes remaining before the high don of the Unione Corse was due to arrive at the rented mountainside chalet. Max's vigilance had increased as he'd peered out the windows for the last hour. Just before the sun set behind the snow-covered mountains, he heard several car doors slam. He adjusted his view from the front window and noticed movement past the top of the driveway, off to the side of the winding road. He stepped outside, armed, peering through the dusk. There was an automobile parked on the side of the road. Two men stood at the front of the car, openly smoking cigarettes, the cherry tips glowing in the gathering darkness. They peered at Max before turning away, obviously unconcerned that he'd seen them.

"Who are they?" Ludivine asked, stepping silently from the house.

"Advance team. They're probably not alone."

"They're with the mob boss?"

"Yeah. Let's go back inside."

Earlier, Max had built a fire and he and Ludivine had eaten a hearty meal from their delivered groceries. He now smoked a cigarette, watching the flames as he pondered how this night would proceed. In Max's estimation, there was a fifty-fifty chance that the don, Gustav, would attempt to simply take the money. Even if Max were to hide it, the don could simply kidnap them both and torture them until they gave up the cash.

So, how to protect against that?

If the amount were smaller—maybe $20,000—the don would kill Max and be done with it. He'd kill Ludivine, too, of course—probably after allowing his men to brutalize her. This would be done in retribution for Max's knocking over the cash rooms. But because the amount of money was so staggering, despite it being counterfeit, Max knew the don would want every single bill and would probably stop at nothing to get it.

So, the question was, how could Max and Ludivine convince the don not to kill them? And furthermore, how could they persuade the don to provide them with the gift of protection? Max knew it was only a matter of time before the rental company's bank in La Clusaz realized the American man in Chalet 23 had passed counterfeit bills that matched the money stolen from the Place de Clichy.

But Max didn't expect the French or the American authorities to arrive first. No. He expected Mr. Winthrop and his people—whoever the hell they were. Thus far, they'd proven that they had all the connections needed to stay several steps ahead of all branches of law enforcement. They'd be the first to react to the counterfeit money.

"What's to prevent this man, the don, from killing us?" Ludivine asked.

"Very little," Max breathed, flicking his cigarette into the fire.

"What does a man like the don want?"

"Power."

"And money?" she asked.

"Oh, yes, he wants money. But power is his greatest desire. With power, he can get virtually anything he wants."

"What about the items from the briefcase?" she asked.

"I thought about it, but I'm not so sure we should consider allowing such a damning piece of evidence to fall into an enemy's hands."

"Is Gustav an enemy of the United States?"

"I'd say he's an enemy of France *and* the United States. Not directly, but he doesn't care about those types of allegiances. He'd probably use the tapes and photos as a bargaining chip. We don't want those tapes and pictures going to the wrong people."

"What else can we provide him?"

Max didn't get a chance to answer the question. There were three solid knocks on the door. He and Ludivine joined eyes.

"What will you do?" she whispered.

"I'm going to appeal to his pragmatic side."

"How?"

"Whatever the situation dictates," Max answered.

The contents of the briefcase were hidden in the attic. They were both confident they wouldn't be found without an extremely thorough search. The money was in the bedroom, stacked behind the drawers of the dresser. In Max's estimation, the cash would be found on a first-pass search.

Hiding places didn't matter, now. The only thing that mattered was appealing to this king criminal's tastes. If Max and Ludivine could somehow solve the enigma, they might make it off this snowy mountain.

But if they failed to impress the man, they would both likely die an agonizing death. In Max's estimation, this had been their best move, appealing to the head of the Unione Corse.

Their best move, earlier…

Now Max couldn't help but doubt himself.

No time for that. Be strong. Be confident.

He walked to the front door and opened it boldly. Standing there were three men. The two flanking men were clearly "muscle." The one in the middle had to be Guillermo "Gustav" Casson. He wore a camel overcoat topped by a handsome wine scarf. His fedora was likely very expensive, and matched the jacket and scarf, right down to the scarlet ibis feather in his hatband. Gustav's tan was rich and his teeth bright white as he smiled and offered his hand.

"Bonsoir, Maximillian."

When Max reached to shake, he saw a shotgun whip up from underneath the left man's overcoat. There was no time to react and, in a fraction of a second, Max felt as if he'd been struck in the chest by a cannonball.

Blown backward, he slid to a stop as his head hit the chimney. Despite the roar of the shotgun, he was aware of Ludivine's piercing shriek.

***

Agent Vann drove Julie north to Philadelphia. They were in Vann's car, a gleaming red Pontiac Tempest with a white convertible top. Though Julie knew and trusted Vann, she'd felt mildly uncomfortable at the beginning of their journey. She'd never driven alone anywhere with anyone from work—

especially a man. Making her more nervous were his dashing looks. They were enough to make any woman flush.

Now, as the miles had worn on, she conversed easily with Vann. He spoke about appropriate subjects, acting in the manner of a perfect gentleman. In fact, not only was he a gentleman, he was also quite funny. Julie was enjoying herself.

Before they'd departed, the director authorized Julie to tell Vann everything she'd learned about the Paris case, right down to the last detail. They'd spent the first hour of the drive getting to know one another, and the last two hours discussing the case. Now, as they made their way into Philadelphia's city limits, Vann had whistled when Julie was finished.

"You discovered all that detail from a typist's testimony about a mysterious briefcase?"

"That, and the man she saw in the courtyard, and the fact that Agent Lang was killed by a bullet that originated on a rooftop. Not to mention what Evelyn Durand heard the shooter say to Agent Lang."

"Any idea who the man in the horned rim glasses is?"

"Mister Winthrop, so said the shooter," Julie answered with a shrug.

"Yeah…Winthrop…I'm sure that's his name."

They were quiet for a few moments.

"Do you know Eddie English personally?" Julie asked.

"Yeah, I know him personally."

The tone in which Vann replied made Julie believe he probably didn't care for him.

"Were you close?" she asked.

Vann looked at her. His expression told her everything.

"Julie, I didn't care for him, nor him me. But I hate what he's going through. I wouldn't wish that on anyone. Maybe you could give me a few minutes alone when we first get there so I can set things right. That is, if we even get to see him."

She agreed. Upon negotiating heavy traffic on Philadelphia's south side, they soon found themselves in the center of the bustling City of Brotherly Love, parking in the deck adjacent to Thomas Jefferson University Hospital, just north of the famed Liberty Bell. A cold wind whipped them both as they made their way into the building. Vann used his credentials to bypass several layers of security and administration. In short order, they were on the mint green 6th floor as the smell of antiseptic assaulted their noses.

Few people enjoy being in hospitals. Julie despised it. She cringed as she heard someone wheezing and gasping for air. As she passed the man's room, she listened as a nurse scolded him, telling him to calm down.

"You get all worked up and it only makes things worse," the nurse said.

"Some place, huh?" Vann asked.

"I could never be a nurse," Julie replied.

"You'd be better as a doctor." He motioned to the door. "Here we are...six-thirty-six. Old Eddie got himself a private room." Vann rapped twice and pushed open the door.

Eddie English was in his bed. Numerous tubes snaked from hanging bottles and the steady rush of oxygen could be heard. Though he was covered in several layers of sheets and blankets, he looked as if he weighed only a hundred pounds. Each breath sounded wet, as if his lungs were full of fluid. Despite his condition, his room was very chilly, primarily because the window was open.

There was a young woman beside his bed. She was approximately 20 years old with a china doll face and tired eyes. The young woman turned and eyed Julie and Vann with surprise.

"Hello, I'm Agent Vann and this is Julie Hedstrom. We're with the Secret Service, up from D.C. I worked overseas with Eddie during the war." Vann offered his hand.

"I'm Meredith English," the young woman said, standing and giving them both a firm handshake. "I'm Eddie's daughter."

"Pleased to meet you," Vann said. "How is he today?"

Pressing her lips together, Meredith shook her head.

"Are you an only child?" Vann asked.

"By *my* mother. But my father has five total children from three wives."

"I see," Vann replied, clearing his throat. "Just you two up here?"

"I've been in this room for the better part of a week. You're the second visitors. The only other visitor was a minister who I asked to come."

"Does Eddie have other relatives nearby?" Vann whispered.

Meredith nodded as her face grew stony. "Oh, yes. They just don't care enough about him to come here."

Julie and Vann were embarrassed. Finally, Vann said, "Can he talk?"

"Yes. He's weak, but he can still talk."

"Would you mind if we have a few minutes with him?"

"Why don't you meet with him first, alone?" Julie suggested to Vann.

Meredith nodded her assent and gently shook her father's arm. Eddie's eyes had been closed. They opened, rheumy and dull, as if there was a glaze over each eyeball. He blinked several times, frowning as he tried to discern who he was viewing.

"Harry Vann," he finally croaked, his chest hitching as if he were trying to chuckle. This set off a bout of explosive coughing. It was agonizing to hear. Eddie finally got settled again as he carefully inhaled long, steady quantities of air. The way he breathed, it seemed as if he knew that sudden sharp breaths would only set him off again.

"Father," Meredith said formally. "These people want to talk with you. Mister Vann, here, wants to speak with you alone, first. Is that okay?"

Eddie nodded. He asked her for water. She gave him a sip and he sent her on her way.

Julie and Meredith left the two men alone and pulled the door shut. Out in the hallway, there was an awkward period of silence. Finally, Julie said, "I bet you could use a hug." She pulled Meredith close and embraced her, feeling her shudders as she cried into Julie's sweater. She must have been utterly exhausted and mentally drained.

This went on for several minutes—Julie held fast in a maternal moment. Finally, Meredith pulled away and dabbed her eyes with a tissue. "I'm sorry I did that."

"We all need a good cry every now and then. You've had a rough time."

"I do feel a little better," Meredith said, a tired smile forming on her mouth. "Would you like some coffee?"

"Sure."

They went to the nurse's station and walked behind the counter. A senior nurse with dark skin smiled politely as she busied herself over a complicated looking form. Meredith poured two mugs of coffee from the pot on the back counter.

"They've been so nice to me up here. They let me do what I want. Cream or sugar?"

"Black is fine." Julie accepted the mug. "Mind telling me about your relationship with your father?"

Meredith added one lump of sugar to her mug but didn't stir it. "I drop the sugar cube in and leave it. Then, by the time I finish, it's like a sweet surprise waiting on me."

Julie felt Meredith was deflecting, as if she didn't want to discuss her father. "Meredith? Are you able to talk about your father?"

She shrugged then nodded. "He and my mom divorced thirteen years ago. His current wife isn't much older than me. She hasn't been up here one single time." Meredith sipped her coffee. "Probably counting the minutes."

"Are you close to him?"

"I've tried. Honestly, I don't think he's ever been close with anyone."

"Why is that?"

Meredith cupped her mug with both hands. "Did you notice how cold the room was?"

"Yes."

"You'll never guess why."

Julie inclined her head.

"The window is open. He said he likes it cold because he knows he's going to burn in hell."

Arching her eyebrows, Julie offered no response. She didn't know what to say to that.

"He told me that very thing just last week. It was one of the rare moments in his life that he showed me any vulnerability."

"Does it upset him that his family isn't here?"

Meredith blew on her coffee. "That would make a nice story, wouldn't it?" She shook her head. "He's not angry, Julie, because he knows he wouldn't be here, either. That man is incapable of loving anyone else. It's cliché, but he's truly got a heart of stone."

"Well…you're good to be here, Meredith. Even if your father is as hard as you claim, I'm sure he appreciates you being by his side."

Vann could be heard calling from down the hallway. "Julie?"

She poked her head around from the nurse's station as he beckoned urgently. Julie turned to Meredith. "You okay?"

"I'm fine. I may go downstairs and get a bite in the cafeteria."

After gently squeezing Meredith's arm, Julie headed down the hallway to room 636, unaware that she would soon learn the complete and disgusting truth about Lucy Thaler's murder.

Chapter Twenty-Three

In a month drenched in agony, what Max currently experienced might have been the most intense pain yet. When he first came to, he heard a strange, animal sound before realizing it was coming from his own mouth. It was akin to a simultaneous howl and growl. The center of his chest burned and throbbed so badly that he was aware of his heart thumping against his ribcage, aching with each pulse.

Boom—boom—boom.

It felt as if someone was rapping his breastbone with a ballpeen hammer. Though his vision was rimmed with red, things began to gradually come clear to him. He was able to make out the split beams supporting the chalet roof. He rotated his head to the right, seeing the window to the rear of the property. The sun had fully set. Other than the blackness of the evening, all Max could discern was a bit of snow on the window frame. Behind his head, Max could feel the intense heat of the fire.

He realized that a portion of his discomfort was due to his neck being wedged against the sharp stone of the hearth. Max adjusted his head again, allowing it to clunk down to the floor. He attempted to move his hands, realizing they were cuffed in front of him. His ankles were bound tightly together, although he couldn't see them. There was no way to sit up—it hurt too much to contract his abdomen. Instead, he rolled slightly left, setting off new flares of pain as everything came clear.

Ludivine was there, sitting on the Ottoman. Her hands were behind her back. She didn't make a sound but fear dominated her face. She attempted to smile bravely at him, but instead her face contorted and she began to cry.

Behind her, sitting in the chair, was one of the men Max had seen at the top of the driveway. He was one chromosome away from being dashingly handsome. It was almost as if half of his near perfect face had been damaged in shipment from the factory, leaving every handsome feature slightly off kilter. One hazel eye was situated slightly lower than the other. His perfect Roman nose was skewed just a bit to the left. The man's full lips had a diagonal scar, top and bottom—probably the result of a knife slash to the face. The left side of his mouth drooped. Even the shape of the man's head was misaligned on his left, giving his skull a rhombus-like appearance. Because his skull was misaligned, it gave the man an appearance drastically different than someone who had suffered a debilitating stroke. The man gave Ludivine's clasped wrists a shake, causing her to chirp.

The only other person in the room was Guillermo "Gustav" Casson. Until moments before, Max had never met him. But he certainly knew who he was. Because Max had made his living robbing Gustav's cash hordes, he'd diligently kept his finger on the pulse of the Unione Corse that Gustav jealously lorded over. Despite keeping a rather low profile at his estate in Corsica, Gustav's photo occasionally appeared in connection with his organization's activities. He also had a penchant for Parisian musicals, and the lithe young dancers that rounded out their casts.

For now, Gustav smoked a brown cigarette, his fedora resting on the table beside him. He also enjoyed a glass of wine. There must have already been wine in the chalet because Max and Ludivine hadn't purchased any. Perhaps he brought his own.

Clear your mind, Max. Fuzzy, unessential contemplations will get you nowhere.

"Well, well, well…you're still alive," Gustav said, speaking his distinct Corsican-accented French. "And how do you feel, Maximillian?"

Max opened his mouth to speak but couldn't generate much sound other than a croak. He swallowed, which caused an entirely new and explosive pain. When he recovered, he tried again.

"Please d-d-don't hurt her."

Gustav chuckled. "Good for you, Maximillian, looking out for the lady. Nevertheless, I don't believe your concern is genuine—I believe it's calculated." Lifted his finger. "But a good move. I commend you."

"Please. Kill me if you want, but let her go. She has nothing to do with anything between us."

"You kill my men, you steal my money, and you still have the audacity to make requests of me?" Gustav frowned and sipped the wine. "I'm deeply insulted by your impudence."

"I've never killed your men."

Gustav turned his head and barely lifted his chin. The Man with the Melted Face stood, crossing the floor heavily. Max wanted to shriek as he saw the man's large wingtip pull back, but there was no time.

The man kicked Max squarely in the chest, squarely at the source of his pain.

Bursts of light blinded Max. His diaphragm heaved, causing him to lose his air as well as the food he'd eaten earlier. As he gasped, Max's mind was awash in the moment.

Is this the end? After I've cheated it so many times, has my death finally come to claim me?

Rolling to his back, acid stinging his throat, Max was treated with visions of his childhood in Chicago, working on steel I-beams, high above the ground, in the clouds and fog. This time, rather than seeing other men fall to their splattering deaths, it was Max who lost his balance. He wind-milled his arms, trying to regain his footing. It was no use. His feet slipped over the edge of the steel. Down, down, down he went.

As he fell, Max remembered...

During their lunch breaks, the steel workers and masons liked to sometimes ponder the result of a long fall. There was no doubt that a human being could occasionally survive a fall of 50 feet. The workers that had been around long enough had seen it happen before. But whoever did survive such a fall would quickly wish they were dead, which usually followed a short time later. But rather than a fall from a "low" height—such as 50 feet—the men preferred to discuss falls of hundreds of feet, during which there was appreciable time to prepare for the impact at the end.

"Five hundred feet takes about seven seconds," one of the men pronounced. "One—two—three—four—five—six—seven. That's quite a bit of time to ponder your demise racing at you. You'd have the chance to think about all sorts of things."

"Ya think ya feel the pain when ya hit?" Max recalled Irish-Ian asking. Irish-Ian had taught Max more about masonry than all the other workers combined. When Max had no food, Irish-Ian fed him. Once, when Max was deathly ill with the flu, Irish-Ian took him to the doctor and paid the bill. A biological father of eight, Irish-Ian fathered many more through teaching and caring.

As they ate their lunch, the others workers would offer up their estimates along with nuggets of experience. The general consensus was, after a long fall, one might feel the pain for only a split second upon hitting the ground. Not even long enough to register.

Tony D'Onfrio, one of the oldest masons, insisted that he'd seen a leather-tough Pole briefly survive a fall of better than 250 feet.

"Poor bastard screamed all the way down. He was saying something, but none of us could make it out. How about that? Your final words were heard by dozens, but not a single fella could understand what you were saying."

"But he lived?" 15 year-old Max had asked.

"Technically, yes. But not for long." Tony pointed north. "We were halfway up the Civic Opera House. Cranes everywhere. Windy that day...damn if it was windy. I'd just gone down to supervise the loading of a full sling of stone when I heard the yells. That Polack had gotten his pants leg caught on a welder's wire. It threw him off balance right when a gust of wind hit from the lake. When I looked up, he was halfway down, kicking his feet and twirling his arms."

Max had been mortified and rapt all at the same time. "And he was yelling?"

"Yelled it three times. I'll never forget what he looked like. He was head down, arms swinging like propellers. Whatever it was, he yelled it three times," Tony said, lifting his fingers—one—two—three—for emphasis. After recounting the horrific tale, Tony had lowered his gaze into his lunch pail.

"Did you see him hit?" Max asked, unable to help himself.

"I did. It was springtime so it was wet. We'd put plywood down everywhere as walk-board. Mud everywhere at the bottom. The reason the pole was swinging his arms was to try to flip himself over, which he did. Tucked over like a gymnast just before he got to the ground. Hit damn near square on his back. I remember his boots almost came off. It was like they were halfway off, tilted upward at an angle. And the sound when he hit that plywood—it was like ten gunshots all at the same time."

One of the other men asked if there was blood.

"Not much. I've heard of men exploding like a ripe tomato, but not that Pole. There was thick mud under the plywood. It probably gave a good six inches. The most bizarre thing was the Pole sat up after he hit, which didn't even seem possible. But he did. He sat up while making this crazy, sad face, before he collapsed backward. It was then I realized the back of his head was mush. He'd smashed the back of his skull."

"Did he talk anymore?" Max asked.

"No. We ran over to him and did what we could. But his eyes were open. Wide open. Unblinking. Wild eyes, looking at each of us, as if he knew the end was near." Tony D'Onfrio, one of the toughest men Max had ever met, had mopped his eyes at this point. "I held his hand until he died. He probably lasted two or three minutes. To this day, it was the strangest thing I've ever seen. They even got a doctor there before he died. He'd been on site giving penicillin shots. The doc didn't really even know where to start. What could he do? By the time they got a stretcher out there that Pole was gone."

Sitting atop that building, eating his lunch, listening to Tony's anguish as he told the tale, had never left Max. He put his arm around Tony before the men changed the subject to lighter fare.

Two years after that, just before Max joined the Army, Tony D'Onfrio and Irish-Ian were killed in a construction collapse. The entire top section of the building they were working on buckled. Thirteen men died, most of them fathers. Thankfully, Max wasn't there that day. But Max had never forgotten either of them.

Max was still falling. Just like that Polish worker, Max knew death was enveloping him and there was nothing he could do about it.

Is there nothing you can do? Are you sure?

As Max adjusted his vision, he again saw his precious Ludivine. Twin streams of tears ran down her full cheeks.

"Don't cry," Max grunted. "We're gonna get through this."

"Maximillian, would you like to get kicked again?" Gustav asked.

Max adjusted his red-rimmed vision, seeing the polished cordovans down by his feet. They shuffled a step closer, the right one slightly behind, ready to kick again. Turning his head back to Gustav, Max spoke.

"Your men in Marseilles weren't killed by me, Gustav. That's part of the reason I called you."

Gustav rolled his eyes.

"I didn't kill them," Max insisted. "I shot them, but I used rubber rounds like I always did. They were alive when I left. That's the truth, whether you believe me or not."

"And how did we do with our rubber shot, Maximillian?" Gustav asked, smoke escaping his mouth with each word. "It took my men a few hours to figure out how to make them, but judging by the results, I'd say the first round worked as prescribed. How does it feel to be shot in the chest?"

"I didn't kill your men in Marseilles," Max repeated.

"They were killed by a man named Mister Winthrop," Ludivine said. "He's been—"

"No!" Max yelled, causing his chest to spasm. He spit up a small quantity of blood and saliva, feeling it hanging in a string from the left side of his mouth.

"You don't feel a woman should intervene in men's business?" Gustav asked, his forehead wrinkled in amusement.

"I just want this to be between us, Gustav. I respect you. And I have a half-million dollars for you."

"Which I intend to get..." Gustav paused. "A half million?"

"Yes."

Resuming his poker face, Gustav gestured to his wine. "As you can see, I'm in no hurry."

"His story might be true," the Man with the Melted Face said. He spoke French, his strong *meridional* accent obvious.

"What?" Gustav snapped.

"When I spoke with the police, they believed the killings were done well after the initial robbery."

"Nonsense," Gustav said dismissively.

You're still falling Max. The plywood is growing much closer. Ten gunshots, all at once...

"But I've got more than half a million, Gustav. Much more."

"More money?"

"No. I have an extra gift for you."

The high don of the Unione Corse wore a bored expression. He crushed out his brown cigarette and sipped his wine. "And what, pray tell, is this divine gift you have to give me?"

"*Puissance.*"

Though the word "puissance" is used in English, Max used the French version. While its precise meaning cannot be directly translated, it suggests power and potency, especially when delivered as a single phrase. And while Gustav seemed unconvinced, he did cock one eyebrow.

Max knew he would get but one chance at this.

"And what is this *puissance*, Maximillian?"

"I'll tell you, but I respectfully request you let me up. And I also request that you consider working *with* me and Ludivine. We need your help and your protection. It's why I contacted you."

Gustav's lips parted as he took this in. Then he laughed uproariously, throwing back his wine afterward. "That's rich."

"Why would I have contacted you?" Max wheezed. "This is a good deal. You'll see."

The don opened his hands. "I can see you're literally dying to tell me, so go ahead. Tell me about this puissance."

"If you'll work with us, I can give you two ranking spies. I'm almost certain they work for the Soviet Union."

Gustav's laughter quieted, but he still chuckled. "Spies?"

"Yes. Men who have long tentacles into the government." Max stared long and hard at Gustav. "This isn't a deception. I'm giving you everything I have."

The high don of the Unione Corse wasn't laughing anymore. "If this is even true, what on earth would I do with two spies?"

"The possibilities are endless, especially since no one will know you have them."

Gustav frowned, but Max could tell he was interested.

"These men know things that no country would *ever* want to get out. What they have in their minds is worth many, many millions of dollars."

A minute later, though still bound, Max was sitting in a chair.

***

Eddie English looked a bit better by the time Julie reentered his hospital room. His color was brighter and he'd propped up on an elbow. He asked Vann to elevate the head of the bed, which Vann did via the crank at the foot of the bed. Once he was sitting up, Eddie gestured to Julie.

"Get that colored nurse for me."

Julie looked at Vann.

"Didn't you hear me, girl? Go down the hall and get that colored nurse."

Julie obeyed, doing her best to shrug off Eddie's characterization. She politely asked the nurse to come to Mr. English's room.

"May I ask why?" the nurse asked, unmoving.

"He requested you come to his room."

"I can only imagine what he called me." Mumbling to herself, the nurse placed her pen on the forms and obliged, moving smartly down the hall. Once in Eddie's room, she checked his I.V. bottles and fussed over his blankets.

"What do you need, Mister English?"

"Absolute privacy. Can't have you or anyone else come in here."

"You called me down here for that?"

"It's important. These two are from the Secret Service." Eddie aimed his needle-bruised hand at Vann. "Show her."

Vann dutifully displayed his credentials.

"See there," Eddie wheezed. "We've got private matters to discuss. No interruptions."

"I'll make sure you have privacy for twenty minutes." The nurse wagged her finger. "No smoking, Mister English."

"Nobody's smoking," he replied, sneering. "Now get on out of here. I'm payin' top dollar for this room—least I can get is some privacy."

Pursing her lips, the nurse pulled the door shut. As soon as she did, Eddie gestured to Vann. "Gimme a coffin nail." Swung his hand to Julie. "Tootsie, you spin that oxygen off."

Julie looked at Vann who shrugged. She walked to the oxygen and spun the knob to the right. The whooshing slowly subsided. Vann shook out a cigarette, handing it to Eddie. He held the cigarette, eyeing it sensually. He sniffed it before turning it and carefully placing it between his cracked lips. Vann lit Eddie's cigarette—the dying man inhaled carefully, exhaling slowly with satisfaction.

"Ahhh. Can't believe they won't let me smoke. At this point, what the hell does it matter?"

While Eddie enjoyed his cigarette, Vann turned to Julie. "I explained to Eddie a bit about what's going on. I also apologized for intruding on him at a time like this. But I didn't tell him anything of what you learned. I'll let you do that."

Eddie took another luxurious drag of his cigarette as he rotated his bloodshot eyes to Julie. He looked her up and down before his lizard's tongue dragged over his dry, fissured lips. "Back in my day, I'd have loved being sent outta town with you."

Julie ignored the insinuation. "Mister English, we need you to assist—"

"Eddie."

"*Eddie*, we need you to assist us with an investigation. We have reason to believe that Clayton Fairchild stored critical information of some sort in a lead-lined briefcase in the Secret Service office of Paris. We believe it had something to do with an OSS agent you took part in handling."

"And that would be one Lucy Thaler."

"Correct," Julie replied, fighting to remain impassive.

"Somebody stole the briefcase?" Eddie asked.

"Yes."

"That ain't good." He grinned and winced at the same time. "Old Fairchild was a real Boy Scout, wasn't he? Had enough dynamite to blow the lid off the entire country, but he never used it."

"Excuse me?" Julie asked.

"You heard me. What he had in that briefcase was enough to change the United States forever, at least as far as the government is concerned." Eddie took a pull on the cigarette as he adjusted his position in the bed. "Fairchild would've used it eventually, which is why we had him killed."

At this point, Julie could no longer control her emotions. "Killed?" she demanded.

His demeanor smug, dying Eddie smoked on.

"Say that again?" Vann asked.

"You heard me. Me and Vic had Clayton Fairchild *killed*."

"He was killed in a car accident," Julie said.

Eddie chuckled. "Exactly." He turned to Vann. "Sharp one, Tootsie is."

"You're claiming that you orchestrated the accident?" Vann asked.

"Ain't no claiming about it. I composed it, arranged it, orchestrated it, and directed it. Cost us a damn fortune, too. You have any idea what kinda rate you gotta pay to murder a man via an innocuous-looking car accident? And beforehand, your killer has to do research to find a spot that has had one too many accidents. Then, your mark has to be at that exact spot, at the right time of day, and no witnesses can be nearby. Not to mention all this had to take place in France. You wouldn't believe what we paid. I think they followed him for twenty-three or twenty-four days before the stars finally lined up."

Vann cursed at Eddie.

"You did this because you were afraid he'd use the evidence?" Julie asked.

"Hell, yes. We didn't even know he had it until about two months before he died. But once we found out, Fairchild had to go." Eddie finished the cigarette, handing the nub of the butt to Vann. "Gimme another."

Though visibly disgusted, Vann obliged, lighting a second cigarette for Eddie.

"What was in the briefcase?" Julie asked.

Eddie frowned, then laughed, setting off his most explosive coughing fit yet. It ended with retching to the point that Julie thought he might get sick. She handed him a clean metal pan from the adjacent table but he pushed it away.

As Eddie calmed down, Vann tried to take the cigarette from him. "Here, let me have that."

"Get your paws th'hell away from my cigarette, boy." Eddie pressed himself back into the thin hospital mattress. A sheen of sweat glistened his forehead. When he'd settled down, he took a careful pull of the cigarette, sighing his satisfaction. Then he looked at Vann, and at Julie.

"You honestly don't know what was in that briefcase?"

"Not precisely, no," Vann said defensively. "But we know it involved Lucy Thaler."

"And her death," Julie said, taking a bit of a calculated risk. She felt if Eddie thought they were fishing, he'd be less inclined to tell them much.

"So, Tootsie, you think she died?" Eddie challenged Julie.

"She died," Julie answered. "We want your viewpoint."

"Yeah," he snorted. Eddie went back to enjoying the cigarette and saying nothing.

"Why won't you tell us?" Vann asked. "Just like the smoking, you've got nothing to lose."

"I've got more than three million bucks to lose."

"Excuse me?" Vann asked.

"I could lose all my money."

"We don't care about your money," Julie said.

"If I tell you what's in that briefcase, you'll care."

"We won't."

Eddie dragged on his cigarette.

Vann and Julie looked at one another.

"Immunity?" Vann finally asked. "You want immunity?"

"More than that."

"What else?" Vann demanded.

"I want your word as a man that you'll act on something for me."

"Without knowing what it is, I can't make you any promises."

"I'll tell you what I want done. Then, if you agree, I'll tell you exactly what is, or was, in that briefcase."

Vann looked at Julie. They both nodded.

"Fair enough," Vann said. "Let's hear it."

"If I tell you what's in the briefcase, you've got to give me your word, and the word of Director-*fuggin*-Lynch, that you'll take down Victor Roach."

"Take him down?"

"Take him down…kill him…I don't care. But I want that sonofabitch to suffer." Eddie, his watery bloodshot eyes blazing, glared at Julie and Vann. "Don't make it quick. Make sure that when he dies, it's slow and painful."

"You know I can't promise that," Vann said, opening his hands plaintively. "And I can guarantee you the director won't promise it."

Eddie English dragged deeply on the cigarette and handed the nub to Julie. "You *can* take him down, and you *will* take him down, when I tell you what I'm gonna tell you. Gimme a'nuther cigarette and call Lynch."

"He won't agree unless you tell me now what's in the briefcase," Vann countered.

Eddie pointed to the phone. "Call him."

Vann allowed Julie to make the phone call. It took her several minutes to wend her way through the general switchboard. When she finally reached someone she knew, they went for the director. Eddie smoked another full cigarette while they waited.

She eventually spoke to the director, sticking to the facts as she told him what had transpired. "Eddie English wants to speak with you."

"You're kidding."

"No, sir."

Lynch muttered a rare curse word. "Put him on."

When Eddie took the phone, he eyed Vann and Julie and spoke two words. "Get out."

***

The negotiation between Max and Gustav took several key turns. Twice, using a low and dangerous tone, Gustav warned Max about taking too strong a stance. Each time, though it didn't come naturally to him, Max apologized. Apologies seemed to go a long way with Gustav Casson. Against Max's wishes, Ludivine provided her own perspective, which turned out to be invaluable. Max's most compelling pitch came at the very end of the back and forth, after Gustav informed Max he had a number of armed men at his disposal around the chalet.

"What do you have to lose, Gustav? The money is here in the chalet. I'm not denying it and you can take it at any time. But the men who've been chasing us will find us soon. And when they do, they'll kill Ludivine and me as sure as you and I are both sitting here. Why won't you at least put your efforts into capturing these men? They can certainly bring you far more than a half-million dollars of counterfeit money."

"They could also make me a sworn enemy of the Soviet Union."

"I'm not *certain* that's who they work for. No matter who they're employed by, I want you to consider the leverage you'll have. They were here, on your territory, robbing a United States Secret Service office for money and, more importantly, for a secret of national security. But, in the end, they got in your way. For all their parent country knows, you'll give them up to either France or the U.S. Do you realize what an imperial power will give up to prevent that from happening?"

"*If* I'm willing to give them back."

As he began to respond, Max suffered a coughing fit, spitting up a bit of blood in the end.

"Max," Ludivine said.

He waved off her concern, continuing his pitch. "If you do decide to give the men up, I believe you'll be able to name your price, Gustav."

The Corsican removed one of his brown cigarettes, fingering it. "What is it they want from you?"

"They want us dead."

"That's not what I asked. What do they *want* from you?"

"They want something we know."

259

A wily grin built on Gustav's face. He pointed the unlit cigarette at Max and spoke a colloquialism Max didn't understand.

"I don't know what that means."

"It's like, 'I wasn't born yesterday,'" Ludivine clarified in English.

"Exactly," Gustav agreed, also in English. He turned to Max. "You see, whatever it is that you know is the *true* value. That's where the treasure lies, tonight. That's why they're pursuing you with such fervor."

"Yes, it is. And I call on your honor when I respectfully ask that you *not* pursue it. What we know involves a deed that lacked honor altogether."

Gustav arched his brows. "Go on."

"All I'll say is that it involved the murder of an innocent woman by two cowardly men. In my mind, what they did is utterly disgusting. That, sir, is the absolute truth."

Gustav lit the cigarette. He remained quiet for a moment. "Maximillian, when might these spies arrive?"

"Could be minutes—could be days."

"Do you have a plan?"

"Yes, I do."

"And the money?"

"Is here."

Gustav's grin was that of the alpha alley cat. "You may have called on my honor, but I'm still getting that money."

"Take it."

"Go get it, *ma crevette*," Gustav said to Ludivine.

"Don't be cute," the Man with the Melted Face warned. He un-cuffed her wrists and pointed his shotgun at her. Ludivine walked away, coming back in several minutes with the duffel bag. She unzipped it and placed it beside Gustav. He removed bills from several stacks.

They watched for more than ten minutes as Gustav carefully examined each bill he'd removed. The Man with the Melted Face removed a leather pouch from his jacket. He unzipped it and placed it beside Gustav's wine.

From the pouch, Gustav used a jeweler's loupe and the light of the lamp to study every square inch of the fugazi American currency. He also felt each one, comparing them, rubbing them between thumb and forefinger. Then he spat on the bills, using a metal instrument to scratch the fibrous paper.

As he waited, Max tensed and relaxed his chest. It had slowly transitioned from throbbing to burning. Several times Max's heart skipped a beat before resuming a normal rhythm.

Finally, Gustav set the bills aside and crossed one leg over another. He turned to his man and nodded. The man put the leather pouch into the duffel and zipped it shut. Keeping his shotgun on Max, he opened the front door and handed the money to the man on the porch, muttering instructions to him.

Gustav treated himself to a fresh glass of wine, which he toasted to Max and Ludivine. After the toast, he said, "We shall remain here until morning. At that time, if your spies haven't come, I will decide if you should live or die."

"I don't agree with those terms," Max replied.

Gustav appeared amused. "I wasn't asking. Now, tell me this plan of yours."

For the next 12 minutes, a very sore but relieved Max Warfield discussed an infantry-style lasso trap. The trap would be aided by the snow, but it would also be made more difficult in the event Max's pursuers noticed the existing tracks. There were other complications, such as the bitter cold, but with 13 vicious members of the Unione Corse on his side, Max was confident the plan would work.

***

Ten long minutes passed as Eddie English spoke on the phone with Director Lynch. The nurse peered down the hallway from the nurse's station, frowning but staying put. Vann and Julie spoke in whispers about what they'd heard.

"Do you think he really knows?" Julie asked.

"Yeah, I do."

"And he had Clayton Fairchild killed because of it?"

"Julie, back during the war, there were a number of men in the OSS, and all branches of the officer corps, who would never ascend to that level today. Ruthless psychopaths who'd gone off the rails years before. But, hey, if you had a degree and could make it through officer candidate school, you were in. We needed warm bodies. And guys like Eddie English and Vic Roach had all the necessary requirements, along with superior intelligence. Lots of criminals have those things, too."

"Why does he want Vic Roach taken down?"

"If I had to guess?"

"Yes."

"Jealousy."

Julie couldn't disagree. Before she could respond, they heard Eddie English calling out to them. When they went in, he was coughing again, followed by retching. Julie was mildly concerned that he might die before telling them about the briefcase's contents. Once he'd settled down again, and as Vann gave him a fourth cigarette, Julie took the phone from Eddie.

"Director, are you still there?"

"Yes, sheesh, I thought he was about to blow out a lung."

"I agree."

"Tell Vann to handwrite a brief contract. We'll make it good with an official immunity agreement later. Once Vann does that, English should tell you what you need to know."

Julie turned in an attempt at privacy. "Did he tell you?"

"No, but he hinted at it."

"Chief, he claims he and Vic Roach *killed* Clayton Fairchild."

"I know what he claims. Today, before you arrived there, I had the deputy director speak with English's doctor. He probably won't live to see Friday. All we're essentially agreeing to is not going after his money along with our agreeing to pursue Victor Roach. This is worth doing, even if whatever he tells us is inconsequential. Make it happen, Julie." The director clicked off.

While Eddie placidly smoked, Vann sat in the visitor's chair and wrote out a contract on the back of a blood pressure form. He scrawled three paragraphs, leaving lines for names, while muttering something about his distaste for attorneys.

"I have a question," Julie said to Eddie. "Your daughter told us you're not at all close with your family. In fact, she said she's the only one who has visited you since…"

"Since I started dying?"

"Yes. So, if you're dying, and at odds with your family, why are you worried about your estate?"

"Because my daughter you met, Meredith, is getting every penny of it."

Vann looked up. Julie shifted her posture, mildly surprised. "Does she know that?"

"Nope. Just me and my attorneys."

"What about the rest of your family?"

"To hell with 'em," Eddie said. "They don't care about me, so why should I give a rat's ass about them?"

Vann finished his scribbling and signed the form. He handed it to Julie, who also signed it as a witness. Then Vann gave Eddie the form and had to retrieve a pair of reading glasses for him. He read the form and asked for the pen. Eddie English scrawled his signature at the bottom of the page.

"Gimme one last cigarette." Once it was lit, Eddie put his left arm behind his head as he propped up his bony knee. "You two ready?"

"Yes," Vann said.

"Can't say I'm proud of it."

"Maybe telling us will make you feel better," Julie offered.

"Knowing Vic Roach is going down is the only thing that'll make me feel better."

"The director assured me," Julie replied.

"Let's get on with it," Vann said.

Eddie told them the full and unadulterated story of Lucy Thaler's murder in the stateroom of the USS Augusta, shortly before President Whitestone and Prime Minister Churchill signed the Atlantic Charter.

Julie was thunderstruck.

"Did Whitestone know?" Vann demanded.

"Not about us killing her."

"But he knew about the coming attack?" Julie asked.

"Sure did," Eddie replied.

Julie and Vann stared at one another.

"We would have rathered he didn't know," Eddie said, his southern accent coming forward. "But later, before he met with Churchill, ole' Prez Whitestone told us to keep our traps shut. He didn't explain nothing. Just told us to pretend we never heard it."

"He wanted war with Japan," Vann said.

"You're a bright one," Eddie sneered. "Gimme another fag."

"Go to hell," Vann replied.

Despite the fact he was dying, Julie berated Eddie English for what he'd done. For the first time since they'd met him, his face displayed remorse.

"Ain't proud of it," he muttered.

"Well, you wouldn't know it from here," Julie replied.

"I've been this way since I was twelve."

"How did Fairchild get the evidence?" Vann asked.

Eddie shrugged. "Carelessness on our parts."

Without any more parting words, Julie and Vann left Eddie's room.

Julie stopped in the hallway when she saw Meredith.

"Did my father help with what you needed?"

"He did, Meredith. I'm sorry about all that's going on. I hate to run, but we're in a hurry."

"It's fine."

"You take care."

Vann and Julie hustled down the stairs.

Twelve minutes later, after using a private lobby payphone and receiving curt instructions from the director, Vann and Julie departed the hospital. Cursing the traffic, Vann made his way east, to the Navy shipyard. Following the gate guard's instruction, they found their idling helicopter on a landing pad at Mustin Field, located within the shipyard.

Julie clenched her eyes shut for the first ten minutes of the flight. Though she'd never flown before, she quickly discovered that she hated flying—especially in a helicopter.

They would be back in D.C. in less than an hour.

Chapter Twenty-Four

The trio of men had spent the last 90 minutes in La Clusaz, searching for employees of the rental company that had rented a chalet to the American man who paid with probable counterfeit bills. Based on what they'd learned from a waiter who worked next door to the rental company, there were three total employees who had worked today—the two managing partners and their clerk. Unfortunately, none of the three employees were at their homes this evening. The Gendarme confirmed this fact, in regard to one of the managing partners, after slipping inside his home with all the skill of a cat burglar. The other partner was away for the evening, confirmed by the man's teenage son, who was home alone. He said his parents would probably be home late but didn't know where they had gone.

Mr. Winthrop pondered breaking into the rental office, but it was located on a busy thoroughfare with a bustling restaurant right next door. And tonight, as fresh snow began to fall, hundreds of brightly dressed skiers caroused and cavorted on the streets of La Clusaz. The Gendarme checked the back door, finding it made of steel and barred from the inside. In addition to the bolstered door, there was too much foot traffic from the back of the restaurant as workers carried out garbage to the dumpster in the alley and milled about, smoking and talking. The only other way in were the rental company's windows, but those were located on the busy thoroughfare. No good. The three men abandoned the idea of breaking into the office—at least for now.

There had been one remaining rental agency employee to check: the clerk, Mathilde Lafièvre. They'd gone to her rental apartment earlier, learning that she'd gone on a date—her "first ever date," according to her giggling roommate. The Gendarme was able to learn this by pretending to be her second cousin, here on a spur-of-the-moment vacation due to the snow. When pressed, the twittering roommate informed the Gendarme that Mathilde had accepted a date with a man named Simon, a young assistant manager from the bank.

The Gendarme lifted his hat and asked the roommate to keep his presence a secret. "I'll stop by her office tomorrow. I'd like to surprise her." He hurried back to the idling car and sat, turning to Winthrop and Timmons.

"She's not here. She's on a date with a man named Simon Martin."

"And?" Winthrop demanded.

"Simon Martin works at the bank...the *Auvergne-Rhône-Alpes Banque*."

"That's where the counterfeit money was passed," Timmons added.

264

"Talk about good fortune," Mr. Winthrop breathed. They drove back into the center of town and Mr. Winthrop made another call from a payphone. When he returned, he handed an address to the Gendarme.

"The bank clerk is a renter at this address. No idea if he's still there, but he was the last time he paid his taxes," Winthrop said.

The Gendarme read the address. "This is on the main road we came in on from Bonneville." He jammed the car in gear and spun the tires through a pile of snow as he whipped onto the wet *Route des Grandes Alpes*.

The address turned out to belong to a sizeable boarding house several kilometers outside of town. It was a large converted home, situated just above the rushing *Ruisseau de la Platton* and surrounded by evergreens dusted in fresh white snow. The home itself was old and white, built of river rock and timber. The fresh whitewash had been done to conceal the fact that it was crumbling, a fact all three men noted by the scattered bits of rock under the eaves. Mr. Winthrop entered first, followed by Timmons and the Gendarme. The home smelled of mothballs and cooked onions.

They found two people in the sitting area, having wine and chatting. The man on the right was tall and thin, with the bookish air of an academic in his late 20s. An older woman sat in the chair to the left, a padded rocker. She didn't stand and seemed mildly perturbed that the threesome had entered without knocking. She had a round face and was rather short, especially when viewed next to her companion. Mr. Winthrop guessed she was in her mid-seventies.

Winthrop looked at the Gendarme and nodded. The Gendarme spoke in his most disarming tone while holding his hat over his stomach.

"Pardon our intrusion, madam, but we need to speak with one of your residents: Monsieur Simon Martin, who works for the *Auvergne-Rhône-Alpes Banque*. Is he in?"

The tall man prepared to speak but the woman silenced him with a flick of her hand. She frowned at the three men, eyeing each one distinctly. "And who are you three to come into my late husband's home, making demands of me?"

Mr. Winthrop spoke up, utilizing his accented French. "You'll pardon us, please. Our friend Pierre here is with the National Police, and we are with the United States Secret Service." He displayed fake credentials for her, which she pulled close and studied.

The woman's face clouded over. "What on earth do you want with Simon?"

"He's in no trouble," the Gendarme replied disarmingly. "We should have told you that before introducing ourselves. It seems someone passed counterfeit American bills at his bank, and we're simply trying to get the man's description before he skips town."

The madam was unimpressed. "And this couldn't have waited until tomorrow? Coming here on a snowy evening and disturbing me and my newest houseguest?"

"We're very sorry, but we've been tracking the counterfeiter for weeks, and time is of the essence," the Gendarme added.

General Timmons stood behind Winthrop and the Gendarme, nodding and smiling in a sycophantic manner that didn't suit him at all.

The woman pursed her lips as she stacked one hand over the other on her lap. She nodded at the academic resident, as if she were too good to utter the words.

The academic cleared his throat. "Simon came in a short time ago and didn't feel well. He went to his room."

"And which room is that?" the Gendarme asked, smoothing his tie.

"We can go get him," the madam said, gripping the arms of her rocker.

"If you don't mind," Mr. Winthrop interjected, "what we need to discuss is rather private." He removed twenty new francs and handed them to the woman. "For your inconvenience."

She held the money as if it were diseased. But after a moment, she opened an ornate carved box located beneath the lamp and placed the money inside. With her lips still pursed, as if she would make this allowance just once, she nodded at her houseguest.

"Last room in the upper hallway," the bookish man said, pointing.

The trio climbed the stairs, their shoes dampened by a threadbare plum carpet runner. Upstairs in the hallway was a narrow table topped by an out-of-place pink pagoda lamp. On each side of the table were two doors. Opposite the table were three doors, the middle of which was open. Then, at the end of the hallway, was the door they'd been directed to.

They stopped outside the door. The Gendarme pulled back his hand to knock, but halted his arm just before it struck the door. Though he could already hear some of it, he put his ear to the door to make his hearing more acute.

Panting. Moaning. Heavy, rhythmic breathing.

The door was thin and loose against the frame, betraying a great deal of sound from inside. The most distinct sound, after the human sounds, was the cadenced sound of a bed squeaking. This was followed by whispering voices.

"You sure you're okay?" A man's voice.

"Yes." A woman's.

"Does it feel good?"

"Oh, yes."

"Does it hurt?"

"Not like the first time."

"So, this one's better?"

"Yes. Keep going please."

The bed started up again. Followed by the heavy breathing.

Frowning, Mr. Winthrop poked the Gendarme. "C'mon and roust them. This isn't a damned peepshow."

As soon as his hand slapped the door, a commotion of whispers and shuffling could be heard inside the room. It was followed by near silence. Finally the man's voice at regular volume.

"Yes?"

"Open up," the Gendarme commanded.

"Who is it?" the voice asked.

"The Sûreté and the United States Secret Service. Open the door *right* now."

There was a brief delay before the man inside opened the door. He was thin and extremely pale with a triangle of reddish hair growing on his breastbone. Sweat ran down his flushed face and neck. Pulling the door shut behind him, he stepped into the hallway, a sheet around his midsection.

"What's this about?" he asked, a shake in his voice.

"Are you Simon Martin?" the Gendarme asked.

Simon nodded.

Mr. Winthrop spoke English. "Is Mathilde Lafièvre in there?"

Mouth agape, the young man didn't answer.

"You either go get her, or we're going in," Timmons added, breaking his brief period of silence.

His large Adam's apple bobbing with a difficult swallow, the young man ducked back into his room and shut the door. A few frenzied, sibilant sounds could be heard followed by the spring of the bed and the thumping of feet.

Just when the Gendarme turned to make a fresh comment, the woman of the house appeared at the top of the stairs. She moved smartly for a woman of her age, her words popping like tommy-gun fire. "Unless you've brought a judge's order, I want you men out of this house right now."

Before anyone could reply, the bedroom door opened, displaying the sweaty young couple in an unkempt stage of dress. The young lady was petite and plain. Her ponytail was cocked sideways. She held her eyeglasses in her hand. Her blouse was buttoned but the buttons were askew, off by one. Her skirt was off center and she held a sweater in her hands. Behind her, Simon hurriedly attempted to tuck in his shirt.

The woman of the house froze, several paces from the room. Her round face looked the couple up and down as she indignantly snapped, "*Qu'est ce qui se passe ici?*"

"Madam," Mr. Winthrop replied with an upheld hand, "we need a word with them first."

The woman's head jerked to Mr. Winthrop. "This is *my* house and I will decide who does what and when." She bulled her way through the men before standing before the amorous young couple and giving Simon what for.

While she berated him, he meekly interjected during several quick breaks, attempting to explain this away as a great misunderstanding.

But the woman of the house was no fool, she pointed to the unmade, sweat-marked bed before she again froze, her eyes focused on something by the bed.

There were several prophylactic packages, two of which had been opened. She then turned to Simon, haughtily lifting her chin. "You have broken my rules. According to the laws of France, I must give you a week to move out. Your week begins today. And you're no longer welcome at any house meals."

The woman of the house turned to Mathilde, looking her up and down before breathing the word "*salope*."

"If you have business to attend to with *her*, you will do it outside," the woman of the house said to the trio.

In what might have been his only good deed in a decade, Mr. Winthrop agreed to drive Mathilde back to her apartment. He sent her and the Gendarme out to the car to wait while he questioned Simon about the counterfeits. In five minutes, they departed with Mathilde in the front passenger seat.

As they drove, they questioned her about the American man who'd passed the counterfeits. Within a few minutes of questioning, Mr. Winthrop was convinced the renter was Max Warfield.

She told them about the man, the woman, the groceries, the money, and the chalet. The only part she left out concerned the prophylactics.

It didn't matter. Mr. Winthrop now knew what he needed to know. There was no reason not to go and take Max tonight.

Outside her apartment, they finished up with a few final questions. Tears glistened in the young woman's eyes as she answered dutifully. Mr. Winthrop saw no other option than to release her back to her life. Once she'd gone, he turned to Timmons.

"We need to hit Max tonight. If we call in the others, they won't be able to get here until tomorrow. And by then that skinny kid Simon, the girl Mathilde, and the old woman will all be talking. We can't afford for him to be forewarned."

Timmons blew cigar smoke at Mr. Winthrop's face and nodded his assent. "Let's ride by a couple of times and case it. Then we'll make our plan."

As the snow fell steadily, the trio of men found the chalet on the map. It was 5 kilometers north of town. Each man armed himself as they drove in that direction.

***

The flight had cost half of Gaspard's life savings. He wasn't concerned.

The flight had cost Detective Roux the contents of his stomach. He was concerned. Deeply.

Now the contents of his stomach were sloshing around in a bag between his feet. Sloshing because the pilot was attempting his second landing at the wind-battered Annecy Mont-Blanc airport, located at the base of the French Alps. Just ahead of them, to the east, resided a massive bank cloud of clouds, churning out snow for the mountains and promising rain and wind for the lowlands. Due to the darkness, they couldn't see the storm—they could only feel the wind. The pilot had listened to the most recent weather report, with winds from the northeast at 25 knots—far beyond the limits of his airplane.

"If I can't put it down this time," the pilot said, "we'll have to head west, away from the weather."

Gaspard found the fuel gauge on the basic instrument panel. They had about ¼ remaining in each tank. He was sitting in the right seat of the Reims FR172, with Roux behind him and the pilot. The FR172 was nearly identical to the Cessna 172, but built by France's Reims Aviation Industries through a license from Cessna. With a bit more power than a traditional Cessna 172, it had managed better than 110 knots to Annecy, taking a grand total of two hours from Paris. 20 minutes before arriving, they encountered the headwind. The powerful gusts made the landing rather difficult, especially for a small craft.

The pilot turned in on final once again, the runway laid out before them. The last time he'd tried to land, they were blown off the left side of the runway before he could touch a single tire to the concrete.

"The trick is using the rudder to face the propeller into the wind," the pilot said over the intercom. "Then, right at the last second, I kick the rudder left to align us with the runway and we land."

Gaspard shrugged and gestured to the runway. "Then just do it. Don't spend your energy telling me about it."

He glanced back at Detective Roux, who appeared to be near death in the scant light of the small airplane. His skin was pallid. His nose was running. He was breathing through his mouth and heaving occasionally.

"You gonna make it?" Gaspard asked with a chuckle.

"I want out of this plane," Roux replied over the intercom. "Kill me now. I don't care if we crash. Just put it down."

"Bad luck to say things like that," the pilot replied.

"Good," Roux answered, heaving afterward.

Gaspard touched the pilot's shoulder and pointed to the runway, which was only about a kilometer away. "You...don't worry about what we're saying. Just land *here*—it's critical."

The wind hadn't abated at all. When the last two-lane road flashed underneath them, just before the field of grass and the runway itself, a renewed blast of wind pushed them slightly left of the runway centerline.

Gaspard watched as the pilot danced with the atmosphere, using his legs and hands to manipulate the controls. By the time they passed the threshold of the runway, they were back over the centerline with the propeller and the aircraft's nose skewed nearly 45 degrees to the runway itself. This time, however, the pilot allowed the aircraft to sink. He kicked the rudder left at the last moment, turning the aircraft.

They landed successfully, albeit a bit abruptly.

All three occupants cheered. Even on the ground, the wind attempted to push them from the runway. But once the aircraft was slowed, they were able to taxi off the runway in the direction of the lighted building to the west.

Ten minutes later, Gaspard was in the minuscule terminal, where he called his lieutenant.

"This is Dimon."

"Lacroix, here. Thanks for the note."

"Where are you?"

"I'm near La Clusaz."

"Holy shit," Lieutenant Dimon hissed. "How'd you get there so fast?"

"You don't want to know. Talk to me. Did you get the chalet address?"

"Yeah, just got it. Apparently, there's someone else down there trying to get it."

"Who?"

"I dunno—was hoping you'd know. The guy I talked to was one of the owners of the rental company. He said his kid told him that three men came by asking questions."

"They say who they were with?"

"His kid didn't know. Said one man was small and spoke native French. Said the other two were silent."

"Descriptions?"

"Lemme grab my notes." Shuffling. "Okay, they were all in suits. The small one was around forty and had dark hair, dark eyes—that's straight from the kid."

"Okay, that doesn't help."

"The second guy had tan skin, was tall with an iron gray crew cut, flat on top. He didn't speak, but smoked a cigar."

"Yeah, nothing."

"The last guy was average height with a roundish face, beady eyes and a sharp nose. He wore horn-rimmed eyeglasses and also didn't—"

"Wait...horn-rimmed eye-glasses?"

"Yeah. That help?"

Gaspard reminded the lieutenant about the man, Mr. Winthrop, in the courtyard at Place de Clichy. As he spoke, he opened his notebook and read Evelyn Durand's description. Average height, average build, suit—and *horn-rimmed* glasses.

"Let me set it straight," Dimon said. "You're thinking that the perpetrator might have been telling the truth to the dead Secret Service agent? That the perp was coerced into robbing that vault, but escaped afterward and now this horn-rimmed guy, Mister Winthrop, is after him to get the money?"

"And the briefcase. There was a briefcase. I believe it's key."

"Lots of people still wear horn-rimmed glasses," the lieutenant reminded Gaspard.

"It's him." Gaspard scratched his day's worth of beard growth. "This thing's got so many layers to it, it's hard to keep up."

"You're sure?"

"Yes. Go ahead with the address."

Lieutenant Dimon read the address and Gaspard jotted it down, reading it back for confirmation.

"Roux with you?" Dimon asked.

"Yeah," Gaspard replied. He viewed Detective Roux through the glass, watching as he took massive inhalations of fresh air outside the terminal. "He was under the weather a bit, but he's improving rapidly."

"Huh?"

"Nothing. Listen, keep this from the captain, please."

"Haven't told him anything but if you screw up…"

"I'm on my own. I know. You haven't told the Americans any of this, have you?"

"Not yet, but I've got to call them now that I know the address. If they find out I held that back, they'll go straight to the chief and my pension's gone."

"Understood. I wouldn't ask you to do that."

"I'll drag my feet, drink a coffee first."

"Thanks."

"You're not gonna go over there and go in heavy, are you?" Dimon asked.

"Not after what all this guy's done," Gaspard said. "Not unless I want to die. We'll reconnoiter the rental. If he moves, and he's vulnerable, then perhaps we'll grab him."

"I can make one phone call and get you all the help you need."

"Let's confirm it's him, first. Thanks for all your help, lieutenant. I owe you several favors."

After hanging up, Gaspard secured the last hired car from the rental agency. He walked outside, finding Roux looking markedly better than he had earlier.

"Feeling okay?"

"Hell, I'm starving now. My stomach's definitely empty."

"You want to fly back when we're done?"

"I believe I'll be taking the train."

Roux drove as rain battered the windshield of the brand new Peugeot, to the point that the wipers could barely keep up. Gaspard used the map light to search for the address on the map. Once he'd found it, he waited for the next road sign. Ten minutes later, after seeing that La Clusaz was 22 kilometers away, he turned to his temporary partner.

"We'll be there in twenty minutes."

"Are we going to try and take this guy?" Roux asked.

"I think not."

Roux twisted his hands on the steering wheel. "So, what are we going to do?"

"In my mind, we have two choices. One is surveillance. We attempt to determine if the renter is indeed our man."

"We know he is."

"We don't know. We just have a strong suspicion."

"Fair enough. What's choice two?"

"Knock on the door."

"*Knock*—on the door? Are you drunk?"

Gaspard smiled.

"If we knock on the door, and don't get shot, then what?"

"Then we talk to him. Get to the bottom of all of this."

Roux turned. "Talk? Get to the bottom?"

Gaspard gestured to the road. "Watch where you're going. You're as bad as that pilot back there."

The two detectives, who were far out of their jurisdiction, decided to go with Gaspard's original idea of surveillance.

Though they had no way of knowing it, their "safe" decision would actually prove to be the most deadly.

***

Julie was mesmerized during the course of the 52-minute helicopter flight from south Philadelphia to Washington D.C. Though she'd been initially terrified, once she felt the stability of the helicopter, she embraced its might and had been all smiles ever since. After providing her with a clean bungee cord to wrap around her legs to keep her skirt from flying up, the crew chief opened the door. Despite the cold wind, Julie held onto the door bar with her head outside the chopper. As the miles wore on, she even leaned her body outside, laughing as she was whipped by the powerful wind. At that point, the crew chief beckoned her back in.

"Looks like we converted another one," he yelled to Vann, who nodded his agreement.

The pilot generally followed the highways, traveling to the southwest just inland of the Delaware Turnpike. After the small towns of Elkton and

Aberdeen, the large city of Baltimore slid into view, meaning they weren't far from their D.C. destination.

Vann did his part, acting as a tour guide. He pointed out the star-shaped Fort McHenry and Memorial Stadium, home to the Baltimore Orioles. They saw Fort Meade off to their left before the helicopter banked to the right.

"Why does anyone drive?" Julie asked, pointing down at Route 1, southwest of Baltimore. "Just look at all that traffic!"

The pilot broke into their chatter. "'Scuse me, Agent Vann?"

"Yes?"

"Just got a call vectoring me to Pershing Park. They don't normally allow us to land there but they've cleared a site."

"Okay, but why?"

"Director Lynch is waiting on you two. Apparently something's happened."

Julie and Vann looked at one another.

"Did they tell you?" Vann asked the pilot.

"All they did was vector me there. We'll be landing in about six minutes. I'm going to need to ask the chief to close the door since we're coming in with such a high profile. I'd appreciate it if you don't mention that we flew with the door open."

"Roger. Understood," Vann replied. "Thanks for the courtesy."

As the crew chief slid the door shut, the situation came rushing back to Julie. Desiring privacy, she removed her headset and leaned to Vann's ear, speaking over the tremendous noise. "I wonder what it could be?"

With his headset around his neck, he spoke in her ear. "It may simply be what we called in. I'm sure after the director digested everything he realized what a time bomb we're dealing with." Vann eyed Julie. "No?"

"I don't think so," she answered. "He's rarely the type to react in such a way. Surely he knew how critical Eddie English's story was the second he heard it."

"True."

"And the pilot said 'something's happened.'"

They grew silent as the pilot began altering course in slight turns.

In a matter of minutes they flew over the familiar sights of northeastern Washington D.C., approaching over the homes and offices of Brentwood and Truxton Circle. They crossed over Chinatown and the northern edge of the Mall before the pilot made a sharp, banking turn to the west and then the north. They were provided breathtaking views of the Capitol and the Washington Monument before the helicopter flared and gently settled onto the unkempt lawn of Pershing Park. A black limousine was parked in the midst of the wind-whipped trash, flanked by two white Ford sedans. Outside the sedans, suit-wearing agents held onto their hats as the helicopter descended and lashed the park in powerful wind.

Director Lynch, hatless, emerged from the back of the limousine, staring stoically as Julie and Vann departed the helicopter. Once clear, the crew gave a quick wave before lifting off, turning and leaving exactly the way they had come. The sudden silence and lack of wind seemed abrupt after the clamorous sound of the helicopter.

"What happened?" Julie asked the director, skipping the formalities with the man she knew so well.

Grim faced, the director motioned to the big Lincoln. "Get in."

Once inside, he made sure the dividing window was up all the way. As the car began moving, he clasped his hands and spoke.

"We received word that a number of counterfeit bills matching our marks were passed this morning in southeastern France. The man who passed them matched the description of your robbery suspect."

"Is there any way to tell if they were the stolen bills from the Place de Clichy?" Julie asked.

"Yes. It's now been confirmed."

Vann lifted his sleeve and looked at his watch.

"Where was this, and can we get someone there?" Julie asked.

"The bills were passed in a small mountain resort known for skiing. It's called La Clusaz, and I've already mobilized men from three locales," the director said, but he appeared worried as he said it.

"Chief, what's wrong?" Julie asked.

"Your man with the horn-rimmed glasses is there, along with reinforcements."

"Shit," Vann breathed.

"How do you know the man with the glasses is there?" Julie asked.

"Intel from the French. Your suspect used the bills to rent a chalet. The man in the horn-rimmed glasses is tracking him."

"Why would the suspect use the counterfeit bills?" Julie asked.

"He was probably desperate and that was the only money he had," Vann surmised.

The director nodded his agreement. "When the rental company took the money to the bank, they realized they were counterfeit," the director added. "Since then, a man matching your Mister Winthrop, with the same horn-rimmed glasses, along with two other men, have been shaking down workers from the bank and rental company."

"Wait," Julie said. "How did he find out our suspect was in this La Clusaz?"

"Good damned question," the director agreed. "I'm assuming the French have a leak somewhere."

Vann was quiet. He settled back into his seat and massaged his eyes.

Julie's mind raced.

As the limousine pulled into the underground parking area of the Treasury Building, the director lifted a sheet of paper from the seat and wagged it. "There's a bit more."

"What is it?" Julie asked.

"Ever heard of the Unione Corse?"

She shook her head. Vann uncovered his eyes and nodded. When the director urged Vann on, he offered a brief explanation.

"The Unione Corse is the French version of La Cosa Nostra...the mob. In many circles, they're believed to be more tight-lipped and ruthless than the Italian mob we're so used to."

The director nodded. "Correct. And they're headed by a man named Guillermo Casson—he goes by Gustav. Speaking of ruthless, old Gustav is about as cold-blooded as they come, even though he did help the Allies a bit during the war. But from what I know, that was out of self-preservation more than anything."

"What about the Unione Corse?" Julie asked.

Right then, the car halted. The director reached for the door handle but stopped. "Gustav and a shitload of Unione Corse muscle arrived in La Clusaz a few hours ago. He flew in and met them."

"Is there a connection?" Vann asked.

"La Clusaz is tiny. There's a million ski resorts between Corsica and La Clusaz, so why there?" The director shook his head. "Too much coincidence for my taste."

"Are you saying this so-called Mister Winthrop, with his horn-rimmed glasses, is with the Unione Corse?" Julie asked.

"I have no way of knowing," the director replied. "But their presence can't be ignored."

"What do we do in the meantime?" Julie asked.

"Not much you can do but wait. I've got to get back to the Dallas investigation. You two get upstairs to the smaller communications room. That will be your situation room from here on. I can give you a few assets and also put you in touch with the teams headed to La Clusaz."

"When will they get there?" Julie asked.

The director checked his watch. "The first one, from Bern, should get there in about ninety minutes." He shooed them away. "Go to it. Update me in an hour."

Julie and Vann skipped the slow elevator and instead took the stairs. When they reached the smaller communications room, Julie asked Vann what he thought the connection was to the Unione Corse.

"Not my specialty, Julie. I don't know much of anything about them other than what I told you."

She battled her own frustration, closing her eyes for a brief moment. "Just give me your best guess, Vann. What do you think the connection is?"

"Your suspect claimed this Mister Winthrop imprisoned him, correct?"

"Yes."

"Maybe Mister Winthrop *is* involved with the Unione Corse. If anyone would have moles inside the French National Police, it'd be them."

"Okay, I agree. But what if he's not?"

"Then my guess would be they somehow found out that there's a half-million high quality American counterfeit bills in that resort town—and they're there to collect."

"Do you think our people will be too late?"

"Yes," Vann replied firmly. "It's well into the night there. If I had to guess, whatever is going down is already over."

Vann was only off the mark by 15 minutes.

Part Four

La defense

Chapter Twenty-Five

As the snow raged, Mr. Winthrop instructed the Gendarme to pull to the left side of the road—if that's what one wanted to call it. The road was more of a cracked asphalt trail, leading off a winding mountain motorway a short distance from La Clusaz. The chalet was 500 meters in front of them, over the crest of the trail and down a steep hill. Mr. Winthrop's hackles were up— he didn't think Max Warfield would just blithely sit in a chalet waiting to be found. They stopped there for a moment, arming themselves and making a plan. Mr. Winthrop was particularly frustrated with himself for wearing polished brogues with little tread on the leather soles.

"Car," the Gendarme warned, staring in his rearview mirror.

Behind them, the twin beams of bright headlights bounced on the rutted road.

"That could be him," General Timmons said, lifting his 1911 as the other car eased forward on their right.

Mr. Winthrop wasn't all that surprised when the car slowed to a stop beside them. Due to the heavy snow, which melted as soon as it touched the warm glass, his vision was obscured to mere shapes and blobs. The driver of the car had rolled down his window, so Mr. Winthrop did the same, ordering the Gendarme to do the talking.

Mr. Winthrop held his Walther a few centimeters below the window's threshold. It was cocked and loaded, and his index finger had already applied a bit of pressure.

Now that his window was down, Mr. Winthrop could see more clearly. Neither man in the car was Max Warfield. The driver had a blade of a nose and the passenger, though obscured in the darkness, seemed to be balding on top. As the Gendarme greeted the two dark figures from across the front seat, the passenger stared only at Mr. Winthrop.

Winthrop saw what appeared to be recognition from the passenger's face.

The passenger said something to the driver and the rear tires spun.

It was too late.

Mr. Winthrop lifted his pistol and unleashed a round from less than two meters. It struck the driver, who immediately slumped. As the car rolled, the passenger returned fire while General Timmons and Mr. Winthrop riddled the interior of the other car with lead. Next to Mr. Winthrop, the Gendarme exited the driver's side of the car and aimed over the snowy hood.

The other car stopped moving.

Four guns were fired from near point blank range. The effect inside the saloon of the car, even with one window down and the rear side window blown out, was utterly deafening.

When Mr. Winthrop and General Timmons had both expended their magazines, the Gendarme rushed around the front of their car.

He yelled that the door to the other car was open and the passenger was gone.

There was enough light from the headlamps of both cars to see a bloody trail leading off the far edge of the road, down into the darkness of the mountain woods.

Cursing openly, Mr. Winthrop wondered what it was about him that the passenger had recognized. Then he slowly removed his eyeglasses from his face, his vision instantly fuzzy as he tried to view them in the snowy night.

"Th'hell are you doing?" Timmons demanded.

"Keep your eyes out for him," Winthrop directed. "He might double back."

The Gendarme and General Timmons extended their pistols over the white automobile. Both men scanned the darkness.

Mr. Winthrop opened the driver's door, lifting the driver. He was dead, shot through the side of his head. One quick check inside his jacket revealed the man to be a Paris Police detective named Roux.

Muttering curse words, Winthrop shut the door and used his jacket to wipe the door handle. As he did, a crashing through underbrush could be heard well down in the ravine.

"There," Timmons pointed. The sounds had come from the car's 1 o'clock. "He went down into that deep ditch and he's climbing back up the other side."

"The road curves up ahead. He's going to rejoin it around the bend," Winthrop said.

"Is he headed to the chalet?" the Gendarme asked.

Winthrop and Timmons nodded at one another.

The three men moved off to the side of the snowy road, following the road's ascent. In 100 meters, at the right curve, the road reached its apex, and the cabin was on the other side of the hill.

To their right, they heard more movement in the woods.

Timmons turned and Winthrop made several hand signals. The general agreed and on the three men crept.

***

Max knew gunshots when he heard them. Even dampened by the snow, the trees and the hills, he heard the pops—many in close succession. Handguns.

A shootout—or a diversion—nearby.

Earlier, before being driven somewhere far safer than the chalet, Gustav from the Unione Corse had driven a hard bargain and had stripped Max and Ludivine of all weapons. This was the only way he would agree to Max's terms. Max and Ludivine were to remain inside the house as his men provided security and dealt with "the spies and their people."

After hearing the gunshots, Max knew Mr. Winthrop had found him. Again. From a primary school in Orléans, to a secluded mountainside in the French Alps, the man in the horn-rimmed glasses had tracked him like a bloodhound.

Despite his hatred for Mr. Winthrop, Max grudgingly respected the man. It's difficult to track a human being—many times harder when the person knows he's being tracked. Apart from Mr. Winthrop's abilities, the fortuitous snowstorm and the terrain might have been enough to tip the odds back toward Max and Ludivine's favor, with the benefit of the Unione Corse gunmen.

Just in case, Max began eyeing implements in the chalet, things that could be used as a weapon.

"Go down into the basement and hide in the crawl space," Max said, lifting the wood poker from the fireplace.

"No."

He turned. Ludivine stared back at him with crossed arms.

"You need to go hide."

"I will not. I'm in this, just like you."

Just as he was about to argue his point, there was an urgent rapping at the back door, a bare hand on glass. Ludivine screamed—it scared the hell out of Max, too. Through the half-window of the rear door, Max saw the Man with the Melted Face. He held his shotgun at the ready and wore a snow-mottled overcoat. He beckoned Max.

"What happened?" Max asked after unlatching the door.

"I don't know," the man replied. "There was shooting up over the hill at the front."

"It wasn't your men?"

"No."

"Well, who was it?"

"That's what I'm asking you. There were two cars. One of my men saw the lights."

"And?"

"We don't know. My man thinks the people in the cars were shooting at each other."

"That's my shotgun," Max said.

"I liked it better than mine."

"Then let me have yours. I'll help and I *won't* turn on you."

"Gustav said no."

Max cursed and asked again. The man held fast.

"Then watch your back," Max said. "The gunshots might be a diversion. Maybe they did that to occupy you while the real assault comes from the other direction."

They heard more gunfire, closer this time. Three pops.

The Man with the Melted Face dropped to his knee and aimed outward with Max's Ithaca. The gunshots were followed by yelling. The yelling came from around front.

"What're they saying?" Max asked.

The man didn't turn. He held his aim toward the back. "Sounds like they said they shot someone. You should go down to the cellar. First, shut this door and lock it."

Max closed the door and locked it, as if the lock would keep everyone out.

"What do we do?" Ludivine asked.

After once again telling her to go to the cellar and hide in the crawlspace, he ran through the house and peered through the curtains of the center window. Off to the side of the walkway, in the brush, Max could see three men standing around a fourth body. The body was prone in the snow. The three men had their guns trained on the body. It was unmoving.

Max opened the front door and asked the men who they'd shot.

The closest Unione Corse shrugged. "He was running toward the chalet."

One of the other men said something about blood, pointing to the trail from the street.

"Check for identification," Max implored.

One of the armed men knelt, removing a wallet from inside the man's jacket. He walked back to the porch, holding the wallet open in the light.

Inside were an identification and badge. The badge was that of the Paris Police. And the identification was for Détective d'homicide Gaspard Lacroix.

The Unione Corse had just shot a policeman.

As Max and the man at the door eyed the identification, gunfire roared from the top of the hill. Triple flashes of gunfire spat at them. The two Unione Corse men fell wounded alongside the downed detective's body, along with the third Unione Corse man at the door. He was joined on the ground by another gunshot victim.

That victim was Max Warfield.

***

Mr. Winthrop slid a full 7-round magazine into his Walther. With one in the chamber, he now had 8 rounds in the weapon and four more magazines in his jacket pockets.

Though he didn't look the part in his tailored gray suits and horn-rimmed eyeglasses, Mr. Winthrop had been a crack-shot with a rifle and pistol since he was a boy. In his teen years, he'd competed on several marksmanship teams. During his time in the military, his shooting prowess was recognized almost immediately. His fastidious nature aligned nicely with the many precise facets of target shooting: the finely-milled metals, the precision bullets with specific uses, the paper targets with clean bullet holes—the physics and science of shooting appealed to Mr. Winthrop, and he excelled at it. During his military service, he'd honed his skills enough that he could have competed internationally. But more appealing than his skills with a weapon was his intelligence quotient.

And his cunning.

Why should he waste his time shooting at paper targets when he could use his intellect for far greater things? But right now his powerful brain was temporarily clouded by disgust.

Disgust with General Timmons, who'd pumped his fist after the sentries fell.

Mr. Winthrop awarded himself credit for the shot that dropped the detective in front of the chalet. He also took down one of the men who'd stood over the body and he was absolutely certain it was he who felled the two men on the porch. If Mr. Winthrop's ear was correct, the Gendarme and Timmons had fired six shots between them, meaning they'd only hit one human target at a maximum range of 40 meters.

Pathetic.

But there was no time to stand around and polish his laurels. Inside that snow-covered chalet resided Max Warfield, along with the little twat he was traveling with. They had to die because of what they knew. Had to. Additionally, the evidence from the briefcase had to be gathered and taken— not destroyed, but taken.

If all that was done, Mr. Winthrop might actually survive this unpleasantness, despite how upset his superiors were. He'd gone dark since being dispatched back to Paris from Vienna—what good would reporting in do? Besides, on the terminally long flight when he and Timmons had flown to France, Mr. Winthrop had meticulously developed a litany of reasons this entire operation had gone south. Most of the blame he would assign to the advance team for not recognizing the potential of escape via the ventilation grate in the courtyard at the Place de Clichy. The advance team had started the operation on the premise that there was one way in, one way out. Despite their reassurances, it was Mr. Winthrop who insisted snipers be placed on the nearby rooftops. Though the snipers didn't prevent Max's escape, they did manage to eliminate a Secret Service agent who presumably took Max's testimony to his grave.

Score one for Mr. Winthrop.

There was a serious flaw with Mr. Winthrop's criticism, however, because he, too, knew the grate existed. He knew it was secured by a lock and hasp. He also knew Max could take a weapon from one of the Secret Service agents. Therefore, since this was his operation, it was ultimately *his* fault. He should have put the possibilities together and taken the proper preventative measures.

Regardless, Mr. Winthrop had learned long ago to pick a story and stick with it. He planned to blame the snipers. Yes, he'd anticipated the escape route and that's why he'd posted the snipers—who hadn't done their jobs. Of course, this wasn't true. The snipers were actually there to prevent Max from shooting Winthrop. Nevertheless, Winthrop would stick with his story so intently that he'd actually begin to believe it himself. Currently, he was living six major lies, all of which he'd carried on so long that he'd forgotten the real truth. Mr. Winthrop was confident he would pass a polygraph—about this, or any of the other lies that made up his identity.

In his experience, the problem would fade away in short order. But he knew he would absolutely have to pass a polygraph when this was over.

Like dropping soft targets at 40 meters—a piece of cake.

But for now, Winthrop was faced with a much greater problem: why were the Paris Police here? And were the other men police, also? If not, who were they and why were they helping Max by guarding the outside of the chalet?

Though he knew Max was desperate, Mr. Winthrop struggled to imagine him turning to the French or the Americans for help. And even if he did, wouldn't they simply take him into protective custody, along with the evidence?

Unless they want to ensnare me.

Me.

A chill ran down Mr. Winthrop's spine. Hiding in the ditch on the far side of the road, he lifted up, able to see the bodies in the yard and on the porch. He could see no movement. Then, from the corner of Winthrop's eye, he saw hand movement to his left—it was the Gendarme. He was also in the ditch, 10 meters away.

Below the cusp of the ditch, the Gendarme showed two fingers and motioned to his 10 and 11 o'clock.

Two men—more targets.

General Timmons, who was between them, adjusted his aim. That quadrant was covered.

Surely there were more? Rather than turn to the left, Mr. Winthrop tactically pivoted to his right, aiming his Walther PPK at his own 2 o'clock.

Right in his zone of fire, compliments of the scant light spilling from the chalet, Mr. Winthrop could see 3 men advancing through the woods. They were coming right at him.

Chapter Twenty-Six

The bullet had struck Max on the right side of his pelvis, almost exactly to the opposite side of his steam burn. The impact had spun him around, making his face hit the doorframe as he fell. Now, on the ground, he fought not to writhe. The shooters were obviously skilled. They'd taken down numerous men, at range, with pistols. Not an easy task. Max silently prayed the Man with the Melted Face was rallying his troops to come around the chalet in a pincer movement, trapping the shooters at the top of the property.

If not...

Slowly adjusting his vision, Max saw a pistol in front of him. It was on the threshold and belonged to the man lying unnaturally in the doorframe. The pistol was very distinctive, one Max knew well, a Stechkin. Designed by the Soviets, the Stechkin was well known due to its fully automatic capability. This one did not have the extending stock from the rear, which made it more similar to a machine pistol. Instead, this Stechkin looked like nearly any other pistol, save for the chunky box magazine that had a capacity of 20 9x18 mm Makarov rounds.

You have to claw your way out of this, Max...for Ludivine.

Max slid his hand outward, moving very slowly, and disentangled the pistol from underneath the Unione Corse's dead hand. Though all was quiet now, the shooters were out there, just over the hill. Max pulled the weapon to him and began to inch his way backward.

The first movement of his torso sent jags of pain through his midsection, making him want to cry out. Despite any amount of pain or discomfort, he had to get out of this doorway. And now he had a weapon. If he could somehow get back inside and—

"Max." A whisper from behind him.

Ludivine.

"Max."

"Go downstairs. I'll be behind you," he hissed.

"Are you hurt?" she whispered.

"Please," he whispered back, "just go downstairs and I *will* be behind you. If they see you they'll shoot."

No sooner had the last word escaped his mouth than multiple gunshots rang out from the road above. Max turned his head, fearful the shots were coming at him. But instead he saw lateral tongues of fire from what appeared to be three pistols. The one on the left fired to Max's left. Steady, measured shots. Pop. Pop. Pop-pop.

The two on the right unleashed what appeared to be full magazines. He saw the barrel rise from both pistols—panic fire. Between the three, there were probably 20 shots fired in all.

This was his chance. Rather than wait around, Max lurched backward and attempted to stand. He fell immediately to the floor as it seemed his right hip socket wouldn't support his weight. New pain flared after he'd fallen, radiating down his leg and up into his stomach.

Ignore it, Max.

He twisted his head and saw Ludivine. She was just out of sight of the front door, standing at the top of the cellar stairs. Again Max attempted to stand. He used the coat closet knob for support, managing to pull himself upright. He began to move, leaning forward and allowing his weight to propel him as a bloody trail followed.

Keep going. Just a few more feet.

Because his leg was dragging, he tripped on the carpet runner. It was just in front of the cellar door.

Ludivine tried to catch Max but couldn't. He went right by her.

Tumbling headfirst down—down into the cellar.

***

"Reload—reload," Mr. Winthrop growled. He'd hit his targets and now craned his neck to make sure the imbeciles to his left had gotten theirs.

Winthrop was able to see one of the men near the top of the driveway, creating a mutated snow angel as he writhed in pain. Knowing he had one remaining 7.65 millimeter bullet in the chamber, Mr. Winthrop calmly leveled the Walther and put the bullet through the wounded man's neck.

The man ceased his movements.

"Status," Winthrop demanded while sliding a new magazine into his pistol. He searched the area to his right. His targets were down and he saw no more. He also could discern no movement from anyone they'd shot.

"Clear here," Timmons replied.

Mr. Winthrop's eyes rotated down to the chalet. Something was different. He peered at the open doorway, lit by a rectangle of maize light coming from inside. Before, there'd been two bodies at the threshold, but now there was only one.

Movement to the right of the house caught Mr. Winthrop's eye. In the dark shadow directly beside the chalet, he could see a man leaning against the corner, behind snow covered bushes. Keeping his movements down in the privacy of the ditch, Mr. Winthrop signaled Timmons and Gendarme that he would take the shot.

He peered over the road again, watching as the man crouched down while he navigated the shrubs. Perhaps this was the man from the doorway.

Winthrop aimed the Walther. It seemed the man was preparing to sprint away from the chalet.

Wait for it…wait for it…

There he went, running to Mr. Winthrop's right, probably hoping to flank up the hill from the woods, the same deadly path the others had attempted.

As soon as the man broke from the shrubs, Mr. Winthrop fired, catching his target broadside. He fell, losing his shotgun or rifle. Winthrop watched—and waited. The man didn't move. Winthrop continued to stare for 20 seconds. When the man didn't so much as flinch, Winthrop turned his attention back to the chalet.

Earlier, he'd definitely hit the two people in the doorway. Whoever he'd just shot wasn't the same man—not moving with such uninjured ease he wasn't.

Therefore, one of the men from the doorway had retreated back inside the chalet.

"There's one still alive inside," Mr. Winthrop warned. He instructed the Gendarme to head to the left and circle the entire house.

"Check the bodies. Kill any that are alive, and shoot anyone else you see. We *cannot* leave witnesses."

Without a word of protest, the dutiful Gendarme popped his magazine out, rechecking that he was locked and loaded before he set out.

"I haven't seen the girl," Timmons remarked.

"She's probably in there. Max, too. We *will* scorch this earth and get what we came for." Winthrop stood, boldly crossing the road steep yard. When he reached the porch, he checked the pulse of the man in the doorway. Dead.

Winthrop turned, finding General Timmons behind him, providing cover.

"Check those men for any pulse," Winthrop commanded. He turned back to the chalet.

There was enough of light to allow him to see a considerable amount of blood in the doorway. The blood trailed into the house. He stepped inside. The trail transitioned to a pool of blood about two meters from the doorway. It was smeared. Then the trail began again.

It led around the corner to an open door.

There was no sign of anyone else in the chalet.

But the amount of trailed blood was significant. Whoever was bleeding might have already bled out. Especially if that person had recently suffered a large knife gash on his head.

***

Next to the chalet, the Man with the Melted Face lay motionless. It wasn't due to a lack of pain. He'd never hurt so badly in his life. But he knew he'd better not move. One of the shooters was checking the bodies. He'd crossed to the left of the chalet before going behind. While he was gone, the Man with the Melted Face slowly turned his head and, sure enough, the same shooter reappeared from the back of the chalet.

He was coming to check his pulse.

On he came, trudging through the snow, blowing on his freezing hands and shaking them.

After a moment, the shooter stopped over the Man with the Melted Face for a moment. The moment dragged on. It was all the Man with the Melted Face could do not to breathe or blink. The shooter watched for a moment before moving back to the front of the chalet, rubbing his hands inside his coat trying to warm them.

Laziness like that can get a man killed.

Or leave a man alive.

The shooter did the same with the bodies at the front of the chalet. He examined them visually, alternating his hand inside his coat and the other on his pistol.

Inventorying his own body, the Man with the Melted Face moved slightly, deducing that the bullet had pierced him just under his ribs on his right side. He slowly adjusted his icy hand to the gunshot, feeling the slick warmth of his own blood. Having survived two years in Libya during the war, he assumed he was a dead man—likely the case even if he made it to a surgery table right now.

Pivoting his dying body, he remained down in the snow. To his left, he saw two of the shooters on the porch. One was keeping watch up toward the road. The other was the one who'd just walked past him. He was talking, speaking English.

They went inside.

The Man with the Melted Face managed to stand, dizzy from his efforts. Thankfully, he needed only go downhill.

One foot in front of the other, he began to move. Zig-zagging, his life's final effort.

In his hands was Max's shotgun—the Ithaca 37.

***

Mr. Winthrop and General Timmons beckoned the shivering Gendarme into the chalet.

"There's no one left outside," the Gendarme reported. "Everyone's dead." His trembling finger pointed down at the floor. "Blood trail?"

Mr. Winthrop touched his finger to his lips. "Whisper. I'd wager that blood is from our old friend, Max." He pointed to the open door at the rear of the chalet, leading to a downward set of stairs. "Cellar."

Still keeping his pistol trained outside, General Timmons asked, "How to proceed?"

"We're going down to get Max. And I want him alive."

"Why?" Timmons hissed.

"Because I have some questions for him, that's why," Winthrop retorted. "He'll die in due time. Let's go. General, watch our back. Pierre, you at the front."

The three men proceeded through the house to the cellar stairs.

This was the moment of truth. Mr. Winthrop liked the setup. If there was a bullet coming, the Gendarme would take it. Then, Winthrop and Timmons could react accordingly.

Mr. Winthrop hesitated...

Think, dammit...will Max be so predictable?

But what else can he do? Guns—knives—Winthrop looked at the furnace grate in the floor—a heating oil bomb?

Max, if you're that industrious, then I deserve to die.

Winthrop thought about the grate in the courtyard at the Place de Clichy. He'll do something unexpected.

"Th'hell?" Timmons whispered. "You got cold feet?"

Winthrop moved forward.

"Ready?" the Gendarme mouthed.

Winthrop nodded. Behind him, General Timmons continued to provide cover to the rear.

Down they went.

***

In Washington, DC, Julie and Vann sat huddled around the military-grade short-wave radio. The radio smelled of burning plastic, a sign that it was working. They listened via relay as their teams approached La Clusaz. One of the teams had reached out to the La Clusaz police and, with help from the French government, had urged the police to move near the chalet but to not intervene.

Ten minutes before, the La Clusaz police reported multiple shots fired from the direction of the chalet. Then, they reported two automobiles on the road, less than a kilometer from the house. Inside one of the autos was a dead man, carrying the identification of a Paris Police detective. There was evidence of a shootout around the cars.

Now, the La Clusaz police reported quiet.

Through his advancing teams, Vann ordered the La Clusaz police to remain in place.

"If anyone tries to leave, they can intervene. But they're *not* to advance on the chalet."

"What do you think happened?" Julie asked him.

Vann set the transmitter down and rubbed his face. "Julie, I have no idea. We've got two cars and one dead Paris detective. We've got a mess of Unione Corse heavies, and this asshole Winthrop and his posse." He opened his hands plaintively. "Shootout at the O.K. Corral, I guess."

"All because of that briefcase," Julie whispered.

"We don't know that's the reason."

She eyed Vann. "I know it."

***

There was a lone window in the cellar. Situated well above the floor, the rectangular window was adjacent to the door that led to the crawlspace. The window communicated through to the backyard of the chalet, located just above the ground line. Though painted shut, the window might open with effort from both in and outside.

And it did, just after it was lightly tapped on with the barrel of a shotgun.

***

At the bottom of the stairs, everything came clear to Mr. Winthrop. As they'd descended, there had been no gunshots, only the soft sounds of a woman crying.

The cellar comprised approximately half of the footprint of the upstairs of the chalet—common for a home cut into the side of the hill. The stairs held a 90-degree turn to the right. At their base was an unfinished room of cinderblock with a concrete floor. Covering much of the floor were cheap throw rugs, and toward the front of the chalet, the large furnace. Surrounding the furnace were boxes, rolls of carpet, floor lamps and the like. At the left side of the basement was an elevated white door that led to the shallower portion of the basement—the crawlspace.

The door was open. Behind it was bare earth and stacks of wood. On the painted white threshold of the door were blood smears.

Below the open door was a petite yet attractive woman. She was the one doing the crying, her cheeks glistening with tear tracks.

Beside her, tightly in her arms, was an ashen and bloodied man. His left hand, wet with glistening blood, lay limp on the concrete. There was a slight pool of blood under his body. It was clear he attempted to make it up into the crawlspace, but failed.

The man, of course, was Max Warfield.

The Gendarme held a steady aim on the woman. Mr. Winthrop leaned to him and told him not to panic and not to shoot. "If she tries something, shoot her knee. But I need to question her."

"Understood."

"You're going to hear something behind you," Winthrop whispered. "Have no fear. Keep her under your aim."

"Yes, sir."

"I mean it. No *matter* what."

"Je comprends."

Satisfied, Mr. Winthrop turned, finding General Timmons on the small landing at the turn of the stairs, still dutifully aiming upward.

"General?"

"Yeah," Timmons answered without turning.

"You shouldn't be here."

"What?" Timmons asked, maintaining his rear guard.

"I was always against bringing you into the fold. I think you're nothing more than a two-bit profiteer, and a traitor to boot."

Frowning, General Timmons turned his head.

Mr. Winthrop issued a vulgar, universally understood two-word insult just before he shot the general in the middle of his forehead. General Timmons' brains scattered across the beams of the basement ceiling, dripping afterward like uncooked eggs. His body thumped off the stairs to the floor as his pistol clattered under the stairs.

Turning, Mr. Winthrop was greeted by the shrieks of the attractive woman. He cocked his head. She was very attractive, indeed.

"Why'd you do that?" the Gendarme yelled.

"He was a traitor," Winthrop yelled, working his mouth after the thunderous gunshot. "Keep her under your aim."

The Gendarme obeyed.

As he did, Mr. Winthrop relaxed. He slid his warm pistol into his pants. Then he removed his last peppermint from his pants pocket. He popped the disc into his mouth, feeling the clicking as it touched his teeth. Then, Winthrop quickly squared the wrapper, pressing it neatly before sliding it into his pocket.

"What's the plan?" the Gendarme yelled over his shoulder, irritation bleeding through in his tone.

"This," Mr. Winthrop replied. He palmed his pistol again and shot the Gendarme in the back of his head. The jacketed 7.65 round scattered the Gendarme's brain matter and cerebrospinal fluid forward, spraying the woman and Max Warfield's corpse.

Despite his temporarily damaged hearing, Mr. Winthrop was able to still detect the woman's screams. Yes, he was too late to question Max Warfield, but perhaps this young woman could mitigate his losses.

Winthrop eyed the Gendarme. *Scorched earth, indeed…*

The woman continued to scream.

Winthrop motioned her to stand.

Both hands were over her ears as she continued to shriek.

Winthrop wagged the pistol to get her up.

She did nothing but scream and press backward into the cinderblock wall. The Gendarme's blood leaked down her face. Perhaps she'd seen too much.

Too bad.

Impatient, Mr. Winthrop lurched forward, using his left arm to yank her up.

It was only then he saw the shotgun he remembered so well—the Ithaca 37. It was held by Max Warfield's right hand and had been hidden under his right leg.

His right hand was no longer limp—and Max Warfield definitely wasn't a corpse.

The shotgun elevated and fired from a range of two feet, directly into Mr. Winthrop's chest.

This shot was far more deafening than the others, and it sent Mr. Winthrop flying across the cellar. His torso led the way, with his arms and legs struggling to catch up.

Mr. Winthrop's brogue shoes stayed put on the concrete floor, and his horn-rimmed glasses tumbled to the ground but did not break.

The peppermint in his mouth shot out, ending up near the entrance to the crawlspace. It would be found hours later by forensic investigators.

Chapter Twenty-Seven

Despite the world-shaking insanity that had occurred over the weekend in Dallas, Texas, the sleepy skiing resort of La Clusaz, France rivaled Dallas for a period of six hours. Though few would ever know it, one of the world's most damning secrets nearly came to light before it was buried forever, via the aid of a Paris police detective and one of the world's most ruthless organized crime syndicates. The key player in this event was a mobster who looked as if he had a melted face. His real name was Olivier. As it turned out, Olivier was 46 years old and a decorated former member of the French Expeditionary Corps. He'd turned to organized crime after his stint in the military due to "shellshock," leaving him unable to cope in normal society.

Whatever his life had been lacking after the war, Olivier had certainly made up for it on the snowy hillside in La Clusaz.

Though no one knew it at the time, there had been one rubber round remaining in the Ithaca. Just before he died outside in the snow as a result of a gunshot wound to the abdomen, Olivier had passed the shotgun to Ludivine through the cellar window. Knowing he had 4 standard buckshot rounds, Max had quickly emptied the Ithaca's tube, finding his rubber round and placing it in the chamber to be fired first. He'd never dreamed that Mr. Winthrop would shoot his own allies first. Although the situation had played out perfectly, Max's situation in the cellar was still grave, even after shooting Mr. Winthrop.

Just as Ludivine made the decision to go for help, the chalet was swarmed by men from several agencies including the local police. Within minutes, three ambulances arrived, coloring the snow red with their flashing lights. The medics hurriedly triaged the numerous bodies, finding three that were still alive, in addition to Max and Ludivine.

One of the survivors was Mr. Winthrop. He'd survived the point blank range rubber-round gunshot to his chest but was currently unable to talk. He could only gasp and his bloodshot eyes seemed they might pop from his head. At the direction of an English speaking man from Geneva, the medics searched Mr. Winthrop and found his weapon, a wad of money, a peppermint candy in his jacket, and a pants pocket full of squared peppermint wrappers. However, they found no identification. He was given his eyeglasses to put back on and his brogues were placed next to him on the gurney.

Next to the house, one of the Unione Corse men had barely survived a gunshot wound to his neck. He was pronounced critical due to loss of blood and was unconscious as he was whisked away to the ambulance where he was given blood on his way to the hospital.

And in the middle of the front yard, a Parisian detective named Gaspard Lacroix was discovered still breathing, albeit barely. He'd suffered two gunshot wounds and also had frostbite on his hands and on the side of his face. The medics felt he would survive if they could get him through the initial period of shock.

Because it had far better trauma capability than any local hospital, the main hospital in Annecy was notified and an advance team sped ahead to the facility to make arrangements for privacy due to security of the state. The French government assisted, even though the reasons behind the shootout and who was involved was still very much unclear.

When the last of the ambulances arrived at Annecy, one of the victims was pronounced dead during transit.

It was not the Unione Corse man who'd received blood transfusions. He would go on to survive.

Detective Gaspard Lacroix survived, also.

The dead man was wheeled from the last ambulance, covered in a white sheet. When the American agent from Geneva pulled the sheet away, he noted the man's horn-rimmed glasses. And despite it being wet with snow and soiled, anyone with a discerning eye could see the dead man's gray suit was finely tailored. The agent pulled the jacket open, finding that the clothing label had been removed.

During a brief examination, a general surgeon removed from the man's mouth the remains of an amber glass ampoule covered in a thin film of rubber. A later examination of residue from inside the ampoule would reveal its contents to have been potassium cyanide. It was never determined where Mr. Winthrop had hidden the ampoule, but it was estimated that he died, quite miserably, within 90 seconds of ingesting the deadly substance.

Perhaps the ampoule had been hidden in his emergency peppermint.

Three days later, the chief surgeon in Annecy declared that all remaining wounded from the incident in La Clusaz should survive. Each person remained isolated in his or her own room. A turn-of-the-century wing of the hospital that was scheduled for demolition in the coming spring had been transformed into a temporary headquarters of sorts. Dozens of security agents were placed around the wing as frowning, important looking men—and one woman—came and went over the balance of the next two weeks.

One of the visitors caused quite a stir among the local constabulary. He arrived via limousine and was made to extinguish his long cigar at the front of the hospital. His name was Guillermo Casson, but was known to the French simply as Gustav. Wearing a gorgeous cashmere overcoat, he flirted relentlessly with the nursing staff as he was escorted to several rooms. When his visit was complete, Gustav exited the hospital and tipped his cap at several waiting police.

Grinning wide enough to display his gold-capped molars, he was chauffeured away, half-a-million dollars wealthier, even though he never received the spies he'd made a deal for.

At the end of the day, Gustav didn't give a damn. He was fine with the money. To him, a half million, even in counterfeit bills, would soon be worth three times as much once he put it out on the streets of Paris and Marseilles.

***

One week later, Max Warfield sat in what had once been an operating room in the old wing of the hospital. A rectangular table had been brought in, along with three chairs. Even though he could now walk, Max sat in a wheelchair on the opposite side of the table.

The room was lit by portable lights since the room's built-in surgery lights couldn't be operated—the special bulbs weren't manufactured anymore. The portable lights revealed the room to be constructed of salmon colored tile— not the hospital mint green that seemed to be used around the rest of the world. The old operating room had dozens of fittings poking out from the tiled wall and numerous electrical connections overhead for various equipment. The floor had a nice drain in the middle. Max numbly wondered how much blood that drain had ingested over the years.

I need a mood adjustment.

Although he had markedly improved, he was still quite sick. Sick of being here. Sick of questions. Sick of talking about Mr. Winthrop and his ridiculous prison. Sick of trying to conjure little details and memories and threads and accents and minutiae and bullshit that no one on earth other than an anally retentive, obsessive compulsive would ever even consider.

Just sick.

But today had the potential to be special. Max was told that, after today, this situation might finally come to an end.

"*Might*" being the key word.

He wasn't sure if he believed it or not.

His first visitors surprised him. Leading the way into the room was a man in a wheelchair. There was an old scar on the man's face, along with fresh bandages on his body. The wheelchair was pushed by a rather statuesque woman. She beamed as if they were all old friends.

"Hello Max, I'm Julie Hedstrom from the United States Secret Service. This is Detective Gaspard Lacroix of the Paris Police."

For a moment, Max couldn't speak. He'd been told he owed both of these people with his life. From what Max had gleaned, Julie had almost magically conjured Mr. Winthrop's motive from her office in Washington

D.C. That, in turn, led to Eddie English, which led her boss to send reinforcements to La Clusaz. Without the quick reaction of the reinforcements, both Max and Gaspard would have died due to blood loss.

And speaking of Gaspard, had he not intervened—breaking numerous rules to do so—it was entirely possible that the Unione Corse wouldn't have been prepared for the assault that came from Mr. Winthrop, General Timmons and the Gendarme.

These two people had helped Max in more ways than he could possibly comprehend.

The three of them spoke for a full hour. The conversation was disjointed at first—all of it in English—but by the end of the hour, the discussion was rich, filled with meaningful accounts and occasional laughter. The best part for Max was watching Julie and Gaspard as they heard the truth about a number of his actions. Little "a-ha" moments when they realized that their intuition had been correct.

Eventually, there was a knock on the door. Julie answered it before informing Max that it was time for them to leave. They each promised to reconnect the following morning.

After allowing Max a five-minute break, three men entered the defunct operating room. Two of them Max recognized. One was Frederick Lynch, the director of the United States Secret Service. The second man Max recognized was Peter Manning, the head of the Central Intelligence Agency. When the men perfunctorily introduced themselves, Max learned the third man, Howard Price, was an active duty lieutenant general and head of the Defense Intelligence Agency.

"I'm not in uniform for obvious reasons," Price said, crossing his hands and growing quiet.

Max joined him in his silence.

"Max, we've read your testimony and spoken to the investigators who've been here since this all ended," Manning said. "And even though we feel you've covered everything, we'd respectfully ask that you tell us the entire story, start to finish, just so we can hear it from you in one sitting."

Manning had asked the question in a kind and reasonable tone. Even though he headed up the CIA, he seemed genuine. Max was sure it was all an act, but he still gave the man credit for playing the part well.

"Where would you like me to begin?"

"Quickly tell us about how you supported yourself by robbing narcotics cash rooms. Then, go into detail about the last cash room you robbed and take that on into your capture, and so on."

Max did as he was asked. Over the past days, he'd recounted a number of details that he likely would have forgotten in time. This retelling was his best yet. It took nearly two hours, ending with his being shot in the side and receiving the gift of his Ithaca 37 from the Man with the Melted Face. Max made sure he gave Ludivine all the credit she deserved. Without her, he'd be dead and the Lucy Thaler secret would be in Mr. Winthrop's hands.

After his retelling, there were a dozen questions, but none that revealed anything new.

General Price, from the Defense Intelligence Agency, went next. He cleared his throat and crossed his hands in front of him as he spoke. "Max, you've presented us with quite a problem. We now have at least two more people who know what transpired on the USS Augusta back in the summer of 1941."

Max said nothing.

"To be frank," General Price said, "we're a bit conflicted about what to do with you."

"I'm more concerned that a president and two intelligence officers allowed a war to happen," Max answered.

The trio had no answer for that.

After adjusting himself in the wheelchair, Max spoke about something he'd not gotten into detail over since all this began.

"General, I don't need to speak about my military record. I hope it demonstrates the type of person I am. At the end of my career, I killed another man in a bar fight. I did. My right hand hit his jaw, and he fell and hit his head on the floor. It was awful. I wish I could go back and allow him to beat on me, instead." Max looked away for a moment. "But I ask you three to consider what happened. I beat him in a game of pool and won three bucks. He didn't want to pay. I didn't touch him; I just told him I wanted my money. As the witnesses stated, he swung at me and missed. I asked again for my money. The next time he swung the pool cue and hit me in my left arm. When he swung it again, I caught it and threw a punch. That was it."

"Why'd you run?" Director Lynch asked.

"We'd all been through a lot, sir. I can't explain where my mind was at that time. But once I got away, and started knocking over cash houses, I grew to like it. Didn't have to answer to anyone and got to do things my way." Max shrugged. "I don't have any other sexy explanation for you. My greatest regret was missing my brothers—my soldiers. But I didn't miss *anything* else."

Mr. Manning from the CIA spoke next. "Max, we cannot allow the information surrounding Lucy Thaler's murder, and the intel she gave, to ever be known."

"I understand," Max replied. "And I agree. And I'd also like to add that I certainly hope each of you are taking steps to make sure that sub-human beings like Eddie English and Victor Roach are never allowed to serve in such positions again."

The three men took the rebuke quiet well. "Your concern is well-founded," Price replied.

Manning continued. "So, Max, the question is this: what can we do to come to an iron clad agreement regarding you and Miss St. Vincent that will ensure you will never breathe a word of any of this to anyone for the balance of your days?"

"Will my crime be expunged?"

The three men joined eyes. Lynch spoke. "That's on the table."

Max shifted in the wheelchair again. His side ached. "Before we talk about all that, I have a question."

"Go ahead," Manning replied.

"Who was Mister Winthrop?"

Blank faces.

Max turned to Price. "General?"

No answer.

"Nobody's going to tell me?"

Silence.

"Who was with him at the chalet?"

Price looked at Manning, who nodded.

"One was a French national who'd once been a policeman—he was nothing more than muscle for hire," General Price said. Then he seemed to bolster himself for what he'd say next. "The other was retired United States Marine Major General Ronald Timmons."

The answer threw Max. He blinked as if he had sand in his eyes. He sipped his water. "A U.S. Marine general?"

Lynch nodded. "Yes."

"Then who was Winthrop?" Max demanded.

"We don't know," Manning replied.

"Like hell you don't," Max shot back.

"I don't expect you to believe us," Manning answered, "but that's the truth."

Mr. Manning of the CIA went on to relay the story of Mr. Winthrop's subterfuge at Panzer Kaserne in Stuttgart, Germany. He told Max all about Winthrop posing as Timothy Pooler, the Assistant Secretary of the Army for Manpower.

"Is that where I was held?"

"It was. I hope you can tell we're being transparent with you. We honestly don't know who Winthrop was or who he was working for."

Flabbergasted, Max said, "So you're telling me that Mister Winthrop fooled the U.S. Army and pulled off an operation for another government right there on our own installation?"

"Part of that is true," Lynch said. "We have no indication whatsoever that Winthrop worked for another government."

"And it's embarrassing that he duped our Army personnel," Price added. "Our security is being changed as we speak."

"What about Timmons?" Max asked.

Manning straightened his tie. "He was obviously recruited by Winthrop's *organization* at some point."

"Do you have any evidence of this?" Max asked.

"We do, but nothing that's been helpful in regard to Winthrop's origin or his organization," Price answered.

"And Timmons' family?"

"He divorced ten years ago," Price continued. "Hadn't spoken to his ex-wife or children in years."

Manning spoke next. "The Marines missed a lot of telltale signs in the general's last few years."

"Was he a communist?" Max asked.

"No, his leanings weren't political," Manning answered. "They were egomaniacal. Our psychologists believe that his mandatory retirement from the Marines sent him off the rails and that's what made him a good target for whomever Winthrop worked for."

"This is why every little detail you can give us helps. Now or later," Lynch added.

"What about the farmhouse?" Max asked, referring to the French farmhouse and property where he trained for the assault on the Place de Clichy Secret Service office.

"We've searched the entire area you gave us," Manning replied. "We've found nothing."

"I can go there and show you."

"We may take you up on that, but we're sure we located the farm you referenced. It's clear there was activity there, and even evidence that a structure was recently removed, but we've learned nothing in the process."

"Who does the farm belong to?" Max asked.

"It's tied up in an estate battle," Lynch answered. "It's been empty for years."

Max shook his head in disgust.

"There's another thing we haven't told you, Max," General Price said. "Your former commander, Philip Ortega, went missing on the Saturday after President Kennedy was killed."

"Went missing?" Max asked.

General Price frowned. "He was stationed in southern Germany and told his wife he had to go to a meeting. He didn't say where, but just said he'd be home late. He never came back."

"All we know is, shortly after he left his home, his car crossed the Austrian border," Manning added. "That's it. Now, both him and his car are missing."

"Winthrop," Max growled.

"We don't know that," Lynch replied.

"I do," Max said. "I escaped Friday night, and Winthrop, or whomever his people were, snatched the man who knew me better than anyone. After they got what they could from him, they killed him." Max rested his head in his hand.

Everyone was quiet for nearly a full minute.

At the end of the pause, Max vigorously rubbed his face. "There's still one colossal question."

"Yes, there is," Lynch agreed.

Max gestured to Director Lynch to go ahead.

"You want to know how Mr. Winthrop knew to knock over our Place de Clichy office minutes after President Kennedy was shot."

"Correct," Max replied. "He told me numerous times leading up to the robbery that any agents who were working would *already* be distracted."

The trio of men were silent.

Max continued. "And, on top of that, how did he know about the money and especially the briefcase?"

No one had an answer. Nor would they ever have an answer. Much like the assassination of President John F. Kennedy, numerous theories were suggested, but none were ever backed up by tangible evidence. There were people who knew, people such as Mr. Vickers—the mystery man who'd acted as Winthrop's and Timmons' puppeteer from his temporary station in Vienna. But none of the men in that defunct operating room knew Vickers existed. Other minor evidence was found over the following months. None of it was helpful—just a few random pieces of an enormous jigsaw puzzle.

The mystery remained unsolved.

But the three men did detail that they believed Mr. Winthrop and his organization *knew* they were going to find evidence in the briefcase that President Reginald S. Whitestone had prior intelligence of the Japanese surprise attack on Hawaii.

Manning spoke next. "Had Clayton Fairchild ever made those tapes and photos public…"

Lynch added, "I'd heard the 'Whitestone-knew-about-Pearl-Harbor' fringe theory for years and I always thought it was utterly ridiculous."

"Very little surprises me anymore," General Price remarked.

Everyone in the room took on a grim expression.

"I have one last question," Max said.

"Go ahead," Price replied.

"Is there any chance that Winthrop, and his organization, could have been part of some runaway sect of the U.S. intelligence community?"

"By God, I pray not," Manning replied.

"But you can't say for sure?"

No one answered. The silence said it all.

On this, the final day of Max's questioning, in that defunct French operating room, the conversation flowed back to the secret Max and Ludivine now held. The trio of U.S. officials asked what they could they do to ensure Max and Ludivine's silence?

It was simple. Max had already spoken about it to Ludivine, and she agreed. Max proposed the idea, touching all the high points in less than a minute. He wanted to be exonerated for his crimes. He wanted Ludivine to come with him to the U.S. and be granted citizenship. He wanted treatment for some of the anguish he'd suffered before all this began. And he wanted the chance to participate in one very specific revenge activity.

It wasn't much to ask.

After a brief conversation in another room, the trio of officials conditionally agreed with Max's requests, as aggressive as they were. Director Lynch mentioned that Max's proposal actually relieved him of certain promises that were made.

Max and Ludivine remained in France for another week. They eventually flew to Andrews Air Force Base, and were taken to a private residence at Bethesda Naval Hospital. There, Max continued to heal while going through processing with various agencies. In the afternoons, he and Ludivine memorized details about their new identities and backgrounds.

It was the beginning of their new life together.

Chapter Twenty-Eight

April, 1964 – Kauai, Hawaii

Max's injuries had almost fully healed. His dark hair was full and lighter in spots, due to the sun. The gunshot wound to his side was nothing more than a lighter colored bump of skin now—not unlike the other scar tissue on his body. His steam burn was hardly noticeable, especially with his suntan. Most of the damage had been internal and had long since healed. The first month had been the most tedious portion. Thankfully, due to the fine medical staff at Bethesda Naval Hospital, Max had quickly passed the critical stage at which point he was able to focus on a full recovery.

Ludivine looked radiant in a blue sundress adorned with white and yellow flowers. Max awaited her on the patio of their Poipu Beach rental home. The smell of jasmine was heavy in the evening air as she stepped outside, twirling for his benefit. An adoring audience of one, he clapped before standing to accept her outstretched hands.

They kissed.

Now that the unpleasantness was over with—it had occurred earlier in the day—they could truly begin their new lives. A month before, Max had termed this date as Day Zero. Tonight, after a meal of seafood and good wine, they would seal their union in their bedroom as the chiffon drapes swirled from the mild open breeze.

Tomorrow, they would fly to Oahu and begin their search for a home. Max had accepted a government position in an advisory capacity. While a number of military personnel might be familiar with his tattoos, his government identity would show him as an honorably discharged major, and he would be paid as such.

Ludivine had begun to fancy opening a French restaurant in Honolulu. She wasn't in a hurry, but planning for it seemed to make her happy. It made Max happy, too.

At least they were together. And alive—now that the "unpleasantness" was done.

To Max, the unpleasantness had actually been quite enjoyable.

***

-One Day Later-
CBS Evening News: 6:36 P.M.

Walter Cronkite, sober and steady: "And from Kauai, Hawaii, comes the news of what is suspected to have been a coordinated, gangland style killing of reclusive billionaire Victor Roach. Roach was found dead on his Kauai estate yesterday, shortly after lunch, by several members of his staff. Making the investigation all the more bizarre, nine members of Victor Roach's estate staff were disabled through the use of what is described as 'high-dollar tranquilizer darts.' Roger Mudd is on the scene in Hawaii."

Roger Mudd – holding his hand over his earpiece: "Thank you, Walter." Camera pans, displaying bursting flora and a large swimming pool with a fountain. "One need only glance behind me to see I am standing in what could be described as paradise. Swaying pineapple trees. Hibiscus. Tropical birds...and murder." Mudd glances at his notes. "Yesterday at 12:44 P.M., Princeville Police, on Kauai's north shore, recorded a distress call from Victor Roach's longtime secretary. She claimed to have been disabled sometime before noon. When she awoke, she discovered other estate staff still in an unconscious state. Then, her gruesome discovery: Victor Roach dead in his study. According to several confirmed reports, Roach had been severely beaten before he was killed with what is described as 'a hunting knife inscribed with Hermann Goering's name on the blade.'"

Mudd eyes the camera and allows a dramatic pause: "Victor Roach is known as the oracle-like investor who gambled and won prior to the Second World War. His earliest financial windfall was in several Pacific shipping companies, followed by successful investments in aviation, rubber, oil and numerous other industries associated with the war effort. By the time the war had ended, he was worth in excess of a hundred million dollars—an amount that continued to grow. His rapid ascent was not without controversy, however, as he was investigated on several occasions. No wrongdoing was ever discovered, but the investigations made him grow more reclusive. The Hawaii State Police are expected to make a statement later today. Sources within the department have told me that, due to the precision disabling of the Roach estate staff, they are concerned over a lack of evidence. They feel the murder was planned well in advance."

Cronkite seems mesmerized: "Roger, do we have any idea who might have wanted to harm Victor Roach?"

Roger Mudd blinks once before he delivers the line he'd practiced for the last two hours: "Walter, I spoke to several sources at the FBI. They each told me that if they were to investigate all of Victor Roach's alleged enemies, it would shut the bureau down for years."

Walter Cronkite, with a barely discernible smug expression on his face: "That certainly is a peculiar case, Roger." *Shakes his head and mutters almost to himself.* "Hermann Goering...my goodness. It seems as if that war will never leave us." *Cronkite shuffles his paper as the news prepares to go to commercial.* "Victor Roach left behind no immediate family. We'll be right back."

The End

**Author's Note

I hope you enjoyed this book and I definitely hope you took it with a grain of salt. You no doubt noticed that I replaced FDR with the fictional American President Whitestone. I simply couldn't suggest FDR knew about the attack on Hawaii, even in a fictional tale. Additionally, I don't subscribe to such a "fringe theory" but I was convicted it could make an interesting story, so I went with it. I do hope you enjoyed it. Please read on for acknowledgments.

Acknowledgments

Many people helped make this book better. If you thought it was lousy, just imagine how bad it was before the following people helped!

Tom Gunther, former Secret Service agent, provided invaluable insight and helped make the Secret Service storyline far more accurate. Tom, thank you so very much, and thank you for your service.

Phillip Day, my trusted early reader, gave me a great deal of help with this book. As always, Phillip, I do appreciate your help and friendship.

Bob Sides, your calm demeanor and sage advice is always welcome. Thank you.

Herr Doktor, your friendship, advice and wise counsel is without equal. Thanks so much for all you do for me.

John Humphries, speed demon, thanks for giving me another honest opinion. I'm proud of your recent accomplishments.

Jane Godwin, you are amazing, utterly amazing. Your passionate support and volunteer marketing has helped me more than I can express. Your enthusiasm is the type of benefit that keeps me writing every single day. I cannot thank you enough.

Dr. David Godwin, I appreciate your help and advice along with your support. You and Jane make an amazing couple.

Don Phillips, you're an incredibly thoughtful and insightful gentleman. I'm thankful to have met you.

Anne Snow, burgeoning book critic, your notes and advice were without equal. Thank you so very much for putting so much thought into the test reading.

Dr. Winston Godwin, I'm flattered that you took the time to read my story and provide me with such excellent feedback. I hope we can work together again.

Elizabeth Latanishen Brazeal, my fantastic editor, I'm so sorry for what you've endured during the edit of this book. I look forward to things normalizing for you and your family. I also can't wait to work together on more books.

Monique Glass, thanks so much for the assistance with French language, and all things French. I'm happy to have met you.

Dina Dryden, your eagle eye is the very best. Thank you so much for your willingness to help. You truly went above and beyond.

Nat Shane, artist extraordinaire, you did it again. I'm in your debt.

To all my readers and supporters, God bless you and thank you. I'm humbled anyone would want to read my stories. I love, Love, <u>LOVE</u> hearing from you. Please drop me a line and I *will* respond: chuck@chuckdriskell.com

We will meet again soon. The sixth Gage novel, currently titled THE CATALYST (and my first ever mystery) should be next. After that, probably a vanishing-wife-suspense-tale set in the 1970s on the French Riviera. So, stay tuned!

About the Author

Chuck Driskell credits the time he spent as a U.S. Army paratrooper for fueling his love of writing. During the week, he works in advertising.

Seven mornings a week, usually very early, he writes. Chuck lives in South Carolina with his tolerant wife and two loving children. *Fringe Theory* is Chuck's twelfth novel.

Made in the USA
Lexington, KY
19 July 2019